MW00772109

Praise for *Saint of the Narrows Street*

"The stunning *Saint of the Narrows Street* is William Boyle's best novel yet, a vibrant, operatic tale of two resilient, big-hearted sisters and the fateful night that sets their life on a path they never intended. Not since Richard Price has a writer brought New York to such vivid, spectacular life, and Boyle's southern Brooklyn is all his own: a neighborhood pulsing with hard-earned humor, dive-bar pleasures and thunderous heartbreak." **—Megan Abbott, *New York Times* bestselling author of *Beware the Woman***

"With *Saint of the Narrows Street*, a magnum opus of family and crime, blood both shared and spilled, William Boyle proves himself once more the poet laureate of Brooklyn, and a writer of true craft and depth. He shows once more how the crime novel can peer as deep into the human heart as any other artform. William Boyle is the real thing. I don't know how else to say it."

—Jordan Harper, author of *Everybody Knows*

"You don't read a William Boyle novel as much as you inhabit his intricately drawn world. *Saint of the Narrows Street* is on par with the best of Pete Dexter, Richard Price, and William Kennedy. This is a tour de force, knockout book; an immediate classic that will stay with you long after you finish the last perfect chapter."

—Ace Atkins, *New York Times* bestselling author of *Don't Let the Devil Ride* and *The Heathens*

"No one can make the everyday vagaries of life feel like Greek tragedies the way William Boyle can. He effortlessly maps the path of desire that moves through the human heart like burning chrome."

—S.A. Cosby, *New York Times* bestselling author of *All the Sinners Bleed*

"*Saint of the Narrows Street* is a hundred-proof shot of tragic love. Nobody writes like William Boyle. Every character has a huge thumping heart. You can smell the skeevy bars and taste the home-cooked lasagna. Boyle deals in details, but this is a big, epic novel, and it's his best yet." **—Eli Cranor, Edgar Award–winning author of *Don't Know Tough***

"A new William Boyle novel is always cause for celebration, and *Saint of the Narrows Street* might be his best work yet. A novel brilliant in structure and in its study of the long-term effects of a single violent crime. Ambitious in scope and impossible to put down. Boyle is that rare writer who is able to walk the line of social commentary and crime thriller." **—Willy Vlautin, author of *The Horse***

"With its rich setting, compelling plot and an unforgettable cast of characters—flawed and fascinating and heartbreakingly real—*Saint of the Narrows Street* will stay with you long after you turn the last page. A classic noir page-turner, it's also a deeply moving story about the dreams that keep us alive—and what happens when those dreams inevitably shatter." **—Alison Gaylin, Edgar Award–winning author of *We Are Watching***

"William Boyle's *Saint of the Narrows Street* is incisive, beautiful, brutal—a book that examines what happens in a small world when big secrets are held down. Set in a neighborhood you will smell and feel as if it's your own, this novel presents a cast of characters you'll swear you've known or known about for years, and yet they'll find a way to surprise you. Death echoes, rumors kill, and the living are cursed on Saint of the Narrows Street."

—Henry Wise, author of *Holy City*

"William Boyle's *Saint of the Narrows Street* drew me in and wrecked me. A powerful story about the ripple effect of violent acts on the lives of good people. Everyone needs to read this book."

—Nikki Dolson, author of *All Things Violent*

Saint of the Narrows Street

ALSO BY THE AUTHOR

Gravesend

Death Don't Have No Mercy

Everything Is Broken (published in France as *Tout est Brisé*)

The Lonely Witness

A Friend Is a Gift You Give Yourself

City of Margins

Shoot the Moonlight Out

Saint of the Narrows Street

William Boyle

Published by
Soho Press, Inc.
227 W 17th Street
New York, NY 10011

This is a work of fiction. Names, characters, places, and incidents either are the product of the author's imagination or are used fictitiously, and any resemblance to actual persons, living or dead, businesses, companies, events, or locales is entirely coincidental.

Library of Congress Cataloging-in-Publication Data
Names: Boyle, William, 1978- author.
Title: Saint of the Narrows Street / William Boyle.
Description: New York, NY : Soho Crime, 2025.
Identifiers: LCCN 2024025625

ISBN 978-1-64129-640-3
eISBN 978-1-64129-641-0

Subjects: LCGFT: Novels.
Classification: LCC PS3602.O973 S25 2025
LC record available at https://lccn.loc.gov/2024025625

Interior design by Janine Agro

Printed in the United States of America

10 9 8 7 6 5 4 3 2 1

To Katie, who makes broken things better

Located on the western edge of Gravesend, Saint of the Narrows Street is something of an anomaly, an oddly named block between Bath Avenue and Benson Avenue, buried amongst the numbered Bay Streets, about a ten-minute walk from the promenade that looks out at the tidal strait separating Brooklyn and Staten Island known as "the Narrows." Ask denizens of the street what the name means, and you'll get a lot of head scratching and confounded looks.

One sunny spring afternoon, as I go from house to house speaking to residents, I stop to talk to a slump-shouldered young man sitting on his front stoop with a can of cheap beer. "Who is the 'saint of the narrows'?" I ask him.

"Who ain't?" he responds, grinning.

—Stephen Grisolia,
Far Reaches: A Walking Tour of Southern Brooklyn

Saint of the Narrows Street

Part 1

FUCK THE SACRAMENTS

Saturday, August 16 & Sunday, August 17

1986

1.

Risa's in the kitchen, crying into a gravy-stained dish towel as she heats up the remaining chicken cutlets on the stove in her cast-iron pan. Her hands are clammy. Sweat beads her hairline. Her purple T-shirt has dusky little circles on it from the popping oil.

Her sister, Giulia, is sitting at the dining room table, holding eight-month-old Fab.

At twenty-eight, a new mother, Risa feels old and worn out already. Giulia's four years younger than her, and she still seems so full of life, like the world can break her and she'll bounce back no problem. She's lithe, tan, looks chic in the acid-wash jeans and blue Oxford shirt she's wearing. Fab's squirming around, playing with the buttons on her shirt, blowing raspberries against her sleeve. Giulia's come over with her own heartbreak—having split with her latest boyfriend, Richie, moved out of their apartment, and shown up here with a suitcase and nowhere else to go—but she hasn't noticed yet that it's Risa who's in tears. Of all nights.

Not that there'd be any good nights with Sav still around. He's out now, thankfully. Probably at that heavy metal club he goes to, L'Amour.

"He's getting big," Giulia says, her focus wholly on cooing Fab. "He's about the cutest baby I've ever seen. I could take a bite out of his little apple cheeks."

"It all happens so fast," Risa says. "I feel like I took him home from the hospital yesterday."

"You really don't have to heat those cutlets up. I'm not that hungry."

"You've got to eat."

"I can't remember the last time I had a home-cooked meal."

"I'm glad you're here. Fab's glad." A break in Risa's voice. The tears apparent in her words.

"What is it, sweetie?" Giulia says. She stands, Fab in her arms, and walks over to Risa at the stove, holding Fab to her chest with one arm, while reaching out with her other and touching Risa on the shoulder.

"You came here because you need help, not to help me," Risa says.

"I'm fine. It's nothing, really. It was just time to move on. What's happening?"

Risa uses a dish towel to dry her eyes and attempts to compose herself. "Sit down and eat," she says. "Please. I'm gonna make you a plate."

Giulia nods and takes Fab back to the table.

Risa met Sav in the summer of 1983 on the beach in Coney Island. Only three years ago, but it feels like another lifetime.

She was twenty-five and mostly happy. Sav approached her and her friends Marta, Lily, and Grace on the sand not far from the boardwalk that day. What did she see in him? He was a year younger than her. Wiry. He seemed a little dangerous, the kind of guy her father had warned her about, and she liked that. She thought he looked like Ralph Macchio in *The Outsiders*, which she'd just seen at the movies—she'd read the book in high school, and Johnny was her favorite then. She liked Sav's voice, sticky with the syrup of the neighborhood, part concrete and part muscle car. She liked his laugh, the way it flattened everything in front of it. They'd gotten married fast and moved into this walk-in apartment on Saint of the Narrows Street between Bath Avenue and Benson Avenue in a three-family house that Sav's parents, Frank and Arlene Franzone, still own. The Franzones lived in the house until Sav was in high school, then they bought a new place on Eighty-Second Street and started renting this one out as three separate apartments. Sav's older brother, Roberto, occupied this unit for a while until he robbed Jimmy Tomasullo's trophy shop and split town for greener pastures with Jimmy's wife, Susie. Roberto was a neighborhood legend in his time—smarmy and charming in his way, a guitarist in a few bands that played at L'Amour, prone to breaking rules and laws—and Sav always seems like he's aching to be his brother.

Sav had revealed himself as a bad man soon after they were married, but it'd been worse since Fab was born and tonight had been the worst of all. The things he'd say and wouldn't say to her, the way he wouldn't meet her eyes, his quiet menace, the way he'd slap her and toss her around—all of it just a boiling prelude to what had happened a short time ago at the very table where Giulia's now sitting with Fab. Sav's friend Double Stevie was there and so was Chooch, Sav's oldest friend from across the street. Sav took out a gun he'd bought on the sly at the Crisscross Cocktail Lounge and was showing it to Double Stevie. Risa told him to get out. He pointed the gun at her and Fab, smiling, and pulled the trigger on an empty chamber. She'd nearly puked up her heart. Her body's still buzzing. Thank God Fab doesn't understand what his father's done.

At the table now, Risa gets Fab situated in his high chair and then sets Giulia up with a plate of cutlets and some semolina bread. To drink, there's wine or water and not much else. Giulia opts for wine, a tall glass filled to the brim. Risa says that the wine's from their former neighbor a few doors down, Mr. Evangelista, who died recently. She says it's strange to have a bunch of wine bottled by a man who's dead. Giulia agrees but drinks it down. "It's good," she says. "And the cutlets are great. They remind me of Mama's."

Risa thinks of their mother's kitchen, oil bubbling on the stove, Mama's hands covered in breadcrumbs and eggs, the apron she always wore. She remembers piping hot cutlets on pink plates. Savoring each bite. She remembers helping Mama. Learning. She has was always been interested in the ways of the kitchen. She kept all their mother's and grandmothers' recipes on index cards in a tin. Things were easier when they were kids at that table with their pink plates. She didn't yet know the sad terrors of the world.

Giulia reaches out and tweaks Fab's cheek. He smiles at her, one of those sweet baby smiles. The way he beams with his whole face. His eyes. Such light.

Risa picks up a napkin from the table. She looks at Giulia

and then at Fab and then looks away, at the wall, at the kitchen, at anything other than them. She's on the verge of tears again. She uses the napkin to blot her eyes. She's turned to the side, faced away from Fab, as if she doesn't want him to see her.

"It's okay," Giulia says. "You let it out." She gets up and comes over to Risa, squatting at her side and placing a hand on her back, palm flat against her spine at first, eventually falling into a rhythm of patting her gently.

Risa can smell the cutlets all over herself. "I don't know if I'm ready to talk about it," she says.

Giulia looks like she wants to say something, but she hesitates and holds back. "Whenever you want to tell me what that bastard did, I'm here," she says.

Risa leans into Giulia, putting her head on her shoulder, sobbing steadily now.

Giulia pulls her into another hug. Fab's watching them, smooshing his thumbs against the tray on his high chair, delighted. "We're gonna take care of each other," Giulia says. "That's what we're gonna do."

As a girl, Risa had daydreamed about being a nun, about helping the sick and poor, about finding real meaning in life. She imagined herself dabbing the heads of dying patients with a wet washcloth, saying not to worry because God was with them. She imagined everyone calling her Sister Risa, which had a nice ring to it. She imagined keeping all her thoughts about God and the world in a journal, all her doubts and fears, everything beautiful and frightening, and she'd write it all down by candlelight in this simple marble notebook with a freshly sharpened pencil. She could have lived a "meditative life of purpose," as her favorite nun ever, Sister Antonella from Our Lady of Perpetual Surrender, would have said.

That dream faded. After high school at Lafayette, where she'd gone instead of Bishop Kearney because her folks couldn't afford the tuition there, she'd attended Staten Island College, getting mostly Bs and Cs in general studies classes, but decided not to go back for her junior year and to forget about her degree. After dropping out, she worked at Villabate Alba for a few years—her father was friends with the owner. It was tough, especially on Sundays and holidays, early mornings and very long lines, people anxious for their cannoli and sfogliatelle and every other beautiful thing behind the gleaming glass in those display cases. If she'd been smarter sooner, perhaps she could have gone down a different road—nurse, social worker, law clerk—but she'd allowed herself to drift until she met Sav that day on the beach. She'd had boyfriends before him but nothing serious, so she didn't know the pitfalls and the signs of serious trouble. She liked that he liked her. If she'd never met Sav, she's not sure where she'd be—maybe still living at home with her folks—but she'd be better off in many ways.

In the last seven months, since watching the *Challenger* blow up on television while home alone with Fab, she's fallen into crying fits daily. Thinking about that poor teacher. Christa McAuliffe. A mother herself. The squiggle of smoke the spaceship made in the Florida sky. Fab was only a few weeks old at the time, but she'd shielded his eyes from the disaster. Maybe they'd happened before, these crying fits, but something about the *Challenger* really set her off. The impermanence of existence. The realization that nothing's promised. Thinking about the tragedy's impact on her makes her feel guilty, but she can't help it.

She's tried so hard to figure out how she and Fab can leave Sav, but every scenario ends badly for them. Alone, tired, with no help. Her father saying it's her duty to stay with her husband, no matter that she'd chosen the wrong guy. The problem, he'd say, was back when she was doing the choosing and not now when she has no choice. He's very old-school, her father. Look at how he's handled Giulia, disowning her when she was seventeen after he walked in on her having sex with her high school boyfriend, Marco LaRocca. One less daughter, no biggie. He'd be angry at Risa for talking to Giulia, let alone knowing she's given her black sheep sister a place to stay. Risa doesn't understand her father. His version of God seems to have nothing to do with love and everything to do with shutting the door.

Risa again looks at Giulia holding Fab. Playing with him. She's such a sweetheart. It's brought her comfort to have her sister's company for this bit of time. It'd be nice if it could be this way all the time. The three of them. Some joy in the room. None of Sav's poison.

Risa dreads Sav returning. She hates to think like this, but she wishes he would stay out. She knows about the other woman, the regular one. Sandra Carbonari. Sav should just stay with her. Risa's not sure why he's so intent on maintaining the facade of their marriage. She hopes he gets arrested. Maybe she'll let him rot in jail. She even thinks—God forgive her—how much easier her life would be if he was dead. She remembers watching that TV movie *The Burning Bed* with Farrah Fawcett a couple of years back. Based on a true story.

Fawcett plays an abused wife who has nowhere to look for help. One night, she reaches her breaking point and sets the bed on fire with her husband in it, escaping with the kids. Risa wishes she had that kind of courage.

She appreciates that Giulia hasn't pushed talking about Sav, especially after her almost instantaneous breakdown. In that moment, she'd felt relief from Giulia's mere presence but also got hung up thinking about how quickly time was passing, how Fab was being raised in an apartment that was half suffused with love and half suffused with hate. She's choking on the idea of talking about what happened earlier with the gun.

"When you were small, I'd pretend you were my baby," Risa says. "I wasn't that much bigger than you, but I'd get you in my lap and feed you your bottle and sing to you."

Giulia makes googly eyes at Fab, burying her face in his neck and giving him a slobbery kiss. "What'd you sing?"

"'Puff the Magic Dragon.'"

"I knew you'd always be a natural as a mother. You were the best big sister."

"When do your memories start?" Risa's asking because she wants to know if it's likely that Fab's first memories will be of Sav's tangled face as he yells. Her own memory kicks in at three. She remembers sitting in a high chair while her mother prepared Sunday gravy—the smells, the sounds, the dancing blue flame of the stovetop, playing with a wooden spoon Mama had given her to occupy herself. She's heard others say five or six.

"My first vivid memory is from kindergarten," Giulia says. "I remember Sister Bernadette scolding me in the hallway. Something about my skirt."

"What an old witch."

"I mostly remember feelings. I remember fearing Pop. I remember feeling loved by you. You know, at church, I used to look up at the stained glass, and I believed that the one of the Virgin Mary was you. I remember thinking, *Wow, they made a window out of Ris.*"

"That makes me happy."

Giulia suddenly looks like she's got something she wants to say again but is afraid to say it. She nuzzles Fab and then passes him back to Risa. She stands and walks over to the china closet, pausing to consider the dusty plates and knickknacks behind the glass. Their grandma on their mother's side had handed down the china closet and everything in it. Nana Candido. She'd given whatever there was to give to Risa. Giulia got nothing. Risa wonders if that's what she's thinking about now as she stares through the glass.

When Giulia turns back to her, there's a different kind of concern on her face. "I'm not sure if I should say anything," she says.

"What is it?" Risa asks.

"Before I came here, I stopped at the Crisscross."

Risa knows where this is going before Giulia even says it. She'd bet anything Sav was carousing with Sandra. Risa's seen Sandra around plenty. She lounges in the front yard outside her building on Benson Avenue on a lawn chair in her bikini, taking the sun. Boys watch her from their windows. She has dark hair and wears hot pink sunglasses. When she's not in her bikini, she's dressed in some skimpy outfit or another. A real airhead. Hair high and hard from spray. A loosey-goosey strut. The kind of girl who blows on a stranger's dice. There's no one she hasn't gone around with. There's even a rumor that she made time with Religious Pete from upstairs the week he fell off the wagon the previous November. Everybody remembers that week because Religious Pete transformed into a madman, turning over garbage cans in the street, getting into brawls at the Crisscross. Risa remembers even more clearly because she was eight months pregnant and watching the action on the block like a TV show. Sandra cooled Religious Pete down with her drunken flirting. Risa remembers seeing them outside the gate, getting a glimpse of how Sandra operated. The touching, the laughing, the shimmying. She's what Sav deserves. Risa doesn't even want to call Sandra the nasty names that are running around her head. Anyway, Sandra is who she is. That's her life. Risa blames Sav, not Sandra. "He was with her, wasn't he?" she says.

"Who?" Giulia says. "No, it wasn't . . . he did say . . . it was . . ."

"It's okay," Risa says. "You can tell me."

"I did see Sav. He was with Chooch and some other meathead."

"Double Stevie Scivetti."

"His name's Double Stevie?"

"Some dumb neighborhood thing. There was a First Stevie and a Triple Stevie, too."

"They came into the bar for a sec. Sav had a quick beer and a shot. I saw that he had . . ." Giulia trails off, afraid or reluctant to say whatever it is she needs to say.

It hits Risa that Giulia saw the gun. Now she'll have to admit that her husband, the man she'd chosen to marry, to spend her life with, had pointed that very weapon at her and their baby. Forget all the other lines he'd crossed. This was way beyond any of that. She'd seen it in Chooch's eyes too, the recognition that his oldest friend, his buddy from the block, had become a new kind of monster. Doesn't matter that the gun wasn't loaded.

"The gun," Risa says.

"You know about it?"

Risa nods. She bites her lower lip. She pulls Fab closer to her. She wants to tell Giulia what he did, but she can't make the words. She starts and stops a few times.

It doesn't take much for Giulia to guess what's going on. "He threatened you with it, didn't he?"

"He was fooling around. He pointed it at me and Fab. He pulled the trigger. It wasn't loaded."

"Jesus Christ, Ris."

"He's never had a gun before."

"This just happened?"

"A couple of hours before you got here."

Giulia gets up, comes over, and squats at Risa's side. She hugs her and Fab like it's the last hug she's ever going to give them. "I'm so sorry."

"Why are *you* sorry?" Risa's crying again. Fab's touching the tears on her cheeks.

"I'm sorry that it happened. I'm sorry you got stuck with Sav. I'm sorry I made this all about me and my problems."

"He wasn't so bad when we first started going together."

Giulia pulls away and stands. "We should go. Pack a bag for you and Fab. You can't stay here."

"Go where?"

"I don't know. We'll figure it out."

"I can't leave. All Fab's stuff is here. Our whole life's in this apartment."

"You can come back and get it another time. You know Dolly Parente from up the block? Her husband Dickie's a cop. Maybe he'll help. You can leave Sav. It's 1986, not 1886."

"I can hear Pop now: 'You made your bed, Ris. Now lie in it.' Marriage is a *sacrament.*"

"Fuck Pop," Giulia says, almost growling, "and fuck the sacraments. Guys like Sav, they start out small with the abuse and it gets bigger and bigger and bigger. Guys like Sav kill their wives all the time. I'm not trying to scare you. It's the truth."

"He wouldn't *kill* me." Risa says it, but she's not sure she believes it.

"You don't know what he's capable of. Please, pack a bag and let's go. I don't care where. You got Dolly's number?" Giulia hustles over to the phone and picks up the receiver.

"This is all happening too fast," Risa says. "Let me think for a sec."

"What about Lola?"

"Marco's mother?"

"Yeah, she's right up the block. She'd happily put us up for a few days while we figure things out, I bet. She's got loads of extra room. You know, she called me for months after Marco broke up with me. Just to check in. We even had coffee a few times. No way Sav will think to look for you there."

"I don't know." Lola's one of the few people on the block who's gone out of her way to be kind. She brought over a gift when Fab was born, a package of onesies, and she made Risa a lasagna and brought a tray of cookies. She wonders if they'd have to tell Lola why they're hiding out. Would Lola be okay with that? Risa's mind turns to Chooch for a moment. He's decent. Sav's his only real friend. She thinks he's the one Sav will wind up hurting the most. Probably get him killed in some mess of a situation. She wonders where Sav and Double Stevie dragged Chooch with that gun in tow. Maybe she *should* have Giulia call the police.

"What do you think?" Giulia asks, trying to prompt her to act.

Risa imagines how it might all go. Cops showing up, asking questions. Dickie Parente. Lola. Mama and Pop getting involved. Sav and Double Stevie holding up a store on Eighty-Sixth Street with ski masks on, pressuring Chooch to keep watch outside. This twisted, confusing life. She cradles Fab in her arms and rocks him, singing "I Won't Last a Day Without You." She loves the version by the Carpenters most of all, but Paul Williams wrote it and did his take too, and Barbra Streisand and Diana Ross also have renditions. It always makes her happy to sing it for Fab. It's their song, even though it's not a song about mothers and sons.

"You have the prettiest voice," Giulia says.

Risa sniffles, swipes at her cheek with her hand to catch a stray tear. "We'll be fine here," she says. "We can't go anywhere."

When Giulia's done eating, Risa takes her plate into the kitchen and washes it. She pours her sister more wine. She contemplates taking a drink herself. She's never been a big drinker, but she's still nursing Fab and thinks it's a bad idea to even sip a little wine. It's after 11 P.M. and she knows she should put Fab down, though he seems wide-eyed. He did take a long nap earlier. Either way, she should get sheets on the couch for Giulia. Maybe they'll watch late-night television. She's still shaky at the notion of Sav waltzing in, but more and more she thinks it's likely he won't bother coming home. Giulia called before he left, so he knows she'll be here and will want to avoid seeing her. He's always hated Giulia, even back in the early days when Risa didn't fully realize who he was yet. He always says she's a bad influence and a bad sister, the way she goes around with so many different guys. Sav is, among other things, despite his overall repulsion toward Risa, also deeply possessive and controlling. He desires saintliness from her but claims that she's too prudish. *This is what happens*, she thinks. He's got her mind wrecked.

A car pulls up outside now, its lights flashing through the front window. She comes back to the table and takes Fab from Giulia.

"He's home already?" Giulia asks.

"Can't be," Risa says.

They hear a car door open and voices chattering and then the door slams shut. The lights move across the apartment as the car pulls away. The sound of feet on the concrete in the front yard. A few seconds pass. The screen door whines. A chill goes through Risa. She recognizes the sound of Sav, drunk, trying to nudge his key into the lock. Giulia reaches out and takes her hand. "We'll leave," Giulia says. "You say the word. He won't stop us."

The main door to the apartment is flung open, the knob slamming hard against the wall.

It's hot in the apartment, and Risa feels her skin flush suddenly. A wave of nausea overtakes her. Sav's drunk and he's got the gun, unless—fingers crossed—Double Stevie took it home. Giulia was right—they should've left, gone wherever. Anywhere's better than here.

Sav stumbles down the hallway, his hands on the wall. She half expects him to be wearing different clothes, but he's still in his jean shorts with frayed edges and his favorite Iron Maiden muscle shirt. A mummy busting through some kind of ancient wall with hieroglyphics on it. He's bedraggled, his hair glistening with sweat, his fly undone. After a minute, he notices them. "Look who it is," he says. "The famous Taverna sisters."

"Why don't you go back out?" Giulia says.

Sav stops moving, falling into a sloppy leaning position against the wall. He's maybe six or seven feet away, but Risa can smell him. The alcohol seeping from his pores. The kind of funk that comes from being in a club packed tight with bodies. "I'm gonna go out for good," Sav says, trying to work his lips into a smile. "Me and Sandra. Just like my brother. I only came home to pack my shit."

"Do it and get the fuck out," Giulia says.

Risa's mind is spinning with possibilities. A little part of her is sickened by the notion of him running away with Sandra, but mostly she feels relief. Maybe the church will see fit to annul her marriage, though he'll have to stay gone. What if he comes back, broke, Sandra having run off, and acts like he wants to reconcile?

Sav trudges forward and pulls out the chair across from Giulia at the table, its legs screeching against the floor. He sits. "Don't rush me," he says.

"Enough, Sav," Risa says, her hands quaking. "I'm done. Just go."

"Tomorrow, I'll be on a plane, headed to a beach somewhere." He plucks some cash out of his pockets. A couple of hundred-dollar bills. Drops them on the table. "Had a windfall."

Risa carries Fab into the living room and puts him in his playpen, setting him up with a couple of toys and his pacifier. He's on his back, lolling about, oblivious, pawing at a soft red block with the letter *F* stitched on the side. She thinks about him growing up fatherless. She thinks about what Sav's abusive behavior has done to him already—even if he doesn't have any idea what's going on, it's seeping in. The way she cries in front of him. He *knows*. He'll carry that. She thinks of ways she might free him from it. She can't erase Sav, though she wishes she could. If only she could go back and tell her younger self not to see in him whatever she saw, to hold off for another guy, a decent and kind guy, because this future she's living in is too painful. She approaches Sav and says, "Wherever you go, whatever you do, whoever you go with, I don't care. I want you gone from my life and from Fab's life. I want an annulment."

Sav reaches under his shirt and takes the gun from where it's tucked into his waistline. He sets it on the table.

Giulia gets up and scrambles into the kitchen. She grabs a bread knife from the knife block on the counter and holds it up, her fingers grasped around the wooden handle.

"Giulia, don't," Risa says.

"Take it," Sav says to Risa, nodding in the direction of the gun. "Let's see what kind of guts you got. Shoot me."

"Shut the fuck up and go," Giulia says.

"Put the knife down," Risa says to her. She looks at the gun on the table next to the crumpled hundreds Sav scattered there and doesn't reach for it.

"No guts," Sav says, standing. His knees hit the edge of the table, nearly toppling the chair as he pushes it back.

In his playpen, Fab starts crying, his face going red and scrunchy.

Sav kicks the chair and continues: "I'll be out of your hair forever, don't worry. Do me a favor and shut the kid up." He lumbers toward the bedroom, reaching out for the wall to stop himself from falling. He passes over the threshold, runs into something, probably the edge of the bed frame, and curses. He proceeds to slam around in there. The sound of drawers being yanked open, the closet door rattling off its track.

Giulia sighs. She holds the knife down at her side and comes over to Risa. "You okay?" she asks.

"I don't know anymore," Risa says, her voice breaking, full of emotion. She's aching to move toward Fab—still crying, his face pressed against the mesh wall of the playpen, his nose smushed—to comfort him.

"Let's hide the gun. He's so out of it, maybe he forgets."

Risa nods in silent agreement.

Giulia keeps the knife in one hand and moves to the table, scooping up the gun by its grip, holding it so it dangles from her hand barrel-down like something diseased. She looks around desperately for somewhere to stash it. A few steps back into the kitchen. She opens the freezer door, finds a half-full bag of frozen peas held shut with two clothespins. She sets the knife down on the edge of the freezer door for a second, takes the clothespins off and buries the gun in the peas and then crinkles the bag shut and puts the clothespins back in place. She nestles the bag behind some steaks from Meats Supreme and a massive box of fish sticks and a stack of Tupperware containers full of frozen food for Fab. She grabs the knife again. Risa nods and then goes to Fab in his playpen and picks him up. The poor kid stops crying instantly.

Sav's really making a racket now. Tangling with the closet door. Lots of slamming noises. When he comes out of the bedroom, he's got a backpack slung over his shoulder, only partially zipped, clothes spilling out.

Risa stands by the table with Fab in her arms. "Don't you want to say goodbye to your son?" she asks, but she regrets the words as soon as they escape her mouth. It's exactly what her mother would do, trying to lay a guilt trip on him. She wants him gone, why prolong this?

"I'll skip it," Sav says. "Never wanted to be anybody's old man. Or husband. Happy to give Giulia a kiss goodbye, though." He flings his backpack to the ground and tumbles toward Giulia, wrapping her in an embrace, nuzzling her neck, laughing. The knife is in her hand, but she's immobilized.

"Get away from her," Risa says. She retreats to the playpen and dumps Fab there again. Much to his dismay. The wailing starts over, leveling up the tension.

But then Sav does back off. Not because of Risa's words, though. Because he notices the blank spot on the table where his gun had been. He approaches it and swipes his hand against the tabletop, as if he's hallucinating that it's missing. "Where is it?" he asks.

"It's gone," Risa says.

He fumbles around, looking for it. Fruit bowl. Hall closet. Countertops. "Where the fuck you hide it?" He's talking to Giulia. He comes back to her. She's waving the knife at him. He grabs her wrist until she drops it. The knife clatters against the floor. Fab's crying so hard it turns to choking.

"I took it outside and threw it down the sewer," Giulia says.

"You didn't have time," Sav says, slurring his words. He moves his right hand up over her belly and chest, pawing at her throat, beginning to squeeze like he plans on strangling the answer he wants out of her.

Giulia's shocked and trembling, her eyes half-shut.

Risa scurries into the kitchen and gets the cast-iron pan from the stove. Protecting Giulia is on her mind, but so is freedom from Sav. She comes up beside him, moving in step with Fab's cries. Gripping the pan tightly by the still-warm handle with both hands, she rears back and swings it at Sav, thwacking him across the side of the head. The sound is awful. An echoey thump. He falls back, smacking his head on the edge of the table on the way down and then sprawling on the floor between them.

Risa drops the pan, breadcrumb-spattered oil puddling on the linoleum. Sav's out cold. He's got a big gash on his forehead where she hit him, and another—one that's almost like an indentation—on his temple where he clipped the table. He's bleeding a lot. The blood is edging up against the oil. Risa steps over him and hugs Giulia, who's trying to catch her breath. Risa's thinking now about destiny, how a series of things happened that led to this moment, and she's wondering what decisions she'll have to make, what price she'll pay. She imagines herself having to help Sav, calling an ambulance, the cops questioning her and Giulia. She imagines a jail cell. She imagines, too, letting him die, letting the blood ooze from him until the whole apartment is flooded red. She imagines setting fire to the apartment, letting him burn up inside like that movie. She looks over at Fab, his anguish having melted into confusion, and gives him a sweet little wave.

2.

Giulia goes straight for the wine. She sits at the table and slugs from the bottle. Risa walks into the living room and picks up Fab and nurses him on the couch. Giulia can hear the slurping sounds. Sav's just a body on the floor, blood pooled under his head and back. The pan is right there next to him. Some of the oil has browned the blood. They don't know how bad it is yet. Seems like he's still breathing. Giulia's not sure what to do. She's a runner by nature. Part of her wants to just take off and let her sister figure this out. But she'd never do that to Risa, who she loves more than anyone. Sav will probably get up and zombie-march out of the apartment, gashes in his head and all. Got what he deserved, anyway. She can still feel his hand closing on her neck. "Jesus Christ, Ris," Giulia says finally, letting out a nervous little laugh. "That was some swing."

"What are we gonna do?" Risa asks, adjusting Fab in her lap.

"Dig a hole in the backyard. Make it deep."

"You don't think he's really dead, do you?"

Giulia senses an edge of desperate excitement in Risa's voice.

"It was just a pan," Risa continues. "I had to do it."

"He hit his head, too." Giulia nods toward a thick smear of blood on the edge of the table, one of his dark black hairs curled in it. "I hope the fucker's dead. Must've felt good to whack him."

Giulia had never been sure why Risa married Sav. As a girl, Risa would spend hours drawing birthday and holiday cards for Giulia. She'd always buy her some thoughtful little gift from one of the stalls on Eighty-Sixth Street—earrings, a bracelet, magnets, stuffed animals, toys that danced, stickers for her sticker book. She was the kind of girl who'd bring Giulia tea and soup in bed when she wasn't feeling well. The way she said things, she was never critical, always supportive. Even after everything went bad with Pop, Giulia always felt like Risa was on her side. Risa even believed in God and went to church in a way that seemed sincere to Giulia, who'd given up on all that shit long ago. That was Risa in a nutshell. Always thinking about how she could make others happy. Everything from the heart.

Sav, on the other hand, Giulia pegged as trouble from day one. Her ex-boyfriend from high school, Marco LaRocca, grew up right here on the same block as Sav, so she'd seen him around a little, heard a few stories. The way he wore his clothes, the way he walked, the way he did his hair, the swagger and indifference, his voice. It was all right there in his eyes—he was searching to take advantage of people and situations, hustling, filled with aimless rage, always walking on ledges. Sure, he'd gotten worse, but he was never good to start with. There's that old saw about opposites attracting, but there's a difference between opposites and people who are just flat-out wrong for each other.

The night before Risa and Sav's wedding a couple of years back, Giulia was sitting with her sister at a table in a bowling alley in Bay Ridge called Yellow Hook Lanes. That was what Risa had wanted to do the night before her fucking wedding—go bowling in Bay Ridge with her maid of honor and bridesmaids. Giulia was her maid of honor, of course, and her girlfriends Marta, Lily, and Grace were her bridesmaids. There was a lot of cackling. They actually bowled. It was a night full of gutter balls, which seemed appropriate in hindsight. Giulia drank cheap beer, whatever swill they had on tap, and Risa and her girlfriends drank soda like teenagers. They were in their mid-twenties, but no one wanted hangovers, except Giulia, who couldn't imagine being at the wedding without a hangover for a variety of reasons, including the fact that it'd be the first time she was in the same place as her father in about five years. After a few plastic cups of beer, Giulia pressed her sister to reconsider this whole fucking marriage-to-Sav thing. "He's not a good guy," Giulia said, slurring her words.

"Don't say that," Risa said. "You don't know him the way I do."

"What do you know that I don't?"

"He can have a sweet side."

"I know his type. He's a loser. He'll go through bad jobs, he'll stay out every night, he'll cheat, he'll be mean as shit."

"My wise old little sister."

"I'm not kidding."

"Why does everyone expect certain things from me?" Risa asked. Like everything with her, it was a sincere question. Giulia could only guess at the time that marrying Sav served as some sort of quiet rebellion against such expectations. Everyone thought she'd find some sweet soft guy at a church mixer, but she went for a neighborhood scoundrel who loved heavy metal and occasionally stole cars for joyrides and dragged around poor Chooch from across the street like a pet.

No surprise, Giulia had gotten him exactly right. In the last couple of years, as Sav showed Risa how terrible he could be, Giulia tried her hardest not to say *I told you so*. She hated seeing her sweet sister suffer, especially during her pregnancy and after Fab was born.

Giulia looks at Risa, watches as she strokes Fab's head as he nurses. She's shaking, that much Giulia can tell. The reality's sinking in.

"I need a cigarette," Giulia says. "You got any?"

Risa shakes her head.

"Sav doesn't have any around?"

"Not that I know of."

"You mind if I go get some? Widow Marie sells them at the bar."

"Right now?"

"I'll be back in five minutes. Give us time to think."

"What if he wakes up?"

"Put Fab down, pick up the pan, and hit him again."

Giulia gets up and leaves the apartment. A family called the Coluccis—husband, wife, two kids—lives upstairs, and a guy everyone knows as Religious Pete is on the floor above them. Giulia looks up and around, as if someone is watching, as if someone knows what's happened inside, as if they can see Sav or smell his blood.

On the brick wall next to the door is a sad and half-busted mailbox, FRANZONE scrawled beneath the lid in white paint marker. Sav's last name. Giulia can't think of it as Risa's last name. She'll always be a Taverna.

The yard's all dead grass and concrete and dried-up plants she doesn't know the names of. The ones that usually have those sleek, curved leaves, but now they look like fountains of burnt brown confetti.

She takes a deep breath and opens the front gate. She's shaking, too.

It's a short walk to the Crisscross Cocktail Lounge, which is right down the block on the corner. Giulia looks up at the street signs on the light post—SAINT OF THE NARROWS ST. and BATH AVE., white letters crowded on the green aluminum—and then at the blue script neon sign over the bar's front door, the cursive after the final *e* transformed into a two-headed arrow with its points aiming in opposite directions. She stopped in on her way to Risa's after ditching Richie and had a beer and a shot. That was when she saw Sav with the gun. She knows the bar well, used to go in all the time with Marco when they were underage.

Giulia's a minor celebrity at the Crisscross. Marco LaRocca's ex-flame. Marco has gone on to become the most famous guy born in the neighborhood. No one expected it and then everyone changed their tune and said they knew he was born for big things. She goes through waves of missing him. She guesses most people feel that way about their high school sweethearts. He'd been tender if not always faithful. He'd written her songs and poems. There was nothing she'd liked more than lying tangled with him on a bed listening to records and smoking. They broke up after graduation, and he moved to the East Village with his friends Kirk, Sammy, and Gabs. They'd been a band in high school called Metric Ton and played a few basements and local bars, but they became the Kickbacks in the city and started playing real shows at CBGB and the Ritz. Joey Ramone was at one of the gigs and liked what he heard. The rest happened fast—opening for the Misfits, a record deal, music videos, fame. Giulia couldn't believe it. She'd figured Marco would struggle with music for a few more years and then give it up and go work at his cousin's pork store on Avenue U. But he'd become a fucking rock star. And here she is, years later, having cycled through losers, stuck in a nightmare situation now with her sister's loser husband, finding respite in a dive on Marco's old block, yearning for what they'd had in high school. She wonders if Marco ever gives one small thought to her, like he's about to start playing on a stage in Paris or Rio de Janeiro, and he remembers her hair or her smell or the way she touched him or the way they sang along to records in his room. There's a signed picture of him up on the wall behind the bar. It always makes her heart hurt to see it.

Inside, Marie Agostara—aka Widow Marie—is still behind the bar. She's a short woman, maybe five-one, and she wears a sweatshirt even in the dead of summer. She has a black wig on because her real hair's thin and she's got bald patches. Giulia's been in before when some drunk or another's plucked the wig from her head and tossed it up on the pool table light. "Look who's back," Widow Marie says.

"Can I have a pack of Marlboro Reds?" Giulia asks.

"Nothing to drink?"

"Okay, I guess. Give me another shot."

Widow Marie slops some Jim Beam—she knows Giulia's drink without asking—into a shot glass cloudy with age and plucks a pack of cigarettes from a carton next to the register. She brings the whiskey and cigarettes over to Giulia and tosses her a matchbook with the two-headed arrow logo above the striker.

Giulia drops a five on the bar, puts back the shot, and rips the cellophane off the smokes, using a match to light one. She's feeling a little drunk now, lost in the surreal swirl of the night, how quickly things went down. She takes a deep drag and looks around the place. Marco's picture. The register. It's mostly empty in the bar. There's an old-timer, Bernadine, whiskers on her chin, rotten teeth, skin flushed red. Another woman, about Giulia's age, who everyone calls Jane the Stain, is on one side of Bernadine. Jane has the look of a distinguished alcoholic—her drink is vodka and ginger ale—even though she's still young. They'd both been here when she was in earlier. Now Jimmy Tomasullo sits on the other side of Bernadine, shelling peanuts and drinking whiskey in a pint glass. A big, oafish bastard. Pit stains and bags under his eyes and his shirt buttoned wrong. Been a couple of years since Sav's brother, Roberto, robbed Jimmy's trophy shop and left town with his wife.

Jimmy downs his whiskey. He knocks the bowl of peanut shells off the bar and staggers into a standing position. Widow Marie curses him for making a mess. Jimmy groans and walks unsteadily toward Giulia, getting right up in her face. "I heard your brother-in-law was here before," Jimmy says.

"Yeah, so?" Giulia says.

"Tell him I gotta ask him something."

Giulia nods, blows her smoke away from him. *Yeah, I'll do that if the fucker makes it through the night.*

Jimmy stumbles to his stool.

It's then that Giulia notices a little horseshoe-shaped spot of blood on the sleeve of her shirt. She dabs it at with a cocktail napkin, darkening it into the blue of her shirt. She scrunches up the napkin and stuffs it in the tight pocket of her jeans. She's not sure how she could've gotten Sav's blood on her, especially there. She kept her distance from what she remembers. She worries that someone might've noticed the blood, that—later—it'll occur to them to be a significant detail. They'll say she was acting twitchy, that something was off, that someone showing up with blood on their clothes always means trouble. Shaking a little, she rolls up her sleeves and cuffs them above her elbows.

After a long minute, she thanks Widow Marie and stands, tucking the pack of Marlboros into the breast pocket of her shirt, and drifting out of the bar.

If she had guts and they had money and passports, she'd try to convince Risa to get a cab to the airport and hop on a plane to Italy. They went once as girls to visit their cousins, and she's always longed to go back. They could have a new life in Naples.

Out on the sidewalk, she takes in a soft summer breeze that seems to waft up the avenue. The smell of salt. The bay's not too far. She finishes her cigarette as she walks and then flicks the butt into the street as she goes in through the gate.

Back inside, everything's the same, except Fab's in his playpen again, having been nursed to sleep, and Risa's put some dark towels over the blood. She's sitting at the table now.

"I'm sorry," Giulia says.

"He's gonna get up, right?" Risa says.

"I don't know."

"I'm gonna call the cops. Tell them he got violent, and it was self-defense."

"That's what you think's best?"

"What if Sandra comes looking for him? He said he was going to meet her."

"You don't think she'd really have the balls to show her face here, do you?"

"We need help. I don't know what to do."

"Say he goes into a coma, or he dies, what then?" Giulia says. "This time we're wasting looks real bad. His mother, his father, you're gonna have to face them."

"Maybe Chooch can help us," Risa says. "He'll understand. He knows how Sav's been. He saw what happened with the gun."

"We can trust him? He's Sav's friend." Giulia knows Chooch a little, knows he adores Risa and Fab, but how's he going to react to this situation?

"We're family to him. He's not like Sav. He got stuck the same way I did. I trust him."

"I hope so," Giulia says.

"Stay with Fab," Risa says, slipping on her shoes. "I'll be right back. Don't answer the door or the phone. If Mr. Colucci comes down from upstairs, just tell him Fab's sick."

"Why would Mr. Colucci come down?"

"He's always got his nose in everybody's business. Sometimes he checks in on me when he hears Sav yelling."

"Jesus."

"I'm sorry, Giulia."

"You've got nothing to be sorry for."

"If Fab wakes up, there's a bottle of apple juice in the fridge. He's okay with that if I'm not around to nurse. Hopefully, I'll only be a minute."

Risa kisses Giulia on the head and checks on Fab, picking up the soft block that's beside him in the playpen, and then she scrambles out of the apartment, closing the door lightly behind her.

Giulia takes the package of cigarettes out of her pocket and puts it on the table. She strikes a match and lights one. She walks close to Sav, toeing the blood line, careful not to step in it. She investigates him for movements. The blood seems like it's in Technicolor. She thought it'd be darker. "Looks like it's just me and you now, fucko," she says, ashing on his body.

3.

Chooch is sitting at the desk in his room working on one of his collages. He cuts up magazines and catalogs using a penknife he got at an art supply store on Eighty-Sixth Street and glues them to a square of cardboard. Then he puts some Scotch tape over the whole thing, making it almost look like it's behind glass. There's really no rhyme or reason to the choices he makes. He just cuts out images he likes—faces, bodies, fields, mountains, planets, products, food—and he combines them in a way that's random. A floating head next to a field of corn and an ad for a fancy little statue of Marilyn Monroe. He's never shown them to anyone. He barely looks at them himself once he's done. The one he's working on now, it's angry. He's cutting out images of burned-out tenements from an old issue of *Life* and he's pasting them next to pictures of devastation from some war magazine he scored in the waiting room of the urology office in Dyker Heights where he works as a file clerk four days a week.

He's got the window open in his room, but it's still hot. Doesn't help that he's wearing jeans and a heavy black T-shirt. His Walkman is on, headphones over his ears, listening to his White Lion *Fight to Survive* tape. Just the act of doing this work brings him some peace.

And he needs some peace after all that happened tonight.

Fucking Sav.

Chooch and Sav go back to day one of kindergarten at Our Lady of Perpetual Surrender when they discovered they lived on the same block. Sister Bernadette was their teacher. She had tight, wrinkled skin, and wore long brown dresses and clean loafers, and she was famous for twisting the ears of children who talked back to her. Sav got put in the corner one day and Chooch got put in the other corner and then Sav whispered they were block brothers *and* corner brothers so that sealed the deal.

That was twenty years ago. They've gone through a lot since then. All of Our Lady of Perpetual Surrender. Sav and his family moving a few blocks away—might as well have been miles. High school at Lafayette. Sav getting married to Risa and moving back to the block and having Fab. Sav treating everyone like shit. Chooch hanging around because he's loyal.

Chooch's given name is Christopher. Sav branded him Chooch in second grade. He lives in a frame house across the street from Sav with his mother, Vi. Even she calls him Chooch. His dad died when he was thirteen. Just a face in crumbling photo albums now. They have a country house up in Sullivan County they stopped going to when his dad passed. Their summers there live in his memory as the happiest time of his life. Swimming in the Delaware River. Having a bonfire in the yard. Walking through the woods. Driving curvy roads and watching hawks in the sky. Eating dinner at the Western Hotel, big bowls of stew chased with cherry 7 Ups in pint glasses, his dad gambling away on a slot machine in the secret room behind the freezer. It's the only time Chooch ever spent away from the city.

Sav grew up in the house where he lives now, though the whole place used to be his family's. They still own it, but his parents are in the house they moved to on Eighty-Second Street, and they rent out the two upstairs apartments here on Saint of the Narrows and let Sav, Risa, and Fab live rent-free in the ground-floor apartment. There were times when the ribbons of blacktop and concrete that separated them felt like sacred ground, but that's changed.

What Sav did to Risa and Fab tonight was a new low. Sav has been a lot of things, but he's never been a gun guy. Chooch left with him after that to be his conscience. He saw big trouble coming, and he was trying to talk sense. Turns out he wasn't wrong. It was like dominoes. After the gun incident, Chooch had trailed Sav and Double Stevie Scivetti to Gilly the Gambler's house up the block. Gilly's in Atlantic City, and they'd somehow overheard at the Crisscross where he leaves his key in the yard for someone to come in and feed his cats. They'd also heard the rumors that Gilly, a widower who likes his blackjack and poker and betting on the horse races, keeps a stash of cash in his attic. So, they went inside and ransacked the attic, Sav knocking over and destroying a crate of old seventy-eights, black shellac splintered everywhere on the wood floor. Finally, they found a tool chest with six grand in it. Then Double Stevie drove them over to L'Amour, the metal club on Sixty-Second Street where they've been regulars for years. A bunch of good acts playing. Sav hooked up with Sandra Carbonari and almost immediately got into a brawl with this guy Squidge over Sandra. Sav showed the gun again. Squidge backed down. That was when Chooch took off. He'd had enough.

He walked all the way back to the block, stopping at the school on the corner, P.S. 101, and climbing up on the roof. He sometimes did that when he needed to make sense of things from above. He knows the way, taught to him by Calvino, one of the janitors at the school. He gets up on the dumpster to access the fire ladder on the side of the building. The building's not that tall, four stories, but it's among the highest in the neighborhood. The roof is big and flat and empty and black. Reminds him of the surface of another planet. What he especially likes is seeing everything from a different angle. The trains rumbling by on the El on Eighty-Sixth Street, a block away, almost at the same level. Dilapidated shingles on sloping roofs of old houses. A weird puddle on the uneven roof of the Benson Arms. Cracked sidewalks. Glittering blacktop. The streetlights reflected in chrome bumpers. Fire escapes where people are sitting and smoking to get out of their hot apartments. Weeds growing wild in yards. Ropes, wires, and buckets in gardens. Tomato plants. The myriad ways people fight for some semblance of privacy: sprawling fig trees, canvases strung up to shield views, fences nudged between houses that are close together. Gates with cement lions. Handwritten signs on mailboxes. NO CIRCULARS. BEWARE OF DOG. PSYCHIC READINGS. Telephone poles like masts on a ship. Sneakers dangling from the wires. So many wires. Stretching and drooping and stitching the sky. The steeple of Our Lady of Perpetual Surrender with its gold cross. The blocks and avenues stretching out. Veins, blood, movement.

While he was up there, Dolly Parente appeared in a high window of the house across the street from the school, where she lives with her cop husband, Dickie. She pushed out the screen, watching it float down to the driveway, and put her elbows on the sill, framed by the darkness around the house. She was wearing a Mets shirt that was too big and had a red bandanna on her head. She was about fifteen or twenty feet below Chooch and didn't notice him. She gazed out over the block. Chooch loves the thrill involved in watching someone who doesn't know you're seeing them. They're not acting. Not aware. Dolly leaned forward, angling her head up, extending her torso out the window as far as it would go. She closed her eyes, took a deep breath, and put her hands over her head. It looked as if she were trying to take flight. Chooch couldn't make sense of what she was doing, but he found it beautiful. Eventually, she disappeared back inside.

It had made him think of Risa. Looking for a breath, a break.

Sav met Risa in the summer of '83, but Chooch had seen her around a lot before that. She'd also gone to Our Lady of Perpetual Surrender and Lafayette, a year ahead of them. Chooch remembers seeing her in the Perpetual Surrender schoolyard in the mornings when they'd say the Pledge of Allegiance. He'd had a crush on her from afar. That black hair. The way she wore her cardigan, the sleeves pulled down over her palms. Stickers on her books. She'd grown up on the other side of Eighty-Sixth Street. The Tavernas. Her sister, Giulia, worked at the Loew's Oriental and dated Marco LaRocca in high school.

Back in the schoolyard, it had just been a crush, but Chooch fell in love with Risa for real after Sav started dating her. He was struck by how wrong Sav seemed for her. The first time Chooch had talked to Risa, really talked to her, was this night they all went to the movies together right after Christmas in '83. Sav wanted to see *Sudden Impact*, but Risa wanted to see *Terms of Endearment*. Because it was only a few months into them going together, Sav yielded, and they went to *Terms of Endearment*. Sav left for popcorn at some point and didn't come back. Chooch watched Risa watch the movie and cry. At some point near the end, when Debra Winger was really on the ropes, Risa put her hand over his and squeezed. It was the most intimate thing he'd ever experienced. He fell for her right then. In the lobby, after the movie was over, they bundled up because it had gotten freezing out and waited for Sav, but he was gone. Chooch walked her home—she was still living with her parents at the time—and they talked about the movie and how sad it was and about what they'd done for Christmas. He made excuses for Sav, said there must've been some emergency. He still remembers the way the cold smelled on their walk, how he could feel her hand on his even after many hours.

Chooch had wanted to tell Risa everything about his life that night. Tell her how he used to cry every morning in the shower until the water got cold. That was when he was a kid at Our Lady of Perpetual Surrender. Tell her about the hollowness he felt when he went to church with his mother. How he hated all that incense in the air and the booming sound of the organ. How the rectory frightened him. How the priests frightened him. How the holy water font and the ushers and the statues and the stained glass all frightened him. How the cardboard taste of a million communion wafers remained in his mouth to this day. How he wore his gym clothes under his uniform in high school because he dreaded the locker room so much. How he hated the hair on his arms and chest and shoulders. How he'd sit in the back of the car when his mother drove them to the Kings Plaza mall for this or that, and they'd be passing so many blurred faces and he'd get this sense of other people's pain. A communal thing. Like the city was a pot. A melting pot, like they said, but not only of so many cultures, of all this pain, and it was swirling in the air and sometimes you could take a breath and it'd absorb into your bones and blood.

He finishes the collage he's working on and sets it aside. He presses stop on his Walkman and takes his headphones off. He goes downstairs for water. His mother is at the sink, taking a sleeping pill and washing it down with a pony bottle of ginger ale. She's in her green floral housedress, her hair pinned up, cold cream on her face. He hadn't seen her when he came in, though he heard the television on in her room.

"Can't sleep?" he asks.

"Nothing to wake up for, and I'm still so restless."

"The pill will help."

"I guess. How was your night?"

"Nothing special." He knows it'd break her heart if he told her all that Sav had done. She's always liked Sav. She has blinders on for him because Sav treated Chooch like a brother when he had no other friends.

"Get some rest," she says.

"You too." He kisses her on the cheek under her cold cream mask. She shuffles off. He takes seven sips of water. It's a superstition he's had since he was a kid—that everything should be done in sevens. It started with his love of Mickey Mantle.

Back in his room, he changes into basketball shorts and his favorite shirt to sleep in, a comfortable blue one with André the Giant on it. He lies down on his bed, staring at the pictures on his wall, pages torn out of magazines and taped there sloppily: an ad for Iron Maiden's *The Number of the Beast*, a mini-poster for Ralph Bakshi's *Fire and Ice*, and a clipping that shows Frank Frazetta's *Moon Maid.* There are posters for *Rambo: First Blood Part II* and *Lifeforce* that he'd gotten from Wolfman's video store when they were taken out of the window. And there's Chooch's greatest joy and shame, a *Billboard* centerfold spread of Olivia Newton-John in a white bikini from when "Physical" was a smash hit. Above that, hanging from a nail, is the old SAINT OF THE NARROWS ST. sign he stole from the corner when they put the new one up—white letters on a black background, the way it used to be in Brooklyn before the green took over the whole city—and he sometimes gets lost exploring its dents and indentions and imagines some city official busting into his room to collar him for the long-ago theft.

He's feeling restless, so he pictures his collection of cassettes, all lined up neatly in their case, alphabetized from Anthrax to Whitesnake, and tries to remember and name every tape he owns. His version of counting sheep.

Something comes flying in his window and lands on his chest, almost giving him a heart attack. He looks at it—a soft block with the letter *F* on it, the kind Fab has in his playpen. He thinks he hears someone calling his name. Risa? Can't be.

He stands and goes to the window and leans out over the

fire escape and sees Risa standing below his window in the alley. "Everything okay?" Chooch asks.

"No," she says.

He puts his black Chucks on and climbs out on the fire escape and carefully goes down the rusty ladder—it's only one floor—to the concrete alleyway next to his house. In high school, he'd snuck out this way a few times to meet Sav.

In the alley, he looks down at the ground under his feet. Weeds crocheted into broken white concrete. A few nearby window air conditioners hum in the night, punctuated with their intermittent condensation drips. A bus wheezes over on the corner. A distant siren bellows.

"What happened?" Chooch asks.

"It's Sav," Risa says in a whisper.

"What'd he do?"

"I need your help."

He realizes she's shaking. "Is it Fab? Did he hurt Fab?" It's the first thought that comes to his mind. Sav, wasted, hitting his baby, or hurting him somehow. Picking him up and dropping him. Collapsing into his playpen or crib. Knocking him from Risa's arms. Or maybe something with the fucking gun. Jesus.

"Fab's fine," she says.

He follows her across the street, passing under the cone of an overhead light, which illuminates the blacktop and the cars parked in front of his house and her apartment. Mr. Vistocci—a few houses down—is out on his front porch, beating the heat with a cold beer, his radio on. Other than that, the neighbors seem to be hiding away inside with their fans or air conditioners.

Before they enter the apartment, Risa tries to say something to him but then she stops herself.

"You can tell me," Chooch says.

"I didn't mean for it to happen," Risa says.

"What happened?"

And then they're inside, moving down the hallway.

Risa's sister, Giulia, is sitting at the table, her sleeves rolled up, smoking a cigarette. She avoids looking at him. Her silence is heavy. She thrums the fingers of her free hand on the tabletop. Sweat glistens on her forehead. The smoke wraps around her.

No sign of Fab—he's probably in his crib asleep since it's so late.

Chooch's eyes travel to the floor where he sees Sav, blood inked under his head, a gash above his brow ridge, another on his temple, a cast-iron pan on the floor next to him, oil threaded into the blood, some dark towels draped over the puddle. Sav's still wearing his favorite Iron Maiden shirt, from their World Slavery Tour last year. Chooch and Sav went to that show together at Radio City Music Hall. Only time Chooch had ever been there other than the Christmas Spectacular once as a kid. They saw Metallica at L'Amour a couple of nights later. The Metal Massacre.

"He was wasted and out of control," Risa says.

Giulia finishes her smoke and drops it into an empty wine bottle on the table. She's nerved up, her eyes now darting from Chooch to Risa and back again. He can tell she doesn't trust him. Whatever happened, she doesn't want him here. Over her shoulder, Chooch finally spots Fab, asleep in his playpen in the living room.

Risa continues: "I hit him with the pan. Then he knocked his head on the table as he fell."

Chooch has barely seen blood at all in his life. Maybe a few schoolyard fights, a split lip, a cut on someone's cheek, scraped knees from when they used to play Kill the Man with the Ball on concrete at P.S. 101. But never blood like *this*. And it's Sav's. He's lying there, haloed by the blood, his body seeming to be an extension of it.

"I need your help," Risa says again. "I don't know what to do."

Chooch buckles to his knees and pukes.

4.

Deep down Risa hopes Sav's dying or already dead. She can't fight the feeling. What more can she hope for than freedom? She stares at his body and imagines him as a cage, his limbs and ears and even his closed eyes making up the bars, and they're fading away as the life drains from him. Perhaps she willed this to happen somehow, wanted it to happen, coaxed a series of events into existence that would lead to this very thing. The whole time she was making the cutlets, maybe she was subconsciously aware that she was holding the hot handle of a murder weapon. She was feeling its heft, knowing that whacking a man in the head with it could probably put an end to him. That, plus a bit of serendipity. Him hitting his head on the table might've been the finishing touch.

Chooch grabs a roll of paper towels from the kitchen. He mops up his vomit and tries to soak up some of the blood, sweating as he moves around.

"I'm sorry I brought you into this," Risa says. The smoke from Giulia's cigarette is collected under the overhead light like a spirit. She feels as if they're being watched.

"I'm glad you did," Chooch says. "I'm thinking, um, I'm thinking maybe we need to call someone. Say it was an accident. Say he was drunk, and he fell. Hit his head. He probably won't even remember."

"Fuck that," Giulia says. "My vote is let him bleed until there's nothing left and then put him out with the trash."

"Giulia," Risa says.

"What? You're the one who believes in God so much. If he didn't kill me, or didn't kill you or Fab, it was coming. He had that gun."

"He said he was leaving."

"Guys like him, they get on the road, they turn around in a day. He would've been back as soon as the money ran out."

"Where's the gun?" Chooch asks.

"In the freezer," Giulia says. "I hid it when he was in the bedroom packing."

"He said he was going away with Sandra," Risa says, pointing to the backpack that Sav had sloppily filled, turned over on its side near the table.

Chooch, on his hands and knees, pauses to take a few deep breaths. She thinks he might puke again, but he sucks in some air, and closes his eyes, and says, "Sav? You hear me? Sav?" In his basketball shorts and wrestling shirt and black Chucks, Chooch looks like an overgrown kid, hunched near the body of this friend he'd been dealt by fate.

Fab wakes up crying. Risa retrieves him from the playpen and cradles him in her arms. She lifts her shirt to nurse him.

Fab latches on and is immediately peaceful again. It also brings peace to her. She looks at his closed eyes, sees how content he is, imagines how awful the night has been for him, his schedule all thrown off. She knows, in the end, he's what matters most.

The room now feels full of silence. Giulia's picking at a napkin and letting the pieces flutter onto the tabletop. Risa knows that the longer they wait, the worse it'll look. "Will you call nine-one-one, Christopher?" she asks. "I can't do it."

Chooch nods. Before he goes to make the call, though, he moves closer to Sav, his knees in the blood, and he reaches out and touches his neck. "I think he might be dead," he says.

In the weeks following her wedding to Sav, Risa realized she'd made a mistake. She'd wake up, and he'd be gone. She'd go to bed, and he'd be gone. He'd come home smelling of booze and cigarettes and stale sweat and perfume. He'd ignore her. He'd call her names and laugh at her. He'd do this in front of others. His mother apologized to her, said she'd talk to him, that he'd straighten up, grow up, but that didn't happen.

She remembers the first time he put his hands on her. It was so casual. Just extended his arm and gave her a smack. She went into their bedroom and put on music. Her favorite Joni Mitchell album, *Court and Spark*, spinning on the Cromwell suitcase record player she'd had since she was a girl. She traced her fingers over the edges of the sleeve and imagined a different life for herself in California or somewhere. Sunshine and health food and flowing dresses. Sav busted into the room and yanked the cord for the record player out of the wall. He screeched the needle across the vinyl and then knocked everything to the ground. She never got the record player fixed, never replaced her copy of *Court and Spark*.

When she was first pregnant with Fab, she had the strangest urge to smell old books—she felt like it kept her from getting sick. Giulia would bring her the oldest books she could find, little crumbling copies of Dickens and Hardy that she'd score at secondhand shops and garage sales. Risa would hold the book up to her nose and take long, deep breaths. It was stupid, but she felt like she was breathing in knowledge. Already she was dreaming of a better life for Fab. She'd do what she had to do to keep him from going down the same road as Sav.

She remembers when Fab was born at Victory Memorial. Sav couldn't even bother to make it. Risa's parents were there for the birth and then Giulia came after they left. Even Chooch showed up and brought a box of Russell Stover chocolates and a gift shop teddy bear. She held Fab and felt simultaneously like she was more connected to someone than she'd ever been but also more alone than she'd ever been. A loneliness without any hope for the future tethered to it. She was pulled between the two feelings. She imagined new mothers with their spouses constantly at their side, doting, in awe. Sav, it turned out, was mixed up in some scheme to sell scrap copper to a junkyard in Coney Island called One Stop Salvage. He and a few other guys—Sweaty Vin, Tall Vin, Rudy the Greek, Charlie Cee's nephew who only goes by Nephew—from another occasional hangout of his, Blue Sticks, had been breaking into abandoned buildings in Sunset Park and ripping copper wires and pipes out of the walls. Giulia stayed with her through the night.

Risa shifts on her feet now, Fab in her arms, her shirt scrunched over him. "He's really dead?" she says to Chooch.

Chooch presses his fingers harder against Sav's neck. There's no movement in Sav's chest, no rise and fall. He places his hand over Sav's mouth and feels for breath, but there seems to be nothing there either. It must've been loss of blood that killed him. They were too slow. They didn't know what to do and so they didn't do anything. This is all very bad. Chooch nods.

Giulia drops another cigarette butt into the empty wine bottle on the table and blows away the smoke that ribbons out. She brings her right hand up to her face and flicks the backs of her fingers under her chin, the old Italian gesture their mother and grandmothers would do to signify not giving a damn.

Risa takes Fab away from her breast and lowers her shirt. She's simply holding her son in her arms, gazing at him in a longing way, as if what's happened will make him somehow disintegrate. Fab reaches out, his little hands fluttering against her. "I'm so sorry," she says to him. She pulls him up against her chest and hugs him tightly, her right palm spread across his back, patting him there. Fab burps. She continues: "I'm so, so sorry, my baby."

"He was leaving you," Giulia says. "We'll tell everyone he left. We'll act like he left."

"How?"

Chooch stands. "Bring him somewhere," he says.

"Like get rid of him?" Giulia asks.

Risa's voice an echo: "Rid of him?" Hope and determination in her tone suddenly. Worse people than her have done worse things than this. Burying it away is possible. She didn't poison him, didn't plan this. He brought this on himself by being who he is . . . *was*. Something guiding her.

"Yeah," Chooch says. "And like Giulia said, you can tell people he took off, act like he took off. Maybe you'll wake up tomorrow and none of this will be real and you'll feel like he really did go away."

"Where? How?"

"I'll borrow my mother's car. Take him upstate. We have that house in Sullivan County. There's woods behind it."

Risa pictures a forest, a grave in the ground, dirt raining over Sav's body. Filling his mouth and nose and ears. Dirt on the wounds in his head. Dirt and blood. Sav left as food for worms and whatever else crawls around in the earth. The image brings her a feeling somewhere between relief and joy.

Chooch wipes his leg with paper towels, catching a smear of blood he's leaned into. The blood soaks into the whiteness of the paper towel, the red spreading fast. "I understand," he says. "Okay? I know what he was like. I know you wouldn't have done this if he'd left you any other options."

Risa nods.

"Give me fifteen minutes. I'm gonna go home and change my clothes and get my mother's keys and a few other things. Get out garbage bags and paper towels and any cleaning supplies you have. Don't do anything else. Try not to look at him. When I get back, we'll put him in the trunk and then clean up."

"Okay." Risa puts her head down.

Chooch goes into the bathroom and strips the beige plastic liner from behind the shower curtain. He brings it back out and covers Sav. "If I leave soon, I can make it up there by two in the morning and then get done in an hour or two and be back home by early morning. My mother took a sleeping pill. She won't even know I'm gone."

Risa tries to picture herself in the shadowy confessional box at church, clutching her rosary beads, talking through the screen to Monsignor Terrone.

She imagines what it'll feel like to hold back the truth. Going to confession as a girl always made her so nervous. When she had no sins to admit to, she made them up, told the priest she had lied or cursed though she hadn't. It was Father Giovanni back in those days. He was sweet and kind and funny. He always made her laugh. She believed he knew she was making up her sins. She was a good girl. Everyone knew she was a good girl. One time, outside the confessional box, he pulled her aside and told her she didn't need to confess things that weren't true. He said it wasn't a sin to lie because she wanted him to think she had the same flaws as the other kids. She nodded and stopped inventing sins.

She turns now and catches a glimpse of her reflection in the glass of the china closet, superimposed over the plates and cups and baubles left to her by Nana Candido, her hand splayed on Fab's back, right below the rolls of his neck. She kisses the soft spot on his head. "Daddy just left us," she says, watching her mouth make the words in the glass, already starting to believe the lie.

5.

Giulia's in awe of Chooch's composure when he returns. He's pulled his mother's Chevy Citation up right out front, lights off, into the same spot where Sav had been dropped not so long ago. He takes the big black garbage bags Risa retrieved from under the sink, the kind often piled on curbs in the fall, filled with leaves from yards and knotted on top like balloons. He's wearing a clean Yankees shirt and a different pair of shorts. He moves with purpose. It's as if he suddenly seems built for this moment. Much different from the guy who'd shown up on the scene and puked.

Risa's rocking Fab at the table—she's distraught in a tangled way. Giulia gets it. Scared he's dead and glad he's dead all at the same time. Emotion and adrenaline making her insides go nuclear.

Chooch asks Giulia for a quick hand in the car.

Outside, under a streetlight, she helps him spread the black plastic bags over the whole interior of the empty trunk. The Chevy has the new white Lady Liberty plates, which shimmer brightly in the darkness. Giulia's had a good amount to drink, but she feels sober. Chooch says he's thankful his mother doesn't keep her trunk full of useless stuff. It looks like a wide coffin in there, except the lining is plastic instead of satin. She tries to picture Sav lying on the plastic, bumping along on his ride upstate.

Chooch looks around. She follows his gaze, knowing he's checking to see if anyone's watching them. The block's full of hawks. Old-timers with nothing better to do than take notice of anything out of the ordinary, a break from routine, a person that doesn't belong, a car parked where or how it shouldn't be, lights and action at a time when lights and action might read as suspicious. She doesn't notice any eyes on them.

"Mr. Vistocci went in," Chooch says. "That's good. He's the only neighbor I saw was out before." He closes the trunk so that it's still open a bit, but the light inside is off. He ducks back into the car and comes out with two boxes of cling wrap.

"You done this before?" Giulia asks.

"I'm just trying to keep Risa out of trouble," Chooch says. "None of this looks any good the way it is. I'm thinking about Fab's future."

"Yeah," Giulia says. She figures folks don't know how they'll react until a thing like this happens, but she doesn't feel bad for Sav. No sympathy or remorse or anything. She's worried about Risa, that's it, doesn't want her to pay any price or have this wreck her soul. She's a good person who had to do something bad.

They go back inside. Risa's singing to Fab. "Blackbird" by the Beatles, a song Giulia's always loved, too. Fab has no idea what's happened. Hopefully he never will. All he knows is the soothing sound of Risa's voice.

Chooch leans over Sav's covered body, about to pull the shower liner back. He sets the cling wrap on the floor next to Sav, an unbloodied spot. He looks over at Risa and then at Giulia and says, "Maybe bring her in the bedroom?"

Giulia nods. She takes Fab from Risa, holding him close to her in the bucket shape her left arm has made and using her free hand to guide Risa into the bedroom. She helps Risa sit down on the bed and then tells her to lie back on the pillows. Risa does.

The bedroom's very simple. A dresser with a lace doily and a lamp on top. A plate for change. A framed picture of Fab that Risa had made at that photo shop on Eighty-Sixth Street. The closet, which is open, half her stuff and half Sav's. A bit of a mess from when Sav was in there earlier grabbing his shit, the door knocked off its sliding track. A table where Risa keeps a red book of prayers, a missalette from Easter, and a bone-like shard of Palm Sunday palm. A crucifix on the wall. An old bed, inherited from their folks. There's no rug on the floor, which is cold even in the hot little room. The rocking chair in the corner, a handmade heart-shaped pillow from Nana Candido propped there. Fab's crib, a mobile hanging over it, his Mickey Mouse sheets. The scent of baby powder and rash cream heavy in the air. "Can I get you anything?" Giulia asks. "A glass of water?"

Risa shakes her head.

"You sure?"

A nod.

"Maybe try to rest. I know it's hard, but try. Me and Chooch, we'll take care of things. You've been through the wringer."

Risa closes her eyes. Swallows hard.

"If I had a voice, I'd sing to you," Giulia says. She brings Fab over to his crib and places him on the mattress, offering him a pacifier, which he takes hungrily, wriggling around and then settling down on his back. His cheeks pinching in with each suck. The rhythm easing him toward sleep. Poor kid must be so tired. Giulia fears what Risa will see when she looks at him from now on. Every moment she'll have to forget what happened here tonight, hide it from him, and that's assuming things go okay, that they don't spin off in some nightmare direction.

"We're doing what we've gotta do," Giulia says. "You know that, right? This isn't our fault. If he wasn't who he was, it wouldn't have happened this way." She's reluctant to even say his name. She wants never to say his name again.

"Is Fab back to sleep?" Risa asks.

"Not quite yet," Giulia says, looking down at Fab's fluttering eyelids. "But he's getting there. I'll shut the light. Rest for a minute. We're going to be okay."

She shuts the light and pulls the door gently behind her as she exits the room.

Chooch has Sav's head and shoulders covered in cling wrap. The bastard's face is all blurred. Blood has collected under the plastic in shapes that resemble continents on a map. Chooch has pushed his body onto the shower liner, and Giulia guesses his intention is to roll him up in that and carry him to the trunk. But he's clearly battling his own queasiness again. He pauses, choking on the foulness of the tasks he's undertaking. She can't imagine what's going through his head. Twenty years he's known Sav, and this is the way it ends.

"You okay?" Giulia asks.

"I don't think so," Chooch says. "I don't know if I'll ever be okay again."

"You were right, though. It's the only thing to do. For Fab's sake. For Risa's."

"I'm gonna wrap him in this shower liner and then will you help me carry him out?"

Giulia nods. She doesn't believe in heaven or hell, but she's never really given much thought to what happens to someone's consciousness after death. Does it fade to black like a movie or does it exist in some hazy dream space? She wishes Sav could see where all his shittiness has led him. That he could float above his own body, wrapped in plastic, about to be carried into a trunk. And he hadn't even been murdered by some mobster he fucked over. Simply brained by his wife's cutlet pan. There was a dark humor in it that Giulia had to keep to herself—she was sure she'd be the only one to ever appreciate it.

"After we get him in the trunk, we'll clean up good," Chooch says. "Use paper towels and bleach on the floor and on the table. Put everything in a garbage bag and throw it in the trunk. I'll bury that stuff. I'm sorry I puked before. I think that's mostly cleaned up."

"Okay."

Chooch rolls him in the liner. Sav's short enough that he fits in there without his feet poking out. Chooch stands and lifts one end. Giulia comes over and gets the other end. They head for the door.

Giulia's struggling. *Dead weight*, that's a term people throw around, and now she knows what it means. She's grabbing at the liner, which has a scummy sheen to it. Little dots of mold and mildew. She drops her end, and Sav's body thuds against the floor. She apologizes to Chooch, and he says forget it, don't worry, and then he says he's going to take the opportunity to prop the doors and open the trunk and to do it fast when they get out there, throw Sav in the trunk and slam it shut, because what they don't want is anybody noticing what they're doing. Past a certain hour, no normal people are putting things into a trunk, certainly not things it takes two people to carry.

He goes out and does that and then they continue, hauling the body quickly to the trunk and depositing it there. Chooch closes the lid hard and somehow almost gets his finger caught, pulling back, holding in a yelp. He looks around again, searching for observers. Giulia knows, as he must know, that most passing people, if there are any, they'll keep their head down, but what you really need to keep an eye out for is those old hawks up in their windows with nothing better to do.

They go back in and Chooch puts the pan in a garbage bag. Then Giulia shows him where the gun is in the freezer, hidden in the frozen peas, and he throws that in the bag, too. He snags Sav's backpack from over by the table, as if taking it as proof that Sav skedaddled. Sav had said he'd had a windfall and tossed that money on the table—Giulia wonders if there truly was more or if he was bullshitting. She resists the urge to search the backpack. Finally, Chooch grabs the box on top of the china closet with the bullets for good measure.

"He had to get this stupid fucking gun," Chooch says. He sets everything on the floor and disappears into the bathroom, locking the door.

Giulia hears the water running. She gets to work on cleaning. She likes to clean when she's drunk, which strikes her as a disturbing observation given the circumstances. The apartment feels so bare and quiet. She starts with the table and then gets down on her knees, using bleach spray and paper towels on the floor, sweating. She thinks of this one time she was walking aimlessly on the block with Marco—*L.A.M.F.* by the Heartbreakers was all he could talk about. They moved languidly. He hung from fences as he preached about Johnny Thunders—John Anthony *Genzale*, Italian like them. He wanted to *be* him. She's fixated on this image of her hand clasped in his hand over the sidewalk, cheap rings they scored from an arcade vending machine on their wedding-ring fingers.

Chooch is in the bathroom for maybe five minutes, though it feels like a lifetime. He comes back out, taking a series of deep breaths.

He helps her finish cleaning. They wipe and scrub and spray until it looks like nothing happened. They fill another garbage bag with bloodied paper towels and knot it tight.

The hard smell of bleach fills Giulia's nose. She feels lightheaded.

"I'm gonna go," Chooch says. "Hopefully, I'm back early enough that my mother doesn't come looking for me. I don't think she'll wake up before I'm back. If she does show up over here whenever, say I went out to see Sav. We'll make it part of the story. Sav was leaving town and he wanted to see me. That was the emergency. That's why I took the car."

Giulia nods. "Thank you," she says. It occurs to her to ask if he wants her to come along, but she doesn't say it.

"I need a flashlight," Chooch says. "You know where there's one?"

Giulia stands and searches in the hall closet where she knows Risa keeps tools and light bulbs and a box of encyclopedias she got suckered into buying. She finds a flashlight. Not one of those fancy ones. A regular person flashlight, more for looking under sofas and beds than making your way through serious dark, but it'll have to do.

Chooch thanks her and picks up the garbage bags and the backpack.

The bedroom door creaks open, and Risa's standing there, holding Fab, who's half-asleep, sucking on his pacifier. "I'm coming with you," she says. "I'm gonna help get rid of him. Giulia, you can stay here if you want."

Chooch sets down what he's carrying and looks at her. His panic barely disguised. "That's not a good idea," he says.

"Gotta say I agree," Giulia says. She tries to imagine Risa in Chooch's mom's car, Sav's body thumping in the trunk. All the dark roads. Carrying him out into the woods to be buried under the moon.

"It's my responsibility," Risa says. "I can't let you do this alone, Christopher."

"Let me take this on for you," Chooch says. "I want to."

"I can't."

"You're not thinking straight."

"I needed your help, and I still do, but I've gotta be there for this part. I'm thinking as straight as I have in a long time."

"What about Fab?" Giulia asks.

"He'll come too, or he can stay here with you," Risa says.

"If you're going, I'm going." Now Giulia pictures them all in the car together, all in the woods together, a bad and necessary deed forged in the fire of desperation. She's been selfish. She'll go with Risa. She'll be there every step of the way. She walks over and puts her arm around her sister. When they were girls, they'd sliced their palms with a kitchen knife and rubbed them together to prove how deep their bond was. They were already blood sisters, but they deduced that actual mingling of their blood took it to another level, to a realm where it could never be broken or disrupted no matter what. Giulia feels it between them now like electricity. "We'll all do this together."

6.

Chooch is driving fast. The Belt Parkway, the BQE, the Gowanus, the Brooklyn Bridge, the West Side Highway—all a blur of lights, flashes of reds and greens and swampy low beams. He can't believe Risa, Giulia, and Fab are with him, huddled in the backseat. Risa is clutching a fast-asleep Fab in her lap. Giulia's smoking. All the windows are rolled down. His mother's Citation has gas, thank God. The St. Christopher medal stuck on the dashboard is making him uneasy. He never wanted the name of a saint. He thinks about what will happen if they break down or get in an accident and then tries to control his mind away from going there.

The breeze from outside is warm against the sweat that's caked on his forehead and neck. He's got the radio on. Whatever station it is, they're playing something new by Van Halen. He should've thought to bring a few tapes. He needs the music to drown out the sound of Sav's body jostling around in the trunk, but he's conscious of Fab's presence and doesn't want to wake him. No one's talking.

At Risa's, before leaving, he'd puked again. This time in the toilet, at least. All that blood. Sav dead. Wrapping him up and carrying him out to the trunk like he'd seen in movies. But this isn't a movie. This is something real that happened, that's happening.

As they cross the George Washington Bridge, he thinks about how the rest of the trip is really what he fears. The Palisades Parkway, the Quickway, the road from Monticello through White Lake and Bethel to the small town of Cochecton, where his family's little country house sits on a hill, unnumbered, on a branch of a road thin with other houses, the Delaware River off in the distance. The drive up is baked into his memory, his father behind the wheel of their 1966 Chrysler Imperial, guiding them, his mother tense in the passenger seat, knitting or busying her hands somehow. Most often, the trip—whether it was going upstate or coming home—had been made in daylight. All the dark he's about to go into, to be swallowed up by, has him reeling. He worries that he's crossing the border into a shadowland, leaving behind the lights of the city for a darkness that he can't escape. He thumbs at the flashlight on the passenger seat, hoping the batteries hold out.

On the first dark stretch of the Palisades, a car rides his tail. He grips the wheel with both hands. He worries it's a cop, that he's going to get pulled over for speeding or because a taillight's out or something stupid. That happens, he needs to play it cool. They all do.

Chooch looks in his rearview mirror to see if he can make

out the shape of the car behind him. There doesn't seem to be a light bar or a cherry light or anything. The driver's got his brights on, illuminating the interior of the Citation.

Giulia turns around and investigates the lights. "I don't think it's a cop," she says.

The car behind him finally makes a move to pass, zooming by in the left lane, spilling its harsh light off into darkness ahead of them.

"I heard a story once," Risa says, in a hushed voice, "about this woman, Joanne Capretti, who poisoned her husband, Tony, using rodenticide with thallium in it. It was odorless and tasteless. She put it in his oatmeal. Took him a few days to die. He was hunched over. Had terrible abdominal pain and was puking in a bucket. She told him he was overreacting; it was only gas. He was a bad man. Really bad. Killed people for the mob. Beat her mercilessly. After he died, Joanne was alone. They didn't have any kids. She started going to mass every day. I heard this story from someone who knew her from church. She tormented herself. Tony deserved to die, but she wasn't a murderer. Eventually, she couldn't take it anymore, and she poisoned herself. The thallium didn't kill her. It brought her to the edge, and she had a vision of hell, and then she was just back in the world, alive. She was afraid to keep living but more afraid to die."

"Don't get fucking philosophical, Ris," Giulia says.

Risa falls silent again, as if she's said all there is to say.

Chooch isn't sure what to make of Risa's story. He thinks about what led him here, the years with Sav tethered to this moment. They were kids once. Sav had become bad, but he wasn't all bad and he wasn't always bad. Back at Perpetual

Surrender, being friends with Sav meant no one else fucked with him. Same at Lafayette. He remembers the way Sav would sometimes get a Coke from the corner store, down it in one long pull, rip a belch, and then throw the bottle up in the air, laughing as it crashed against the concrete. He never gave any thought to how that glass scattered, the problems it could cause for others. Sav did it this one afternoon—maybe late during their freshman year of high school—and Chooch felt guilty and went back to the spot after Sav had returned home and cleaned up the glass piece by piece. The guy who owned the store came out and thanked him. He should've had more guts around Sav. Should've said more about how shitty he was to Risa, should've told him to love Fab or he'd regret it. No fucking guts. Maybe he could've stopped something like this. It would've been better if Sav just pulled a Roberto. Chooch's thoughts go haywire. He's wondering if he really loves Risa and why he's doing this. He's wondering what else he might do for her. He wants to say something true. Anything true. He wants to know who he is, who he's ever been. He's not sure he has an identity of his own. In this moment, at least, he has a purpose.

Another car passes in the left lane, coming out of nowhere, probably doing about ninety, brights blaring. The interior of the car is lit up again.

Chooch tries to focus on the road. His headlights dance across the blackness. The radio's getting fuzzy. A song's playing, but he can't make out what it is.

He looks in the rearview mirror, a few miles up the road, as they're passing a well-lit gas station, and he feels like he sees someone sitting between Risa and Giulia in the back. It's

Sav as a boy in his Our Lady of Perpetual Surrender uniform. Powder-blue button-up shirt. Clip-on tie emblazoned with the parish logo. His hair combed like he's headed in for school pictures. This is the kid who took Chooch under his wing when no one else would.

Chooch almost loses control of the car and hits the rumble strip. He moves his hand on the wheel and straightens the car out.

Giulia leans forward and puts her hand on his shoulder. "What's up?" she asks.

"Thought I saw someone," he says. "It was nothing."

When they arrive at the house, it's swallowed up in the darkest dark Chooch can ever remember seeing. He turns off Route 97 onto the little turnpike—he can't remember the name—that leads to Parsonage Road, where he makes a sharp left. And it's an even sharper left into the long driveway, which is all uphill, and overgrown with knee-high weeds and broken branches. The surrounding woods are full of country noises. Crickets and tree frogs and owls and whatever else hoots and bellows. The headlights brighten the weeds.

Chooch guns it up the driveway, kicking up pebbles and dirt, hoping there's not a camouflaged boulder in his path. Something darts in front of the car, an animal, a possum, or maybe a raccoon, and he hits it, feels the thump of the creature against his bumper.

He stops the car. He curses, throws it into park mid-driveway, and gets out with the flashlight. Giulia opens her door and follows him. Risa stays with Fab. Chooch looks behind the car and sees the animal lying there in the flattened weeds, tire-tracked, bleeding, gasping its last breaths.

"Jesus Christ, what is that?" Giulia asks.

"A possum." He knows it's a possum because he remembers seeing them up here as a kid. He's never seen one back in Brooklyn and he's not sure they exist in the city, but he remembers his old man giving him lessons on the kinds of animals that inhabit the country. Once, there'd been one in the attic of the house, and his dad had trapped it in a cage and brought it to a field ten miles away to release it. He remembers liking that his dad hadn't killed it.

They stand there in the red glow of the Citation's taillights, Chooch's flashlight shaking over the body of the possum, and he wishes he could put it out of its misery. He cries as he watches it die. "I'm sorry," he says to the possum. "I didn't see you."

Giulia puts a hand on his shoulder. "It wasn't your fault," she says.

He leans forward and pulls the neck of his shirt up to his face to dry his tears.

They get back into the car.

"What was it?" Risa asks.

"Possum, I guess," Giulia says. "I'd never seen one."

"Poor thing."

Chooch is rattled, trying to erase the image of the dead possum from his mind. He didn't want to hit it. He's never hit an animal of any kind. One of his greatest fears has always been hitting someone's dog that got loose from a yard and then having to go up to their front door and report what had happened. He keeps seeing the possum in his mind's eye and keeps imagining what it must've felt like to die that way. He thinks that animals must feel things the way humans do, at least to a certain extent. If tonight hadn't happened and he hadn't sped up the driveway at this hour, the possum would be fine, going about its business in the dark, searching for food.

He goes slower the rest of the length of the driveway, pulling onto the flat bed of concrete next to the cellar hatch where his dad used to park the Imperial. He cuts his lights and tries to prepare himself for what they've got to do. "Maybe I should go back and bury the possum," he says. "It's not right to leave it there like that."

"If you think we have time," Giulia says.

He nods. "Maybe."

"Bury it with Sav. Possums are rodents, right? They'll get along."

"Possums are marsupials," Risa says.

"How the fuck do you know that?" Giulia says, shaking her head.

"My encyclopedias."

Chooch shuts the car. With the lights and engine off now, the stillness is unsettling. He hopes the hidden key is still where they used to leave it.

He gets out again, following the beam of the flashlight around to the front of the car, where he searches the bumper for possum blood. Nothing that he can see. His mother doesn't check the odometer on the car religiously or anything, but he knows she'll know he used the car. Even if he keeps the trunk clean of Sav's blood and the bumper doesn't show any signs of having been involved in running over a possum, it'll be hard to erase the stink. The smell of fear and death bleeding into every inch of the upholstery. He tells himself he needs to stop at a gas station on the way home to fill the tank and buy one of those pine tree–scented air fresheners. Instead of hanging it from the rearview mirror, he'll leave it on the floor—maybe she'll think she bought it at some point and forgot to put it up.

Giulia emerges from the car next and then Risa follows, adjusting to hold Fab against her chest, his head smooshed between her neck and shoulder. It's almost as if they've all forgotten they have one extra passenger.

"I've gotta get the key," Chooch says.

He guides them with the light as they walk to the propane tank at the rear corner of the house. The closest neighbor is three hundred, maybe four hundred feet away. He keeps the flashlight aimed at the ground so it's not wandering wildly across the yard. Behind the house, there are woods that are at least a half-mile deep, edging up against Route 97 where it loops down in the direction of Narrowsburg. He used to take walks back there with his dad and marvel at how different it was to walk in the woods instead of on sidewalks and across streets, to not see any houses and stores, only trees and dirt and leaves. They carved their names into a beech tree with a pocketknife his dad always carried when he was upstate. They also often buried garbage in the woods—the garbage they couldn't burn—before going home to Brooklyn, which is why, Chooch guesses, he thought of this place when trying to decide where to bring Sav.

He finds the key where his father always kept it, in a red-and-gold Christmas tin wedged under the propane tank. It's blackened with age. There's nothing else in the tin.

He leads them around to the front of the house, up the rotting steps, and opens the front door, nudging his hip against the knob and clearing away some spiderwebs before entering.

Dust swirls in his flashlight beam as it passes over mouse turds in the corner of the foyer and a toppled coatrack and debris on the floor from a patch of ceiling that's collapsed. He tries the light switch on the wall, though he knows his mother stopped paying the electric bill years ago. It's not a very big house, two bedrooms and a kitchen and what his mom called a drawing room where there's a player piano inherited from a dive bar called Rubythroat's in Callicoon. The coldness of winter has somehow been contained. Chooch feels it in his bones. He also senses that others have been in the house since he was last up here. Break-ins, that kind of thing. They go into the kitchen, and he sees that the cabinets are open, picked clean of the relatively worthless plates and bowls and glasses that once filled them. The pots and pans are missing, too. Even the toaster's gone. There hadn't been much to steal, so the thieves scavenged what they could. Chooch notices that the window over the sink is broken. Glass scattered in the drain and on the linoleum. Probably how they got in. He wonders if they slept in the house or what. Maybe it was local kids turning it into a party spot.

"So, this is the country," Giulia says. "Can I smoke?"

"I don't think anybody'll mind," Chooch says. "Just don't start a fire. Last thing we need."

She sits at the table on a chair with a bad leg, takes out her cigarettes, and lights one. She finds a chipped porcelain coffee mug on the table, thick residue coating its bottom, and uses it as an ashtray.

Risa sits at the table, too, in a better chair, and she shushes Fab as he stirs.

Chooch finds a candle and borrows Giulia's matches to light

it. He puts it on the table between them. "I'm just gonna get some stuff from the utility room," he says.

He makes a left down a dark hallway at the far end of the kitchen, following the flashlight beam. His father always worked under the assumption that a house that stayed mostly vacant would get broken into now and again, so he kept a combination lock on the utility room where the only real valuable stuff was stashed. And, even still, there wasn't much. Some cleaning supplies and tools—saws, loppers, hammers, screwdrivers, a headlamp, buckets, a mop, bottles of Pine-Sol for the wood floors, Mr. Clean, Ajax, Clorox, fat rolls of Scott paper towels. Shovels and a wheelbarrow, which is what Chooch is after. The water heater's also in that room.

The combination on the utility room lock is his mother's birthday. He holds the flashlight under his chin as he fingers the combo on the dial. *Three, twelve, thirty-two.* The doorjamb seems to have been tampered with a bit. Someone must've picked at the frame around the plate, the wood splintered there, but they hadn't gotten very far. Chooch removes the lock and undoes the latch. He enters the room. Everything is as his dad left it.

He puts on the headlamp, amazed it still works. It'd been sitting unused for years. He would've assumed that the batteries would have exploded and gone crusty. He thumbs off Risa's flashlight and stashes it in the pocket of his shorts, no longer needing to waste a hand on it—he'll give it to Giulia to hold when he gets back to the kitchen. The headlamp's glow is wider and brighter. He turns the wheelbarrow over and rests the shovels on top of it and then pushes it to the kitchen.

Giulia and Risa cringe at the intensity of the brightness

coming from the headlamp. "I'm sorry," he says, parking the wheelbarrow. They avoid looking at him, shielding their eyes in the crooks of their arms. He hands Giulia the other flashlight, and she flicks it back on. She finishes her cigarette and extinguishes it in the cup. He blows out the candle. The smoke from the cigarette and the candle dance together over the table, forming a wispy gray tusk before dissipating in the darkness.

Chooch opens the back door, and he pushes the wheelbarrow straight outside. No stairs this way. Again, Giulia and Risa trail him. Communication seems less and less necessary. They're following his lead. He's trying not to feel, only do what needs doing. He locks the door behind them.

In no time at all, they've edged around the rear of the house, avoiding fallen branches and a woebegone wood pile, and they're back at the car. He positions the wheelbarrow right behind the trunk. He pops the lid. He stares at Sav's wrapped body.

Risa comes over and stands next to him. She gives Fab to Giulia and takes the flashlight in return. "Okay," she says.

"You sure you want to do this?" Chooch asks. "Maybe you should go back in the house."

She shakes her head. "I'm doing it."

"You can probably put the flashlight down. I think the headlamp's enough." She shuts it and places it tenderly on a jutting piece of concrete on the ground.

Chooch moves the shovels from atop the wheelbarrow. He and Risa hoist Sav out of the trunk and drop him into—really *onto*—the wheelbarrow. Chooch collects the other stuff he needs to bury: the bag he took from home with his dirty clothes, the ones that he'd gotten Sav's blood on; the bag with the pan and the gun hidden in the now-defrosted peas; the bag of bloody paper towels; the backpack; the bags he'd spread to protect the trunk. He stuffs everything under Sav and begins the lurching procession into the woods, trying to keep the wheelbarrow balanced so the body doesn't fall off, following the bouncing light that the headlamp cones across the trees. Risa's beside him, carrying the shovels. Giulia's last in line, not as natural about holding Fab, keeping him in an awkward position like someone carrying a heavy sack of rice. Chooch is worried about what happens if the kid wakes up and starts howling.

He counts seventy-seven paces from where he enters the woods. His arms hurt as he works the handles of the wheelbarrow to keep it steady. Dropping Sav would be a hassle. He leads them between trees. Branches and shells crunch under their feet.

The moon's enormous in the sky. Not quite full, but bright. He's seeing it the way he never sees it in the city, unobscured, casting down its silvery light.

He looks around at the trees. He's trying to remember the one where he and his father carved their names. Impossible to make sense of the exact location in the dark.

He chooses a spot, a bare patch between a triangle of oaks, and sets the wheelbarrow down, its black legs and thick black wheel pressing down into the dirt, cocooned Sav sprawling over the edges. "Here's good," Chooch says.

Risa gives him one of the shovels. She wastes no time and begins digging with the other, chunking up clumps of earth and tossing them to the side.

Chooch joins her. He watches her as she digs, the muscles

in her arms, the sweat beading her brow. He watches the way their shovels knife open slots in the ground.

"I guess I'm on baby detail," Giulia says, going over and sitting against the oak at the top of the triangle, Fab splayed across her lap.

Chooch digs in bursts of seven. He counts under his breath as he digs. *One-two-three-four-five-six-seven.* Reset. Repeat.

His gaze drifts back to Risa.

All the fury in her eyes. He'd only ever seen her one way and now there's this other side to her. "I'm doing it," she'd said to him, and she is, digging fiercely, angrily, not just digging but building down, creating.

Aside from hitting some tough, sinewy roots, the digging isn't too awful. The ground is soft. He keeps getting hung up thinking about the potential consequences of all that's gone down. What he's doing, he could go to jail for. Big time. He wouldn't make it. He's way too soft. He would've figured himself as too soft for what he's doing now but necessity dictates action. It's all for Risa and Fab. The lie might not hold. Saying Sav ran off. He's got to at least consider that option. Or the body gets dug up by dogs or something and it's on his upstate property, there's only one answer. If it comes out that Sav's dead, people will build a narrative. They'll think it was premeditated. Maybe he and Risa had a thing and acted together. That's the story the world would want. The truth is messier. It'd be hard to explain. Risa seems incapable of violence, but she'd swung that pan. There might be some sympathy for her, but how far would it go? Too much to think about. They can only hope. The lie's got to hold. This is the right decision.

The digging takes a while. They've been going at it for at

least an hour. He's lost track of time. No one has a watch. He doesn't know what's not deep enough or how deep is too deep. They're standing thigh-deep in the wide hole now, each shovelful more burdensome. He's out of breath, panting. He should've thought to bring water for them. The house is part of a shared town well so the water works even when the power's off, but turning it on involves finding a lever in the cellar. On his trips up here as a kid, the cellar scared the shit out of him. Still does. It's not like their cellar at home in Brooklyn. This one's more like a dank underground prison. It always made him think of that Edgar Allan Poe story he'd read in school, the guy buried in the wall. Ironic to remember that now given the circumstances.

Risa looks like a different woman from another era, dirt streaked across her face, suddenly older. She's fighting blisters on both hands from the handle of the shovel, wincing.

"I think that's enough," Chooch says, working to square the edges.

"Yeah?" Risa says. "Maybe we should do more."

"Your hands are a mess, and I'm beat to shit. Plus, we've still got to fill it back in."

"If it's not deep enough, maybe some animals'll dig him up."

"It's good."

She nods and climbs out of the hole and drops the shovel to the ground. She stares at her hands. Chooch can tell that she's worrying about tomorrow, thinking that someone will come by to visit—maybe Sav's mother, Arlene—and Risa will have to say that Sav never came home, and she'll have to concoct some lie about her hands.

"Say you burned them on the stove," Giulia says, obviously reading Risa's mind, too.

Risa staggers over to where Giulia's sitting against the tree and collapses next to her, putting her head on her sister's shoulder. Giulia reaches out and strokes her hair, cleans some dirt from her check.

Fab's eyes open suddenly. It's as if he's been pretending to be asleep. He can tell something's different. The night air and nature noises and the light of the moon. He's not crying yet, just confused. Giulia gives him her right hand. He tries to suck on the tip of her thumb, and she keeps pulling it away and tweaking his nose. "Go back to sleep, little one," she says. "Nothing to see here."

Chooch remembers the money that Sav stole from Gilly. He knows he's got to unwrap the shower liner and go into Sav's pockets to get it. He should return it to Gilly. He'll do it anonymously. Put it in an envelope and stuff it through Gilly's mail slot. It's probably not all the money—Double Stevie must have some, and Sav spent a bunch at L'Amour—but Chooch can only do what he can do. And what if it gets back to Double Stevie that part of the money's been returned? That piece of shit will likely know something's up. Sav would never give the money back before splitting town when it was *for* leaving town. Too many ways for this all to collapse.

Chooch swishes what little spit he has around in his mouth. His teeth are so dry. He licks his lips to moisten them. He goes to Sav, pushes him from the wheelbarrow to the ground, and then hovers over him, peeling back the liner.

One last look. Sav hasn't stopped being dead. His face is still hard to make out through the cling wrap, which helps Chooch remain detached.

"What are you doing?" Risa asks.

"I forgot about the money," Chooch says. "He stole it from Gilly."

"That's where he got it?"

"Yeah, him and Double Stevie broke in. Well, they knew where the key was. I tried to talk them out of it." Chooch reaches into the pockets of Sav's shorts and takes whatever money he can find, stuffing it into his own pockets. Seems like a couple thousand bucks. He leans away from the body and retches. Nothing left in him to puke up. He puts the liner back in place. Finally, he uses his feet to prod Sav into the hole. The body lands on its side. He can only think of it as *the body* now. He steps into the hole and twists it onto its back.

As he climbs out, Risa stands and goes over to the wheelbarrow and empties everything else—the bags and the backpack—into the hole on top of the body. He believes, for a moment, that he sees the body move as one of the bags lands on it. He knows that can't be. He felt for a pulse earlier. He stares at the shape under the plastic, looking for a rise and fall of the chest, a jolt of the arm. Nothing.

He concludes it'll be easier if they shovel dirt into the wheelbarrow and then empty it into the hole.

"Let me shovel a little," Giulia says. She puts Fab down. He's fully awake, still not crying, curious. He crawls around. He touches the bark on the oak tree. He finds a branch on the ground and goes to put it in his mouth.

Risa races over and snatches the branch away from him. She squats next to him and says, "How's my baby doing out here in the dark? Do you like nature? Maybe you'll be the outdoorsy type. Not me." She pauses. "We're almost done. We'll be going home soon."

Chooch and Giulia get to work on filling the wheelbarrow.

The first cartful isn't bad. By the third, his arms feel like they're going to fall off. He fears he won't be able to make the drive home, that he'll fall asleep on the road, especially on the dark country roads that lead back to the Quickway. He'll need something. Coffee. NoDoz. Maybe Giulia can drive. He knows Risa doesn't have a license.

When they're done, they tamp down the dirt with the shovels. Chooch pushes some debris over the spot, branches and leaves and rocks, and then smudges out the obvious shape of the grave.

Giulia sinks the blade of her shovel into the ground and finds her cigarettes in her pocket, lighting one, and blowing smoke out in an exasperated exhale.

Chooch collapses. He lies on his back, looking up at the dark treetops, the dark sky, the three-quarter moon. His body racked with aches and pains.

"Are you okay, Christopher?" Risa asks.

"I feel like I'm gonna have a heart attack," he says.

"Try not to," Giulia says. "Last thing we need to do is wind up at some Podunk hospital."

He lies still for a few minutes and gets his breath back and feels his strength returning. He stands up and shakes dirt from his back. "I'll bring the wheelbarrow and shovels in," he says. "I'll see if I can get the water on. If you need to use the bathroom or anything, I guess just try to go outside. Do you want to come in with me?"

"We'll stay here," Risa says.

Giulia shrugs and looks at her like, *What the fuck?*

Chooch removes Giulia's shovel from the ground and sets it and the one he'd used with their blades facing down in the tray of the wheelbarrow. The handles line up over his right shoulder as he pushes the wheelbarrow to the house. Stray dirt skitters between the shovels.

He opens the back door and enters with the wheelbarrow and shovels. He pauses to lock the door behind him. He goes through the dark hallway to the utility room, following the light from the headlamp. He'll keep the headlamp because he's decided he's going to go down to the cellar to try to turn the water on. He props the shovels in the corner of the utility room and turns the wheelbarrow on its side. He stands there. Just him and the light shining from his head, a glowing circle on the wall in front of him. He thinks of Risa, Fab, and Giulia in the woods. Risa wanted to stay there. Did she want to say something she didn't want him present for? He feels the promise of new possibilities. What will their lives look like after this? Risa needed his help tonight, and maybe she'll continue needing his help. He thinks of her hand on his at *Terms of Endearment*. Maybe he can be the father Fab never had.

The hours and days and weeks ahead will be hard. Risa will have to begin to act—sooner rather than later—surprised and horrified that Sav's disappeared. Sandra will be pissed that he split town without her. Double Stevie will come sniffing around. Frank and Arlene, Sav's folks, will be gutted, yet another son having run off in the middle of the night, leaving no forwarding address, no explanation, no hint or clue of his reasoning, nothing to go on. Leaving his wife and young child like that wouldn't be a shocker. They'd never entertain the notion that he's dead, buried in a grave in the Sullivan County woods, struck down with a cutlet pan by sweet Risa. Still, Chooch wonders if he should forge a note as Sav, say he's off on some adventure like Roberto, go to Atlantic City, send it from there. Give them some hope. He knows one thing. Comes down to it, anything ever happens where the truth emerges, he'll take the fall for Risa. Say he killed Sav to protect her and Fab. He won't let her go to jail.

He leaves the utility room, putting the lock back on the door, and follows the light through the hallway and kitchen into the alcove that leads to the cellar. He knows he must face it. He needs water.

The cellar door is heavy, the knob rusty and difficult to turn. He finally gets it open, the wood whining. When a door hasn't been opened in years, it sounds like a ghost. He takes the steps down carefully, aware that they might have rotted. His breathing intensifies.

His light bounces around. He sees the dirt floor, cobwebs everywhere, an ancient bed frame, two broken mirrors. Stacks of cinder blocks line the walls. A series of mousetraps set in a circle, all of them snapped and empty.

In the corner are a disconnected washing machine, a scattering of ancient storm windows, and the oil tank, cluttered there. He thinks he remembers his father saying there's a lever on the wall to turn on the water. He finds it—his father has labeled it in Sharpie on a peeling piece of gray duct tape—and switches it on.

He goes back upstairs into the kitchen and finds an empty jug. He turns on the cold water in the sink. It sputters to life slowly and then starts gushing. After letting it run for a few minutes, he leans over and drinks straight from the tap. The water is cold, but it doesn't taste anywhere near as good as city water. He pulls away, water spilling down his chin, feeling reinvigorated. He thinks he's probably dehydrated. He's not sure if he's ever been dehydrated before. He fills the jug and sets it on the counter. Finally, he races back down to the cellar to switch the lever off. When he returns, he's winded again.

He pockets Giulia's cigarette butt from the coffee cup on the table. He thinks about what other evidence they might've left. Prints everywhere. Traces of Sav on the wheelbarrow—his hair, possibly blood. Too much to worry about right now. One day, in the future, maybe he'll sneak back up here for a cleanup mission. Until then, they'll just have to hope that the house and land keep their secret safe.

He goes out through the front door, locking it and then double-checking that it's locked. He brings the key back to the tin under the propane tank, picks up the flashlight Risa put down, and waits by the car with the jug of water.

7.

Risa watches Fab crawling around on the ground in the woods. It's darker without Chooch's headlamp, but the column of moonlight they're standing in is enough for them to see clearly. Fab's really moving, curious to explore, touching everything there is to touch, including an empty turtle shell he uncovers and what looks like a squirrel skull. Risa takes both things away from him with her hurt hands. Fab blabbers, almost seems like he's making an argument for why he should get to keep these objects.

Giulia paces, finishing her cigarette. "You ready?" she asks.

"I don't know," Risa says. If they leave, that's it. Standing in the woods makes her feel like she's in some in-between place, between done and undone, between reality and dream.

Fab crawls toward his father's grave. The edges of the hole are apparent—the soil turned over within those lines is blacker, richer. Fab stops in the center and sits there and then flops over onto his side and begins digging. He scoops up dirt and passes it between his hands. Before Risa can stop him, he puts some in his mouth, mashing it around and spitting it out.

"Jesus Christ," Giulia says.

Risa knocks the dirt from Fab's hands and cleans his mouth, but he quickly gets back to digging, dirt marking his chin like an upside-down Ash Wednesday. She wonders if he can feel his father interred below. It's a game to him. Time to unbury Daddy. *No, sweetie, sorry. He's gotta stay buried.*

She thinks about going to church tomorrow. *Today*. It's Sunday already. Can she sit in a pew again? Can she go for Communion? She's hopes it's Monsignor Terrone serving mass and not that awful, young Father Tim. She'll see Arlene there, no doubt. Can she perpetuate the lie that Sav's alive and missing, that he's run off and left her and Fab, without her skin and soul going cold? Or will everyone somehow know she killed Sav and buried him and let their son eat dirt from his grave?

Giulia flicks her filter away and comes over to pick up Fab. She cleans more dirt from him. He makes happy noises. "Let's go," she says.

They walk to the car and find Chooch waiting there with a jug of water. Risa drinks hungrily. The water is cold and earthy. She passes it to Giulia, who drinks and then pours some in her hands and splashes it over her face. Chooch takes the jug and does the same thing. It seems to give him new energy. Risa doesn't need to do it. She feels more awake than she's ever felt.

They all get in the car, Risa in the front this time, Giulia holding Fab in the back.

Chooch starts the engine. He puts the car in reverse and

pulls off the cement slab and then turns around in the yard. He rolls slowly down the driveway.

Risa remembers the possum. Fab had been asleep in her arms, so she hadn't seen it. "Stop," she says.

Chooch slams on the brakes. "What'd you forget?"

"The possum. We should bury it like you said."

"I put the shovels away in the house."

"I'll just dig a little hole with my feet. It's the right thing to do." She turns to Giulia. "You stay in here with Fab. I'll be right back."

She gets out of the car and walks over to the possum, lying right in the path of the headlight beams. A tragic sight. She walks a few paces into the weeds on the side of the driveway facing the yard and the woods, away from the road. She begins nudging the heel of her sneaker into the dirt. Her hands are useless.

Chooch joins her and falls to his knees and uses his hands as cups to scoop dirt. Risa kicks farther into the hole that begins to take shape.

It starts to rain. A slight drizzle at first.

When they've done enough, Chooch retrieves an extra black garbage bag from the trunk and holds it inside-out over the possum, picking it up by touching it only through the heavy plastic. He lets the air out of the bag and wraps the remaining part around the possum, tying the top in a sloppy, halfhearted knot. He drops the possum in the hole and begins to kick the dirt over the bag.

Risa pushes the dirt with her toe more gently. What they're doing isn't much, but it's better than leaving the poor thing in the road. The death of this possum is Sav's fault, too. She feels worse about it than she does about Sav. She imagines that it lived in a hollow tree trunk in the woods, that its life here was very peaceful, no cars ever in the driveway, no one to chase it away. Then they'd come along and ruined that.

Chooch looks at her and says, "Listen, we need to get straight what we're gonna say. He ran off on you. He said so direct to you and me. He ran off on everybody. Stevie. Sandra. His family. They're gonna feel like he should've told them. We act mystified. They'll believe it. Maybe he got in some trouble no one knows about. Between the booze and the drugs and the stealing. Comes out—all three of us witnessing it, Stevie confirming it—he had this gun. Plenty of people at L'Amour heard him talking about running away. No one will think it means anything he ditched Sandra. He had to disappear, that's it. Said he was gonna be gone for good. Roberto all over again, except worse because Sav's abandoned his wife, his baby."

"Okay," Risa says.

"Me and Giulia gotta be on the same page with you. There can't be different things we say. There can't be truths we let slip to certain people. I'm vowing I won't let anything slip to my mother. She's the only person close to me. You can't talk to Monsignor Terrone or to your folks and expect to confide in them, okay? There's me, you, and Giulia in this together."

Risa nods. When the lie starts making the rounds, people will treat her like a widow. They'll bring casseroles and pastries. They'll ask what they can do to help. They'll say how terrible it is, a young man walking out on his family. They'll tell her to pray. They'll say God has His reasons, that He has a plan for her and Fab. She'll nod and nod and nod. She'll say, "Thank you so much." She'll learn to believe the lie. She'll teach Fab to believe the lie. She'll remember this possum. How it would've been fine forever if Sav hadn't been such a bad man.

The bag's showing through the dirt, but it's mostly covered. Rain plinks against the creases in the plastic.

Chooch finds a large white rock a few feet away, using whatever energy he has left to haul it over and placing it atop the spot like a lid. It reminds Risa of some of the old graves at St. John Cemetery in Queens where much of her family is buried, the ones that have concrete grave mound covers.

Two burials in one night.

"Sorry I hit you," Chooch says to the possum.

Risa touches the rock with her foot. She sees all the dirt from the night caked on her sneakers. She doesn't say anything.

They rush back to the car as the rain begins to fall harder. Risa gets in the front—she'd like to stay there if she can.

"I can't believe you buried that fucking possum," Giulia says.

"How's Fab?" Risa asks.

"Oh, he's very interested in the floor back here. Found an ice scraper under the seat he tried to gnaw on."

"He's teething."

Chooch shifts the car into drive and switches on the windshield wipers. He takes the rest of the driveway slow. "I think there are some napkins in the glove compartment, if you need them," he tells Risa.

She opens it and finds a stack of stiff napkins from Dunkin' Donuts amid the maps and manuals. She hands a couple to Chooch, and he dries his face. She uses one to wipe the rain and sweat from her face, too.

They're back on Route 97. The dark seems even more

hypnotic than before because of the rain. The only lights anywhere are theirs, painted across the blacktop in front of them.

Chooch is white knuckling the wheel, his eyes scanning the whole road for any other animals that might leap out. He's keeping the car perfectly straight between the double-yellows and the white line of the shoulder.

Risa fiddles with the radio. She searches for a station that's playing something good but nothing's coming in clear.

As they pass through Bethel, Chooch points out where Woodstock happened, breaking the silence, making small talk in a way he hadn't seemed to consider on the drive up. "We were up at the house that weekend," he says. "I was ten. We must've come up a different route because of the traffic. I don't remember. My father wasn't happy about it. I remember hearing a lot of helicopters."

Risa tries to imagine it. All those people spreading out over the hills, dancing, muddy, happy, free. She's never been to a gathering like that. Probably never will be. All the different lives she could've led haunt her.

"If there was such a thing as a time machine, I'd check out Woodstock," Giulia says. "Hendrix, Janis, Joan Baez. I would've killed to see Melanie—nobody talks about Melanie anymore." She holds Fab close to her and nuzzles his neck. He giggles.

Risa smiles at the sound of her son's laugh. She thought the sound of that pan hitting Sav's head would linger in her memory forever, but she's already forgetting it.

Part 2

BLOOD'S BLOOD

Wednesday, February 20

1991

1.

Giulia's been trying to learn Italian. She knows a few words from around the house growing up, but she wants to be better. If she ever gets back to Naples—and it's still a big dream of hers to return—she doesn't want to embarrass herself. She wants to be able to hold a conversation, to listen and understand, to say things in a natural way. She'd gone to a bookstore in Bay Ridge a month ago, the closest bookstore she knows of, and bought a thick Italian dictionary and a book called *Basic Italian Conversation*, which was apparently co-written by some guy from the neighborhood. She's been waking up early in the morning and going into the dining room to study. Risa's usually up already, too, making coffee, and they sit there quietly at the table together while Fab sleeps, Risa reading a mystery novel from the library or piecing together a puzzle while Giulia runs through a couple of practice exercises from her book.

Giulia sits at the table now, a steaming cup of coffee in front of her in Sav's old favorite mug from Belmont Park. Sav hadn't been big on betting the horses, but he got into it occasionally if his second cousin, Switchyard Mike, twisted his arm. This mug, though it isn't anything special—white with BELMONT PARK in green print and a green racehorse under that, caught midstride—was Sav's go-to for morning coffee. Now it's hers.

She's hung up on the exercise she's looking at, keeps rereading the same directions and phrases repeatedly to no avail. Morning light is filtering in through the slats in the new blinds Risa put up. Risa is across from her, working on a puzzle, eating a pretzel stick, her usual breakfast, and drinking her own coffee from a mug that says BEST MOM EVER on it, something she'd bought herself as a gift from Fab last Christmas. She stirs the pretzel in her coffee, which always grosses Giulia out for some reason. Fab's a late sleeper, curled up in the little race car bed Risa had replaced his crib with a few years back.

Sometimes Giulia's overwhelmed by how happy her life is here with Risa and Fab. Sure, she's twenty-eight years old and sleeping on a couch, but it feels like the most comfortable place she's ever slept most nights. She's got a job around the corner at Sid and Eddie's garage, she helps pay bills and chips in for groceries, and she gets to spend the bulk of her free time with Risa and Fab. She'll have a few drinks at the Crisscross four or five nights a week but that's her only vice. Everyone believed Risa when she reported that Sav took off. Everyone thought it made sense that her sister should move in with her to help with Fab and everything else. When they're out in the real world, people feel bad for Risa, think she's just this sad wife and mother whose husband has abandoned her, but here—in their private little universe—she's content, and so is Giulia. They've woven a protection spell around themselves. What happened here, the way Sav died, they thought the place might be haunted by it, but it hasn't been. The opposite's true. It feels cleansed.

"It's Chooch's birthday," Risa says, biting her coffee-softened pretzel. "I'm going to have a cake for him later. Probably around seven."

"Should I buy him something?" Giulia asks.

"You don't need to."

"What'd you get him?"

"Fab and I took the bus to Kings Plaza. I got him a shirt for this band Tesla he loves. Fab picked out a little nameplate that says CHRISTOPHER."

"I'll just get him some scratch-offs and hard rolls from Augie's."

"He'll love that."

Giulia closes her book—she doesn't feel like she's learning anything today—and drinks down the last of her coffee. She brings the mug over to the sink and rinses it and sets it in the dish drain. She goes into the bathroom and brushes her teeth and changes from her sweats into her clothes for work, a red turtleneck sweater Risa knitted her for Christmas and a pair of jeans. She never eats anything for breakfast. She doesn't have to be in to work for a few hours but one of her other morning routines involves taking a slow hike down by the water. She likes to walk on the promenade, sit on a bench, smoke a cigarette or three, and stare out at Gravesend Bay and the Narrows and the Verrazano Bridge.

When she comes out, Risa tries to convince her to eat, of course. She offers to make her an egg sandwich or French toast. Giulia says, "Nope, I'm good, thanks."

In the hall closet, she finds a wool hat she borrowed from her mother and never returned. It's been strange and nice having her folks back in her life. They go over there as a family on Sundays. Her old man doesn't look her in the eye, but he's dropped the holier-than-thou act and given her a second chance because of how she's stepped up and helped Risa.

She comes back over to the table and gives Risa a kiss on the top of her head as she fits another piece into her puzzle. Risa's only a quarter of the way through it, but Giulia can tell the picture is a garden by Monet.

Risa leans back and reaches up, giving Giulia's shoulder a little squeeze. "Enjoy your walk," she says. "Have a good day at work. Let me know if you want me to bring you over a sandwich."

"I'll be fine, thanks," Giulia says. "Say good morning to Fab for me." He hasn't started talking yet—a late bloomer—but one of these days, she selfishly hopes that "Good morning, Aunt Giulia" is the first thing he says.

She puts on her boots and coat by the door and steps outside.

It's not frigid, but there's an icy edge to the air. She knows it'll be chillier down by the water. She pulls up the collar on her coat and walks to the end of the block, crossing Bath Avenue and heading for Cropsey, where she takes a right. From there, it's a few blocks to Bay Parkway, where she hooks a left and watches the line of rush-hour cars backing up in the right lane to get on the Belt.

Walking through the Belt underpass tunnel, she looks up and sees pigeons huddled on the ledge by the cement wall. She takes in some of the graffiti. Nonsensical tags, a puffy dick shooting out numbers that must be some secret code, a memorial painting for this kid Rico killed by a drunk driver in '89.

She passes Ceasar's Bay Bazaar and crosses over by the tennis courts and the baseball fields right on the bay, walking a short distance up the promenade before settling on a bench, taking out her smokes and lighting one.

She stares at the sunlight on the choppy water. When their grandparents came over from Italy, they passed here in those massive steamships on the way to Ellis Island. She always finds herself thinking about what that entrance must've been like. Maybe they were standing out on the deck, staring at this very spot, considering what waited for them on the land. No Verrazano then. The Statue of Liberty off in the distance. How scared they must've been. How excited. Entering the unknown. Leaving behind all they loved. Two of their grandparents—the Tavernas, Nonno Alfredo and Nana Sabina, whose maiden name was Pellegrina—came over in the early 1900s to escape grinding poverty in Naples and Salerno and eventually met in downtown Brooklyn, on Court Street, where they both lived. When they married, he was twenty-four and she was eighteen. Their other two grandparents—the Candidos, Nonno Natale and Nana Giulia, her namesake, previously a Badalla—came over in early 1909 as refugees after the Messina earthquake on December 28, 1908, rocked Sicily and Calabria. They met on the ship. All of it part of what she's seen called the Great Arrival. She always has a hard time imagining what their journeys were like. The world must've seemed so much bigger and quieter and more frightening then.

Her world is small. She loves what she's built with Risa, but she also feels trapped by the neighborhood. She barely goes outside of about a twenty-block radius anymore. Everything cool's in the city, but it might as well be Mars.

She scans the promenade and sees a few people walking. An old couple in matching sweat suits and balaclavas. A hunched man with a shopping cart full of plastic bottles. A tall woman doing strange stretches as she hustles along. It's then that she notices the guy maybe fifty feet away, sitting on the backrest of another bench, his feet up on the seat. He's got a hoodie on, and he's very skinny with a bit of a curved posture. He's also smoking a cigarette, but he's doing it a lot more aggressively than her, really pulling in the smoke, ashing like he's trying to bust through the paper and rain tobacco everywhere. He's not looking in her direction, he's just staring out at the water, but she can swear it's Sav. Something about this fucking stronzo.

She averts her gaze, finishes her cigarette, and drops the butt on the ground. She stands and walks back the way she came, shaking off what she figures is some kind of trick her eyes are playing on her. Can't be him, of course. Must just be one of those mornings where she's losing her goddamn mind.

2.

Chooch is in the back room of the urology office where he still works, alphabetizing files. It's just after one in the afternoon, and he'll be getting off in a few minutes. They have no patients this afternoon because Dr. Ranieri and Dr. Geraci are attending some charity golf thing. Chooch sits on a rolling chair, slowly and methodically inserting manila folders where they belong in the giant wall of color-coded files. He likes saying the names of patients in his head: *Biagini*, *D'Angelo*, *Esposito*, *Joyce*, *Petito*, *Suarez*, *Ventimiglia.* Occasionally, he opens a folder and reads a chart, knowing he shouldn't. He's worked here for thirteen years now. Four days a week. A simple, nothing job. His mother got it for him when he was eighteen, and it was meant to be the kind of gig he kept for a little while during college before getting a real job. Except he didn't go to college, and he never got a real job.

Bertie, the office manager, sticks her head into the room and says, "Will you come up to the front for a sec?"

"Sure," he says, stuffing one last folder into the rack and following Bertie down the long hallway to the front of the office.

Dr. Ranieri and Dr. Geraci are there in their white lab coats. So are the techs, Domenica and Kathryn, and the high school girl who just started in the office, Marilu. As he approaches, they all start singing "Happy Birthday" to him. He's always surprised that Bertie remembers. They've ordered a couple of pizzas from Krispy to celebrate.

When they're done singing, Chooch puts his right arm across his chest, a nervous maneuver. He wishes they hadn't done this again. It used to be nice, but now it just feels like another meaningless routine. "You guys shouldn't have," he says.

"The big three-one," Dr. Geraci says. He has a neatly manicured beard and big, glittering gold rings on several of his fingers. He's got a few patients who are in the Gambino crime family, and he tries to act like a mobster himself. He shakes Chooch's hand, passing him something.

Chooch looks down at his palm and sees a folded fifty-dollar bill there. "Dr. Geraci, thanks, but that's not—" Chooch starts.

Dr. Geraci stops him. "You deserve it. You're a good kid. Not a kid anymore, I guess. Take Mom out for a nice dinner."

Chooch nods.

Dr. Ranieri fancies himself a comedian, and he gives Chooch a shirt with a cartoon drawing of Saddam Hussein getting kicked in the ass by Uncle Sam. Bertie gives him a box of chocolates. Domenica and Kathryn give him a bottle of wine wrapped in a cloth bag even though he feels certain they know he doesn't drink. Marilu's gift is a candle that smells like birthday cake. They stand around, eating pizza and talking for fifteen minutes or so, but everyone is impatient to leave since it's a half day.

Chooch skips the bus and walks home from Dyker Heights. It's cold out but not freezing. His big plans for the rest of the day involve renting a few videos from Wolfman's, working on a collage, and going over to Risa's later. She's invited him and his mother to join her, Giulia, and Fab for cake. Giulia's been living with them since that night almost five years back. Everyone thought Sav ran off on his family, so it seemed natural that her sister should move in to help. She's got a job at Sid and Eddie's garage and jokingly calls herself Risa's replacement husband. Fab's grown so much. He doesn't remember his father. He's got a mop of black hair on his head and a bike with streamers he rides up and down the sidewalk—the corner by the Crisscross being one boundary, P.S. 101 being the other—and he loves his G.I. Joes and wrestling figures and watching TV. He's not big on words, doesn't talk at all, but that'll change soon. Risa's kept him out of pre-K at Our Lady of Perpetual Surrender, but later this year he's going to start kindergarten, where Sister Bernadette still rules with an iron hand, and she'll get him yapping away.

Chooch avoids the big avenues and stays on the quiet tree-lined back streets, Eighty-Third mostly, all the way to his neighborhood. It's a long walk, thirty or forty minutes, depending on his pace.

Today, he's taking his time. Studying front yards with their Mary statues and fig trees wrapped in tarps. He's noticing stuff he hasn't noticed before. Broken windows. Signs taped to doors that say NO SOLICITORS. The way a tree's roots have lifted and broken part of the sidewalk. Dripping pipes. Vinyl siding gone rusty. Wires and cables that seem to have no purpose. Some of the oldest houses are being torn down and replaced by boxy, redbrick condos. Everything feels different to him. Decaying. Dying. He's heard at the office that a lot of people are getting out, moving to New Jersey or Long Island. He wonders what's different in those places. He pictures sprawling lawns, obscene U-shaped driveways, inground pools, and grills on wooden decks.

His mind goes to the house upstate. Lately, his mom has been talking about selling it. The taxes are getting to be too much. He hasn't told Risa or Giulia. His mom wants him to go up there with her to do a walk-through and see if there's anything worth saving and to visit a realtor over in Callicoon who might begin the process of putting the house on the market. She doesn't think they'll get much for the place, but the size of the property is significant, and a semifamous writer—Chooch can't remember her name—apparently bought another house on Parsonage Road and restored it, so his mother has the idea that yuppies from the city and downtown Brooklyn might be getting in line to snatch up such properties. There's also talk of a casino opening by the Monticello Raceway, which could change things. Chooch keeps distracting her away from going up by focusing on the good times they once had there, taking out photo albums from trips where they spent days swimming in the Delaware and having cookouts in the yard and driving into Callicoon for groceries or to eat at the Western. He'd gone up there only once since what happened—a few weeks after the fact, a day when his mom had taken the bus to Atlantic

City—to check out how messy they'd been. He came away concluding they were safe unless something out of the ordinary occurred. If they get rid of the house now, drastic action will need to be taken. Moving what's left of Sav. Thankfully, his mother's talk of selling has come in waves and then she's drifted on to other things.

On Bay Parkway, he stops at his favorite bodega and browses the magazines. He's looking for something he can cut up. He notices Marco LaRocca on the cover of *Rolling Stone*. The Kickbacks had a big hit on the radio the year before, and Marco's more famous than ever. He's dating this hot young actress Hysteria Wilkins, and they're always in the tabloids. Big block news. Lola has become something of a recluse as his fame has grown. Chooch wonders if Giulia's seen the *Rolling Stone*. He knows it'll probably upset her. He picks out issues of *Popular Photography* and *Outside* and brings them to the counter.

The guy behind the counter, Johnny Musacchio, he's owned the place forever, rattles on about Mayor Dinkins, saying the city's going even more to shit than ever. Chooch avoids the conversation and pays. He has a gym bag with him—emblazoned with a logo for a new drug from Merck, given as promo to the office by a pharmaceutical rep named Kirsten—containing the gifts from Bertie and the crew. He takes it off his shoulder, unzips it, and places the magazines neatly on top of the other stuff. He walks out of the bodega with Johnny still prattling on about Dinkins.

Wolfman's is off the corner of Bay Thirty-Fourth on Eighty-Sixth Street. It's next to the Pigeon Club Laundromat and across from the place where Chooch used to get his Little League baseball uniforms. Everyone calls it Wolfman's—even though the actual name of the store is DeeLite Video—because the owner has hairy arms and hairy hands and a big beard and wild sideburns and a small, knotted tusk of hair bursting up from his shirt collar. The rumor is that he keeps himself chained to the floor behind the register when it's a full moon because that's when he goes full wolf. Wolfman's is Chooch's go-to video place because the selection is good, and the three-for-two deal is a bargain. He's always liked movies but likes them even more now since his mother got him a TV/VCR combo as a gift last year and he can watch them in his room. The only other option in the neighborhood is K&D on Cropsey, and they have worse tapes than the library.

He walks into the store and sees Wolfman hunched behind the counter doing a crossword puzzle, glasses low on his nose, picking apart an orange, his beard ornamented with pith. The porn room is to the left behind saloon doors. The new releases are on the wall right next to the counter. The racks lining the aisles of the store are stacked with classics, horror, action, comedies, a little bit of everything.

Chooch picks out two recent releases—*The Freshman* and *Die Hard 2*—as well as an older movie, *Honey*, for his freebie. He puts the stack of boxes on the counter.

"This *Honey* is real sexy stuff," Wolfman says. "Don't watch it with Mama Chooch."

Chooch's cheeks go flush. "I won't."

Wolfman shuffles off into the back to retrieve the tapes. He returns and rings Chooch up. "You hear anything on your buddy Sav?" Wolfman asks. Whether it's been a while since Chooch has come in or he's come in five days in a row, Wolfman always gets around to bringing up Sav.

"Still nothing," Chooch says.

"I'd like to get my hands on that guy," Wolfman says. "Nothing lower than robbing old Gilly and walking out on your wife and kid without a word."

Chooch nods. The lie has become gospel. It's careened off in many directions, sprouted many other lies. Word got around that Sav and Double Stevie had broken into Gilly the Gambler's house and stolen some cash. Double Stevie had shot his mouth off at L'Amour, though he apparently hadn't mentioned to anyone that Chooch was along for the ride. Chooch never returned the money he took from Sav to Gilly as he'd initially planned because he thought it would cause problems, raise questions that couldn't be answered. Gilly was more upset about his records being destroyed, and he died not long after that, leaving his house to a distant niece who sold it to developers for condos. A burglary like that was—at least in part—an explanation for Sav's sudden departure. Just like his brother, the bum. Once word started spreading about what they'd done, Double Stevie left Brooklyn under cover of night for who knows where—having already blown his half of the dough—before Gilly could sic the cops on him. It was the best possible outcome, wiping Double Stevie out of the equation and making it appear as though both he and Sav were on the lam. Sav abandoning his family became the accepted narrative in the neighborhood to such an extent that even his own parents hadn't once questioned its validity, doting on Risa and Fab, trying to make up for Sav's shittiness through gifts and apologetic posturing. Chooch knows how much that kills Risa, how she can barely look at them when they're around visiting her and Fab, but she's kept her cool repeatedly in difficult situations. Chooch carries some of the same weight as Risa, but he doesn't have to confront it in the ways she does.

He leaves Wolfman's with the tapes and heads home.

His mom is at the door to greet him, as if she knew the exact moment he'd arrive somehow. It's more likely that she's just been standing there, waiting on him. She pushes open the door and smiles. "How's the birthday boy?" she asks.

"Fine," he says, pecking her cheek.

"Exciting day at work?"

"Oh, thrilling. I accidentally bent a file folder, so I put it under some heavy manuals and flattened it out and it looked almost normal after a couple of hours. They pay me the big bucks for that kind of ingenuity."

"Smart *and* funny."

"Yeah, a real prize. How's everything been here?"

"Same old, same old. Come into the kitchen. I've got something for you."

"Ma, you didn't have to get me a present."

"Oh, hush up."

He follows her into the kitchen. Two wrapped presents sit on the table, one in a big box, the other smaller. He puts his bag on the floor and sits in front of the presents, opening the big one first. It's a Sony boombox with a CD player. "Ma, you shouldn't have," he says.

"I know you wanted it," his mother says, sitting next to him.

"I got all my tapes."

"The guy at Sam Goody said tapes are out and everybody's only gonna be listening to CDs now."

"Thank you." He leans forward and gives her another kiss on the cheek.

"Open the other one."

He unwraps the other present. It's a shoebox. He takes the top off and there's a fluff of blue tissue paper inside. He digs around and finds a stack of shrink-wrapped CDs: Motörhead's *1916*, Cinderella's *Heartbreak Station*, Tesla's *Five Man Acoustical Jam*, Steve Vai's *Passion and Warfare*, Iron Maiden's *No Prayer for the Dying*, Megadeth's *Rust in Peace*, and AC/DC's *The Razors Edge*. He has a couple of these on tape already, but he's excited to see the CDs with their sharp-edged jewel cases.

"Seven to get you started," his mother says. "I know how you love seven."

"You picked these out?" Chooch asks.

"I listen to you when you talk. I know what bands you like. It's not Sinatra or the Andrews Sisters, but to each his own."

"This must've cost you a fortune."

She waves him off. "You're such a good son. Always doing for me and others." She pauses. "How's thirty-one feel so far?"

A lot of men—millions of men—have lived full lives by the time they're thirty-one. Gone to war. Gotten married. Had kids. Been working a real job for years. His father, for one. By the time his old man was thirty-one, he'd fought in the Korean War, gone to school on the G.I. Bill, gotten married to his mom and then landed a gig with the Department of City Planning, bought their house on the block, had Chooch, and then bought that second house upstate. Chooch takes a quick inventory of what he's accomplished. Not fucking much. Guys he went to high school with are working on Wall Street, teaching high school, doing the lawyer thing, coaching sports, taking over their fathers' landscaping businesses or pork stores, and there's even one, Davey Cantalupo, who's a soldier and did some heroic shit in Operation Desert Storm the month before. All Chooch knows with any certainty is that he wishes he could be Risa's husband. He wishes he could be a father to Fab. He wants that to be his legacy. "Feels good," he says. "Thanks for the presents."

The phone rings. His mother scrambles to answer it. "Hello?" she says. Someone else is speaking on the other end. His mother begins to walk toward him, the long cord threaded several feet from the base on the wall. She holds her hand over the mouthpiece. "It's Risa. She sounds upset."

This concerns him. He can't remember the last time she called. Anything's eating away at Risa, she can usually wait until he checks in, which he does at least once or twice a day. He stands and takes the phone from his mother, who leans against the stove, trying to eavesdrop. "Ris, what's wrong?" Chooch asks, curling toward the wall, yearning for a bit of privacy.

Risa's voice is a whisper, edged with panic. "I can't believe this," she says.

"What is it?" he asks. "Is Fab sick? What can I do?"

"It's not Fab. He's fine. Roberto's here."

"Sav's brother Roberto?"

"Yeah, he's back. He's looking for Sav. He's asking for money and saying he wants to stay here. I'm sorry—I should've said happy birthday first. Happy birthday. What do I do, Christopher? What do I tell him?"

Chooch hasn't seen Roberto since he split town seven years ago. His arrival back in the neighborhood will be big news. He can also throw off the order of things in a significant way. Horn in where he doesn't need to. Put the squeeze on Risa. Say he starts believing Sav's disappearance is fishy. He and Sav hadn't been in touch since Roberto left. Chooch is sure of that because

Sav talked often about how much he wanted to link up with his brother again. Roberto was his hero, and Sav was always trying to figure out where the crafty fucker might've escaped to. He imagined him on beaches and in tiki bars. Running scams. Cavorting with tanned women in bikinis. Chooch is worried by Roberto's sudden appearance but relieved that Risa has called him for help. "I'll be right over," he says.

3.

Risa hasn't seen Roberto since the week before he left Brooklyn all those years ago. He looks different, sitting across from her at the kitchen table, bopping Fab around on his knee. Starvation skinny and desperate in the eyes. Stubble on his face. He smells of cigarettes and cheap aftershave. He's wearing acid-washed jeans and a blue hoodie that says SECOND ANNUAL BIG BITCH FEST. People used to say he and Sav were like twins. That resemblance is still there, but he looks more destitute than Sav ever did. If she saw him walking on Eighty-Sixth Street, not knowing who he was, she'd clutch her purse tighter. She should probably still clutch her purse, even here in her kitchen, not that she's got much for him to beg after. Still, despite Roberto's sketchiness, Fab's looking at his uncle adoringly, as if this is the man he's been waiting for. She hopes Chooch will show up soon.

"I was sorry to hear my brother left you like that," Roberto says, shaking Fab from his knee and patting him on the back.

Fab takes a seat at the table—well, climbs up on the chair and kneels there—and pulls the box of rainbow cookies from Villabate Alba that Risa has set out close to him. The cookies are arranged in thick rows, the chocolate coating on top glistening, the layers bright and fresh-looking. He rummages through the box and takes two rainbows, shoving one in his mouth and keeping the other clasped in his palm as he chews.

Risa puts her hand on Fab's arm as if to warn him to take it easy. "How'd you know?" she asks Roberto.

"I went to see my folks first."

"They must be happy you're home."

"My mom about had a conniption fit," Roberto says. "I thought she was gonna shit. Excuse my French. Gone all these years. Probably figured me for dead. My parents, God love them, they never had an iota of faith in my abilities. Didn't think I could survive on my own. They don't know how hard I hustle."

"What became of Jimmy Tomasullo's wife?"

"Susie and I had our differences. We broke up amicably down in Miami. She went her own way. Took up with some Cuban gangster."

"And what about Jimmy? Now you're back, you don't think he'll come after you? Or call the cops?"

"I was hoping Jimmy would be dead, to tell you the truth. I fully expect him to come knocking. But I decided I had to see my folks. I wanted to see Sav before I knew the story about what happened. When my folks told me you and my brother had a kid, I knew I had to meet the rug rat. Ain't every day you find out you're an uncle." He tousles Fab's hair. "Family's all you got in the end. That's one thing I learned out in the world. Blood's blood. What about you? How're things? You hanging in there?"

"We get by. Giulia lives with us. She got a job at a garage right over here. Really pitches in. That's why I don't think you can stay. We have a full house already. She sleeps on the couch."

Roberto bites his knuckle. "I remember Giulia. Real looker, that one." He pauses. "And I hear Chooch Gardini's over all the time."

"Who told you that?"

"My folks."

"Christopher helps me a lot."

"*Christopher*. That's his real name, huh? I forgot. He still lives at home with his mother across the street?"

"Yeah. He's coming over now."

"That's who you called in the bedroom? Don't want to be alone too long with the Big Bad Wolf?"

"It's not like that."

Roberto turns to Fab, who's digging into his second rainbow, gnawing the chocolate off the top and then separating the pink layer from the jelly and eating it in small bites. "Mommy here doesn't trust Uncle Roberto," he says to Fab. "Thinks I'm coming around with my hand out, begging for money, begging for a place to crash. Got real comfortable in this new life without my brother."

"Sav *abandoned us*," Risa says, her voice on the verge of cracking from the emphasis she puts on the last two words. It's not an all-the-way lie. He'd certainly abandoned them in his heart before everything that happened. Getting defensive is the hand she thinks it best to play. She's done it before when others have insinuated that she's moved on too readily. It seems true to the way she'd respond if Sav had actually split. She never had any interest in being an actress—not even in high school when her favorite teacher, Mr. Mangiello, urged her to try out for the school production of *You Can't Take It with You*—but now she feels like she's acting all the time. Except she's not acting the way actors do, drawing on real emotions to connect with the work; instead, she's acting to keep the truth hidden. She thought it would be tiring and taxing, but she finds she doesn't mind the charade in most circumstances. But facing down Roberto like this is different. It's got her all nerved up. She wants him gone from her apartment and from the neighborhood and from the state. She wants to keep forgetting about his existence. Looking at him is like looking at a lost piece of Sav.

"Sure, okay," Roberto says. "My brother's a no-good bum, I'll buy that. Off partying it up while his wife raises his kid. You gonna get an annulment? You talk to the priest? Must be within your rights."

"No, he's still my husband," Risa says. In all actuality, she's thought long and hard about this very thing. She knows that abandonment isn't grounds for annulment in the eyes of the church, so she'd have to find some other way to invalidate the marriage if she hopes to keep his death secret. She has no interest in getting remarried, so her thinking is she'll let Fab get older and then she'll figure out what other options she has. Fidelity is just another act she puts on.

"That's nice. Very forgiving of you."

"I'm not trying to be forgiving. It's what I believe."

Roberto leans forward and hovers over the open box of

rainbows. He wafts his hands over the cookies and takes a deep breath. "Been a decade at least since I had one of these. They should bottle that smell. The almond paste. I'd carry it around with me, open the bottle, and take a whiff when I need a hit of sunshine. I used to be like a junkie with these things. I could sit here, eat the whole box."

"Have a few," Risa says.

Roberto grabs one and pops it in his mouth and chews noisily, moaning with pleasure. Fab watches him and laughs. "I got another idea," Roberto says. "Rainbow cookie air fresheners for the car. Instead of pine or whatever. You got a big picture of a rainbow hanging on your rearview, and you've got that smell in your nose the whole time you're driving. Happiness factor goes through the roof." He pauses, chomps on another, then hands one to Fab. "Let me ask you something, Ris. I'm sitting here, I'm a natural observer, and I'm observing that your little guy don't talk. What's up with that? Cat got his tongue or he one of those mute types?"

"He's a late bloomer," Risa says. "He knows his words, but he has trouble saying what he wants to say. Dr. Bernardi says he'll be fine."

Fab comes over to Risa and presses his body against hers. He paws at her chest. He'd nursed until he was almost four and it had been a long year of weaning him off. He still wants to nurse often, especially when he's tired or worried, and Risa breaks his heart every time and reminds him they've crossed a line where it's no longer acceptable. In fact, maybe they crossed that line a while before stopping. Acceptable to whom exactly, she's not sure, but she knows she doesn't want to do long-term damage. Truth is, she misses nursing Fab. She'd let it go on longer than she should've because it brought her such peace of mind. It made her feel like a mother should feel. When she stopped nursing him, she'd grown sad, knowing there'd never be another time like that in her life.

"He's still on the tit?" Roberto asks.

Risa feels her face flush. This bastard has some nerve talking like that. She snaps back: "You, always with the inappropriate questions."

He puts his hands up. "Just curious. They're like drunks when you let them go too long. Knew this kid down in Florida. Him and his mom lived at the same motel as me. Kid was seven and still on the tit. Craziest thing to see. He was over four feet tall, and his mom was about five-three, and he'd walk up and press on one of her nipples like it was a soda fountain, and she'd lift her shirt and let him have at it, standing up. They didn't have much dough, so nutrition-wise, I guess it was a good deal, though she smoked like a goddamn chimney."

The doorbell rings. Chooch, finally. *Thank God.*

Fab rushes to the door and yanks it open. Chooch already has the storm door propped. He enters. Fab embraces him and makes a series of small noises that sound almost like "Uncle Chooch," though Risa's encouraged him to go with "Uncle Christopher" instead. He's trying, her poor boy. He'll get it down. Once he's in kindergarten, he'll blossom. Being a parent, she's discovered, is in large part about hoping everything turns out the way it's supposed to and holding back the despair that comes with realizing there's a good chance stuff might actually go wrong. Bad thoughts often assail her: *What if he doesn't talk? What if he never talks? What if his fate was sealed that night in the woods? He ate dirt from his father's grave, and it made him mute.*

Chooch puts his hands behind his back and then holds out his closed fists. "Got something for you," he says to Fab.

Fab's vibrating with excitement. He slaps Chooch's right hand. Chooch turns it over palm up and there's one of those small bouncy balls from a grocery store vending machine. A swirl of green and purple. Fab grabs it and hugs Chooch around the waist and turns to Risa. He holds it up and groans toward the door. He's asking if he can go outside.

"Okay, but stay right in front of the apartment," she says. "And *do not* chase the ball into the street."

Fab nods and clatters outside.

"Cute how you two got your own little language," Roberto says.

Risa lets the comment pass.

Chooch lumbers up to the table and shakes Roberto's hand. "Been what, seven years?" Chooch asks.

"Something like that," Roberto says.

"It's good you're back."

"Yeah?"

"Why not? Your folks must be happy. They know you're here, right? They've been broken up since Sav split. Both of youse gone."

"I reunited with them earlier. It was an emotional scene. But how happy can they be? It's not like I'm Mr. Successful or anything, coming home with my fancy car and fancy wife and wads of dough. I've been bouncing around flea-infested motels for the better part of a decade." He pauses. "You're what, a bodyguard for Risa over here? I show up, she's on the horn to you immediately."

"It's not like that."

"You moving in on Sav's family?"

"It's not like that either."

"Christopher has been a great friend to us," Risa says.

"You must like she calls you Christopher instead of Chooch, huh?" Roberto says. "How old are you now? What kind of job you got?"

"Thirty-one today," Chooch says. "Me and Sav were four years behind you in school. My job's nothing special. I work in a doctor's office. I do filing, that kind of thing."

"Shit, happy birthday, kid. Filing? I've worked some shit jobs, but I've never filed anything."

"I put the folders with the charts in alphabetical order on the shelves. It's a lot to keep track of. I've got a good head for names. I do other stuff there, too. I carry in deliveries. They send me out for lunch. I make runs to the lab."

"Thrilling. Risa, I take it you're a full-time mom. How're the bills around here?"

"We get by," Risa says.

"I'll tell you what," Roberto says. "I miss this apartment. My room was upstairs growing up, but I'm sure you remember I lived down here on my own a while. Those years, this place was party central. It wasn't all titty milk and rainbow cookies. Right on this very table—best night of my life—me and Ginny Saggese went to town. We could've been a porno, that's how memorable it was."

"On the table?" Chooch asks. "Why not go into the bedroom?"

"Sometimes you want it on a table. Ginny was a fucking hoot-and-a-half."

"She's married now," Risa says, looking down, away from the table, which has been desecrated forever in her mind. She'll have to plot for its replacement.

"To who?"

"Benny Picciotto. You remember him? They've got four kids."

"Oh, madone. Four goddamn rug rats? She ain't fucking on tables no more, I guarantee that." He laughs and shakes his head. "Ginny with four kids. Hard to imagine. Used to say she couldn't stand kids. Used to say she'd rather have fun than ever have kids."

Risa isn't friends with Ginny. Knows her to say hi, that's it. Sees her at church with Benny and their children, in the back pew of the crying room, or sees her up on Eighty-Sixth Street shopping at Meats Supreme. "Maybe you'll run into her," Risa says.

"Maybe," Roberto says.

Silence swelters in the room for a few minutes. Risa goes and checks on Fab. He's bouncing the ball against the brick front of the building and chasing it into the weeds in the small garden. She opens the door and asks, "You being careful?"

He nods and holds the ball up like he's rediscovered it.

"Too cold?"

He shakes his head. He's one of those kids, in the summer he puts on layers, and in the winter, he strips them off. He's wearing a T-shirt and jeans and it's not *that* cold, but she's thinking she should force him to put a jacket on if he stays out much longer.

Risa smiles. "Stay away from the street," she says again. Two weeks before, a kid from P.S. 101 had been hit by a car while running out into the street after a football during recess. Cars fly on the block. Kids think they're immortal. She's trying to really make Fab hyperaware of his surroundings. A city like this, you've got to have eyes in the back of your head, always be paying attention. He's so little still, but she needs to build up a healthy sense of fear in him.

Back at the table, Chooch and Roberto have fallen into a whispery conversation. Roberto's pulled his hood on over his head.

"What's going on?" Risa asks.

"I was saying to Roberto it's not a good idea for him to try to stay here," Chooch says. "With Giulia and Fab and everything, it's too much. I was saying for him to stay with his parents. They'd be happy to have him."

"I get the message loud and clear," Roberto says. "You brought in your representative here to really drive the point home. I'm not welcome."

"It's not that you're not welcome," Risa says.

"I don't feel welcome." Roberto stands.

"I can't help how you feel."

"Don't worry. I won't ask for money again neither. I come to my family for a touch to get back on my feet, but I ain't a beggar and I don't expect jack shit."

"What about Jimmy?" Chooch asks. "He hasn't forgotten you. Talk to anybody who knows him, they say getting revenge on you is all he talks about."

"What about him? I'm sick of hearing about this fuck. He comes for me, I'll give him a slap. You think I'm scared of some jabroni trophy shop owner?"

"Scared enough you ran away for all those years."

"I left so I didn't get pinched for knocking off his store, not because I was shitting my shorts over what Jimmy might do to me. Anyhow, it's been great catching up. Chooch, you ain't fucking Risa, are you?" He shakes his own question off. "Nah.

She's a woman in mourning for her failed marriage, right?" With that, Roberto cinches his hoodie tighter around his head and leaves.

Risa goes back to the door and watches as he passes Fab, hunched over a storm drain in the concrete, swirling the ball around on the cover, trying to get the ball to balance on one of the tiny holes. Roberto kneels next to Fab and says something to him. Risa's going to let it pass, but Roberto keeps talking for thirty seconds and then a minute, and it's too much for her to take, to wonder about, so she throws open the door and says, "What are you saying to him?"

Roberto looks at her and smiles. "I'm telling him about his pop. No harm in that. Looks more like him than I do. That must kill you. Looking at Fab and seeing Sav."

Fab resembles Sav enough that folks bring it up all the time. *He's the spitting image of his old man.* She tries not to see it, but it's often unavoidable. She doesn't say anything to Fab now. She won't know exactly what Roberto said to Fab or if Fab truly understood any of it. "Fab, come in now, okay?" she says. "It's too cold to be outside with no jacket."

Roberto tousles Fab's hair again.

Fab collects his ball and scampers inside under her outstretched arm holding open the door.

Roberto stands, gives her one last nasty grin. "Be seeing you," he says.

Risa closes the storm door and then the interior door, thumbing the lock shut. She leans against the wall, gripping her left wrist with her right hand and anxiously twisting it.

Fab quickly establishes a perch in the living room, on the floor next to the couch, turning on the television to cartoons, rolling his ball around on the carpet. It seems like the encounter hasn't had much of an impact on him, after all.

Risa comes back to the table and sits across from Chooch, exasperated, shredding the sports pages of the *Daily News* on the table for something to do with her hands. She likes to tear up the paper when she's nervous. The sound. The action. "He knows something," she says. She's talking about Roberto, but she doesn't need to say his name.

"There's nothing he could know," Chooch says.

"Maybe he feels something's off. I couldn't even look at him."

"Take it easy."

"I can't believe he's back. He was talking to Fab outside. He could've been saying anything. And my table. I've gotta think about what him and Ginny did on it every time I look at it now."

"Roberto's a lot of things, but smart's not one of them. And I'm sure he's lying about the table. Or exaggerating."

"He's gonna be hanging around. I can't take that." Her voice falls to a whisper: "I'll break. Eventually. Or you or Giulia will."

"You won't. I won't. Giulia won't. We'll be okay."

Risa can't see how any of this will be okay. Roberto's poison, and once poison starts spreading, it's hard to stop. He'll turn his and Sav's folks against her—she can see it now. He'll say something's not right about her story. He'll say the way she and Chooch act together isn't right. He'll keep sniffing around her door. Other people will start asking questions. "I'm not sure if we will be," Risa says. "Maybe I don't deserve to be."

"Don't say that," Chooch says. "You're a good person who's been put in a bad spot. It ain't your fault. We'll figure out a way to take care of this."

"I don't want to see him again. I really don't." Risa collects the shredded pieces of newspaper and stacks them in a pile. "You want something to eat? I've got mortadella and provolone."

"Sure, that'd be great."

She asks Fab if he's hungry and he shakes his head. Too many rainbows. She pushes away from the table and goes into the kitchen and starts making the sandwich. The semolina bread's fresh from that morning. She takes the mortadella and provolone out of the Tupperware container where she keeps her cold cuts. She remembers that she has some leftover broccoli rabe and asks Chooch if she should heat that up and put it on the sandwich too. He gives her an enthusiastic yes, so she takes out a pot from under the stove and puts it on the burner and heats up what remains of the broccoli rabe, which isn't much since both Giulia and Fab love it so much. While she's waiting, she cuts off a nice piece of bread and slices it in half. She spreads it open on a plate and layers mortadella and provolone on the bottom half. Back at the stove, she gets lost staring at the green leaves and soft garlic bulbs swirling in olive oil and water. She makes her broccoli rabe with a lot of liquid. Once it boils, she forks out some and places it atop the mortadella and provolone on the bread. It begins to melt the cheese immediately. She shuts the gas, removing the pot from the hot burner and shuffling it over to one of the cool ones. She puts the top piece of bread on the sandwich and brings it over to the table, and she watches Chooch eat his sandwich while Fab dances around in the living room.

4.

Giulia works in the front office of Sid and Eddie's garage on the corner of Bay Thirty-Fourth Street and Bath Avenue, right around the block from Risa's place on Saint of the Narrows—her place too—and just a few storefronts down from the Crisscross, where she finds herself many nights after locking up the garage. She came in early today after racing away from the promenade, mistaking that guy on the bench for Sav. Spooky shit.

She's had the job for a while, and it's not the best or anything, but it feels good to contribute. Sid and Eddie aren't terrible, all told. They throw some lighthearted harassment her way, call her *doll* and *baby* and say they want to leave their wives for her, but they're generally respectful, holding doors for her, saying *please* and *thank you*, the basic stuff. They pay her in cash, which is a plus, and sometimes give her little bonuses when they've had a particularly solid week. They say she's invaluable in the office. They say a lot of guys bring their cars to them just to see her.

The customers, that's another story. Some of them are nice enough. Others are hounds. Many bring her gifts. Flowers, cookies, jewelry, scratch-offs, the works. This one, Mr. Vixama from over on Cropsey Avenue, he always brings her these little porcelain figurines. She's not sure if there's a name for them or if there's a story involved, but they look to be out of a country scene. Farmers and kids chewing hay. Some of them decked out in overalls. Some clutching fruit and vegetables and gardening tools. The figurines are about three or four inches high. Painted with a light touch. They're very professional. Mr. Vixama wears track suits and only speaks Italian. His car's not even getting worked on most of the times he comes in. He talks to her nonstop when he's in the office, and she can grasp a word here and there but mostly she has no idea what he's saying. She tries to use it as an opportunity to practice Italian, but he's too much of a pain in the ass. He's probably telling her all about the figurines. He's bringing her a whole collection piece by piece. She keeps them set up on the bookshelf behind her, and she's starting to imagine them as characters in a story she'll make sense of someday.

She has an overcrowded desk with a typewriter, a lamp, an adding machine, and lots of stacks of receipts, mostly related to parts they've had to buy. Other than the figurines from Mr. Vixama, her decorations are scarce. A framed picture of Risa and Fab. A calendar from the hair salon she sometimes goes to. In her top drawer, she has a picture of Marco clipped from the cover of the most recent *Rolling Stone*. He's standing on a subway platform with his shirt open. She's been staring at the picture a lot lately and daydreaming about meeting up with him. She imagines a scenario where they have a tryst at the Chelsea Hotel and she tells him all about what happened with Sav and about what it's been like to move in with Risa and Fab, and he admits to her that fame is overrated and he longs for the kind of love he had with her. Men don't talk to her about him a ton, but women always ask what it was like to be his girlfriend. She brushes the question off and insists they were just kids.

The rest of the office is stacked with boxes. Parts mostly. Engine oil. Whatever else. The walls are a tribute to the Italian soccer team that won the World Cup in '82. Giulia doesn't know shit about soccer, but Sid and Eddie are diehards. A squat steel safe cabinet is on the floor next to the desk, camouflaged by all the stuff stacked on top of it—they keep some important documents in there, as well as a loaded Beretta pistol in case of trouble. Sid and Eddie took Giulia out to a shooting range in Staten Island one day to show her how to handle it.

It stays cold in the office in the winter with the doors constantly opening and closing—one from the street side and one from the garage side—so she bundles up in sweaters and leggings and wool caps and can often see her breath. It's not that cold today, but it's certainly not warm either. She's wearing the sweater from Risa and has kept her mother's wool hat on.

Her job mostly consists of taking calls, writing invoices, bookkeeping, and filing, though their system—if it could rightfully be called a system—consists of stacking folders in big white bank boxes and piling them in the closet on the far end of the garage.

From what she can tell, Sid's an ace mechanic but has no bedside manner. Eddie's all bedside manner.

She's not sure what to expect out of the day—she always feels like anyone can walk in at any given time and start busting her chops, so she stays on her toes—but she's certainly not expecting, as she sits there behind the desk trying to do the math on a parts order from some dealer in Coney Island, that Sav's fucking brother, Roberto, would bounce into the office. She instantly realizes that he's who she'd seen down on the promenade and mistaken for Sav. She's not sure why the thought hadn't occurred to her. She'd forgotten how much they resemble each other.

Bad fucking news.

There's no one else in the office, unfortunately. Sid and Eddie are tangling with Mr. Pascione's Caddy in the garage, and no customers have drifted in for about forty-five minutes. Now would be the perfect time for Mr. Vixama to come around with a figurine or for Irish Georgie to bring her a coffee from McDonald's. She thinks about the gun in the safe in case she needs to run him off.

Roberto's standing there in front of her, skinny in an anguished way, wearing that ragged hoodie, his hands in his pockets, looking like a bunch of different scroungy scumbags got Frankensteined into one super-scroungy scumbag. "You remember me?" he asks.

"I saw you down by the water this morning," she says. "I thought you were Sav for a second."

"Yeah? I didn't see you."

"You're back?"

"I'm back."

"I'm busy," Giulia says, trying not to act too shocked by the fact that he is who he is. He's also been assumed dead by many people. More than that, he's a major subject of neighborhood lore. Sav always wanted to have that sort of juice when he was still around. People always saying, *You remember the time Roberto Franzone did this or that?* When Sav finally became a guy people talked about that way, it was because of his disappearance, and even in that regard he played second banana to Roberto, who'd disappeared first and more dramatically.

"You don't look too busy."

"This is my job."

"Risa said you were working around here in a garage. I figured Sid and Eddie's. Came around the side so I didn't pass the Crisscross. Never know who's hanging out there. A lot of women, they get less hot as they get older, but I think you're getting hotter. I've always admired maturity in a woman. You're what, close to thirty now?"

"What do you want?"

"Seven years gone, and I'm being treated like a pariah. Thought they'd roll out the red carpet."

Sid comes into the office through the door from the garage, grease smeared on his face and coveralls, wool skullcap pulled tight over his bald head, writing something in a tiny memo book with a golf pencil as he walks. He's tall and imposing and she's hoping his presence is enough to chase Roberto off. Then again, it seems like Roberto maybe knows him from before.

Sure enough, when Sid looks up and sees Roberto, his face breaks into a glow. "Roberto? Holy shit, man, you're home?"

"Here I am," Roberto says.

Sid goes over and bear-hugs him. "Me and this guy, we have some wild stories to tell," Sid says to Giulia. "We go back. All the way back. This one time, Iggy Imbriano bet Roberto a hundred bucks he wouldn't go naked with a hard-on into Lenny's to order a slice and a soda. He's what, maybe eighteen at the time? Not only does he do it, he stays in there and eats the slice and sucks down his soda, and he maintains the hard-on the entire time. The guys behind the counter, they're so shocked, dumbfounded, whatever, they don't even react. Later, they says they thought they were on a dirty version of *Candid Camera*. How'd you keep that wood going the whole time you was standing there eating pizza?"

"Easy enough," Roberto says. "Just thought about your mother."

Sid laughs and throws an arm around Roberto's shoulder. "Don't joke around. My mother always loved you."

"I'll be your stepdaddy when the time comes."

"This fucking guy." Sid turns the way he's holding Roberto into something resembling a quick headlock and then lets him go. "What the hell you doing home? I thought you was on the lam. Jimmy Tomasullo still wants you stuffed and mounted on his wall. He hangs out at the Crisscross all the time. You're probably about a hundred feet away from him right now."

"I came back to hit on your secretary here."

"Join the club. Ninety percent of our business is guys hitting on Giulia. Not sure what we'd do if we hadn't hired her." Sid wipes his hands on a blue cloth, grease coming off in long streaks. "You ain't seen Sav out in the big wide world, have you? Always wondered if he ran off to meet you somewhere."

"I ain't seen him. Until I got back, I didn't know he'd even split. We hadn't been in touch since I left. My fault. Him being gone dashed my hopes of teaming up with him on a couple of business ventures I had in mind."

"Business ventures? The Franzone Brothers? Man, oh, man. Hey, you know the dirty movie theater farther down on Bath Avenue? You need a job, I think they're looking for help. Someone to mop up all the jizz." Sid swats Roberto on the back. "You need some meat on your bones, you know that? You been eating anything wherever you been or what? You're not a dope fiend, are you? Where the hell *have* you been?"

"Miami, mostly. A few other places. And you know I don't fuck with needles."

Sid sings it like the part from Lou Reed's "Walk on the Wild Side": "'Miami, F-L-A.'"

"Beaches and broads in bikinis."

"Both foreign concepts to me."

"You get married?"

"Christ, don't get me started."

"Who?"

"Lizzie LaRusso."

"Lizzie the Lezzie?"

"She was never a lezzie, come on." Sid heads toward the garage, looking down at the cloth in his hands, all the grease.

Giulia knows he's sensitive about his wife, who was—by all accounts—a well-known lesbian at Bishop Kearney before shocking everyone and marrying Sid and bearing him two children.

"I've gotta get back to work," Sid says. "It was good to see you, Roberto. Giulia, let me know if that Bay Ridge guy calls."

Giulia nods.

"Something I said?" Roberto laughs. "He married Lizzie the Lezzie. I don't give a shit. That's funny. It's like marrying Tony the Tiger or something. She was, like, on the box of cereal every

Catholic school girl lesbian in Brooklyn ate for breakfast. She was on the fucking recruiting posters. That's how famous she was as a lesbian."

"I wouldn't say those things, I was you," Giulia says.

Roberto comes closer, sits on the edge of her desk. "Okay, enough about Lizzie the Lezzie. Tell me about you. You live with Risa and Fab since my brother went AWOL? What's that like, being your sister's new husband?"

What's she supposed to say? Moving in with Risa has been one of the best things that's happened to her in a long damn time. Risa feels the same way. Though they've had to tend to their lie, the last four and a half years have largely been devoted to renewal and joy. Sav's death made it possible, but their bond as sisters makes it work. She doesn't even dignify Roberto's question with a response. "Can you please fucking leave?" she says. "I've got a million things to do."

"Chooch Gardini comes over a lot, huh? What's going on over there? You can tell me. Mute five-year-old kid still hunting for the tit. Chooch trying to act like the muscle in the family. Risa nervous as hell. Something's off big time. How do *you* fit into all of it?"

Giulia picks up the receiver of her phone and uses the eraser end of a pencil to rotate the dial, checking the number against what she has written down on the invoice in front of her. She doesn't really need to make this call desperately, but she's trying to encourage Roberto's departure. She's unsettled. What he's saying now, he sounds so suspicious about everything. Instead of accepting their arrangement as the rest of the neighborhood mostly has—Giulia and Chooch banding together to help Risa and Fab in their time of great need—Roberto seems to be suggesting that it's all bullshit.

"I get it," Roberto says. "I'll tell you what. I'm not skilled at much, not really, but I can smell a lie like a fart in a closed closet, and I'm gonna start shaking some trees around here and see what the fuck's really going on." He leaves the office, the door clanging loudly behind him.

Giulia hangs up the receiver before completing the call to the dealer she didn't really need to talk to. Instead, she dials home, wanting to share her panic with Risa about this Roberto situation they've got to deal with now. He's another guy she wouldn't mind seeing gone forever. The first time, fate helped them out. Maybe this time, they'd need to give fate a hand.

5.

Chooch knows how consequences spread out. All this time between them and the night Sav died. All this time living with what went down, and they'd expected to continue to just live with it, but they hadn't anticipated a curveball like this. Chooch knows Roberto well enough—or knew him, at least—to recognize the fact that he can sense something's not right. Maybe it's instinct or maybe Sandra Carbonari got in his ear—she's been one of the people who's always insisted something's rotten in Denmark. Either way, Chooch knows he needs to act.

Risa's reluctant to let him leave, and she becomes even more stressed out after Giulia calls from the garage and says Roberto paid her a visit over there, hammering her with questions. Chooch tells her she'll be okay, to keep her head up, and try not to worry too much. He reiterates that Roberto's more a nuisance than anything else, but he doesn't really believe that. "This guy's just a minor league dirtbag," Chooch says.

Risa nods, picks at her fingernails. "I'm sorry this has to ruin your birthday," she says.

"It's not."

"I'm still making you that carrot cake. I'm sure Vi's excited to come over and see Fab."

"You know my mother loves spending time with him," Chooch says, and he gets up, bringing his plate to the sink. He puts some dish soap on the sponge and washes the plate and then gives it a good rinse before fitting it into a notch in the dish drain. "Thanks for the sandwich."

"Don't thank me."

He comes back and stands by the table. Fab runs up and latches on to his leg and stands on his right foot. He wants Chooch to do the thing where he walks around with him balanced on his foot. Chooch does it for a minute, bobbling awkwardly around the dining room, and Fab laughs. "What time's cake?" Chooch asks.

"Sevenish sound good?" Risa says.

"We'll be over then." Chooch pries Fab from his leg. He hesitates but then pecks Risa on the cheek, leaning in close, wanting to hug her and tell her not to worry, but he knows there's a lot to worry about.

After leaving Risa and Fab, Chooch goes to the corner and takes a few deep breaths. He watches a bus kneel on the other side of Bath Avenue to let off an old woman in a shabby black puffer jacket. He knows he needs to talk to Giulia about Roberto.

He walks over to the garage. As if she's been waiting for him, Giulia stands behind her desk and says, "What the fuck are we gonna do?" Concern threaded in her voice.

"I don't know," Chooch says.

Giulia sticks her head into the garage and shouts to Sid and Eddie that she's going for smokes. She tells Chooch to take a walk with her.

They go outside and amble toward the corner. She removes a brand-new pack of Marlboro Reds from her pocket and lights one with a yellow Bic.

"You didn't actually need cigarettes," Chooch says.

"You're a regular Columbo," Giulia says.

They linger on the corner of Bay Thirty-Fourth by the stop sign. Chooch looks down at the square of grass between the sidewalk and the curb. An empty potato chip bag, a squashed quarter water bottle, a couple of dark mounds of dog shit. "It's not good he's sniffing around," Chooch says. "It's like he knows something's up."

"I saw him down by the water this morning," Giulia says. "From a distance, I thought it was Sav and freaked out. Then he shows up at the fucking garage. He's definitely gonna start making noise. Guy like that, maybe he can smell it on us."

"He couldn't just stay away."

"We should keep Risa out of this."

"Out of what?"

"I was thinking maybe it wouldn't be a bad idea to let Jimmy Tomasullo know about Roberto's arrival back in town."

"He's gonna find out one way or another."

Giulia takes a long drag on her cigarette. "He could use a

little prodding. The sooner Jimmy goes after Roberto, the more beneficial it is to our situation."

Chooch nods. "You're talking about Jimmy chasing him out of town again."

"Or whatever."

Chooch thinks about what Giulia's suggesting. Roberto's more trouble than he's worth. He's expendable. There's a built-in method to deal with him. He thinks about the way Roberto was talking to Fab out in the yard. He didn't like that at all. Roberto keeps turning over rocks, whispering things about how fucked up their arrangement seems, the whole house of cards comes crumbling down. The life Risa, Giulia, and Fab have built over there. Any shot he's got at making Risa think about him as husband material. "You think Jimmy's at the Crisscross now?" he asks.

She finishes her smoke and drops the butt on the sidewalk, stomping out the still-smoldering cherry with the heel of her boot. "He's over there all the time. If he's not there, he's at his shop."

"I'll do it," Chooch says.

Giulia reaches out and puts her hand on his shoulder. "Just putting the wheels in motion, that's it."

He nods and then walks her back to Sid and Eddie's.

Chooch hasn't been inside the Crisscross since the night Sav died. He wonders if there's a chance Jimmy has somehow already encountered Roberto, who probably passed the bar on his way to see Giulia. He hopes so. Take the onus off him.

He pushes in through the scarred and weather-aged front

door under the neon sign. Feels like time's stood still in there. Widow Marie's behind the bar, shorter and wearier than ever. Jane the Stain's sitting on a stool up front. Chooch has heard she's been dating Frannie Zu from around the corner. She's wearing fancy slacks and a black pullover sweater. Jimmy's down at the far end with a bowl of peanuts, a pint glass of whiskey, smoking a fat stogie. The place smells like his smoke. He's wearing a yellow dress shirt that's tight around his bulging belly. Chooch has only seen him a handful of times in recent years, always seeming to bump into him at the annual Eighteenth Avenue Feast. Still, it's a different thing to pass him out on the street than it is to see him here again in his regular dive. It hits Chooch how much older Jimmy looks. The guy can't be more than forty, but he looks fifty-five or sixty. He's lost a lot of his hair. His skin is pockmarked, his nose bulbous. Jimmy, always a big drinker, had hit the bottle even more recklessly after Roberto robbed him and took off with Susie, and the damage is apparent. Stare at him hard enough now—in his yellow shirt, with his bad skin—and he vaguely resembles a misshapen, half-melted trophy.

"Chooch Gardini," Jimmy says, stubbing out his stogie in a glass ashtray on the bar top crowded with other butts. The burning end sizzles down to a black streak. "What brings you here?"

"Haven't seen you in here since Sav split," Widow Marie says.

"That's right," Jimmy says. "Years since you graced us with your presence." He lifts the pint glass to his lips and sips the whiskey.

Chooch isn't sure exactly what time it is, but it's still early in the day.

"Excuse me while I imbibe my special vitamins," Jimmy says, and he takes a longer sip, making slurping noises, the glass looking fragile in his meaty hand. "This right here might look like mere whiskey, but it's really a magic potion that keeps me from putting a bullet in my fucking brain. You know what I deal with all day when I'm not here? Coaches and managers. Enthusiastic fucks. Happy for the kids on their team. Or that floozy runs a bowling tournament over at Yellow Hook Lanes. Bubbly, bright. A trophy joint's about the worst kind of shop to operate when you're in my frame of mind. Thank Christ I got Dina Petrocelli in there working. Excuse me—I'm on a talking rampage here."

"You want a drink?" Widow Marie asks.

Chooch shakes his head. "Just a club soda if you've got it."

Widow Marie reaches under the counter and comes out with a warm pony bottle of Schweppes club soda. She then gives him a highball glass filled with ice. "On the house," she says. "You must really have something on your mind, you're pounding club soda this time of day."

Leaning at the bar, Chooch unscrews the cap on the bottle and pours some of the soda water over the ice in his glass. It's flat. "Sav's brother is back," he says, looking down at the bar top, trying not to lock eyes with Jimmy. "He was just over at Risa's, causing problems." He's thinking from Jimmy's expression that word hasn't reached him yet.

"Roberto's back?" Jimmy says, his voice gone gravelly in anger.

"Don't know why the hell he came back. You hadn't heard?"

Jimmy shakes his head. "I'm sure I'll hear from others soon. A lot of people been waiting a long time to deliver this news to me. Susie back, too?"

"No, he's alone. Says him and Susie broke up down in Florida."

Jimmy nods and downs the rest of his whiskey. He's gripping his glass so hard, Chooch thinks it might damn well break in his hand. "Roberto's not a pal of yours?"

"He's no friend of mine."

"But his brother was."

"We grew up together." In his mind's eye, Chooch sees them as kids out on the block, riding bikes, playing stoopball and stickball, hanging from telephone poles, wrenching open fire hydrants, performing burials for action figures in Chooch's backyard.

"Roberto's staying where?"

"I'm assuming with his folks. He was trying to convince Risa to let him crash, but she put her foot down."

"A lot of years I've dreamed about getting revenge on that fuck," Jimmy says, looking at the mirror behind the bar, squinting, his forehead scrunched. He's trembling. "But, as much time as I've spent thinking about how good it'd be to shoot him in the throat and watch him choke on his blood, I've thought about offing myself even more. What'd Susie want that I didn't have? How'd I let myself get taken like Roberto took me? I used to be smart. Many a night I took out the piece I bought from Slug Kelly's brother, and I put it in my mouth. Couldn't pull the trigger. Imagined my own funeral, saw my old man wailing, saw my sister angry at me."

Chooch looks at the floor. He's been there. Sometimes he'd remember Sav's body in the wheelbarrow or down in that hole, and he'd think he should slice his wrists open in the bathtub. Other times, he'd tell himself he should go back to the country house and dig up Sav and get that gun and—if it still worked—shoot himself right there and throw his body down in the dirt and take his last breaths as Sav's bones protruded into him. He figures that's what Sav is now, just bones, worms and bugs wriggling over what's left of him. He knows he'd never have the guts to do that.

Jimmy has tears in his eyes and motions for Widow Marie to refill his glass, slugging from it, emptying the booze down his throat in a constant stream, coughing, almost choking. "My Susie," he continues, clearing his voice as he says the words. "I miss her so goddamn much. She never sent me a note. Nothing."

Chooch has done what he came to do. He begins backing up toward the door.

"Fucking Roberto," Jimmy says, slamming his left hand on the bar. It comes down hard on the ashtray, crinkled butts firing off in all directions, the glass shattering under his closed fist. He holds his hand up and it's bleeding, blood soaking into the sleeve of his yellow shirt. The blood is dripping onto the heap of cigar and cigarette butts. Jimmy gets off his stool and disappears into the bathroom, coming out with a roll of brown paper towels. He wraps his hand until the roll's down to the inner tube. The blood isn't visible now, except on his sleeve. "What the fuck you looking at?" Jimmy asks.

Widow Marie curses Jimmy and Chooch. She grabs a broom and dustpan and gets to work cleaning up the mess on the floor. Then she moves to Jimmy's spot and starts piling the broken pieces of the ashtray in the dustpan. Jane the Stain gets up and helps her.

"I'm sorry," Chooch says, and he leaves the bar, walking fast to the corner and heading home without looking back. He's not quite sure how this will all play out. He'll go to his room and cut up the magazines he bought and work on a collage. Maybe he'll put on a movie while he works, or he'll open the boombox and one of the CDs. *Passion and Warfare.* That's what this is. Warfare. Strategy. Maybe by the time he's blowing out candles on his cake at Risa's, Roberto will be on the train into the city and then catching a bus at the Port Authority. At least that's the best-case scenario. He's not sure what Jimmy's capable of.

6.

Roberto's eating spaghetti and meatballs his mother made. Trying anyway. He's swirling a few strands of spaghetti around the tines of his fork, taking small bites of meatball. It's delicious, the gravy full of garlic and basil, and he hasn't had a real home-cooked meal like this in a long time, but he doesn't have much of an appetite these days. He's not sure what the hell he's doing back home. Ran out of options. His mother's sitting across from him in the kitchen of the house where they moved when he was finishing high school. He'd visited Risa and Fab earlier in the house where he grew up—they're in the apartment downstairs where he lived solo before taking off with Susie. His mother looks brittle. Poppy's in the living room, watching TV. Some Western with that actor he remembers from *The Omen*. Guy's younger in this one. The smell of the gravy his mother heated up on the stove heavy in the air.

"Never would've figured you two for getting cable," Roberto says to his mother.

"We were bored with the regular channels," Ma says. She's got whiskers on her chin. Lines crisscross her face. Her eyes are glassy. Her hair's frizzled and ghostly white. Her hands are liver-spotted. "All junk. I like romances and your father likes Westerns, so we keep the old movie channel on. They don't make them like that anymore."

Roberto's not even sure how old she is. Sixty-five? Which means his old man's close to seventy. While he was gone, he thought of them occasionally but hardly at all.

Ma continues: "I didn't ask you before, but I'm gonna ask you now. Where've you been? What've you been doing? People talk. You brought a lot of shame on this family. Knocking off Jimmy's shop. Stealing Susie. I see Jimmy around still. He's been a mess."

"I didn't 'steal' Susie," Roberto says. "She's a grown woman. She wanted to come away with me. And pinching that money from his safe was her idea."

"I raised you like that? To be a thief and an adulterer? You're lucky you didn't get thrown in jail. Who knows? Maybe you'll still wind up behind bars. Been seven years, but nobody forgets the kind of things you did."

"The cops knock on your door, you hold them off, okay?" he says, smiling. "I'll escape out the back window."

"It's all a big joke to you."

"Tell me more about Sav."

"What's there to tell? He went the way of his wise older brother. Left without saying anything. Word is he and that Double Stevie broke into Gilly the Gambler's and caused some havoc."

"I hadn't heard that."

"Apparently, some cash went missing, but Gilly was more upset about the albums of his that were broken."

"Albums?"

"Seventy-eights. Gilly's dead now. His house got torn down. And, of course, your brother didn't steal anybody's wife that we know of, but he did leave his wife and son behind. Poor Risa. Poor Fab. That boy still doesn't talk."

"I noticed."

"You went over there?"

Roberto pushes his plate away. "For a few minutes. I wasn't too well received."

"You're not hungry? Eat up. You're awfully skinny."

"Ain't got the stomach anymore."

Ma stands and collects his plate. She scrapes what's left into the garbage and rinses it in the sink.

Roberto takes in the rest of the kitchen, which hasn't changed at all. The cuckoo clock someone gave them. The wood paneling. The framed pictures of Pope John Paul II and Mother Teresa. Cards from various holidays. Pictures of cousins, people he remembers from when he was little who'd gone on to get married and have kids of their own, arranging these shitty little families of theirs on beaches or in front of big fucking trees, and sending along glossy snapshots that captured their glorious goddamn happiness. The only picture of Roberto and Sav up on the wall is from Sav's eighth birthday party in the driveway of the house on Saint of the Narrows Street. Big table, cake from Villabate Alba, party hats. Roberto was twelve at the time. No shirt. Elbow leaning on his brother's shoulder. Sav jokingly wincing. It's weird to have that little Sav staring at him from the picture, clawing at his memory. His brother's got to be thirty-one now too, like Chooch. Last time Roberto saw him was right after they'd celebrated Sav's twenty-fourth birthday. That had been a much different party. A strip joint in the city named Error of My Ways, all those poles and glowing girls in the golden night, his brother's dopey grin. Getting in a fight in the parking lot with some Irish mooks from the Bronx. Doing blow while they drove back in that sweet old inherited Caddy of his to Brooklyn. Dancing at the club in Bay Ridge that was popular at the time with Edie Valentino and her half-sister Corinne—what was that place called? Going down and parking the Caddy by Shore Road, him and Edie stretched out in the front seat, Sav and Corinne in the back, steaming up the windows. That'd been a night for the books.

"How about some coffee?" Ma asks.

"Okay, sure," Roberto says, thinking a cup of hot coffee will warm him up. He's been cold since he got back. His own fault for coming back in the winter. Couldn't be helped the way things had wound up in Tampa. He'd gotten chased out of there like he'd gotten chased out of Miami, Daytona Beach, Key West, and Fort Myers. Get run out of enough places and home's the only place to go. It's been a long stretch of bad trouble. Drugs, gambling, the wrong women. The usual line. He'd had some trouble here too but nothing he couldn't snake out of. Running away had been more about starting over with Susie than being scared. He's sure Jimmy Tomasullo will make a move on him, but Jimmy's Winnie the Pooh next to the guys down in Florida on his tail. He might've gone somewhere else—that would've been smart—but there's no money for that, no bridge he hasn't burned. Here, he's got shelter, and he knows

Ma and Poppy will give him handouts even as they yap in his ear about finding a job, about not being too old to take the civil service test or whatever the fuck. He's not worried about the Florida trouble finding him. He went by Robby Vasquez down there, having had the good fortune to take up early on with a guy named Rick the Operator who did IDs and shit like that, but Roberto had smartly figured that a phony identity meant he'd always have something to escape back to. All the nasty stuff he got into in Florida, he regrets none of it. The one thing he does regret is Susie. Not because he did Jimmy wrong. Because he loved Susie. Really fucking loved her. What happened was, once they hit Miami, she started working at some high-end club and took up with this rich fuck, Felix. *Felix.* Had a boat and wore white linen suits. Roberto was a ticket out to Susie, that's it. Jimmy was a hole she'd fallen into, Roberto was the ladder, and now she was in the life she wanted all along. Broke his heart. Never again. He isn't the heartbroken type.

Ma takes the pot out of the cabinet and gets to work on making the coffee. The sounds of scooping and settling, the tap running, the pot clinking against the burner grate on the stove, the gas flicking on.

"Let me ask you something," Roberto says to his mother.

"What is it?" she asks, her voice edged with suspicion.

"You think everything's on the level over there at Risa's? You think their story is for real?"

"What do you mean?"

"You think Sav split on them like everyone says?"

"What else could it be? Risa's a saint. God love your brother, but he didn't deserve her. Always running around. Making a spectacle with that Sandra Carbonari. Poor Risa tolerated his hijinks for long enough. And with a baby at home. Have you seen her with Fab? Every kid should be so lucky to have a mother like that."

"Sav was seeing Sandra Carbonari on the side?"

"That puttana. I blame her. I hear she's over at the Wrong Number every night now dancing on the bar. A rotten influence on your brother. I wish he'd gotten that wildness out of his system and been content with the life he had. A small, happy life, that's the most we can ask for from God. A family. A roof over our heads. You and Sav are chasing something else. I don't know what. You both got bit by some bug." She pauses, turns up the gas. The blue flame grows under the pot. "Why? What do you think? You think Risa's lying about something?"

"A feeling I got. I don't know. Chooch came around, and they looked like they were hiding something. Kind of communicating with their eyes about things they knew I didn't."

"Chooch is your brother's best friend. I've known him since he's six, seven years old. You think him and Risa are in cahoots on some evil scheme? You've got the wrong two."

"Probably."

The coffee boils, and Ma brings over a cup. He spoons in enough sugar to make her go wide-eyed and then stirs his coffee with the butt end of a plastic knife until some slops over the edges of the cup onto the tablecloth.

Ma's there instantly to mop it up with a dishrag. "You don't change," she says, sitting back down. "You stir your coffee like a thunderstorm. And all that sugar. Minchia."

They sit there in silence, and Roberto drinks his coffee. The sounds of his slurping fill the kitchen. A couple of conversations with his mother, and he's run out of shit to say. He could ask about her and Poppy, and she'll go on about the prices at the markets on Eighty-Sixth, how much they're charging a pound for broccoli rabe, and she'll tell him about this person or that person from church who died of cancer, probably her weekly pinochle game with the group of biddies she hangs out with. The new medicines she and Poppy are on. Gossip. An avalanche of bad news and secondhand tragedies. Same as ever.

"You want some Entenmann's?" Ma asks. "I have crumb cake."

He shakes his head. "I'm good, thanks." He downs the rest of his coffee, the sugary sludge at the bottom of his cup lingering on his tongue for a moment before he swallows it. He feels warmer. The sugar and caffeine have lit up his insides. He reaches out and clasps his right hand over his mother's folded hands on the table. She's ice-cold, the raised veins above her wrists tender and blue. "I'm happy to be back."

"You've always got a home with us."

He nods. "I know. Feels like it. Haven't had a home this whole time I've been gone. Maybe that's what I've been looking for."

"You can straighten up. I know you can."

"I'll do it for you, Ma." He pats the back of her hand.

After a while, he stands and goes into the living room and watches about fifteen minutes of the Western with Poppy, who's in and out of sleep. The TV's big. It sits on top of a smallish table that appears to be sagging from the weight. Poppy has the remote in his lap. They used to have a different TV. He remembers sitting here watching episodes of *All in the Family* and football on Sundays. He wonders if Poppy still roots for the Jets. The carpet's the same. Green shag. All the life's been flattened from it. Pictures on the wall in the living room mostly tell Sav's story: Communion, confirmation, graduations, at a ball game with Chooch, his wedding to Risa, little Fab as an infant in the bathtub and a toddler in the park.

But there's one of Roberto. He's with his grandparents at some wedding. Probably a distant cousin. He's maybe eleven, twelve. Barely recognizes himself. He misses his grandparents. They were kind to him. His grandpa died a few years before he split town, his grandma only two or three weeks before. He remembers specifically going to the Harbor Motor Inn with Susie the night of his grandma's funeral and starting to make plans.

The Western on the TV ends, and another one begins. Poppy's snoring. His mom's clanging dishes around in the sink. Running the water. Opening and closing cabinets. He remembers how she's always got to keep herself busy. Maybe she's washing some ancient plates that haven't been washed in a long time or getting ready to scrub the floor.

He's tired. The trip up on the Greyhound bus had been brutal. He sat next to a woman who wouldn't stop talking.

He goes upstairs. He hasn't been in his room yet, and he's worried what he'll find.

He checks Sav's room first, and it's still the same. Single bed with a black comforter. Kiss and Black Sabbath and Cheryl Tiegs posters. Albums in crates. Eight-track tapes and cassettes. A basketball in a wicker basket. Fucking Sav. Where is he out there in the big wide world? Be something if he's down in Florida.

He opens the door to his room. As if on cue and as if aware of his every move, Ma comes to the base of the stairs and calls up to him: "There are towels in the hall closet if you want to take a shower. You remember where the bathroom is, right?"

"Of course," he says.

"I don't know what people forget," Ma says. "If you need anything, let me know. Relax. Take a load off."

"Thanks, Ma," he says, and he enters his room, honestly surprised it's also as he left it all those years ago before moving into the apartment on Saint of the Narrows. He would've thought he'd be the brother whose room got turned into an office or storage space. Hasn't been touched, though. Same bed. Worn brown carpet. A dresser full of his old clothes, probably huge on him now. A Rangers pennant on the wall. Pictures of Corvettes. His *Rocky* and *Rocky II* posters. Those movies hit him like not much else ever had. Saw both about twenty times at the Loew's Oriental.

He remembers something then. His stash of porno mags in the closet. He kept them under the carpet. His mother never found them that he knows of, even though she's always been a hound and was perpetually in his room vacuuming and going through shit. Even when he was eighteen, nineteen, early twenties. He peels back the corner of the carpet, and they're hidden there. Issues of *Gallery*, *High Society*, *Hustler*, *SCREW*, *Swank*, and *Gent*.

He brings them back to the bed and lies down, the magazines spread out next to him, his head propped on the pillows, and he starts going through them one at a time beginning with an issue of *Swank* from June 1975 with a picture of a girl bending over a beachball on the cover, wearing sunglasses, her ass in the air.

He thinks maybe tomorrow he'll go to the porno theater

on Bath Avenue that Sid mentioned. The De-Luxe. He's surprised it's still there, but it is. He likes sitting in a theater and watching people fuck on a big screen. He likes the seediness of it all. He likes how it feels to walk outside after being in a theater like that. He thinks of that scene in *Taxi Driver*, De Niro bringing Cybill to see a porno. He wants to do that. Maybe he'll go back and ask Giulia if she wants to go to the De-Luxe with him. She'll toss hot coffee in his face. The idea of her tossing hot coffee in his face makes him excited. Forget the pictures in the magazine he's looking at. He likes the idea of Giulia punishing him, burning him because he deserves it.

Now his mind turns to Sandra Carbonari. He remembers her well. When he was around, everyone knew Sandra—the old guys, the young guys, the women. Sav and Sandra. Interesting. Always dancing on the bar at the Wrong Number, his mother said. He's thinking maybe he should go over there and see if she's around, see what she's got to say about his brother.

The Wrong Number is a neighborhood institution on the corner of Avenue T and West Seventh. A dive with a great sign—multicolored letters spelling out the name of the bar and a tipped cocktail glass on a black background—and not much else. As soon as Roberto gets there, it's as if he never left. It's only late afternoon, but it's four in the morning inside. The bartender is an old-timer who looks like he got dug out of the rubble of a building crushed by a wrecking ball. The clientele is a mix of mangy alkies and mismatched goons. He finds Sandra Carbonari camped out alone at a booth in the corner. When he left town, she was a hot young thing. She's about his age, mid-thirties, maybe a little younger, but she's at the beginning of a descent into looking tragic. A nice bloat going from all the booze. Cigarette skin. Her hair's all spritzed up, hard and high but also obviously thinning. She's wearing a pink faux fur coat. Her mascara's running down her cheeks. Her lipstick is smeared across her teeth. She's drinking whiskey. Even just sitting there, she's aging her ass off. He's one to talk. He's lived rough and looks rough, too.

"What the fuck you looking at?" Sandra asks, as he approaches the table.

"You remember me?" he asks. "Sav's brother."

She does a double take. "Roberto?"

"The one and only."

"Is Sav with you?" She asks it so gently, he feels bad for her. There's a real woman in there. He bets a lot of people ignore that and treat her like nothing. It's apparent in how she carries herself. She's battered, beat down. All her interactions are rooted in desperation. She knows better than anyone how savage the world can be.

"I didn't even know he was gone. I came back hoping to see him. Mind if I join you?"

"Go ahead."

He sits across from her. "So, he just split back in August of eighty-six?"

"We were supposed to split together. Had big plans."

"And what happened?"

"He never came to get me. Word on the street the next day was he abandoned Risa and the kid and lit out for parts unknown. Figured he didn't want to haul me around with him."

"Nothing fishy about it to you?"

"Over time, I started to wonder about things."

"What kinds of things?"

"Risa and Chooch being so chummy." She pauses. "I watch a lot of cheap movies. My mind starts going to crime of passion scenarios. She knew I was fucking her husband, so she suckered Chooch into offing him. If anybody's a patsy, Chooch is a patsy."

"You really think that?" Roberto asks, taking out his pack of Old Golds and lighting one.

She nods toward the pack, asking to bum a cigarette without saying the words.

He passes her one and lights it for her with the Zippo he stole off some guy on the bus.

She shrugs, finally getting around to his question. "Who the fuck knows what I believe anymore? Now you're back, what're you gonna do?"

"I don't know. Maybe I'll be a fireman."

Sandra laughs so hard it turns into a coughing fit.

Roberto smiles. "Come on, I can do it. Run into burning buildings, carry out cats."

"I'd like to see that. Guy who starts the fires doesn't usually put them out."

"That fire I started at Space Odyssey was an accident."

"A couple of burnt-up disco freaks wasn't nobody's idea of a big deal."

They both laugh. Smoke hovers between them. Someone puts Poison's "Ride the Wind" on the jukebox.

"I take it you never heard from Sav?" Roberto asks her.

"Nope," Sandra says, throwing back the last of her whiskey.

He goes up to the bar and buys a round, whiskey for her, tequila for him. He keeps waiting for others to recognize him, to welcome him back with open arms and free drinks and propositions to make some dough, but nobody recognizes him, and nobody seems to give a shit he's there. He used to be somebody in the neighborhood. He guesses time erased a lot of that.

He brings the drinks back to the table, and they toast Sav. Sandra looks like she might weep. Roberto feels as lost as he's ever felt, but the fact that the situation with Risa isn't kosher is giving him a sense of purpose. Maybe it didn't happen exactly how Sandra said, but there's something there, some fucking thing ain't right about Sav's disappearance, and he's gonna get to the bottom of it.

7.

Risa takes the carrot cake out of the oven. She puts it on a wire rack to cool and then goes into the living room to check on Fab. He's asleep on the couch, his arms bent awkwardly, his legs scrunched up, clutching Giulia's pillow. Probably crashing from all the sugar. She's glad he's taking a little nap. She doesn't want him going wild while Vi's around. She puts a checkered wool blanket over him and adjusts his head a bit.

She imagines Fab as an older kid. In the year 2000, he'll turn fourteen and she'll turn forty-two. She wonders where he'll go to high school. If she can get the money together, she'd rather send him to Narrows Academy than Lafayette, which isn't much of a school anymore. She can see him in that cute Catholic school uniform. The year 2000. *Imagine that.* She remembers being a girl and thinking the year 2000 was forever away, that it sounded like some science-fiction story full of flying cars and computers that talked. She's getting ahead of herself—there's still nine years left in the nineties—but she knows how fast time can go. She's not that old yet but she's getting there.

Sometimes, she just makes lists in her mind of all the things she needs to teach Fab about the world. There's so much to prepare him for. All the trouble out there. She'll teach him not to carry too much money or to flaunt gifts he's gotten, so he doesn't make himself a target. She'll teach him to be unassuming, to know where trouble is and avoid it, to keep his head down, mind his own business. She wonders often if she'll ever have the guts to tell him the truth about his father. Now that Roberto's back, she can't predict how things will play out. Exactly the kind of trouble she's worried about. Someone's not there and then they are, and the earth is shaking right down to its bones. She can't tell Fab anything now. He's too young. She needs more time. She needs Roberto to steer clear of them.

She tries to picture Fab as an adult. According to everyone and their mothers, it's mostly Sav he looks like. When they're young, she's been told, who kids look like can shift. Maybe he'll start looking more like her down the road. She wonders if he'll want to get out of the neighborhood. Maybe he'll want to go to college far away. Probably he'll work in the city. What if he wants to join the military? She doubts it, but what if he does and there's something else like this Gulf War business that goes down? She can't picture him that way. Buzz cut, dressed in camouflage, carrying a gun in the desert. Not Fab. She wonders if he'll be an artist like her cousin from Queens, Giuseppa, who makes these wild sculptures of tangled bodies. The way she works so hard on them in her garage. Hands in clay. Molding, shaping. It's a different kind of life, creating like that.

Before she goes back to the kitchen to begin work on the cream cheese frosting, Risa stops in the bedroom and sits on the edge of her bed. She used to talk to God. She doesn't so much anymore. She sits there in the silence of the room, staring at the crucifix on the wall. She can still feel Roberto in the apartment. If they get through him being back without anything disastrous happening, she's going to try to go back to school. Maybe Kingsborough this time. Maybe nursing. She can imagine herself in scrubs, tending to patients.

Her eyes wander over to Fab's race car bed. How long until he's too old for it? A few years tops. He'll start being embarrassed by little-kid things. He'll stop wanting to hug her. School will change his whole demeanor. Maybe she's got kindergarten and first grade to enjoy walking him to school in the mornings and home in the afternoons without him asking her to wait on the corner. She knows kids will say things to him about his father. It's not easy to survive if anything's different about your life. She already feels the weight of what's to come.

The doorbell rings. She checks the alarm clock on the dresser. Just after five thirty. Can't be Chooch and Vi yet, and Giulia has a key. Her heart jumps in her chest. She assumes it's Roberto again. He's got nothing else to do, no one else to bother, so he'll keep showing up like a hungry dog.

She hopes the bell hasn't woken Fab up. She checks on him. It hasn't. He's still out cold, whimpering a little against the pillow. She can't imagine what he dreams about.

She goes down the hallway and presses her left palm against the doorjamb while she twists the knob slowly with her right hand. She's relieved to see Religious Pete from upstairs standing behind the glass storm door. He's holding a paper Pathmark bag, the top crinkled in his fist. He's a lanky man whose rumpled clothes fit him like a scarecrow. He's got a pallid countenance, and he wears a large wooden cross on a piece of twine around his neck, letting it hang over his jacket. Risa wears a small gold cross and likes it under her shirt, against her skin. She thinks Religious Pete's cross is off-putting and aggressive.

She pushes the button on the latch and opens the door outward, whispering, "Everything okay, Pete?"

"Sure," he says.

"Fab's taking a nap, otherwise I'd invite you in."

"I just wanted to give this to you," he says, holding out the bag.

"What is it?" she asks, accepting the bag and holding it close to her chest.

"I was working at Perpetual Surrender, volunteering, helping Father Tim and Andy O'Hagan clean up the Reilly room downstairs. They get a lot of donations, you know, and that's where they keep them. There was a big box of children's books. Some of them were in bad condition, musty and water-damaged, but I took the best ones. Thought you might want them for Fab. I don't know what's what, but they looked good."

"That's nice of you." She pushes open the top of the bag and gazes in at a pile of old paperbacks. *Stuart Little*, *Watership Down*, and *The Little Prince* are the three on top.

"You don't mind me saying," Religious Pete says, "I heard Roberto Franzone is back?"

There it is. The books merely an excuse to come nosing around about Roberto. "He is," Risa says.

"But no Sav?"

"Nope."

"Watch that guy is my advice. One time, I saw him kick a dog. I'd heard about men who kicked dogs, but I'd never seen it happen. It was Rudy the Greek's dog. Very upsetting. Roberto should've stayed gone."

Risa knows she can't respond by echoing the sentiment. "I'm sure Frank and Arlene are glad to have him back," she says.

"That's a positive outlook. Poor Arlene."

Risa thinks for a second that the right thing to do, the neighborly thing, would be to invite Religious Pete to Chooch's party. But—God forgive her—she doesn't want to. She hates having people who aren't Fab, Giulia, and Chooch in the apartment. Vi she'll make an exception for. "Thanks again," she says, pulling the door shut.

He gives her a wave through the glass, turns, and walks around the side of the building to the stairs. She lets out a breath. She brings the bag into the kitchen and puts it on the table, unloading the books into two equal stacks. They're in decent shape, but the smell of muffa hangs in the air.

One of the books is *The Outsiders*. It's the same red Laurel-Leaf edition she had in high school. Five shadowy figures on the cover, a couple of them wearing sunglasses, looking like a mediocre rock band. Not at all what she imagined when she first read the book. The movie's much closer. The author's name, S. E. Hinton, is centered close to the top edge in a simple yellow font. Risa remembers Mr. Mangiello saying Hinton was sixteen or seventeen when she started writing it, nineteen when it was published. She never could wrap her head around that. She's tried to keep journals her whole life, but she never sticks with it. Part of her blames this book for Sav. If she hadn't read it and loved it and hadn't gone to see the Coppola movie when it was released and hadn't thought that Sav looked like Ralph Macchio as Johnny, maybe she could have avoided years of heartache. Maybe Sav could've been some other woman's problem.

She flips through the browning pages with their green trim carefully, a couple of wispy corners flaking off. The binding is tight, and there's no writing inside. She wonders how old Fab will be when he reads *The Outsiders*. Will they still be reading it in high school in the early 2000s, or will she have to force it on him? She can see him turning out to be something like Ponyboy.

She returns to the kitchen to work on the frosting. The ingredients are already on the counter: a brick of cream cheese, unsalted butter, powdered sugar, and vanilla extract. She gets out her yellow ceramic mixing bowl and electric mixer.

Sometimes, when Giulia's not around, the quiet of the apartment overwhelms her. Even when he's not sleeping, Fab's inability to talk makes the silence oppressive. She empties the package of cream cheese into the mixing bowl and begins to beat it. The whir of the electric mixer fills the silence. Next, she'll add in the butter and then the sugar and vanilla. She thinks again of hours spent baking with her mother and grandmothers. Sometimes she worries that she wants to move backward, to bring Fab into the past with her, the years before Sav, instead of into a future of their own. Back in the past, she hadn't done what she'd done to Sav. It was safer there.

Fab stirs on the couch, the mixer loud enough to wake him. Giulia should be home soon, and Chooch and Vi will probably show up right at seven. She pictures Roberto bouncing around the neighborhood, asking questions about Sav, fearing yet again that he'll bounce right back to her.

8.

Giulia stops into the Crisscross on the way home from the garage, and she's relieved to see that Jimmy Tomasullo isn't there. She wonders if he ever was. She guesses Chooch will fill her in when she shows up for his little birthday get-together. Either that or she'll hear all about it from Widow Marie and Jane the Stain, the only two currently in the joint, both stationed down at the far end of the bar. Giulia reminds herself she needs to go buy Chooch's scratch-offs and hard rolls. He'll get a kick out of gifts like that. She's just gonna have a quick drink or three first.

Widow Marie brings her a Budweiser and pours her a shot of Beam. "Chooch was in here earlier," she says. "A real rare sighting. Like a bald eagle, but boring."

"Yeah, so?" Giulia says, her eyes drifting to the picture of Marco behind the bar, trying to play it cool.

"He was getting Jimmy all fired up about Roberto Franzone being back."

She plays it dumb. "Roberto's back? I don't think Jimmy would need much firing up about that."

Widow Marie shrugs. "Maybe not. None of my fucking business anyway."

The TV is on over the bar. *CBS Evening News with Dan Rather*. Something about that disaster at the Los Angeles airport—two planes crashing into each other on the runway, one landing, the other taking off. The only time Giulia's ever flown was to Italy, and she hated being in the air. When she goes back one day, it's going to be on a ship. She's not sure if the *Queen Mary* goes to Italy but something like that's gonna be how she gets there—cabins, a bar, maybe a show, a nice little touch of seasickness. She's seen enough old movies to know people live whole other lives on those massive transatlantic journeys. Solve murders, fall in love, evade things that need evading. Give her time to cram with her Italian books, too.

She listens to Rather. Looks like what happened with the planes in LA was a fuckup in the air control tower. Air traffic wasn't heavy, but the controller was distracted. The plane coming in—a 737 with about ninety occupants—was given the green light, while the plane taxiing to take off, a smaller turboprop aircraft, accidentally shut off its tower frequency. When the 737 landed, it crushed and dragged the smaller plane. Thirty-five fatalities.

Giulia puts back her shot and chases it with a sip of beer. She's never sure what to do with bad news like that. This fucking world. Terror everywhere. Every goddamn second someone somewhere getting killed or abused, left behind, accidents and natural disasters, random violence, a fucking ticker tape of shit that could go wrong.

She hates to make this runway disaster about their lives, their situation, but it's like a metaphor for this whole thing with Roberto. He's the plane that's landing. They're the smaller plane that's about to be crushed and dragged. Only way to stop it is situational awareness. Protect thine own ass. She hopes her idea to have Chooch sic Jimmy on Roberto expeditiously can help avert a crisis.

Cursed Roy comes strutting into the place just as Giulia motions to Widow Marie for another shot. He smells strongly of Ben-Gay and sauerkraut. He eats sauerkraut sandwiches. Puts sauerkraut in his eggs and on his pizza. He's a goddamn sauerkraut fiend. He's called Cursed Roy because Alma Ruotolo's mother put the evil eye on him when he dumped Alma. The clientele of the Crisscross is humble, but the stories there are rich. "You seen a little fucking idiot about yea high?" he says, using his hand to demonstrate a height coming up to just above his waist. "My niece. I don't know where the hell she got off to."

"You have a niece, and someone let you care for her?" Jane the Stain says from down at the other end of the bar.

"My sister Lucy's kid. Frankie's her name. Messy hair, like somebody emptied a pot of spaghetti on her head."

"Ain't seen her," Widow Marie says.

"Why would you be looking here?" Giulia asks.

"We were at the park over by Cavallaro," Cursed Roy says. "When we left, she raced ahead. I told her to wait for me right outside here. Truth is, I figured I'd come in, wet my whistle, maybe order her a Shirley Temple."

"I don't do Shirley Temples," Widow Marie says, as if that's the most important lesson to take away from this.

"You lost her between Cavallaro and here?" Jane the Stain asks. "That's what, a couple hundred feet?"

"I got distracted," Cursed Roy says.

"Like that air traffic controller at LAX," Giulia says.

Cursed Roy looks at her like she's got twenty thousand heads. "Can I have a whiskey, please?" he says to Widow Marie.

Widow Marie pours him a double without asking, and he stands at the bar and drinks it down in a monstrous gulp, whiskey slopping out of the sides of his mouth, down his chin, and onto his United Steelworkers hunter-green fleece pullover. Giulia wonders where he got the shirt. No way the guy's ever come close to doing whatever the fuck it is that steelworkers do.

A few seconds later, a kid who can only be Frankie comes into the bar, holding two ragged action figures and smashing them together. She's maybe seven. Messy blond hair, a down jacket patched with silver duct tape, black sweatpants, lilac winter boots. Cute kid. Head in the clouds.

Cursed Roy lets out a groan of relief. "Where'd you go?" he asks her.

"Nowhere good," she says.

Giulia, Widow Marie, and Jane the Stain have a nice laugh over that.

Cursed Roy sets Frankie up on the stool next to Giulia and introduces her. Frankie sticks out her little hand, dirt caked under her nails, and Giulia shakes it. She wonders how she looks to Frankie. Whiskey on her breath, bloodshot eyes, the smell of the garage all over her. Twenty-eight years old might as well be fifty-eight to a kid.

"Watch out for this one," Cursed Roy says to Giulia, motioning toward Frankie. "She's a little grifter. Get her around a deck of cards, you'll think she wants to play Go Fish, but she'll hustle you out of your dough with a round or two of Three-Card Monte."

"Well, you're a lot cooler than me," Giulia says to Frankie.

"Probably am," Frankie says.

"Marie, can we get my niece here something to drink?" Cursed Roy says. "You're too good for Shirley Temples, what else you got up your sleeve?"

"I've got some milk in the fridge," Widow Marie says.

"You think I'm gonna let Frankie drink milk in a dive like this?"

"Ginger ale?"

"Sure, give the lady a ginger ale."

Widow Marie grabs a pony bottle of ginger ale from under the bar. She screws the cap off and sets it in front of Frankie on a cocktail napkin.

"Thanks," Frankie says, taking a sip. "But it's warm."

"Oh, she wants cold ginger ale," Widow Marie says. "We're in the presence of royalty."

"You keep the milk in the fridge, you should keep the ginger ale there," Cursed Roy says.

Widow Marie gets Frankie a glass of ice. "I look like I give a shit where I keep the ginger ale? The kid can drink it, or she can go play in traffic far as I'm concerned. Why don't you take her over to Carvel?"

"You wanna go to Carvel, ballbuster?" Cursed Roy asks Frankie. "Get you a vanilla cone with sprinkles?"

"I don't like ice cream," Frankie says, pouring the ginger ale over the ice.

"This kid's a riot," Jane the Stain says.

"What kind of kid don't like ice cream?" Cursed Roy asks, genuinely flabbergasted. "I give up."

Giulia looks at Frankie, her hands up on the bar, taking a sip of the ginger ale from the glass and then pushing it away, rejecting it. As much as Giulia loves Fab, she can't imagine having a child of her own. All the stuff people need to get and do when they have a kid. Crib, playpen, potty, diapers, changing table, toys, clothes, a million things she doesn't even know about. Overwhelming shit. Never mind feeding them, changing them, waking up with them in the middle of the night, burping them, teaching them about right and wrong, watching over their every move for years and years until they're finally able to do a few things on their own. Not for her. Can't picture herself doing any of that as a mother. As an aunt, she's happy to help, to fill in, knowing full well that Risa will do all the mothering and that she's only gotta make the kid laugh, maybe take him to the park.

Also, to have a kid, she'd probably have to get hitched and that's not happening. She's settled into the idea that marriage just isn't for her. As she gets older, she doesn't even like going home with anyone for more than a couple of hours. She'll hook up, but she won't spend the night. She likes to be back on her couch soon as she can. Marriage is a far-off distant land she doesn't understand. Now, if Marco LaRocca was to show up tomorrow and get down on one knee and say he'd been pining for her all these years, as he traveled from arena to arena with his guitars and bandmates, that'd be another story. But that's a fucking fairy tale.

Cursed Roy takes Frankie out of the place, Giulia giving her a little wave as she goes, the kind of wave—it occurs to her—that drunk people give little kids thinking they're being sweet when they just look like unnatural morons. But she's not drunk. Not yet. She finally puts back the second shot Widow Marie brought her.

Her mind drifts to Jimmy Tomasullo. Roberto's a fucking nobody. A loser. He shouldn't have come home to shake things up. *Go get him, Jimmy. Make him pay.* She thinks about her Italian book, the list of sayings she was studying earlier. One comes to mind: *Il fine giustifica i mezzi.*

9.

After leaving the Wrong Number, Roberto comes home to lie down in his room. He has a headache from the bottom-shelf tequila. Ma gives him some Tylenol and puts a wet washcloth on his forehead. He's feeling better now, flipping through the magazines he found earlier, thinking about what Sandra said and about going back over to confront Risa and Chooch. Maybe he should head there a little later, try to knife this thing open right away, see what else spills out.

A racket downstairs. He wonders what the hell's going on. His mother's voice muffled but loud. Probably an argument. Maybe Poppy woke up angry or got pissed she was cleaning and wouldn't let him rest. Their fights were centerpieces of his childhood. They've really got some chops when it comes to brawling. Poppy was never violent, but he could sure say some mean shit to Ma. Some funny things, too. Ma's fighting style was mostly to express disgust and frustration. A lot of nights he spent like this, lying on his bed while they went at it downstairs.

But maybe it's not that. There's another voice, and it doesn't sound like Poppy.

Roberto leaves the magazines on the bed and goes back out into the hall. That voice he's hearing is *not* Poppy. Another man, banging around, angry.

When he gets down to the kitchen, he sees that Jimmy Tomasullo's standing there in a puffy unzipped winter jacket with a gun in his right hand, his left hand bandaged in paper towels, a wool hat drawn low over his forehead, and that he's corralled Ma and Poppy to the kitchen table where he has them sitting with their hands stretched out in front of them. Even though Jimmy's changed—looks like he's aged about thirty years—Roberto knows it's him. Sweaty, desperate, ready to blow.

"There he is," Jimmy says, giving Roberto the once-over. "You got some balls coming back."

Roberto had anticipated a reaction from Jimmy but not one of this magnitude. His mother's on the verge of weeping. Poppy's eyes are vacant—he'd still been asleep and is trying to get a grasp of the situation. Roberto knows he needs to handle this right. "Let my folks go, and we can sit down and talk, okay?"

"'Sit down and talk,' he says. You ruined my life, you know that? Where's Susie? You chucked her once you got tired of her?"

"She dumped *me*."

"Jimmy, don't do this," Ma says.

Jimmy motions with the gun for Roberto to join his folks at the table.

Roberto sits at the far end across from Ma, while Jimmy takes the last seat and leans back in the chair, its legs digging into the linoleum. "I bought this gun to off myself," he says. "Never had the guts. Then Chooch mentions you're back, and I get to thinking, 'Why I gotta get stepped on like a bug my whole life? Why don't I do some of the stepping?'"

"Chooch told you?" Roberto asks, thinking Sandra's right, his impulse is right. Something's up with Chooch and Risa and the Sav situation. Why else would Chooch rush to Jimmy to report Roberto's reemergence? Must've been hoping Jimmy would chase Roberto out of town again, get him off their backs. Roberto's mind goes back to what Sandra said. Maybe Chooch and Risa *are* having an affair and they killed Sav and their convoluted way of covering it up has been to say he disappeared and to act like Risa and Fab have been victimized. Despite what he's in the middle of here, he almost laughs at the thought. *Chooch and Risa ain't got it in them.*

Jimmy lets the question about Chooch go, and he continues talking: "When I got married, it was the happiest day of my life. I remember, me and Susie were in bed that night, after the ceremony and the reception and all that, and she's asleep, and I had a thought about us in fifty years, our grown kids coming home at Christmas, a bunch of grandkids lining up to kiss us hello. That was the happiest part of my happiest day. Handful of years down the line, I spent my nights wondering where the fuck my wife was. Why she wasn't home. Who she was out with. Started hearing things in the shop and out on the street. She's been with Roberto at this club or that club. Hit me like a cement slab to the goddamn chest. Then you two rob my safe and hit the road. And I'm left here, looking like an idiot, everybody giving me that fucking sympathetic head tilt. Embarrassed for me. Ashamed."

"He did you wrong," Ma says. "There's no denying that."

"Ma, let me talk," Roberto says.

"Yeah, let your smart boy shoot his mouth off all he wants," Jimmy says. "Thinks he can talk his way out of this."

"I don't think that at all. I think you're right to be pissed."

"That's nice." Jimmy taps the butt of the gun against the tabletop.

"Susie played me. It was all her idea. Robbing the shop. Taking off. I was a ticket out, that's it." What Roberto's saying is true, but he hopes it doesn't piss off Jimmy worse.

"That's your approach? Susie's some coldhearted and calculating broad, and you're the poor patsy who got played?"

"It's true. Listen, Jimmy, I got nothing. It's not like I did what I did, and I went on to live some fucking dream life. I've got other guys on my tail for gambling debts. I've spent the last seven years jumping from cheap motel to cheap motel. I'm barely hanging on by a thread. That's why I'm home. I'm trying to straighten out. I'm gonna get a real job, and I'm gonna contribute and be here for my folks as they get older. You want me to help you find Susie, I can do that. She went off with this guy Felix. I can point you in her direction, no problem. Ease up with the piece, and let's go somewhere and talk, just me and you."

"You think I'm gonna believe a single word out of your rat mouth?" Jimmy asks.

Poppy hasn't said anything yet, but he clears his throat now, still dumbfounded by the whole thing, and says, "My son's a bum, Jimmy, but I don't think killing him would accomplish anything."

"You're gonna slaughter me and my folks?" Roberto says to Jimmy, ignoring his old man's jab. "Come on. Punishment don't fit the crime. I'll tell you what. I get a wife, you can have a crack at stealing her. I open a shop, you can rob me blind."

Ma reaches out and slaps the back of his hand. "Stop with the smart mouth, would you?"

"Here's what I'm thinking," Jimmy says, looking down at the gun, beads of sweat dribbling from under his hat and down his jawline, falling from his chin into his lap. "I'm thinking I plug your folks in front of you. After that, a goodbye bullet in the chest for you, and one in the head for me, and here we stay, gathered at this table for a feast of death."

"Oh, don't you talk like that, Jimmy," Ma says. "What would your mother or your grandmother say, they heard you talking like that?"

Jimmy's face twists up at the mention of his mother and grandmother. Libby and Jean were their names, from what Roberto remembers, and they both died in a bad accident over by New Utrecht High School around the time Jimmy married Susie. "Leave them out of it," he says.

"They were wonderful ladies. I'm sure they'd be turning over in their graves to know they raised a savage does something like this."

He lifts the gun and shoots her in the chest nonchalantly. She falls back in her chair. In one smooth motion, before Poppy even has time to react, the gun's on him and Jimmy pulls the trigger and shoots him in the throat and he collapses forward, blood rivering out on the tabletop.

Roberto stands and pushes his chair back. His instinct is to cross his arms over his chest. He can't believe Jimmy's done what he's done. He can't believe he's just standing there. He looks over at his mother—her chair has toppled back, and she's still sitting in it, leaning against the wall, lifeless—and then at his father, who looks like he's napping in a pool of blood. He can't believe any of it.

"Nobody ever takes me serious," Jimmy says, turning the gun on Roberto now.

"Why my folks?" Roberto asks.

Jimmy doesn't answer. He pulls the trigger.

Roberto sees a flash from the muzzle of the gun. The bullet comes at him in slow motion. A searing pain explodes in his chest as he feels the bullet enter near his heart. His body bangs back against the wood paneling. The world instantly becomes hazy. Jimmy says something else, but Roberto can't hear it. His hands are on the cold linoleum. He's not bullshitting his way out of this. The last thing he sees is Jimmy putting the gun in his own mouth and pulling the trigger—his body jerking back, his brains splashing the air—and then everything goes dark.

10.

Risa opens the door for Chooch and Vi. Fab's awake now and he runs up to greet them. Risa's wondering where Giulia can be. Probably stopped off for a drink at the Crisscross. Outside, there's a swarm of sirens. Passing close. Rushing somewhere. She can't really distinguish between cops and fire trucks and ambulances, but she thinks it sounds like all of them. Sirens are a part of living—they register, but unless they're headed for Saint of the Narrows, she doesn't pay them any special notice.

"Uffa, this noise is giving me a headache," Vi says, wiping her feet on the doormat. A guilty look on her face suddenly. She crosses herself and continues, rapid fire: "I pray everybody's all right. Probably an accident, the way these animals drive. What a nice celebration this is, Risa."

"Oh, it's nothing," Risa says. "It's just cake."

Vi sits at the table. Chooch kneels on the floor nearby,

playing with some action figures Fab has dragged over to him. They're smashing them together, making impact noises, pretending that there's a big battle.

Risa moves the books that Religious Pete brought her to the china closet and then brings the cake to the table. She doesn't have a cake stand—she's always wanted one—but it looks pretty good even just on one of her regular old plates.

Vi claps her hands together under her chin. "What a lovely cake," she says. "Thanks for going to all the trouble. I try to make a cake like that, forget about it. I've always been a disaster with desserts."

"No trouble at all."

"You should open a bakery, no kidding. That's a professional cake."

"It is a beauty," Chooch says. "Thanks a ton, Ris."

Risa blushes. She's not great with compliments. Makes her feel good, but she's not sure what to do with that feeling. People say things like *You should open a bakery* all the time, even to those who should never open a bakery. Just a way of being kind. She tries to picture herself running a bakery, waking up at the crack of dawn to knead dough and mix batter, sliding her creations into an oven and then decorating them and placing them on trays in display cases like the ones they have at Villabate Alba. When she worked there, it was stressful but only because she was at the counter, dealing with customers. If she was the one in the kitchen, maybe that'd be a different story. "You mind if we wait a few minutes before we blow out the candles?" she asks. "Giulia's on her way, I'm sure."

Vi leans forward in her chair, elbows on her knees. She snaps her fingers at Fab, trying to distract his attention away from

Chooch. "You, Fabbie, come on over and visit with Granny Vi," she says.

Fab obliges. He comes over and sits on her lap.

Vi digs around in her pocket and takes out a Dum-Dums, the kind they have in glass bowls on the counter at Williamsburgh Savings Bank and sell loose for ten cents at Augie's.

He grabs at the lollipop, but she pulls it away.

"What do you say?" Vi asks.

He makes a deep noise in his throat.

"Close enough," she says, handing over the pop. "Cherry. That's all I had."

Fab looks to Risa to see if he's allowed. All those rainbows and cake to come, but what's she supposed to say? She likes seeing him happy. She nods.

He tears off the wrapper and jams it between his lips, clanging the candy against his teeth, his eyes lighting up.

"You get his hearing checked?" Vi asks her.

Every time Risa sees Vi, they go through this same song and dance. It's exhausting. "Dr. Bernardi says he'll be fine," Risa says. Her scripted response.

Vi continues with a variation on her typical follow-up: "I'm sure he'll be yapping away soon enough. You'll be praying for some peace and quiet."

Chooch stands and comes over to the table, pulling out a chair and sitting. At first, Risa thought he seemed cool and relaxed but now she notices that he's tapping his foot against the floor, drumming his hands against his thighs. Roberto's got him rattled. He lets out a nervous breath, fiddles with a fork that's on the table.

A rumbling outside the front door.

Giulia comes in, clutching a white plastic bag. Scratch-offs and hard rolls for Chooch, no doubt. Risa hasn't spoken to her since she called to report that Roberto had shown up at the garage and that she'd also, in retrospect, seen him down by the water this morning, thinking she was hallucinating Sav.

"Where you been?" Risa asks. "We've been waiting to blow out the candles." Acting like they'd been waiting hours.

Giulia's frantic. "Did you hear what happened?"

"What is it?" Risa asks.

"Turn on the TV."

They go into the living room.

"Maybe send Fab outside," Giulia continues. "I'm not sure he should see this."

Fab puts up a protest, crossing his arms over his chest and pouting, but Vi calms him and helps him put on his jacket and hat, accompanying him out into the front yard. Chooch and Risa sit down on the couch. Giulia remains standing by the television. Vi comes back in a few seconds later, leaving Fab to his own devices, joining them on the couch.

Risa's thinking it must be some tragedy like the *Challenger* blowing up or John Lennon getting shot or maybe an earthquake or volcano. She was only five when President Kennedy was murdered, but she remembers everyone gathering around the television like this. She was sitting on the carpet, staring deep into the curved screen of that ancient television her folks had, wondering how the tube inside transmitted images, how it could transport terrible news like this to parents and their children. She remembers the pall that was cast over the neighborhood in the wake of Kennedy's death, the city, the country, the world. Everyone grieving together, crying in the streets. Changed everything. She remembers the same thing when Martin Luther King Jr. was shot—she was ten when that happened. Ten for Bobby Kennedy, too. She's thinking this is something like that.

Giulia turns on the television and flips through channels until she finds the news. A blowsy reporter in a black jacket clutches a microphone in her hand and speaks into the camera. It takes Risa a minute to realize she's standing in front of Frank and Arlene's house. The reporter's name, Megan Murphy, comes up on the screen, floating above the network's logo. "Before turning the gun on himself, detectives of the Sixty-Second Precinct tell me that Jimmy Tomasullo sought revenge on Roberto Franzone," the reporter says. "In this unassuming house behind me on a block that marks the border of the southern Brooklyn neighborhoods of Gravesend and Bensonhurst, today Jimmy Tomasullo slaughtered not only Roberto Franzone but also his parents, Frank and Arlene, who I'm told were parishioners at Our Lady of Perpetual Surrender and upstanding pillars of the community."

"Oh my God," Risa says.

"Holy fuck," Chooch says.

"Poor Arlene," Vi says.

The reporter continues: "They had lived in this house on this quiet tree-lined street for almost fifteen years, having moved here—I'm told—from just a few blocks away, where they resided for many years before that. Well, terror found them here tonight. They were, as Monsignor Terrone from Our Lady of Perpetual Surrender tells me, 'quiet, respectful, lovely people.' Frank was an usher at church. Arlene was a fixture at weekly bingo games in the basement. Their two sons, on the other hand, have had difficult lives. Both—Roberto, and his brother, Saverio—left town after getting into trouble. Roberto had just returned, desperate for help from his parents, but Tomasullo tracked him down quickly. Authorities aren't yet revealing what Tomasullo's motive was for revenge." She takes a breath. "It is a heartbreaking scene here as neighbors gather together on the block to try to make sense of this violent, senseless tragedy."

The camera pans around to show a crowd gathered on the block behind yellow crime scene tape strung between telephone poles. Spinning lights from ambulances and cop cars cover them in a red glow. Risa knows every person in the crowd. She spent a handful of Christmases and Thanksgivings and Easters in that house and was over there on most Sundays in the early days of her marriage to Sav. When Fab was in his stroller, she'd stop by on her walks some afternoons and sit and talk to Arlene. Whatever Sav and Roberto were, their folks were nothing like them. They were sweet and gentle and devoted. Arlene wasn't a big gossip. Frank was stoic. They hadn't doubted her one bit after Sav disappeared. They liked her more than they liked Sav, it seemed. They said they knew she had her own wonderful parents, and they didn't want to cross any lines, but they wanted to be like parents to her too, they wanted to be active grandparents in Fab's life, whether Sav was around or not, and they wanted to help as much as she'd allow them to. They had no idea how much it hurt her to be around them, how much it reminded her of what had happened, what she'd taken from them.

"Oh my God," Risa says again, and she suddenly realizes she's digging her fingernails into her legs through her pants.

She thinks of Fab outside, hunched in the cold, probably playing war, burying toy soldiers he left out there in the dirt and weeds, hanging them from the chain-link mesh of the fence. How's she going to tell him? His grandparents. His uncle, who he just met for the first time. Is she going to be able to keep him from the true horror of it all? Will she be able to pass it off as natural causes? Maybe she can say a gas leak got them. Maybe she can keep him away from the news. She can already imagine the *Daily News* and *Post* headlines, stuff like SOUTHERN BROOKLYN BLOODBATH and TROPHY TERROR REVENGE.

The reporter keeps talking: "A source tells me that Tomasullo had grown unhinged in recent months and that Franzone's sudden return to the neighborhood sent him over the edge. Reporting from southern Brooklyn, this is Megan Murphy, and we will keep you updated on this grisly story as more information becomes available."

"Shut it off, please," Risa says to Giulia.

Giulia obliges. She turns the knob and the screen fades to darkness.

Chooch stands and places his hand on his mother's shoulder. "I'm gonna take you home, Ma," he says. "This is a lot."

She nods. She's got tears in her eyes. "You stay here, see if Risa needs any help. I can make my own way home." She pauses. Something seems to occur to her. "Those sirens—they were for the Franzones." She crosses herself again and leaves the apartment.

Risa imagines Vi stooping to say goodbye to Fab on her way out of the yard, but she knows she won't say anything to him.

A look passes between Chooch and Giulia. Risa catches it.

"What is it?" Risa asks.

"Nothing," Chooch says. Risa realizes that he's crying. He was close with Frank and Arlene his whole life.

"I didn't wish this on him and his family or anything," Giulia says. "Certainly not his family. But he had bad intentions. No doubt about that. The whole time he was in the garage, he was freaking me out."

Chooch paws at his cheek with the heel of his hand, swiping at a couple of slow-crawling tears. He turns to Risa. "Me and Giulia talked earlier. I went over to the Crisscross. Jimmy was there. I said we were stressed out Roberto was back. Just talking. Could've been anybody spreading the word. I was thinking maybe he'd find him and threaten him, that's it. He was in rough shape, but I didn't think it was gonna go down like this. I didn't think he was gonna even hurt Roberto. I had no idea he'd go after Frank and Arlene. I figured he'd shake a stick, you know, and Roberto would beg Arlene for some money to leave again. That's it."

"We've got nothing to feel guilty about," Giulia says. "Word travels fast. Someone would've told Jimmy if it wasn't you. Sid's got the biggest fucking mouth in Brooklyn. Maybe you were first, but I bet Jimmy was getting it from all sides. Maybe that's what set him off."

"Religious Pete brought me some books that were donated to Perpetual Surrender, and he was asking about Roberto being back," Risa says, though it's dawning on her that she might've put this in motion when she called Chooch for help.

"Roberto was all over the place, acting crazy," Giulia says.

Risa's trying to keep some pictures out of her head, but she can't. Sav's harmless old parents executed in their house. She's seeing blood on the floor. She's imagining their bodies wheeled out on gurneys under white sheets. She's thinking about what people will be saying about Sav, probably expecting that he'll hear what happened and come home for the funerals. She's dreading every encounter up on Eighty-Sixth Street and at church with every person she half-knows, expressing their grief over what's happened, touching her hand. And she'll have to respond with restraint. Hold in her tears. Say what's expected. *Such a tragedy. I can't believe it. They were wonderful people. I'm thankful they were my in-laws. What kind of world is this?* Invariably, the person will ask if there's any word from Sav, and she will shake her head, and whoever it is will feel for her, and she'll be on fire with shame. "I should go over there," Risa says.

"And do what?" Giulia asks.

"I don't know. Stand there. Talk to their neighbors. Talk to Monsignor Terrone. How's it look if I don't go?" She hates herself for saying that last part, but it's true. No matter what Sav's done, she's too good to care about poor Frank and Arlene? "Can you watch Fab for a bit?"

"Of course."

Risa goes to the hall closet, taking out her mohair jacket and scarf and a hat that Arlene knitted for her the first year of her marriage to Sav. It'd been Arlene who made her want to learn to knit. She gets bundled up. The hat makes her sad. She thinks of Arlene's hands holding the knitting needles. The way she'd sit in her chair with a ball of yarn in her lap and make a hat or sweater out of nothing. "If Mama or Daddy call, are you good to talk to them?" she asks Giulia.

"I'll tell them you went over there. They'll probably show up. This might be the thing that gets them out of the house."

Chooch hasn't moved. He's sitting on the couch, stiff, frozen in place. He's stopped crying, but he seems shell-shocked.

"Christopher, I'm going over there," Risa says. "Okay? I need to."

He finally moves, nodding his head slightly.

"Are you coming?"

"I can't," he says.

"I'm sorry we didn't get to eat your cake. I have gifts for you. Giulia does, too."

"Forget it. Another time."

She walks outside. It's dark, but the yard is bathed in golden streetlight. Fab is kneeling over a small pile of things he's unearthed from the garden. The rusted handle of an ancient pair of shears. A brass amusement park token. A long sliver of blackened Styrofoam. A losing lottery ticket. Fab likes to dig. She thinks of him digging that night in the woods. "That's some collection you've got there," she says, her breath in front of her. "Maybe you'll be an archaeologist." She pauses. "I'll be back in an hour or so, okay? I've gotta pick up a few things at the store. Stay with Aunt Giulia. Listen to everything she says. Maybe you should go inside now. It's cold. And no TV. Not tonight. Read a book."

He smiles, and it lifts her heart to see such a genuine, sweet smile from him. Her boy. She kisses him on the forehead and begins walking up the block.

The cold feels good on her face. She's shaking. She's angry at herself and she's angry at Jimmy Tomasullo and she's angry at Sav and Roberto. Life's a game show. You choose a door and get stuck with what's behind it. She chose the wrong door. Why'd Sav talk to her that day in Coney Island? Why *her*? Her nose is dripping. She can feel it on her upper lip. She takes a disintegrating tissue out of her jacket pocket and dabs at her face.

Sav's parents' house is only a few blocks away. They also own the house where her apartment is, charging her no rent—she's responsible for water, gas, oil, and electric—and charging more normal prices from the tenants upstairs. They've been so good to her. Especially since Sav disappeared, often saying they're happy to help with bills if she and Giulia don't have the money. If only they'd known the truth. What had happened in that apartment, what they'd done with Sav's body. The cost of her freedom. In most ways, she thinks, her freedom's been worth it, but she'd trade it for their lives. They didn't deserve to die.

When she gets to the crime scene, she's greeted almost immediately by Monsignor Terrone, who wraps her in a hug. He's wearing a peacoat over his clerical clothes. His silver hair is up in his trademark bouffant, swaying in the cold air like a Jell-O mold. His cheeks are ruddy. He's wearing black leather gloves. He's tall for a priest, that's always the first thing everyone says about him. "Oh, Risa, this is so terrible," he says.

"I just saw on the news," she says. "I can't believe it."

She overhears a woman in the nearby crowd say, "One of those boys finally got their parents killed." Probably Mrs. Routledge or Mrs. Annio, both notorious gossips on the block.

"What a senseless tragedy," Monsignor Terrone continues. "I never would've expected something like this from Jimmy. I knew he was troubled, but I only ever worried that he'd hurt himself. God has His reasons."

Father Tim joins them. He's wearing a jacket with a fur

collar and leather gloves. He has dramatic sideburns and movie-star good looks. He's younger than any other priest that's been at Our Lady of Perpetual Surrender in her lifetime. Everyone's always telling his story: the street kid orphan turned priest. He always makes Risa uneasy, and now's no different. He hugs her, and it's unpleasant. "You okay?" he asks.

She says she doesn't know if she's okay. She says this seems like a nightmare. She's watching red and blue lights bounce off the Franzone house. She's watching detectives and regular cops and the medical examiner walk in and out of the front door like they own the place. She's picturing Sav up in the window of the room he spent his later teen years in, overlooking the crowd.

"Had you seen Roberto since he got back?" Monsignor Terrone asks. "I hate to say it, I really do, but I wish he'd stayed away."

"Very briefly," Risa says. "He came by to meet Fab."

"They got dealt a tough hand with Roberto and Sav, but they were awfully lucky to have you as a daughter-in-law and to have a grandson like Fab. How is Fab, by the way? You haven't talked to him about all this yet?"

She shakes her head.

"There's no way around it. But you can't lie to him. Can't tell him Frank and Arlene have gone on a long vacation. It's better for him to know they're in heaven."

"Kids are more resilient than we give them credit for," Father Tim adds.

A man Risa recognizes—Mr. Capelli, who owns the neighborhood funeral home—comes up to them, greets Monsignor Terrone and Father Tim first, and then bows his head to her. He's wearing a black suit, the padded shoulders dusted with dandruff, a red rose pinned on the lapel. A forest-green scarf is wrapped around his neck. His cheeks match the rose. He's got on one of those silly wool trapper hats that look out of place in Brooklyn—it's like something someone might wear in Minnesota or Alaska. His shoes are unnaturally shiny. "My condolences, Mrs. Franzone," he says. "I'm Mr. Capelli. I know Saverio since he's knee-high to a grasshopper. Frank and Arlene were longtime acquaintances. I've seen you at several wakes over the years, but I don't know if we've been formally introduced."

"Yes, of course," Risa says.

He takes a business card out of his pocket and holds it out to her. "As far as funeral arrangements go," he continues, "I don't know if you're running the show or what, but I wanted to pass along my card. Things start moving very fast."

"Mr. Capelli is the best at what he does," Monsignor Terrone says.

She looks at the card, which says his name and that he's a funeral director, and then there's the address of Capelli's, though everyone knows where it is. It protrudes like a garish hood ornament from the corner of Eighteenth and New Utrecht. The upper left section of the card is filled by an embossed drawing of a golden harp and a dove in the act of flying away.

Will this all fall to her? Dealing with wakes and funerals for Frank, Arlene, and Roberto? Dealing with the house and bank accounts and insurance policies? Will she inherit their belongings? Will she inherit both houses?

She feels sick to her stomach. She hopes there's someone else. Technically, it'll be Sav who's inheriting everything, but—since he's AWOL—she's worried it'll be her.

Oh God. The nausea is counterbalanced by the sensation that she might faint.

Father Tim puts a gloved hand on her shoulder to steady her. "What's wrong?"

She shakes her head. "I'm not equipped to deal with any of this. There's gotta be someone else."

"You have no idea where Sav is?" Mr. Capelli asks. "He really needs to be here. He shouldn't let this all come crashing down on your shoulders."

"Maybe now's not the time," Monsignor Terrone says.

"Of course. I'm sorry for your losses, Mrs. Franzone." Mr. Capelli disappears between pressing bodies as quickly as he appeared, his trapper hat visible for a minute before being swallowed up.

"I think I need to sit down for a minute," Risa says.

Monsignor Terrone and Father Tim guide her to the opposite curb, away from the crowd, and they find the unoccupied front stoop of a small two-family house. They help her sit comfortably and then both linger in front of her. "You want me to go get you a hot chocolate?" Father Tim asks.

"No, thank you," she says.

"Something else to warm you up?" He flashes a flask from his inner pocket.

She shakes her head. "Arlene's got a sister. And Frank has two brothers."

"Everything that needs to be taken care of will be taken care of," Monsignor Terrone says. "I'll help. Father Tim will help. We've built a community of helpers. You aren't alone."

Risa closes her eyes to escape the scene. She focuses her energy on popping her ears and it creates a sound like ocean waves that fills her head. It's loud enough to drown out everything around her—Monsignor Terrone and Father Tim, the mumbling crowd, the sirens—and to send a sandy feeling coursing through her jawline. She's not even thinking about precious Fab now. She only feels the weight of everything bad that's happened.

11.

Chooch lingers as Giulia gets Fab settled on the couch. She'd discovered a stack of books set atop the china closet—probably what Religious Pete brought over—and says she's going to read to Fab from *The Little Prince*, a book she loves but hasn't read in forever.

Fab waits for her while she comes over to Chooch. She hands him a bag.

He looks inside. Hard rolls and scratch-off lotto tickets.

"Happy birthday," Giulia says, smiling.

"Thanks."

She lowers her voice down to a whisper. "It's not our fault," she says. "We couldn't have known it'd go like that. Roberto's one thing. Even if we'd wished the worst on him, there's no way . . ." She looks back over her shoulder at Fab. "There's no fucking way we figured on this with Frank and Arlene. Don't take it on."

"Collateral damage, you're saying," Chooch says.

"I'm not saying that. A senseless tragedy. No predicting something like this."

He nods. "I know. I just—"

She puts a hand on his shoulder. "You're a good guy."

On his way out of the apartment, Chooch can't even look at Fab. His world's been what it's been, and they've kept what they've kept from him about Sav, but there will be no hiding this. The news will be everywhere. He almost cries again thinking of Fab's little-kid mind trying to make any sense of it.

He stumbles home. Quickly crossing a square of sidewalk, nudging himself between two parked cars, racing across the thick ribbon of blacktop, and then seeing his feet on the sidewalk again, head down. The whole short way, he's picturing Risa outside the Franzone house. He should've gone over. He should be there.

Sav and Roberto turned out rotten, sure, but Frank and Arlene were good folks. They'd always been so kind to him. Since the beginning. Weird to think he's known them most of his life. Weird to think they're dead now. Weirder still to know there are gonna be wakes—he's gonna see their embalmed bodies, lying there—and funerals, and he's gonna have to shake hands and hug Franzone relatives and everyone will be whispering about Sav's absence. He's already steeling himself against the questions and comments that will be hurled at him nonstop. *Is Sav gonna show? Isn't there any way you can let him know? Someone must have information on where he is. He needs to be here to mourn his family.* He'll shake his head—as he's done under different, less brutal circumstances over the last four-plus years—and assure them that if he had any idea where Sav was, he'd contact him.

Before walking through his front door, he notices Sandra Carbonari coming out of the Crisscross on the corner. Back in her old haunts for whatever reason. Maybe hunting gossip about Jimmy and Roberto. Wasted. Alone. That high hair. Bundled in a faux fur coat. Her face bloated. She's trying to light a cigarette with a Bic that won't spark. He gets inside before she even notices him.

His mom. He hasn't even given a moment's thought to her since she left Risa's, but here she is in the kitchen, sitting at the table, crying, a box of tissues at the ready. She's got her little blue prayer book and a stack of laminated funeral memorial cards she keeps rubber-banded around it and a few rosaries she stores in a shoebox. This is her ritual when there's a death that hits close to home. She sits there and worries her fingers over the beads and touches the laminated cards and remembers the dead and prays.

The TV is on in the living room, tuned to a different channel, where the murder-suicide remains the main topic of conversation. Chooch hears a reporter say that "the neighborhood of Gravesend has been rocked by a shocking act of violent retribution."

"I just can't believe it," his mother says. "And on your birthday. What is this world coming to? Poor Frank and Arlene. You know, when you were little, I was very protective. I didn't like to let you go over to friends' houses. I worried my head off. You never know, after all. Whose mother's a lush? Whose father's fond of the belt? With Frank and Arlene, I never worried. I knew you were in good hands over there."

It makes him sick to hear that. He always felt comfortable with Frank and Arlene. Especially Arlene. Sometimes, when he'd be over at their place and he was meant to be playing with Sav in his bedroom, he'd instead wind up sitting with Arlene in the kitchen and she'd give him a slice of Entenmann's crumb cake or a Ding Dong and a glass of milk and she'd ask him questions about himself.

His mother furiously thumbs one of her rosaries, seeming to rub the color from the dark beads. "And now, here we are," she says. "It's a regular February day. I'm alive, and they're dead. I don't understand."

Chooch wants to explain how it's all his fault, how he went over to the Crisscross and basically told Jimmy to go after Roberto, but he holds his tongue and sits down across from her and puts his hand over her hand on the table.

"You're freezing cold," she says.

"You are, too."

"There's no way to tell Saverio?"

He looks down at their entwined hands on the table. "You know no one has any idea where he is."

"Frank and Arlene tried with those boys. They really did. Roberto had it all going for him. Before what happened with Jimmy, he was like a celebrity around here. So handsome. Half the women I knew were throwing their daughters at him. Who's to say how and why people turn out the way they do? Saverio was always sweet enough to me but treating Risa and Fab the way he did, and then leaving them behind, such disgraceful behavior. And Arlene told me some of the things he said to her over the years. She put up with a lot, God bless her. She can rest now. I'm very lucky you're the kind of son who doesn't bring me any heartache." The tears come harder. She grabs a tissue and dabs at her cheeks.

"Take it easy," Chooch says.

"I really think I'm in shock. Look at us, sitting at the table, and them killed like that at their table. That's what they're saying on the news. Jimmy had them seated like it was a dinner."

"Thinking about it won't do any good."

"You're absolutely right." She pauses. "But what if someone comes in here and shoots us where we sit?"

"Ma, that was a personal thing Jimmy had against Roberto. He was sick. It's not gonna happen random like that."

"I can't help thinking this way. Every noise, I'm on the edge of my seat. Maybe I'll live out the rest of my days afraid. Maybe we're supposed to be afraid."

"Stop."

"If it's not a madman with a gun, maybe it'll be cancer. You know Peggy Quinn from over by Highlawn? One day, she's fine, feeling great, pushing her grandson around in his stroller, taking him for ice cream at Carvel. Next day, she's diagnosed with stage-four lung cancer. Doesn't even smoke."

"You're spiraling, Ma. This is terrible, what happened. A tragedy. But what—"

She cuts him off. "Don't 'but what' me." And then she puts her head in her hands. "I'm sorry, Chrissy. My Chrissy. I shouldn't talk like that."

"You want to take a pill to help you sleep? Lie down. Try not to think about any of this. You don't need agita on top of everything else."

She shakes her head. "I need to show you something in the cellar. Please shut off the TV."

"Okay, Ma." He goes into the living room, trying not to look at the screen, not wanting to catch another glimpse of the house where he spent so much time when the Franzones moved there during his and Sav's junior year of high school. So many lunches and dinners. Pitchers of Kool-Aid and Tang. Arlene's homemade pizza. Frank yelling about some bastard blocking the driveway. Chooch turns the knob on the television and watches the blackness take over the screen.

He follows his mother into the hallway at the back of the house. She grabs a skeleton key on a loop of red yarn they keep hanging on a hook next to the light switch at the entrance to the hallway. The cellar door is kitty-corner to the back door. She opens it using the key, which is black with age. He remembers his father soldering it once, years before, when it snapped.

They traverse the rickety stairs down, his mother holding the railing as she takes each step sideways, one foot following the other.

"Be careful," Chooch says. "I don't need you to fall on top of everything else."

"Mannaggia," she says. "I'm fine."

The cellar is cold, almost frigid. The burner's humming. Old bicycles are lined up against the far wall. A few different ones he rode around on as a kid, though he never much liked riding his bike.

In the back part of the cellar is his father's workbench. Tools and boxes of manuals. Crates full of parts that Chooch doesn't know the names of. He'd been handy with house stuff and car stuff and anything there was to be handy with, his old man. Next to one of the crates is an old AM/FM radio still plugged into the same drooping brown outlet as a long-corded drop light. His father used to listen to some AM station that played crooners and big band hits while he worked.

"Since we're down here," his mother says, "remind me to check the gauge on the burner. We need to, we'll call the oil man. They'll probably be able to come tomorrow."

"What are we doing?"

"Anything happens to me, I want you to know where a few things are."

"Nothing's gonna happen to you."

A sagging white shelf next to his father's workbench is filled with television tubes and needles for record players. Underneath it, nudged into a tight space, is a heavy cardboard box that says it contains an Olivetti adding machine. His mother pulls the box out and carries it over to the workbench, opening the flaps. She takes out some plastic and Styrofoam and there's an actual adding machine, which looks like it's never been used. She sets that off to the side. At the bottom, there's something wrapped in black plastic. She takes it out and peels the plastic away to reveal a metal safe with a handle on it.

"What is this?" Chooch asks.

She opens the lid, and it's stuffed full of cash. "Your father always liked to hide money in the cellar. He said it was better than the bank. There are five other spots, too. I'll show you. We have money in the bank, of course, and your name's on those accounts, and we have a few grand in the safe deposit box in the vault, but I wanted you to know about this too."

"How much?"

"Down here? Maybe forty."

"Forty *thousand*?"

"You know your father was paranoid. I've continued the tradition."

"You have the oil guy down here all the time. Meter readers. What if someone finds it?"

"They won't. They'd have to have some idea."

"Jesus, Ma. Where'd it all come from?"

"Some from your father's side jobs. A lot from gambling. He always preferred cash around. I've contributed. I've been wanting to tell you, but I didn't want you to think about me dying. This is for emergencies, okay? Health or house crises. I don't touch it."

He nods.

She shows him the other hiding spots: a manila envelope tucked into a hole in the ceiling next to an oxidized pipe; a record case for forty-fives in a metal locker across from the workbench; a wooden liquor crate nudged behind the bikes; a cookie tin on the table next to the washing machine; and an old fur coat in the closet wrapped in a beige garment protector, the inner and outer pockets stuffed with cash.

"I wish you weren't showing me any of this," Chooch says.

"See, it upsets you," his mother says. "You're old enough now—more than old enough—where I need to prepare you for a life without me."

"You're not that old."

"You never know. Look at today. On the floor in the closet in my room, there's a big tin container. That's where all the important papers are. You know that already, right? We'll go through it again. Birth certificates, Social Security cards, vaccine records, bankbooks, the deed to this house and the house upstate, insurance policies, and the like. There's also an envelope full of cash in there. When I die, that's the money for my funeral."

"Ma."

"Tomorrow, we'll go to the bank. We'll talk to Bonnie. She's nice. Confirm your name's on everything it needs to be on. Make sure you won't have any hassle. And we really need to get rid of that house upstate. The taxes are killing us."

Chooch feels like he's on the verge of hyperventilating.

"Stai bene?" his mother asks.

"I don't know." He crouches down into a squatting position and then sits on the cold floor, his back against the wall.

"What are you doing?"

"I need to sit a minute." His head's spinning. His heart's beating fast. Arlene and Frank and Roberto and Sav, all dead. A whole family wiped out. Blood on his hands. That house. Those memories. This house. Hidden money. Upstate. Sav buried in the woods. Bones in dirt. Deeds. Funerals. Risa, standing in the cold, gazing up at the Franzone house. Little Fab with his grunts and groans. Giulia, who'd said that Jimmy could use a little prodding, that the sooner he went after Roberto, the more beneficial it would be to their situation. Those words on repeat in his head. She couldn't have known Jimmy would go this far. He didn't know, obviously, or he never would've gone into the Crisscross with that plan. He takes a few deep breaths and scrunches his eyes closed tightly as if he might be able to pressure the thoughts away.

He imagines Frank's and Arlene's obituaries. An article about them in the church bulletin. What good parishioners they were. How they grew up in the neighborhood and remained there their whole lives. Their joys and accomplishments. How both of their boys leaving hurt them but how they endured. How much they loved their only grandson.

"Let's go back upstairs," his mother says. "I'll make a pot of coffee."

"I don't want coffee," Chooch says.

"Okay, well, maybe it's best to lie down."

"I think I need to."

She helps him to his feet, and they walk upstairs. He takes each step slowly. One day, after his mother's gone, he'll have to come down to the cellar on his own, and he thinks of himself tumbling down the stairs, breaking his neck, no one finding him for days.

He lies down on the couch in the living room. He's got those tapes from Wolfman's, but he just wants regular old television right now. His mother turns on the set and flips it to a channel that's not the news. This one's showing a made-for-TV movie of some kind. A man and a woman in a trailer in the desert. Both sweaty. A beer clutched in the man's hand. The woman tense, uneasy. She's blond, slight, and she's got heartbreak in her eyes. He recognizes the actress. It's that Hysteria Wilkins who Marco LaRocca is dating. Chooch likes to fall in love with actresses in movies, and he does that now, lets his sudden crush drown out everything else for a moment. In a different timeline, he's the kind of guy who gets in his car and drives out to Los Angeles and lives a life full of adventure. He knew guys in high school who read that *On the Road* book and lit out by car or by bus and he's sure they fell in love and slept on beaches and saw all the things he'll never see.

His mother brings him a couple of Tylenol and a small

glass of ginger ale. Tells him to sit up and take the pills and drink the soda and maybe it'll make him feel better. He obliges and then leaves the glass on a Yankees coaster atop the coffee table.

"Did Risa go over there?" his mother asks, and he's surprised it's taken her so long.

He nods.

"She didn't bring Fab?"

"Of course not."

"I feel for that kid, I really do." She pauses. "He reminds me of you when you were little. Shy. Withdrawn. I see him playing in his yard, all to himself, and I think of you in our yard with your figures and your imaginary ballgames."

"Both only children. We've got that in common."

"I wish you could've had brothers and sisters."

His mother has never talked about this to him before. He knows that something happened after he was born and that she couldn't have more kids, but he doesn't know what it was exactly. He's never asked. Certain things you don't say to mothers. Certain things you don't bring up. She's got a wistful look on her face now. Regret crossing her eyes like a black storm. She sits on the edge of the couch and touches his feet. He doesn't respond. She doesn't elaborate.

They sit there and watch the drama play out on the TV screen. Hysteria Wilkins pulling a gun on the guy with the beer. The guy laughing, setting his beer down on a counter and putting his hands up, saying, "Whoa, now."

"Who is this actress?" his mother asks.

"She's the one who dates Marco LaRocca," Chooch says. "Hysteria Wilkins."

"What kind of name is Hysteria? Anyhow, I like her. She's exciting to watch." She squeezes his ankle. "I need to take a hot shower. You want anything else?"

He shakes his head. "I'm good."

His mother heads for the bathroom, and he knows she'll take a long shower and really steam it up in there, and she'll take a sleeping pill and be out of it for the rest of the night.

He's left alone with the movie. Hysteria has prevailed. The man is gone from the trailer. She's exhausted. Crying into her hands. Chooch likes to come into a movie in the middle of a scene like this, not having any idea what the hell's going on, who any of the characters are supposed to be.

Trying to make sense of things takes his mind off the tragic aftermath that's playing out a few blocks away. Investigations, questions, a piecing together of events.

He thinks back to Jimmy at the Crisscross with his peanuts and his stogie and his pint glass of whiskey. The gun Jimmy talked about. The one he said he put in his own mouth. That was probably the gun he used. Widow Marie and Jane the Stain had overheard their conversation. They know it's not a coincidence he stumbled in there for the first time in almost five years for a fucking club soda. They know what his intention was. Maybe if Chooch hadn't gone to see him, Jimmy wouldn't have found out about Roberto when he was quite so hammered, and he would've had more time to think it all through rationally. Then again, Jimmy was probably hammered all the time.

Chooch thinks of the beautiful birthday cake Risa made for him, just sitting on her table across the street, the same table Roberto said he once fucked Ginny Saggese on. He can't imagine they'll find any cause to sit around and eat slices in the wake of what's happened. It's selfish, but he's thinking every year his birthday will mark the anniversary of this tragedy.

Something else is happening in the movie now. Hysteria is driving a white pickup truck in the dark. Headlights bouncing across the road. On the run. Perhaps from the man. Running to something or someone else. Chooch can't make heads or tails of it. She blows a strand of hair out of her face. He wishes he could be in that truck with her.

Part 3

THE FUTURE SEEMS IMPOSSIBLE SOME NIGHTS

Friday, November 13

1998

1.

Father Tim is in for it now.

Monsignor Terrone sits across from him at the table in the back room of the rectory, hands clasped over a folded copy of *The Tablet*, a constipated expression on his face. "Father, consider this an intervention," Terrone says, that fake compassionate tenor in his voice he so excels at. "You're in free fall. It might not be apparent to everyone—you put on a decent performance at mass—but it's clear to me. The drinking. Spending hours a day at that pub. Playing cards. Forsaking your duties. I know you had a rough life before the priesthood found you, but this behavior needs to stop."

Father Tim rubs down some wrinkles in his jeans. He's not dressed in his clerical clothes. He's taken to not wearing them lately, opting for Levis and flannel shirts. "You were supposed to go to that dinner for the Taverna girl tonight," he says to Terrone. "What happened?"

"That's not what I'm talking about."

"Tell me why you're not going."

"Giulia didn't want me there. Risa only invited me for their parents' sake. Let's get back to the issue at hand."

"My behavior."

"Precisely." Terrone pauses. "I heard from a concerned parishioner that they saw you browsing in the pornographic section of Wolfman's video store."

All these years, Father Tim's had to put on an act around Terrone. Be subservient, full of awe. Meanwhile, this disgust's been boiling under the surface. "I'd rather be a degenerate than a phony," he says. "Besides, I was just looking at the boxes. We don't even have a VCR in this dump."

Terrone looks like he's been smacked in the face with a shovel. "Excuse me?"

Father Tim takes his flask out of his pocket. It's full of cheap Canadian whiskey. He unscrews the cap, pulls a quick sip, and wipes his mouth on the back of his hand. "What time is that dinner?" he asks.

"Why this interest in the Taverna girls?"

It's funny to him that he runs an AA meeting and that, in one of those meetings about a month ago, Risa's neighbor, Pete Parisi, mentioned—out of the blue—how he'd overheard something he shouldn't have because he was being nosy, overheard Risa and Giulia talking about Sav like he was dead, like they *knew* he was dead, saying he didn't want to gossip but it didn't sit right, saying worrying over it was making him want to drink again, because everything's a lie and holing up with a bottle's the only answer. Father Tim had nodded and listened, not saying much in response, but silently agreeing with that last part. Pete fell off the wagon a few days after that meeting and then fell off the map. Last Father Tim had heard, the poor sucker was drying out in some clinic upstate, and Risa was stressing about what to do with his vacated apartment. Father Tim's got real trouble of his own—beyond Terrone, way bigger than that—and he's latched onto this information about Risa and Sav as a possible solution. Privately, in the confines of the confessional, he'd acted the detective and pressed Pete for any other details, but it was just those whispers. He let his imagination build from there. It wasn't hard. Something had never sat right about Risa's handling of her husband's disappearance and the annihilation of his family by Jimmy Tomasullo.

Terrone continues: "Where are you, Father? I asked you a question, and you don't have an answer for me."

"No crime in being curious," Father Tim says.

A dramatic exhale from Terrone. "You're waging a war against yourself and against God. You'll wind up on the streets. I've seen it happen."

Father Tim doesn't think about where he'll *wind up* the way he once did. He used to fear ramifications, used to care what Terrone and the people of the parish and diocese thought and said, but now he only thinks about the moment. It's a strange thing to be a priest without faith, to have had that faith simply dissolve. A strange thing to fear the void more than he ever feared hell. He wants to keep spiraling, wants to live long enough to see how far he can fall but wants to stop himself before splattering on the rocks below. Having Charlie Cee and Carmine Perasso on his tail for this debt he's accrued playing cards is no joke.

"Do you want me to hear your confession?" Terrone asks.

Father Tim takes another hit from his flask. "Maybe some other time," he says, standing and pushing away from the table. He goes over to the closet and yanks his black peacoat off a wooden hanger, slipping into it. He finds his wool beanie and puts it on. This rectory with its sad light and its scuffed linoleum floors and its holy smells. He's sick of it, just as he's sick of Terrone. He leaves with his head held high.

Late afternoon walking the sidewalks of the neighborhood. The sun is bright in a cold way. He tries to remember when and how this shift in him began. Perhaps it had been there all along, lying dormant. Like that priest he knew once, Father McDermott, who'd been exposed to tuberculosis by his father when he was a child and then he got sick in his forties and the TB somehow activated and he wouldn't go to the doctor, thinking it was something more regular, so he died struggling for breath. Father Tim's sickness is different, but it had been lying in wait for many years. His exposure to so much evil as a boy had built black rooms in his soul where things were buried. The sickness was patient but present. The scent of sin finally breathed life back into it.

He heads to Blue Sticks Bar down on Bath Avenue past Bay Parkway, hoping they'll have a card game going in the back room. High rollers assemble there. Mickey Banh, Slop O'Brien, Artie DiMonda, and Andy Adesso, who'd played in the World Series of Poker. Pots are substantial. They get a kick out of having a priest playing cards with them. When they call him *Father*, they really emphasize the word, so it's dripping with sarcasm, so they're testifying to the oxymoronic nature of playing poker with a priest, whether he's deranged or a degenerate or whatever. Father Tim's already in the hole to Charlie Cee and Carmine Perasso—mobsters who operate out of Blue Sticks and run the game—for spotting him upward of ten grand to pay off his losses. He shouldn't have the guts to show up here, definitely shouldn't beg for more dough, shouldn't keep digging deeper.

He's barely across the threshold of the place when he's stopped by Charlie and Carmine's main goon, Giuseppe Senzamica, aka Joey Sends. In his mid-sixties but trim and tough, Joey's got on a pristine black Fila tracksuit and his famous black porkpie hat. He's also wearing potent aftershave. He puts a hand on Father Tim's chest to stop him from entering the place. "You got some balls showing up here, Father," Joey says.

"Charlie and Carmine spot me fifty, I can win back what I owe," Father Tim says.

Joey moves closer and speaks in a monotone voice, looking him square in the eye. "Sooner or later, I'm gonna have to put one in the back of your head. They're giving you extra rope right now because you're a man of God. Nobody wants to see a priest face down in Coney Island Creek. Least of all me, who'd have to put you there. Got enough bad shit on my conscience." He pauses. "Plus, Father, it's Friday the thirteenth, you don't mind me saying, you got rocks in your fucking head? You're already the unluckiest bastard I know, and you think you're gonna strut in here *today* and *win*?"

Father Tim lets out a breath. "If I pay off what I owe, they'll let me in the game?"

Joey scratches his chin. "Sure, Father. Don't go knocking off church funds, though."

Father Tim nods and steps back outside. He thinks about

Risa and what she might be covering up. The money she came into after the Franzones got slaughtered. Her sister involved—the one who's getting married tomorrow. That dinner tonight. He can threaten Risa, say he knows what she did or what they did, bleed some money from her. He knows the tricks of confession, knows that people want so badly to admit what they've done wrong. He paws at his flask and drinks deeply. It's a plan forged in desperation but nonetheless a plan. A way in or out or through. Time to act.

2.

Giulia's smoking a cigarette in the bathroom of this house that's been her home for a while, but still doesn't feel like home. She's wearing jeans and a shimmery pink pull-over sweater from Joyce Leslie, though she should be getting changed and doing her hair and putting on her makeup. Instead, she's sitting on the toilet, lid closed, leaning over and ashing into the sink, looking at herself in the mirror. She had her hair dyed the day before at Bensonhurst Dolls, so the gray starting to thread through the black is gone, but the laugh lines around her mouth and eyes are still bugging her.

She's thinking about Marco. When he died of an overdose at a club in Los Angeles a few years before, it was big, heart-breaking news. Reporters and camera crews engulfed Lola's house. Giulia sent a card, but she'd never had the guts to go see Lola. She didn't go to the memorial mass, and she'd hated herself for that. Occasionally, she walked past the house after leaving Risa's, and she'd see some shrines left by fans on the sidewalk in front of the gate, and she'd avoid looking at the windows for fear of allowing her memories of Marco to destroy her. Lola's house has begun to crumble around her. The babble among neighborhood crones is that disconsolate old Mrs. LaRocca never goes out, not even to church or to the shops on the avenue. Giulia's still haunted—all these years later—by what could've been. She saw something special in Marco before anyone else did. People know his name more than ever. College kids put his poster on their dorm room walls. She read somewhere that they're trying to make a movie about his life. Lola put the kibosh on that, but she won't be able to hold them off forever. Eventually, she'll die, or she'll move out of the house and into an assisted living facility or something, and the estate will fall into the control of a person who only sees dollar signs. When it finally happens, Giulia wonders if someone will play her. A young actress she's unfamiliar with. If she was smart, she'd write a book about her time with Marco. No one knows that story. No one else can tell it. Prefame Marco. Two kids in love. But she can't write well, and she doesn't want to be one of those vampires who simply feeds off his memory.

She supposes she's thinking about Marco now because she's marrying Stan Zajac at Villa Monaco on Avenue U tomorrow. They're keeping it small. Not getting married in church. Just doing the ceremony at the little chapel they have at the Villa Monaco and then going straight to the reception area. Maybe a hundred and fifty people. Stan wanted to do it today—Friday the thirteenth—because it was so much cheaper, but Giulia talked him into tomorrow. Her parents are only coming because Risa is forcing them to. They're not happy it's not at Our Lady of Perpetual Surrender or in some other church. They're less happy Stan's Polish. Risa is her matron of honor, of course, and she insisted on saying "matron" instead of "maid" for the sake of appearances. Her cousins and one of Stan's friends make up the rest of the bridesmaids. Fab's an usher. Stan's best man and groomsmen are a bunch of his electrician buddies. They've all been drunk for weeks since the Yankees won the World Series against the Padres.

Giulia met Stan a little over two years ago at the Crisscross, and they went on a three-day bender together. There was a lot of passion between them right out of the gate. Their first fuck was in the ladies' restroom, drunk off their asses. She started going home with him, abandoning her couch at Risa's, and it only took about two months for her to move into this house of Stan's on Harway Avenue. He's five years younger than her. Thirty-one. Handsome with his Virgin Mary blue eyes. Likes to read and has tons of books about the history of the borough. He's always pointing things out to her, like the place where Moe Howard from the Three Stooges lived and the house where Ruth Bader Ginsburg grew up. He's said some sketchy shit about Monica Lewinsky in the last nine months or so since that news broke about her and Clinton, but he's a man after all. She's opened up to him, spilled her guts many drunken nights, talked about her parents and Risa and Fab and how she sometimes feels trapped in this place. Cornered. The closest she's ever come to betraying the bond of silence about Sav is with Stan. The words were on her lips once—the impulse to spill the whole sordid tale, to unburden herself. She wonders what Stan would've made of it, how he might've reacted. No matter—she kept the secret safe. They still go to the Crisscross together all the time, drinking way too much, and Stan's a solid listener. He'll listen forever if she's going on and on about something after one too many whiskeys. He encouraged her to keep trying with Italian, saying he'd take her to Naples one day—not on their honeymoon, they couldn't afford it—but she'd abandoned her books recently, feeling frustrated she was getting nowhere, that she was thirty-six and could only say the most basic shit. She doubts Stan will ever take her to Naples.

Tonight, they're doing a dinner at some hole-in-the-wall restaurant on Avenue T. They've got a private room. Just their immediate families. Risa had wanted Monsignor Terrone to come, probably to get in Giulia's ear about the importance of baptizing a kid if they had one. Terrone didn't think it was his place to horn in—*good fucking call, Monsignor*. Anyhow, she doesn't ever want kids. She can't imagine a life of diapers and bottles and burping and strollers and whatever the fuck else.

She's nervous as hell. She can feel it in her stomach and in her bones and in her blood. The cigarette's helping to calm her but not as much as she'd like. She keeps thinking of her and Stan getting older together. Time passes fast. He'll get heavier. His hair will turn gray and fall out, and he'll have hairy ears and nostrils. He'll walk around the house in stained sweatpants. She's already going gray. All the booze and cigarettes are taking their toll. She still works in the office at Sid and Eddie's garage and doesn't see her professional outlook improving. Never thought she'd fall into this shit. Always thought she was better than the suckers. She should walk away. She can still walk away.

Stan calls up to her: "What time you want to leave for this dinner thing?" His voice has never sounded so jagged, so awful, so like the voice of someone who has never done or said one interesting thing in his fucking dumb ox life. It isn't the voice of the man she met at the Crisscross who told her about the famous architect Calvert Vaux accidentally drowning in Gravesend Bay in 1895. She imagines him saying *I do* during their vows and wants to puke.

She gets up and opens the door a crack. "What time is it now?"

"I don't know. Four thirty maybe."

"An hour, I guess. We should get there first."

He grunts in acknowledgment. "I gotta wear a suit, you think?"

"Wear what you want." She closes the door.

She takes one last drag of her cigarette and then opens the toilet lid and flicks the butt into the scummy water. She thumbs the hemline of the new blue square neck midi dress hanging from the shower rod. It's what she plans on wearing tonight. She bought it the week before. Looks nice on her. She checks out all her stuff sitting on the counter next to the sink. Eye shadow, concealer, rouge, foundation, mascara, blush. A can of hairspray. A vanity mirror. Tweezers, manicure scissors, Q-tips, cotton balls. A few bottles of nail polish. She puts her arm out in front of herself and swipes everything onto the hard tile floor. The glass in the mirror shatters. The glass bottles of nail polish too, inking out across the tile like something small shot dead. Whatever's plastic breaks.

Stan calls up to her: "The fuck was that?"

"Nothing," Giulia shouts back. "Just dropped something."

She goes to the window and unlatches the lock and pushes it up. The sun's going down, and darkness is settling over the neighborhood. It's chilly. She steps onto the fire escape, shutting the window behind her.

She climbs down the ladder into the backyard and then edges up against the house, hoping to avoid Stan's field of vision if he happens to glance out.

She tries not to think about the turmoil that her absence at the dinner will cause. Worse than that, what her sudden disappearance from the bathroom will do to Stan. The havoc it'll wreak on his nerves. Everyone will be freaking out about tomorrow. If she's not at the dinner, will she blow off the wedding? Did she get cold feet and hit the road? Truth is, she's got no idea what she's going to do. She only knows she can't go to this dinner.

Out on the sidewalk, she looks around. Her breath hazy in front of her face. The sweater she's wearing is warm, but she could use a coat and a hat.

Giulia's overwhelmed suddenly by the urge to see Lola, to talk to her about Marco, to forget the present and the future for a few hours and open the curtains onto the past. All those same what-ifs sparking in her mind. She crosses her arms over her chest—a half-hearted attempt to warm herself—and heads there.

3.

When Father Tim shows up at her door, Risa's surprised. He's not in his usual black clerical clothes either. Instead, he's dressed like a civilian. Black peacoat, flannel shirt, blue jeans, shiny brown boots. Looks like he's wobbling in place.

What the hell kind of priest shows up unannounced?

"Why are you here?" Risa asks, not even pretending to hide her disdain.

"Tonight's the big dinner, no?" Father Tim says. "I know you invited Monsignor Terrone, and he shot you down. Thought I'd take his place. Can I come in?"

Father Tim has rubbed Risa the wrong way since he first came to the parish fifteen years ago. She remembers his arrival precisely because it coincided with her meeting Sav. A few weeks apart. At the time, she'd never met a priest who was around her age. Everyone was thrilled that he was young and lively. They thought he'd bring new life to the parish with his sweaters and sideburns and his soft voice. They figured the kids at the school would be happy to have a priest around who wasn't as old as Methuselah. But he skeeved Risa out almost immediately. His voice, the way he moved, his steely gaze. She's always thought he looks like the kind of guy who washes his hands for about twenty minutes, until they're red and raw, even scrubbing at the tips of his fingers with a wire brush. Mary Redden from church—she's gone now—used to say he reminded her of Anthony Perkins in *Psycho*. She still hears that music in her head when he's around. Early on, she went to him for confession occasionally, but she stopped that within a few short years and would only go if it was Monsignor Terrone. Father Tim hovered in an unsettling way on the other side of that screen in the confessional box. Breathed strangely. And he's given Risa the creeps even more since the night Jimmy Tomasullo killed the Franzones. His sinister bearing. Kindness masking treachery. He's underhanded and insincere. Just *off*. People in the parish continue to fall for his sweetheart act. Doesn't help that he seems to view her suspiciously. "I don't think that's a good idea," Risa says. "It's not what Giulia would want."

"Fair enough," he says. "Do you have just a few minutes before you go? There's something sensitive I'd like to discuss with you."

Risa sighs. She steps aside and waves him in. She's unsettled by the word *sensitive*. All she can think is Fab's in trouble at school. Maybe he broke into the rectory and drank Communion wine.

Father Tim takes off his coat and hangs it on a wall hook.

He pulls out a chair at the dining room table. "I'll take a load off, if you don't mind." He sits. Takes a flask out of his coat pocket and drains it dry and then puts it back. "Been nipping at this whiskey to keep warm—it's cold out. You have anything else to drink? Wine perhaps? I'd love a glass if you have some."

Jesus, so he's already got a load on. What is this?

Still, to be polite, she searches in the kitchen cabinets for a stray bottle of wine. She finds a jug of something cheap Giulia left behind. Screw-top. Label half peeled off. She takes it out and sets it on the counter and finds a glass for Father Tim. She pours the wine and brings it to him, and he takes a nice, long belt.

Serving wine to Father Tim in her apartment is an unusual situation at best, an alarming one at worst. Word gets around the neighborhood, she'll be painted as some sort of seductress. Her husband gone like he is. Trying to get Father Tim loaded to take advantage of him. She should have the guts to tell him to go but decides not to rock the boat.

Hopefully Fab will come bursting in soon. Risa's on edge because Fab was supposed to be home from school a while ago. Probably off with that friend of his. Justin. Troubled kid. Risa doesn't like Fab hanging around with him. Lives with his grandfather over in one of those big, slate-gray apartment buildings on Cropsey.

"You don't mind me saying," Father Tim says, "you look very nice."

She's been ready for an hour. She's wearing a gold blouse, black slacks, and a heavy white shawl. She dyed her hair this afternoon, and she's put on more makeup than she's had on in a long time. Giulia's wedding is a big deal. It's not something

Risa anticipated ever happening during all the years Giulia lived with them. She never figured on being her sister's matron of honor. *Matron*. She knew the rules—the church would identify her as a matron of honor whether she was still married, divorced, or widowed, so she's insisted on being called that even though it'll be a nonreligious ceremony, and no one really cares how she's identified. Giulia even said she hated the term either way and would rather call her the *best lady*. She deflects the compliment from Father Tim. "I don't know where Fab could be," she says. "He's supposed to be home. I'm a little distracted. Worried about him. He's off with that Justin."

"Boys will be boys," Father Tim says. "He'll be here. So, how's school?"

Risa looks at her stack of brick-thick textbooks on the china closet and thinks about the night classes she's been taking at Kingsborough Community College. The stuffy classrooms, the other students who are mostly younger than her, her gruff teacher who wears corduroy blazers and crooked bow ties. She'd started volunteering at a nursing home on Stillwell Avenue when Fab went into first grade and, enjoying her time there thoroughly, feeling useful, she's since decided she wants to be a nursing assistant. She wants to continue to help old people but in a more official fashion. Be kind to them and bring a little light into their lives. She's good at it. She'd inherited this house after Frank and Arlene died, and she and Fab kept their apartment and she became a landlord for the other tenants, which is a strange thing to be. She also got the house where Frank and Arlene and Roberto had been murdered, and no one wanted to live there, of course, so she sold it to some developers who knocked it down and built condos, which is something that's been happening all over the neighborhood. Old houses, houses from back when the neighborhood was first settled, these gargantuan and beautiful structures with *stories*, are getting demolished, and these sleek multifamily, interchangeable condos with driveways cemented over gardens and yards are replacing them. It started a while back, but it's amped up recently, as more and more people sell their places and leave, saying the city's too hectic, too crowded, looking for peace in Jersey or on Long Island. A lot of old Italians moving together to retirement communities out at the end of Long Island, by that nuclear power plant, disturbed by the changing face of the neighborhood. The Italian majority starting to give way to an influx of Chinese and Russian immigrants. The most ancient and superstitious of these folks think the end of the century might mean the end of the world, and they want to be far away from the chaos of a collapsing city, even if Giuliani's been mayor now for the last few years, an Italian that mostly makes them proud, as well as being a law-and-order type.

Whatever other money Frank and Arlene had left behind also got handed to Risa. In the immediate aftermath, she used some for the funerals and wakes, and she's had to use a lot for Fab's tuition at Our Lady of Perpetual Surrender over the years. Now she's using it for her own tuition at Kingsborough. She also donated some to the church in Frank and Arlene's name, which Monsignor Terrone thanked her for profusely—and the bulk of what remains she put in a CD account for Fab at Republic National Bank. Over thirty grand. He doesn't know about it. Her intention is that he'll use it for college down the road.

As for her own future, if she can't get a job at the home

where she volunteers, there's another home a block away on Cropsey, others in Coney Island, at least one over in Bay Ridge, and another on Thirteenth Avenue she knows of, the Norwegian place, and she figures some of them are probably desperate for CNAs. Her college classes have been difficult. Science especially. And the program she's in is intensive. She takes a million notes and stays up late most nights, reading and studying. She was never great in school but finds herself much more capable at forty than she ever did at eighteen or nineteen. She's able to fight through the struggle. Still, she doesn't want to crack those textbooks once this weekend if she can help it. "It's going fine," she says.

"I really admire you for doing that. A lot of people, they settle into their lives, they don't pursue their dreams anymore. With all that you've been through, it's even more impressive."

Risa flinches when Father Tim mentions *all that she's been through.*

Father Tim sips his wine. "It's nice to be here. I don't mean to belabor it. If I can be frank, I mostly spend time outside the church in the kitchens and dining rooms of women like Honey Grimaldi and Grazia Sanfratello, who serve me pound cake and want me to meet their still-single daughters. I'll never for the life of me understand why these old, devout women are trying to matchmake their lonely daughters with a man . . . like me."

Risa's getting angry. *Where's this going?*

The phone rings in the kitchen. "Excuse me," she says to Father Tim, and she rushes over and picks it up, fearing the worst. Fab's had an accident, or he's gotten into a predicament with Justin. Fab's begun to change so much. His sweet phase over. Always boiling with turmoil or indifference these days.

Hormones, people say. She knows it's more than that. Trouble in his blood. His father breaking through in him maybe. The influence of Justin, drawing that stuff out. But when she picks up the phone, it's not Fab or someone with a report of Fab, it's Stan. He's melting down. Shouting. "She's gone," he says. "Went out the window."

"Take it easy," Risa says. "What are you talking about?"

"Giulia. She went AWOL. Escaped the house through the bathroom window. Dinner's off, Ris. Wedding might be off too, for all I know. You haven't seen her?" His voice cracking.

Risa likes Stan, and she feels bad for him. What he's describing sounds like something from the Giulia Taverna playbook. Cold feet. Panic. One last chance to walk away. "Take it easy, okay?" she says. "She's not here. She's probably just nervous. She'll come back."

"Dinner's off," he says. "Can you call your family? I already called the restaurant and my people. I told them Giulia's not feeling well, and she needs to rest up for tomorrow. The restaurant's keeping the deposit, you believe that?"

"Maybe we should wait a half hour. She could've just gone for a walk to clear her mind."

"Someone's going for a walk, they don't make a fucking mess knocking all their shit all over the floor and escape out the bathroom window. I got all dressed, too. I was always scared she'd make a sucker out of me somehow. 'Out of my league,' my buddies said. 'She'll break your goddamn heart,' they said."

"Cancel the dinner, I get it, but this doesn't mean the wedding's off. It's normal to panic the night before a wedding."

"Yeah, maybe," Stan says, clearly dejected, probably

wondering what his future will look like if Giulia splits for good. Not only cancels the wedding but moves out. He hangs up.

Risa presses down the hook and then dials Chooch's number. He picks up after a couple of rings. "Don't bother getting Vi out of the house," she says. "Giulia's on the lam and the dinner's off."

"What do you mean?" Chooch asks. "She okay?"

"I don't know anything else. She snuck out through the bathroom window like a kid breaking curfew. Stan's freaking out. He's worried she'll bail on the wedding too."

"Geez. Okay. You need anything, let me know."

"I'm a little worried about Fab. I'm afraid he's at Justin's again. I've got Father Tim over here," she adds, her voice aching with resentment, "but I'll have to go look for him at some point."

"What's Father Tim doing there?" Chooch asks.

"Still trying to figure that out," Risa says.

"I can go get Fab, if you want."

"Yeah?"

"No problem at all."

"Thank you so much, Christopher. That's a massive help. It's one of those gray buildings on Cropsey. Building number two, apartment four-D. Justin lives with his grandpa." She's not sure how Fab will react to being wrangled by Chooch, but so be it.

When she's done talking to Chooch, she makes a few more quick calls to her folks and her cousins and tells them the dinner's not happening. None of them are shocked. "What'd Giulia do to screw it up?" her father asks.

She puts the receiver on the hook and comes back to the table. "The dinner's off," she says to Father Tim.

"Gives us more time to talk," Father Tim says.

"I have other stuff to do. I'm sorry. I've gotta find my son."

"Chooch is going to get him, isn't that what I overheard?"

"It's just not a good time. I've gotta see where Giulia went."

"Do you have anything to eat here?" Father Tim asks. "I'm starving. I know you're a great cook. The trays of ziti and lasagna you've left at the rectory for Monsignor Terrone—he often shares those with me."

The gall. She bites down on what she really wants to say. "I have lasagna in the freezer," she says. "You can take it to the rectory."

"I'd rather stay here. As I said, I want to discuss something with you."

She feels cornered, but she's not sure how to handle him. She takes a deep breath. Giulia's fine—a grown woman. She's not missing, just nervous. Chooch will bring Fab home shortly. If she's got to muscle through this awkwardness for a bit longer, she'll do it. What could he possibly want to talk to her about? If it's not about Fab, maybe they're planning on some renovations at the church, and he intends on hitting her up for a donation, knowing she's still got some of that Franzone inheritance.

She goes over to the freezer and takes out a tin tray of lasagna, wrapped in plastic and foil. She removes both and puts it in the oven at three-fifty. "It'll probably take about thirty or forty minutes to heat up," she says, closing the oven door, dreading the wait.

"That's okay," Father Tim says. "We've got wine. Speaking of which, I'd love a bit more. You won't have any?"

"No," she says, bringing the jug to the table and refilling his glass. "What do you want to talk to me about?"

"I want to know the truth, Risa," he says.

"What truth?" she asks, sitting.

"I want you to tell me the truth about what happened to Sav."

4.

Fab takes a cigarette from Justin, who lights it for him. Justin opens the window a crack and lights his own. Cool air drifts into the room. The cigarette feels weird between Fab's lips. His first. That hard little filter. He gags on the smoke. Justin cracks up.

"Fuck off," Fab says.

They're in Justin's room listening to Mobb Deep's *Hell on Earth*. Justin's drawing tags in his black sketchbook with a paint marker, the cigarette dangling from his mouth. His grandfather Knucks is asleep out in the living room, the Spice Channel blaring on the television.

Fab ashes into an empty Coke can and notices through the slats in the blinds on the window that it's starting to get dark out. "I've gotta go soon," he says. "Got this dinner for my aunt." He doesn't want to go. And he especially doesn't want to go to Aunt Giulia's wedding tomorrow because that means putting on the shitty black suit his mother got him. He's twelve, but the suit makes him feel younger. It's like the suit he wore to Uncle Roberto and Nana and Poppy Franzone's funerals when he was five. He also just doesn't like that Aunt Giulia's getting married. When he was an infant, his old man had gone missing—he had no memory of the guy—and Aunt Giulia and Uncle Chooch had attempted to double-team that role. His hope has been that she'll come to her senses, dump Stan, and move back in with him and his mom.

"You can hide here if you don't wanna go," Justin says. "Knucks won't care."

Fab's not sure why Justin's grandfather goes by Knucks. He's also not sure how he wound up with just his grandfather. He doesn't know a lot in life, but he knows there are certain questions that don't get asked. He's played through the many answers to that question, and he can only figure on some combination of death, prison, and abandonment. He knows all about abandonment because of his old man, and he knows something about death because of what happened to his dad's parents and brother. People in the neighborhood still throw him a lot of sympathy for that. *Oh, you're the Franzones' grandkid.* Then they get weepy. *What a tragedy.* "I don't know," Fab finally says to Justin.

Fab's sure his mom's sitting at their kitchen table now, jacket on, deciding whether she should give him a little space to do the right thing or whether she should come and grab him. She doesn't like Justin. Thinks Knucks has no idea how to raise a boy because he plays cards and bets the horses. She's banned Fab time and again from going over to Justin's after school, and he's continued to ignore her. Justin's got a sweetness that he hides. The way he's always working on his tags in that book. The way he bounces his head along to the music, like he's doing now.

"You want to go up to the roof?" Justin asks. "Your mom comes looking for you, she won't think to look up there."

Fab feels conflicted. What's he gonna do? Ruin the dinner? Ruin the night? Could be perceived as a protest, as a message. *Aunt Gee, don't do it.* "Okay," he says.

They drop their cigarettes in the soda can with a sad fizzle and put their coats and hats on.

Justin gathers a few things—the pack of Winstons, two more paint markers and a different sketchbook, and his boombox, which is battery operated—and they head out of the apartment, leaving Knucks still asleep somehow in front of his porn.

They head to the stairwell and go beyond the sixth floor into the restricted zone. There's a fire door that opens out onto the roof. One of those silver bars across the middle of it. A warning sign saying an alarm will sound when it's pushed. But everyone knows it's forever busted.

The roof's peaceful. The sky's dusky, purple at the edges, the sun setting, but it's still bright enough to see. There's a pigeon coop with a slatted tin roof and wire grates for walls over at the back end. A makeshift clothesline strung from an exhaust vent to a railing on the edge. "Girl jumped off last week," Justin says.

"No way," Fab says.

"Sarah Magnuso. Apartment three-B. She's sixteen. Goes to Lafayette. Lost her mind or something. Tried to fly."

"She died?"

"No idea."

Fab gets as close as he can to the front edge and thinks about hitting the concrete in the courtyard below from seven stories up. If the fall didn't kill her, surely every bone in her body shattered and she's a vegetable somewhere.

They move to the back of the roof, settling by the coop with its open door and huddled masses of pigeons. He loves watching and listening to them. He wishes he knew more about pigeons. He wishes he grew up with an old man who tended to pigeons and maybe even raced them. He knows that's a thing people do. There's a storefront club not too far down on Cropsey. He imagines these people meet on roofs with their pigeons and big black flags and race them across the city. He's not sure who looks after the pigeons up here. Maybe the super of Justin's building. Guy named Ganz. Looks the type.

On this side, there's another building from the apartment complex very close by. A looming antenna that resembles pieces of scaffolding arranged into a point ornaments the other roof. There's maybe six or seven feet between the two buildings. A slim chasm. Fab gazes down into a weed-strewn alley dotted with massive condenser units.

"I say we go back to school and bust into the convent tonight," Justin says.

Fab laughs a little. He imagines putting on ski masks and trying to break into the school like robbers when all they ever want is to get out of the place. He imagines going up to the mysterious convent on the top floor where all the nuns live. Another kid in their class, Rocco Salcedo, had been up there once—Rocco's dad is a plumber and the nuns thought maybe Rocco could fix their clogged sink—and he said they had a *Basic Instinct* tape out on the coffee table. "Why?" Fab asks.

Justin shrugs. “I heard Sister Val is a Nazi. That she used to be, like, an SS guard or whatever. Want to see for myself.”

Sister Val is an angry beast of a nun with flaming red cheeks and see-through eyebrows and rotten yellow teeth. Wears glasses so thick they magnify her eyes. She’s got the rough hands of a rip-off mechanic. Has pints of whiskey hidden throughout the convent and school. The kids can always smell it on her. She *is* old, probably in her fifties, but not old enough to have been an actual Nazi, and he’s pretty sure she’s from Boston. Got that New England accent, roots for the Red Sox.

“She’s not even German,” Fab says. “She’s Irish. Who’d you hear that from?”

“Janey Balotelli said she saw her wearing some Nazi regalia,” Justin says, half-smiling.

“*Regalia*? What’s that mean?”

“I don’t know. Like Nazi jewelry or whatever. I bet she prays under a big-ass Nazi flag. Has a framed picture of Hitler on her nightstand.” Justin’s eyes travel to the roof opposite them. “I’ll give you ten bucks if you jump from my building to that one,” he says, out of nowhere, motioning with his head.

“I wouldn’t eat something I hated for ten bucks,” Fab says.

Justin puts down his book, his markers, and his pack of cigarettes. Takes off his coat. Cracks his knuckles. Pigeons cluck around nearby, a few strutting out of the coop and exploring. “I’ll do it for nothing,” he says.

“Do what?” Fab says.

“Jump from over here to over there.”

“You’re crazy.”

“I always wanted to do it. It’s nothing. I make it, you’re my witness.”

"Don't fuck around. Let's chill."

Justin backs up beyond the coop and gets into a starting position. He seems to be checking the wind and really examining the distance he'll have to clear. On top of that, there's a lip on the back edge of this roof and a one-foot wall on the opposite roof. He takes a deep breath and grins.

Fab's taking him less seriously now. No way he'll do it. He shakes his head. "Stop fucking around," he says.

"If I croak, promise me you'll find out if Sister Val's really a Nazi," Justin says, and he starts running toward the edge.

Fab's heart is in his throat.

5.

Giulia can't remember the last time she saw Lola. A handful of glances from a distance when she was living on the block with Risa and Fab. A few waves on the avenue in passing over the years. The last time they'd *talk*-talked had to be something like eighteen years before, in the wake of Marco dumping Giulia, when Lola would call to check in and ask her out to coffee and express her anger at Marco for putting his music first and breaking Giulia's heart. How strange to be able to live in dangerous proximity to such a big piece of her past and manage to mostly avoid it. Physically, anyhow. She feels guilt. She should've come sooner. Especially after Marco's death.

Lola looks fragile. She can't be much older than her late fifties or early sixties, but she's gaunt. Sunken cheeks. Paper-thin skin. Arms bony and jagged. She's wearing a plain blue sweatshirt covered in pills of lint and burgundy grandma pants. Her hair's cut short. Seems like she did a hatchet job on herself, the line scissored unevenly. She's smoking a long, slim cigarette. One of those brands that resemble a lollipop stick. The white filter smudged with dark lipstick. An overflowing ashtray on the table in front of her amid a wild scatter of bills and catalogs and church bulletins. The outside of the house is bad—the facade crumbling, the garden overgrown, cement cracked dramatically, the windows to the walk-in apartment downstairs boarded up since she quit having tenants—but the interior is even worse. Dusty and funky and foul. They're sitting in the kitchen. The wallpaper's peeling off, and the linoleum floor's curling up at the edges. The sink's dripping. The ceiling's caved in a bit where there must've been a leak. An exposed pipe is visible through a gaping hole in the plaster. It's incredibly drafty where they're sitting and very cold in the place overall, as if the oil burner's barely churning out any warmth. The heat pipes on the wall are ragged, the bone-white paint tasseling off in large strips. A pile of dirt on the floor looks like it's from a knocked-over plant, but no pot is in sight. There must've been money after Marco's death, but Lola either didn't care and didn't use it or somehow got screwed over by his record label or management.

"I know it's a hellhole in here," Lola says. "I don't get many guests."

"I'm sorry I didn't come sooner," Giulia says. "I should've come to pay my respects after Marco died. I was a coward."

"Honey, we're all cowards. You want anything to eat or drink?" She reconsiders the question. "Well, you want anything to drink? I don't have much to offer in the way of food. I've got scotch and brandy, that's about it."

"Whatever you're having, I'll have."

Lola stands unsteadily, the cigarette quivering between her lips, ash falling on her sweatshirt and the floor. She dodders over to a cabinet, grabbing a bottle of brandy from above the sink and then finding two glasses in the dish rack and coming back. Her frail hand trembles as she fills both glasses. Giulia thanks her.

"How're your sister and her son?" Lola asks. "I see them from my window now and then."

"Risa's okay. She went back to school for a nursing assistant program. Fab's twelve already."

"That bum husband of hers is still gone, huh?"

"Yeah." That's all she can say on that matter. The state she's in, she's worried about what she may let slip. "You're hanging in there?"

"Everything ended for me after Marco died," Lola says. She's stoic. There's no despair in her voice. "Now I'm waiting around to croak myself."

"You need help?" Giulia asks.

"Help dying?" Lola smiles. "I forsake all help." She raises her glass and urges Giulia to do the same.

They toast.

Lola takes a long drink.

Giulia does, too. The brandy warms her. It's fruity and sweet. "I'm supposed to get married tomorrow," she says.

"Oh yeah?"

"To Stan Zajac. You know him?"

"I don't know nobody no more. Even old, lonely Mrs. Gardini stopped passing by after the funeral. I quit going to church."

"Stan's a nice guy."

"Sounds like you're very enthusiastic."

"I love him, I do. I don't know. I'm just not sure marriage is for me. I feel like I'm settling into a life that's *typical.* I always promised myself I wouldn't be typical."

"And you came to me for my wisdom?"

"We were supposed to have a big dinner tonight, and I escaped out the bathroom window and decided to blow it off. I didn't know where to go. Then I had the thought that I should come here. I think about Marco all the time. You were always so kind to me, even after we broke up. I don't know why I came. I'm sorry to bother you. I shouldn't have. I'm selfish, that's it."

"I understand."

"You do?"

Lola downs her brandy and pours more. "Sure. In a parallel world, Marco stayed with you and you two got married and there was no big music career and, even then, a life with Marco wouldn't have been typical. You're asking yourself, if that happened, would you have been happy? Marco might've loved you the way he loved you—your first and best love—but would he have been happy if the music thing didn't work out? Is anybody ever happy? In that world, he's alive. The idea of that makes *me* happy."

"I guess you're right. What I felt with him I never felt again."

"There's no easy solution. No escape from what you're feeling. This Stan's a nice enough guy? Treats you well? Go for it. That's my advice. My Rosario died of a heart attack when Marco was ten, you know? He was no big romantic, but he was a fine husband."

Giulia drinks her brandy in one big gulp. "Can we go up to Marco's room for a minute?" she asks.

"Why not?" Lola says.

They get up from the table and traverse an obstacle course of boxes and crates in the hallway, heading upstairs. Pictures of Marco in high school and on stage at various concerts line the walls. This staircase. Giulia feels like she's sixteen again, Marco leading her up to his room while Lola's at work.

Lola opens the door to Marco's room. It's cobwebby and cold but otherwise just as he left it when he split for the city. A battered acoustic guitar. His posters on the wall: the Heartbreakers, Television, New York Dolls. His books. His slim twin bed with black sheets and a black comforter. The window—that little rip in the screen, the grime on the sill, the exact spot where they sat and smoked with forever in front of them. She'd fallen in love with him the second they met. It was outside Benny's Fish and Beer. She was with her friends. He was alone. He talked to her. He convinced her to go out with him. He wasn't like other boys she'd known. He was full of confidence. He acted like a man. She was drawn first to his eyes. The way he was dressed. Jeans, red T-shirt, leather jacket. Looked like one of the Ramones, except handsome. And he saw her as she was. Saw through her. The posturing with her friends. The bubblegum and bullshit. Saw straight to her heart. Knew the songs she loved before she ever even heard them. In hindsight, she was a dumb kid blasted to pieces by his charm. Marco was simply all promise. And that promise drifted away with him when he left. His death has made her feel less human somehow—she hasn't fully processed that yet. What's gone is gone. Real fairy tales end in the gutter. No amount of trying to live regular can bring back the fireworks.

"You know, after his death," Lola says, "I swore I'd never come in here again. I was so mad at him for dying. I still am."

"Thanks for letting me see it. Brings back a lot of memories."

"You two being alone in here when you shouldn't have been."

Giulia laughs a little. "Sorry about that."

"You want to stay here the night, you can. It's cold and dusty, but you're the only person I'd ever let sleep in Marco's bed."

"Yeah?" The invitation makes Giulia want to weep.

"Why not? One day, this room will be gone, and I'll be gone, and all those memories will seem even further away."

Giulia nods. "You wanna come to my wedding tomorrow, Lola?"

6.

Chooch knocks on the door of the apartment where Risa told him Fab would be. He's winded from the stairs since the elevator's out of service. He's passed by this cluster of buildings on Cropsey a million times on his way to Waldbaum's or the Belt Parkway, but this is his first time inside one. So many places like that in the neighborhood. Both familiar and foreign.

He can hear some noise coming from the apartment. Sounds like a television. Thinks maybe he's hearing moaning. His first guess is Fab and his buddy are watching porn. The grandpa's out, and they're having at it. But there's no movement to speak of on the other side of the door. He waits a couple of minutes and knocks again, harder this time.

The volume fades. Some thrashing around. Feet clomping on the floor. A grizzled voice echoes out: "Who the fuck's that?"

Must be the grandpa. "My name's Christopher," Chooch says. "I'm looking for Fab."

The door's thrust open, and a stocky, skeezy old man's standing there. Chooch is certain he's seen this guy around the neighborhood somewhere, but he can't put a finger on it. Those glasses. That shiny head. He's wearing a green T-shirt that says BOBBY "WIGGLES" IANESCO MEMORIAL GOLF TOURNAMENT in white iron-on letters and black sweatpants. The heat's blasting in the apartment and pulses from the open door. "Who'd you say you are?" he asks.

"Christopher. You're Justin's grandfather, right? I'm looking for my nephew, Fab."

"The kid in trouble?"

"His mom wants him home. Said he might be over here. I'm helping her out."

The old man turns around and mock searches the apartment. "I don't see him. You see him?"

"I don't."

"Could be they're in Justin's room, I guess." He waves Chooch in. "Call me Knucks."

Chooch follows him. Feels like he's walked into a sauna. The whole joint smells like stale smoke and old man ointments. It's a mess. A bachelor-pad type situation, but even worse. He feels sweat blooming on his neck and under his arms. He's wearing a lot of clothes. A thermal shirt and a winter coat. Heavy jeans. Timberland boots his mother bought him the Christmas before. He's got a wool beanie pulled low on his head. He's hoping Fab's in the bedroom, and they can get out of there quickly.

"I know you from somewhere?" Knucks asks, as they walk down the hallway.

"I was thinking I've seen you around," Chooch says.

"Did you used to go to the De-Luxe?"

Chooch is taken aback, being asked if he ever frequented a porn theater. He always figured that to be something guys don't talk about aloud. He'd passed the De-Luxe often before it closed a few years ago and had thought about going in once or twice when he was feeling especially desperate, but he never could cross that line. "Nope, not me."

"I seen you in the Hostess outlet over there on Stillwell maybe?"

"Could be."

"I'm a Ho Hos man myself. Also like those Suzy Q's. What's your poison? I bet you're a Sno Balls boy."

Chooch takes that as an insult. That's what he looks like? A goddamn *Sno Balls boy*? "I like Ding Dongs," he says.

They get to Justin's door, and Knucks slams his elbow against it. "Justy, you in there?"

No answer.

Knucks turns the knob and pushes the door open. The room's empty. A couple of folding chairs across from the bed. Swimsuit centerfolds on the wall. The lingering smell of cigarette smoke. A draft coming from the window, which is lifted enough to get some fresh air.

"No dice," Knucks says. He goes over and closes the window. "Hundred fucking times I gotta tell him the heat's going right out."

"You know of any other place they might be?" Chooch asks.

"You could check the roof. My grandson—Einstein that he is—thinks I don't know he likes to hide out up there." Knucks pauses. "I know where I know you from. The kid's not your real nephew. His old man—the one who split town all those years ago, Saverio—you used to run around with him, right?

Gilly was a pal of mine. I heard a few stories. They call you something."

"Chooch."

"Right. Chooch. Seems like the name fits. You're over here doing grunt work for this Franzone dame, huh? You gonna pick up her laundry and do her grocery shopping next?"

"I'm sorry I bothered you." Chooch walks out the way he came in.

Knucks is fast on his heels. His voice gets louder as he gives Chooch an earful on the way out: "You woke me up and disturbed my movie, so I'd say you did bother me pretty goddamn good." He slams the door behind Chooch as he crosses the threshold.

Chooch exhales in the forlorn hallway. He's always hated hallways like this in apartment buildings like this. The sad light and the sad walls and the sad doors. What Knucks said about him being Risa's errand boy, that's something he's touchy about. Maybe that's all he is. He shakes it off and goes back to the stairs.

He walks the few floors up to the roof, arriving at an emergency door at the top. There are warnings about alarms, but he doesn't heed them, not knowing much in this life, but knowing that nine times out of ten such alarms are busted.

He exits onto the roof. It's dark out now, and the roof only has one light, a floodlight right above the door he's walked through. In the shadows, he sees Fab, standing maybe a foot from the back edge, just beyond what looks like a handmade pigeon coop with a tin roof and screened-in walls. He calls out his name.

Fab turns. "Uncle Chooch?" he says.

"Your mom wants you home, kiddo," Chooch says.

"How'd you find me?"

"She figured you'd be over here. Justin's grandpa told me to check the roof."

"I don't wanna go to Aunt Gee's dinner."

Chooch shakes his head and walks closer to Fab. Doesn't seem that long ago that Fab wasn't talking and now his voice is cracking, getting deeper. "Dinner's off," Chooch says. "Why don't you back away from the edge a little?"

"Why's the dinner off?" Fab asks.

"Aunt Giulia got cold feet."

"The whole wedding's off?" Fab sounds happier.

"Yet to be seen. Come on, now. Back up from the edge. Where's your buddy, Justin? You're up here alone?"

Fab motions out toward the darkness. Chooch hadn't even noticed the almost-adjoining roof of a nearby building in the complex. Two red pinpricks of light blink on a large skeletal antenna. A shape emerges there. The other boy. Justin. "He's about to come back over," Fab says.

"What do you mean?" Chooch says.

"He jumped over there and he's coming back. He's done it three times already."

"You did it too?"

"No way."

"In the dark he's gonna do it?" Chooch moves a little closer. Figures there's maybe a six-foot gap between the buildings. "Stay over there," he calls out to Justin. "I'll tell your grandpa to come get you."

"Fuck off!" Justin yells in response, his sawed-off voice thick with hormones and recklessness. He cackles and then backpedals a few feet before bolting forward and launching himself over the crevice.

"What the hell?" Chooch says.

Justin lands like a cat on his haunches, clearing the gap by almost a foot, and then he rolls forward. He comes up laughing. "That's some Evel Knievel shit right there," he says. "Four for four."

"You stood by letting him do this?" Chooch asks Fab.

Fab shrugs. "What'd you want me to do?"

"I got superpowers, don't worry," Justin says.

"Yeah, until you're dead on the ground down there," Chooch says.

"Why don't you try to make the jump?" Justin asks, smirking.

"I don't think so." Chooch has never met Justin before tonight, but he's heard about him from Risa. He feels an intense dislike for the kid that he usually reserves for a certain kind of adult. Just what he needs. Him with gray in his hair now, twenty pounds extra on his gut, aches and pains he never had before, and a fucking snot-nosed middle schooler's giving him agita. Aside from Fab, Chooch doesn't even like to be around kids. Especially as he's gotten older. He gets filled with regret and thinks about missed opportunities from his own childhood. He doesn't have the patience to watch them disregard their futures the way he disregarded his. He should've learned another language. Should've thought about applying to CUNY. Had those collages he used to make. Gave that up. Maybe he could've done something with that, gone to art school. A lot of days, he feels swallowed by the neighborhood. A small world in this big city. What they had to do back in '86 hovering like heavy weather over their lives, so it became easier to hide, to retreat, to cower, to stay trapped. Looking at this smug little shit Justin is making him sick.

"If we don't got the dinner, why do I have to leave?" Fab asks.

"Just come on," Chooch says. He's always been nice to Fab. Always tried to treat him the way he would've treated his own son. He thinks of himself as the closest Fab will ever have to an old man. Knowing what he knows, having done what he did, Chooch feels a huge responsibility for the kid. It always flattered him that Risa insisted Fab call him Uncle Christopher. Of course, that transformed quickly into Uncle Chooch, but so be it. It hurts that he can never actually be his old man, his *stepdad* or whatever, that he can't take on that role in an official capacity. Nothing's ever changed on that front and probably never will. He's a friend to Risa, a confidant, someone she trusts to the bone, but he's come to terms with the fact there won't ever be anything else between them. She doesn't and won't think about him the way he wishes she would. She said once he's like a brother to her, the death knell to any romantic dreams he might've harbored. There won't be any big, dramatic realization that they were always meant for each other, no camera swooping down as they embrace and fall into a twirling kiss in the middle of Saint of the Narrows Street.

Fab shrugs and says, "Okay."

"Mommy wants you home for dinner," Justin says, laughing.

Fab shrinks. Looks at the ground. Obviously feels embarrassed.

Chooch shakes his head and puts his hand on Fab's shoulder.

Fab recoils. Doesn't want to be touched. Doesn't want to be treated like a loser.

Chooch gets it. He draws his hand back.

They walk to the door and head downstairs. Both are quiet the first couple of flights.

Chooch finally breaks the silence: "You okay? You seem down."

"I don't know," Fab says. "I guess."

Chooch remembers this age so well, not knowing how to say things, not really, giving the shortest answers possible.

They get to the ground floor and head back outside.

Fab's looking up, trying to see if he can catch a glimpse of Justin on the roof. Probably wondering if he'll see his dark shape skittering through the air from rooftop to rooftop.

They continue west on Cropsey. It's not far back to the block.

"Used to be a roof I'd go up on," Chooch says. "P.S. 101 on our corner, you know? I'd sit and listen to music. Watch the stars. Look down at everything. Being up there just now reminded me of it." He pauses. "I can't believe that kid was jumping. I'm not trying to be overbearing, but you've really gotta be careful around someone like that. Worst-case scenario, they get you killed. Make you do stupid things. I'm glad you had the smarts not to follow his lead. What if he'd fallen? What would you have done? Then you got that on your conscience."

"He wouldn't have done it if it was super dangerous."

"You don't think that's super dangerous? Like I said, I won't tell your mom, but I gotta give you a little lecture. You gonna retain this information?"

Fab nods.

Chooch digs around in his pocket and comes out with a folded five-dollar bill. He presses it into Fab's palm.

"What's this for?" Fab asks.

"Take it. Buy yourself the new *X-Men* comic."

7.

All these years Risa's had her freedom, and that's a good thing, but the kind of freedom she's had, she's never truly free and can't be, and now it's coming back to bite her in the ass the way she's feared since that hot August night twelve years ago. Someone got suspicious enough to ask the question. For whatever reason. And that someone's Father fucking Tim of all fucking people. "What do you mean, 'the truth about what happened to Sav'?" she asks him, mock innocence in her voice.

"Come now," Father Tim says, sitting there looking like any old chump, his voice laced with menace.

Risa pours herself some wine. Her first drink in she can't remember how long. This stuff is cheap, heavy on the sweetness, and the first few sips give her goose pimples on her arms. "What's that mean?" she asks.

He finishes his own glass of wine and grabs the jug and pours himself another one. "You don't mind, do you?" he asks.

"I don't know what you're asking me."

"I'm asking for the truth. And I'm assuming you want that truth to remain where it is. Buried."

She sits with her silence. She's wondering if this is some magic priest thing. Whether he's awful or not, maybe he's got the ability to see that someone's conscience is weighing them down, that they're carrying around a burden from something wrong they did, some sin they committed. Stare at someone like her long enough, maybe it's apparent she's got secrets. Him, with all his wicked experience in the confessional. Probably it's that she wears her guilt like perfume, and he's got a good nose. All these years, though, why now? Why the night before Giulia's wedding? What he said just then. *Remain where it is.* He's trying to blackmail her?

"You don't drink much, do you?" Father Tim asks.

Risa shakes her head, stands, and goes over to the oven. She opens the door and looks in on the lasagna. She's not sure how long exactly it's been heating up, but she thinks it needs a bit more time. Probably still cold in the center. This situation with Father Tim is at the front of her mind, but she's also getting worried that Chooch hasn't come back with Fab yet. She's trying not to panic. Knowing Chooch, he's letting Knucks talk his ear off. "The lasagna needs more time," she says.

"I'm thinking about your sister," Father Tim says. "It's a very normal thing to get cold feet the night before your wedding. I'm sure you were nervous before you married Sav."

"I don't want to talk about him," she says.

"What really happened that night twelve years ago?" Father Tim asks.

"You're asking me that like you don't know the answer," Risa says. "You know what happened. You've known all along. He left us. He went away."

"You know what it means to be a priest?" He pauses and looks around, waits for her to respond.

"Dedicating your life to the church."

"Sure. And you know what God gives men like me? A built-in lie detector. It's like playing poker. I played poker a lot back in seminary even though I wasn't supposed to. I got good." He puts his finger up to his lips. "I still love to play. Don't be a stoolie. People have their tells."

"I don't know what you're talking about."

"Okay." Father Tim raises his hands in surrender and then quickly snatches up his glass and downs a mouthful of wine. He follows it immediately with another long gulp and pours himself a third glass. "I'm in trouble, Risa, and I need money. How your situation came to my attention's not important; it just did. I know you got that significant inheritance from your in-laws. I thought my silence might be worth something."

"You're trying to blackmail me?" Risa asks, her voice trembling. "I think you should leave."

"But the lasagna," he says.

God help her, she imagines a scenario where what she did to Sav, she does to Father Tim. Gets her replacement cast-iron pan and clocks him across the head with it and then deals with the fallout.

She scoots her chair and stands again and races back to the oven, retrieving an oven mitt from a nearby drawer. She's taking this thing out now whether it's hot enough or not. She busies herself by setting the lasagna tray on the stove and unfolding a couple of kitchen towels in the center of the table. She gets plates and forks and napkins. Father Tim watches her. She brings the tray to the table and sets it on the towels. The lasagna is steaming, its edges crispy, the sauce bubbling at the corners, the mozzarella on top browned, almost blackened. She realizes she forgot a knife to cut it and a spatula to serve it. She goes back for both and then returns to the lasagna, cutting it rather haphazardly, using the spatula to take out a sloppy piece, putting it on a plate and shoving it toward Father Tim, the mozzarella and ricotta melting from between the layers. "There," she says. "Eat and get out."

He holds it up in front of his face and wafts his hands over it.

She sits down across from him.

He pours more wine for them both, even though her glass is half full. He lifts his glass. "To the cook," he says. He clinks her glass and drinks.

She sips from hers.

"I suppose I should also say a blessing," Father Tim continues. "Bless us, O Lord, for these thy gifts . . ." He drifts off before completing the prayer. "You know what my friend Gus in the orphanage used to say? 'Rub-a-dub-dub, thanks for the grub!'" He smiles drunkenly and digs in. He eats like a man possessed, forking large portions of the lasagna up to his mouth and moaning with each bite.

Risa gulps down more wine.

"You're not hungry?" Father Tim asks, his mouth full as he talks.

"No," she says. She wants so badly for this to be over. It feels like a nightmare. She's wondering how she can get out of it. Just continue with the denial? Give him money and hope he stays quiet? That's an admission of guilt. Plus, she's read enough stories to know blackmail is never-ending.

8.

Fab's been asking more and more about his dad lately, getting curious, and Uncle Chooch is the only one who sometimes seems like he might be willing to reminisce, to let his guard down enough to tell a story, to forgive the bastard for splitting for just a few measly minutes.

As they cut through the Cavallaro schoolyard on the way to Bath Avenue, Fab turns to Uncle Chooch and asks, "You have anything of my dad's you can give me?"

"I don't," Uncle Chooch says. "Ain't even got pictures anymore."

"That's okay. I thought maybe. Can I ask you something about him?"

"I don't know if that's a great idea. You know it upsets your mom."

"Yeah, right."

Uncle Chooch stops in his tracks and says, "I guess we've got a few minutes. Your mother's occupied with Father Tim."

"Father Tim?" Fab says. "Why's he over?" Fab sees Father Tim around the halls at school and in church. Always thinks he moves like a snake. He hides a lot of meanness behind how handsome he is. Has a real vicious streak. Fab has heard stories from older people, his mom and aunt and others, about priests and nuns hitting kids in school back in the day, but that's mostly a thing of the past. Except for the time he saw Father Tim take a yardstick to Gianluca Mannino's backside for stealing a package of unconsecrated Communion wafers. Sick fuck took pleasure in it. Creeps Fab out bad to imagine the guy chilling in his apartment.

"Probably hunting a meal," Uncle Chooch says. He takes a beat, scratches his chin, and then sits down on a bench across from the rusted, rickety jungle gym.

Fab sits next to him, space for another person between them. An overflowing garbage can nearby perfumes the air with the smell of bagged dog shit.

Uncle Chooch continues: "How about asking me one thing about your old man? We'll keep it between us, okay? I'll try my best to give you a good answer."

Fab thinks hard about it. He's never really questioned anything about the story surrounding his dad's disappearance. Some information would be nice. He'd eavesdropped on a few conversations along the way. Heard neighborhood gossip. Saw some wedding photos and snapshots from when he was a baby, but his mother had cut his old man out of most of the pictures. Without his dad was just the way he'd grown up. "You think he loved me?" Fab asks. "Did he run off because he didn't want a kid?"

The corners of Uncle Chooch's mouth turn up into

something resembling a strained grin. He looks almost like he's going to cry. "He loved you. He didn't leave because of you. He had his own thing he was chasing. The block was too small."

Something about the way Uncle Chooch says it gives Fab pause. There's a lie in there, but he doesn't know exactly what it is. Probably the lie is just that his old man loved him. Uncle Chooch is likely holding back because he's continuing to try to protect Fab from the fact that having a kid is exactly why his dad ran away. Guy like that doesn't want a kid dragging him down.

For the first time, Fab has a wild thought. He's of the age where his brain's working different ways. What if his old man had to get out of town for another reason? Trouble. Same as with Uncle Roberto. Someone wanted him dead—he stole money or something else—and there's no way he could show his face around here without getting killed. What happened with his brother only cemented that. But why not be in touch? Why not send a postcard from a place he no longer was?

"We won't count that as a question," Uncle Chooch says. "I'll give you one more."

Fab scrambles to think of something good to ask. He can ask if he's like his old man. People say he looks like him, but is he *like* him? He can ask about the music his father loved—he knows about a few of the bands because Uncle Chooch loves the same stuff. He can ask what his father and mother were like together. He can't picture it. He can't picture his mother with any guy. "You promise you'll tell the truth?" he asks Uncle Chooch.

Uncle Chooch nods. "Sure thing, pal."

Fab shoots from the hip as the questions teletype through

his mind: "Do you know where he is? Have you been in contact with him? Is there a way to find him?"

Uncle Chooch hesitates, lets out a sigh. "Nope, nope, and nope. I'm sorry."

Fab feels stupid for wasting his question on something he already knew the answer to.

Uncle Chooch reaches over and musses his hair.

Fab hates when people touch his head. He draws back, trying to escape Uncle Chooch's hand.

"Too old for that now, I guess," Uncle Chooch says. "Let's get you home."

9.

Giulia leaves Lola's after Lola surprisingly agrees to come to the wedding, saying she'll stay for the cocktail hour and see how it goes. It's tempting to spend the night in Marco's room, but Giulia can't do it. She's not ready for that level of aloneness confronting the past—lying in Marco's bed, listening and watching for ghosts.

She's made up her mind about some things, but she's not ready to return to Stan, so she heads to Risa's. She's ready to unleash a million emotions onto her sister—try to explain why she snuck out the window, what going to see Lola and standing in Marco's old room did to her—but instead Risa lets her into the apartment and leads her to the table, and Giulia's totally thrown off by the unsettling scene she's stumbled into.

Weirdo Father Tim is there, and he's drunk. He's out of costume and his cheeks are flushed. A tray of lasagna is in the center of the table. Father Tim's plate is wiped clean. Risa seems to be drinking, too. There's a half-full glass of wine in front of her, and her teeth are stained purple. Giulia can't remember the last time she saw Risa have a drink. Normally, she'd think it's maybe a good thing—Risa finally taking an opportunity to unwind—but instead it looks like she's in a situation she doesn't want to be in and is only drinking to calm her nerves.

"There she is," Father Tim says. "The lady of the hour."

"What's going on here?" Giulia asks in a halting voice.

"Well, Risa heated up a nice lasagna and we're drinking some wine in lieu of your canceled dinner."

Giulia ignores Father Tim and turns to Risa. "You okay?" she asks.

"I don't know," Risa says.

Giulia pulls Risa into the living room, leans in close, and whispers to her: "What's going on?"

Risa's shaken. She speaks so low that she's almost only mouthing the words. "He's asking about Sav."

"Asking what exactly about Sav?"

"Saying he knows something and that he wants money to keep quiet."

Giulia nods, takes a few deep breaths, and pats Risa on the shoulder. She goes back into the dining room and approaches Father Tim with fire in her eyes. "Get the fuck out of here, would you?" she says, her voice thrumming with anger and frustration. "Night before my wedding, you come around to upset my sister? I don't know what you got in your head, I don't know who put it there, and I don't know what your endgame is, but you're gonna go home to your little rectory and you're gonna take your big ideas with you. Okay?"

"Touchy," Father Tim says, giving the impression of an

unspooled ribbon in both manner and speech. "So, Giulia, how are you feeling about the big day tomorrow? Better? Getting over the cold feet?" He pauses. "You still studying your Italian? I remember hearing about that. Bevi un bicchiere di vino con noi. Per favore. We'll talk this all out. Don't want you to wind up in the same position as Risa here."

"Vaffanculo. Got that one down. And I know all about you. Betraying people's trust in the AA meetings you run. Using information that's shared privately against them. Angel Roncagliolo told me your MO. You got no morals, *Father*. I bet you heard someone talking trash about Risa, and you latched on to it like the leech you are."

"Pete Parisi told me what he heard."

"*Religious Pete*?" Giulia says, letting out a nervous laugh. Her eyes dart to Risa, who shuffles back into the room, anxiety defining her posture. Could he have heard something, been eavesdropping, hearing their voices drift up through vents or pipes? "He's a nut. He fell off the wagon and he's drying out upstate."

"Pete has a lot of problems," Risa adds.

"All I'm saying is I think you can help me with the trouble I'm in," Father Tim says to Risa. "My silence is worth something."

"What is it, *Father*?" Giulia asks, moving closer to him. "What'd Religious Pete tell you? What kind of trouble you in?"

"I simply asked Risa what the truth is," Father Tim says, looking down at the table, tapping his fingers against the tines of his fork.

"You know something, or you don't?"

"He said something about playing poker," Risa says.

"I'm beginning to understand," Giulia says. "You owe on some gambling debt, Pete insinuated something somewhere along the way, and you figured Risa for a sucker. Figured she's got money from Frank and Arlene you can tap into, soft as she is. You're full of shit." Giulia goes into the kitchen, where she gets a coffee mug out of the cabinet, and then comes back to the table, filling it to the brim with wine. It's the final pour from the large jug of cheap red, one she'd left behind when she lived here. She takes a seat. She's not going to let this unravel. She's not going to let this fucking shangad priest break Risa and bring the whole thing crashing down. She'll be strong. She's got to be. She'll chase him away like a scared bird.

"I like a woman who drinks wine from a coffee mug," Father Tim says. He's trying to mask the desperation, but it's bleeding through now. "Let's calm our jets and reevaluate the situation."

Risa's new approach seems to be to ignore his presence. "Are you hungry?" she asks Giulia. "You want a plate? I can reheat the lasagna."

"No, thanks," Giulia says. "Couldn't eat if I wanted to. Where's Fab?" Looking around, hoping he's not holed up in the bedroom, having to endure this Father Tim bullshit. Last thing they need is for Fab to get suspicious and start wondering if the truth's not actually the truth.

"Christopher went to find him. Probably at his friend Justin's."

"He was avoiding the dinner too, huh?"

"You're feeling better about things?" Risa asks.

Giulia nods, focusing in on Risa for a moment, trying to forget about Father Tim. "I went to see Lola. I don't know why.

But it helped. I can't do the dinner, but I'm gonna go through with the wedding."

"You should call Stan. He's probably a nervous wreck."

"Let him sweat a little."

Father Tim butts in: "Nice to witness such a bond between sisters. Not much you two keep from each other, is there?"

"Fuck off," Giulia says.

The front door opens, and Fab comes charging in, followed by Chooch.

Risa stands. "You were at Justin's?" she asks.

"Yeah," Fab says.

"I've asked you not to go there. You should've come straight home from school. We had the dinner." She pauses, sniffs around him. "Were you smoking?"

"Knucks was smoking. Dinner's off is what Uncle Chooch said. Why you wearing so much makeup?"

"Forget my makeup. You didn't know the dinner was canceled. Say hello to Aunt Giulia."

Fab moves over in front of Giulia and hugs her. "You're not getting married?" he asks.

"I still am," Giulia says.

His expression goes from cheerful to downcast on a dime. "Oh."

"You're disappointed?"

"I don't want to get dressed up."

"Me either. You should see me trying to get into my stupid dress."

"Say hi to Father Tim too, I guess," Risa says. Risa, always going through the motions of respectability. What they should really do with this drunk priest is dump him out in the gutter.

Fab gives a slight nod and then goes over to greet Father Tim. He sticks out his hand, and Father Tim shakes it heartily and then acts as if Fab's grip has wounded him. "I'm used to all these limp handshakes," Father Tim says. "You shake like a man."

Fab isn't charmed. Giulia's noticed that he seems to hate nothing more than when people treat him, at twelve, as they might've treated him at six or seven.

Chooch joins them at the table. He says hi to Giulia and gives Father Tim a wary look.

Fab takes off his coat and hat and stuffs them in the hall closet. He stands off to the side, bored, irritated.

"Thanks for going to get him," Risa says.

"No problem at all," Chooch says. "I think he's nervous about having a job at the ceremony tomorrow."

"You want some food? I can reheat the lasagna."

"Sure, thanks, but no need to put it in the oven. I don't mind if it's a little cold."

Risa gets Chooch a fork and plate and then cuts him a big piece of lasagna. "You want water? Ginger ale?"

"Ginger ale. Thanks."

She grabs a can from the fridge and brings it back to him. The can's beaded with condensation. He digs into the lasagna.

Father Tim finishes his glass of wine and goes to pour another, nearly flopping out of his chair as he reaches for the empty jug.

Giulia notices Chooch becoming aware that Father Tim's got one hell of a load on, that something's not right in this situation. She'd like to commiserate privately with Chooch but doesn't want to make a scene by pulling him aside.

Risa sips her wine. Another thing Giulia witnesses Chooch trying to make sense of.

"Christopher Gardini," Father Tim says, his boozy breath fuming across the table. "I know your mother very well, but I don't really know you the way I'd like to. Chooch." His usual plaintive homily tone having totally given way to this loudly performative grandiloquence. Really drawing out the *oo* in *Chooch*. Sounding vicious.

Chooch doesn't respond. He stares down at his plate as he chews.

Father Tim continues: "Tell me something about yourself. Yankees or Mets? Giants or Jets? Do you read Shakespeare in your spare time? Play checkers with your mother? How's that office you still work at after all these years? A *file clerk*, that's your job, correct? Not exactly the stuff that dreams are made of."

Giulia sees in Chooch's eyes that he's immediately filled with rage by Father Tim giving him shit.

"Man, go to hell," Chooch says.

Risa, sensing things are coming to some kind of head, stands and leads Fab to the bedroom. "Go into the bedroom and shut the door," she says. "Okay? Father Tim's had a little too much to drink."

"I'm only asking what the truth is about Sav," Father Tim blurts out.

"What about my father?" Fab asks.

Father Tim attempts to stand, knocking his knees into the underside of the table, rattling everyone's wine, before settling into an unsteady stance. "I'm trying to help you and get help for myself," he says, slurring his words. "Risa obviously has something she wants to get off her chest. Confession's cleansing. And I could use some minor support in trying to wrangle out of this debt I've managed to accrue. A small price to pay. You scratch my back, et cetera."

"What truth?" Fab asks.

"He's very drunk," Risa says, pushing Fab into the bedroom and shutting the door. Then to Giulia and Chooch: "He was drinking from a flask when he first got here."

Giulia's aware that whatever Father Tim thinks he knows, whatever exactly he heard from Religious Pete, is incomplete. A fragment of some overheard conversation that made Religious Pete's ears perk up. The fuck. Nothing better to do than to nose in and then go acting tortured to Father Tim.

"What's he talking about?" Chooch asks.

"He thinks Risa's not telling the truth about Sav," Giulia says. "He says Religious Pete told him something. He's lost it."

"Something what?"

"Even if you did something to protect yourself, even if you're in the right, a mortal sin's still a mortal sin," Father Tim says. He takes out his flask and tries to drink from it, but it's empty. "My silence on the matter is valuable."

"There are no mortal sins in this apartment," Risa says, calmly now, standing, wiping crumbs from the table with a napkin to busy herself and avoid eye contact with him. "I need you to leave, Father. Giulia's getting married tomorrow, and we have a lot we need to do."

"I won't be so kind as my sister," Giulia says. "Get the fuck out of here, you drunk asshole. You've gotta be kidding with this mortal sin shit."

Father Tim takes a deep breath and exhales. "We'll talk

again," he says. He makes a quick turn on his heels, agitated, seeming like he's heading for the front door but instead flopping forward onto his hands and knees on the floor.

"Priest down," Giulia says, lifting the mug of wine to her lips.

10.

Chooch pushes back from the table and goes over to Father Tim, who's in a crawling position on the floor. The guy's maybe four feet from where Sav went down that summer night twelve years ago. His empty flask is beside him.

Giulia rushes to the cabinet in the kitchen, opens it, and feels around inside behind some pots and pans. She finds a stashed pint of whiskey. "Give him some more booze," she says, unscrewing the cap. "Let him fucking choke on it." She rushes over to Father Tim and splashes some of the whiskey on his head, as if she's anointing him.

"Stop," he says.

"You fucking lush," she says. "You're an embarrassment. Who's gonna listen to anything you say?"

"Guys like you are the reason I stopped going to church," Chooch says. "Coming around here with some bullshit accusations. I'm gonna tell my mother about your little show tonight. She'll report you to Monsignor Terrone."

"Oh no, he's gonna run and tattle to his mother," Father Tim says.

Fab pokes his head out of the bedroom, trying to understand the unfolding drama. In a serious mom voice, Risa demands he go back into the bedroom. He hesitates but obeys.

Chooch gets Father Tim to his feet and then begins to move him toward the front door as if he's a bouncer tossing someone who's been eighty-sixed. He's never thought of himself as tough, but he feels that way now.

"What's your relationship with Risa, Chooch?" Father Tim asks. "You were involved, weren't you?" Spitting the questions.

Risa has her face in her hands.

Chooch knows what she's thinking. This is the way it ends. What happened with Roberto was a false start, and now Father Tim's come to complete the job. It'll never end. Nothing stays buried. Even if no one takes Father Tim seriously or if he drops out of the picture, how do they know he doesn't say something to someone else? Soon enough, questions lead to that still-deserted house in Sullivan County, that grave in the woods. He has Father Tim by the arm and pushes him the last few steps down the hallway to the door.

Risa throws his coat after him. Chooch picks it up and stuffs the coat into the crook of Father Tim's arm.

"Ten thousand dollars is all I need," Father Tim says, his blustery voice gone broken.

With his free hand, Chooch pulls the door in and then opens the storm door and shoves Father Tim into the front yard.

Father Tim stumbles and almost falls again but regains his balance and attempts to regain his composure. He has trouble putting on his coat, getting his right arm stuck somehow but finally forcing his hand out through the sleeve and then running through the routine with the other arm. "You think you can treat a man of the cloth like this?" he asks.

"Time to go home now, Father," Chooch says, letting the storm door rattle shut and closing the interior door.

They gather back around the table and speak in whispers so Fab can't hear them. Risa turns on the radio for a little noise to drown out the quiet.

"What're we gonna do?" Risa asks.

"Maybe he'll get hit by a car," Giulia says.

"We can't wish that."

"Blackmailed by a priest. What a world."

Risa shushes her. "Fab's right there. Please." She pauses. "What could Pete have told him?"

"People talk. They say crazy things all the time."

"You've heard these things?"

"I hear all kinds of stuff at the bar."

"Like?"

"Like one or two crazy fucks have suggested that you and Chooch have had a thing all this time and that you banded together to get rid of Sav. Maybe Religious Pete heard something like that and took it as gospel. Sandra Carbonari was a great one for talking before she split."

"Come on," Risa says.

"That's why he said what he said at the end?" Chooch asks.

Giulia shrugs. "I'm just guessing."

"You're drinking?" Chooch asks Risa out of nowhere.

"I didn't know what else to do," Risa says.

"It's a relief, frankly," Giulia says, reaching out and tapping her mug against Risa's glass. "I've been wanting my sister as a drinking partner."

Risa asks, "You think he'll come back?"

"Sweetie, I think he'll go to the rectory with his tail between his legs. Someone's after him for money he owes, maybe he winds up with his legs busted or worse come morning." Giulia takes one last long slug of wine and then looks down into the white ceramic mug. Chooch notices how the wine feathers the rim in faded brushstrokes, smudged brightly over deep-wrought coffee stains.

"What if he starts talking and people believe him?"

The bedroom door opens, and Fab's standing there.

They fall to a hush.

"He's gone?" Fab asks.

"Sure is," Giulia says.

"I didn't know priests got drunk."

"Oh boy, do they."

Fab joins them at the table. "What was he saying about my father?"

"Nothing," Risa says, her voice hard.

Chooch can see how dissatisfied Fab is by this response. He thinks maybe he should step up, take the load off Risa a little. He works through a Rolodex of lies in his mind. What could he possibly say that would make sense and satisfy Fab? Something else to keep track of. Probably ill-advised to just pull something out of the air. "Everyone knows Father Tim grew up in an orphanage, but what they don't know is that, before he was a priest, he was in a mental institution. Had electric shock therapy. You know what that is, Fab? Something they do to people whose minds aren't in such good shape."

Giulia looks at him and almost smiles.

"But why would he talk about my father?" Fab asks.

"He knew your father," Chooch says. "He's been around a while now. He's a disturbed individual. People with the problems he's got, they imagine stuff that didn't really happen."

Risa's looking down at the tabletop.

Fab's sitting there, obviously trying to compute this information. "So, what's he imagining about my father?" he asks finally.

"We don't even know," Chooch says. "Mind like that, you can't make sense of. Nothing clear. Nothing specific." He's digging in deeper and deeper, picturing Fab at school, telling his classmates that Father Tim's a nutcase who got electric shock therapy and was rotten drunk in their apartment. So be it.

"I think I'm gonna be sick," Risa says.

"You okay, Ma?" Fab asks. He's straying from her—trying to be tough like he's gotta be to survive in school and out on the streets, trying to grow up—but that little-kid love is still there. It's obvious he hates to see her like this. Chooch wonders if, one day, the kid's gonna find out the truth, either on his own or from Risa telling him. He knows Risa can hold on to things tight. Maybe on her deathbed, she holds Fab's hand and finally lets it all out. She lives a nice long life, say to eighty-five or ninety, that's many years down the road, in the fucking 2040s or thereabouts. Fab'll be older at that point than they all are now. The future seems impossible some nights.

Risa reaches across and puts her hand over Fab's. "I'm okay, sweetie. Thank you."

"I've got an idea," Giulia says, putting her hands flat on the table, trying to lighten up the mood. She's still got that pint of whiskey. She didn't pour it all on Father Tim. She takes a pull.

"What?" Risa asks.

"Since you're my maid of honor—*matron* of honor—I think you and me should go to the Crisscross for a little bachelorette party. Girls' night out. Have a few drinks. Talk. Shake off all this shit. What do you say?"

"I don't think so. I don't go to bars."

"Come on. It's special. A onetime thing. I had a crisis tonight and then Father Tim threw a wrench into everything, but I'm getting married tomorrow. Let's celebrate."

"What about Fab?"

"Chooch, maybe you wouldn't mind sitting with Fab for a few hours?" Giulia asks. "I'll call Stan—I'll let him know we're still on—but that I need some time with my sister."

"I don't mind," Chooch says. "You two stay out as long as you want. I can just sleep on the couch here tonight."

"We won't be out that late," Risa says.

"Really," Chooch says. "Whatever. We'll be good. Don't worry." He doesn't mind at all, that's not a lie. The idea of Risa drinking with Giulia freaks him out a little, but maybe it's what she needs. And it's Giulia's big weekend, so he's sure not going to horn in and say it sounds like a dumb idea.

"It's settled," Giulia says. She stands and hustles over to the phone, taking the receiver off the hook and keeping her finger perched over the dial. "I'm gonna call Stan real quick. Put on your coat. Kiss Fab good night. I don't want you second-guessing yourself."

"What if Father Tim comes back?" Risa asks.

"He's not coming back," Giulia says. "He does, Chooch'll chase him off."

Giulia uses her pinky to pull the numbers on the rotary dial, her nail clanking against the finger stop on each of the seven numbers. The slow sound fills the room.

Chooch listens in on Giulia's conversation with Stan while he finishes eating his lasagna. The guy's simultaneously upset and relieved—Chooch can hear pretty much everything he's saying because he's yelling. Giulia talks him down with tender declarations. Says what she went through is normal—a little touch of panic—but she's over it. The dinner's no major loss, and she's going to do a minibachelorette thing with Risa. Eventually, Stan calms down and buys into the plan. The wedding's on, that's all that matters. He tells her not to drink too much, he doesn't want her hungover on their wedding day, and she says it's club soda all the way tonight, as she finishes the pint of whiskey and tosses it in the trash. She hangs up the phone and disappears into the bathroom.

Risa returns to the closet and puts on her coat. She kneels by Fab. "You don't mind me going out for a bit?" she asks. "I need some time with Aunt Giulia."

He shrugs. "I'm just glad I don't have to go to the dinner," he says. "I'm sorry about Justin's."

"It's okay, sweetie. Uncle Christopher will be here. Any emergencies, we're right at the Crisscross." Risa kisses him on the head. "Are you hungry?"

Another shrug from Fab. "Not really."

"I'll make you a plate, leave it in the fridge. You can heat it up if you want."

Soon enough, Giulia's out of the bathroom, and she and

Risa are leaving the apartment in a frenzy, as if they're late for a Broadway show. Risa thanks Chooch again for watching Fab. He waves her off. Giulia reiterates that it means a lot, the night before her wedding like this, to get her sister to herself for a few hours. No problem, he insists, he's happy to help. Risa reminds him they'll be right at the Crisscross if there are any emergencies or if Father Tim shows back up. He nods. He says if Father Tim shows up, he might have to go all Daniel LaRusso on him, give him a crane kick to the face.

And just like that, they're gone. The Taverna sisters out on the town. He tries to think if he's ever been in the apartment without Risa being there. Maybe a few times when Sav was still around, and they were hanging out while Risa was at the store or church.

Fab disappears into the bedroom without saying anything.

Chooch follows him. A curtain is drawn down the center of the room. He enters Risa's side, her stuff compressed there—bed, table, rocking chair, a stand with another phone—and pulls back the curtain to find Fab on his side, sprawled on his twin bed with his hands behind his head. Chooch sits on the cast-iron radiator by the window. It's warm, the radiator. Feels nice on the backs of his thighs. Fab's side of the room is spare. A few milk crates full of clothes. A small dresser. The five-dollar bill Chooch gave him pinned down under the edge of the lamp atop the dresser. Stacks of Mylar-covered comic books. Baseball cards. Stray candy wrappers on the floor.

"I'm gonna go watch a movie in the living room," Chooch says. "You should eat. The lasagna's good."

"I'm not hungry," Fab says.

"You want to watch the movie with me, come on out. I'm not sure what's on. Channel eleven's always got something."

Fab nods against the pillow.

Chooch goes to the living room and settles on the couch. He finds the remote nestled between the cushions and turns on the television. He clicks around until he comes to whatever movie's playing on channel 11. Nothing that seems very good. He only wants something to look at. He's having a hard time picturing Risa in the Crisscross. It'd be like seeing a nun on a bench in a needle park or a spiffed-up movie star at L'Amour back in the day. People in places they don't belong. He can't fixate. He thinks about Father Tim instead. Hopes the bastard passes out on the sidewalk outside the rectory, wakes up in a puddle of puke, and forgets whatever the fuck it is he thinks he knows.

11.

Risa can't recall if she's ever actually stepped foot in the Crisscross Cocktail Lounge. Maybe once or twice, when she was pregnant with Fab, she poked her head in the door if she was searching for Sav. Aside from that, it's always been a place that's so close and yet so incredibly distant, a place that she walks past daily and has never felt much of a sense of mystery about. It represents, to her, what was instead of what might've been. She knows Giulia started frequenting the place in high school with Marco, stopped in almost every night when she lived on the block, and still hangs out here a good amount. She supposes enough time has passed that she can put her grudge against the bar to rest. Besides, Sandra Carbonari finally left the neighborhood a couple of years before—bloated, her hair thinning, overcome by defeat—so there's no chance of running into her.

The Crisscross has what strikes Risa as a peculiar layout,

though she hasn't been in many bars in her life to compare it to. Bars have never interested her. This one doesn't interest her now. It smells like an old coin. Neon lights cast a sad glow over an assembly of regulars hunched on stools at the bar. Five people. Three men, two women. A few of them old-timers, a couple a little younger. The owner, Widow Marie, is leaning against the register. Risa starts thinking about how Chooch shared the news to Jimmy Tomasullo that Roberto had returned right in here, at Giulia's urging, something he might not have done if Risa hadn't asked him for help, and she senses the ghost of Jimmy's rage in the air. She notices a picture of Marco LaRocca—gritty with age, the frame dusty, the glass cracked in one corner and smudged with fingerprints—hanging behind the bar. She imagines that Giulia just comes in a lot of times and stares at Marco, gets misty and nostalgic.

"I thought you and Stan were getting hitched," Widow Marie says to Giulia.

A guy at the bar—maybe mid-forties, a wool hat pulled low over his forehead, his hangdog eyes crusty, his lips chapped—turns and says, "And none of us invited."

"I was," Giulia says. "I *am*. Tomorrow. I'm sorry about not inviting you guys. It's a small thing. No bar friends allowed."

"It's okay," he says. "I understand. I've got a small thing." He cackles, his throaty laugh making it sound like he gargles with gravel.

Giulia nods as if she's walked straight into a trap. "Anyhow, everybody, this is my sister, Risa. Risa, this is everybody." She points as she goes around and gives their names: "Widow Marie, Cursed Roy with the small thing, All Bad Allie, Jane the Stain, Cyclone Archie, and George." None of them seem to fit their handles. The regulars all groan in response, except Jane the Stain, who flutters a soft hello.

"The famous Risa Franzone," Widow Marie says.

Risa's not sure what to say. An angry voice runs through her head: *Yeah, let's get it over with. My husband used to come in here and cheat on me with Sandra. Yeah, he disappeared. No, no one's heard from him. Yeah, twelve years later, I'm still acting like he's coming back.* The whole routine. Instead, Risa smiles and says, "It's nice to meet you."

"What do you want to drink?"

"I'm fine."

"Come on, have a drink with me," Giulia says.

Widow Marie is already in the process of getting Giulia's drinks—she doesn't even need to order. She sets them on the bar.

"My sister will have the same as me," Giulia says to Widow Marie.

Risa doesn't put up a fight. Under normal circumstances, she'd insist that she doesn't want anything, that she doesn't really drink, but not tonight. After all that's happened with Father Tim and in celebration of Giulia's impending nuptials—with the help of the wine she's already had—she decides to go with the flow. Her whole life, she's tried to do the right thing in every situation. And look where it's gotten her. Maybe she needs to do the wrong thing more often.

Widow Marie retrieves a second beer and pours another shot of whiskey. "Where's your buddy Chooch?" she asks. "Last time I saw him, he was getting Crazy Jimmy Tomasullo all fired up about Roberto. Next thing you know, the fucking maniac's gunned down every Franzone in the neighborhood that's not you."

"It wasn't like that," Risa says, giving Giulia a quick look like she's not prepared for this and doesn't want to deal with it.

"Hey, I keep my nose in my own business."

Giulia pays. They carry their drinks over to a booth in the back and sit down.

"I know this place is a hellhole," Giulia says, "but it's my hellhole. Forget Marie. Don't worry about her. She's all talk. I walk in here, and—I don't know—a feeling of contentment comes over me. Probably what you feel in church." She pauses. "Sorry—I shouldn't bring up church. Fucking Father Tim. What balls."

"What're we gonna do?" Risa asks, keeping her voice down. "I don't give him money, maybe he starts talking to others. The way it looks—me getting everything after Frank, Arlene, and Roberto died—isn't good. Never has been. Not gonna be a stretch for people to say I'm some kind of conniving monster, especially if it's a priest doing the insinuating."

"He's a degenerate, and he's off the rails. If he's in deep gambling, it's probably Charlie Cee and Carmine Perasso he owes. Guy might be done for." She pauses. "Sandra's talk never swayed anyone, like I said. Of course, Sandra's Sandra. I tell you about the time I got in a fight with her in here? Some hair-pulling was involved. I won."

"I didn't know about that."

"Defending your honor. She pulled a razor on me, but she was too drunk to use it. Not like one of those old-style razors with a handle they use in barbershops. Just a flimsy little blade. Pinched it between her thumb and index finger and swiped at my throat."

"You'd think you'd tell me something like that."

"Fab was maybe three at the time. Didn't want to upset the works."

"Maybe I'll just report Father Tim to Monsignor Terrone. Maybe he'll get reassigned and that'll be the end of it. The monsignor's a good man. He'll believe me."

"I say we kill him," Giulia says, the edges of her lips turning up into a smile. "Poison a tray of ziti. Slip into the rectory and press a pillow over his face while he sleeps. He wants to play hardball, let's teach him what the Taverna sisters are made of. It goes well, we can start a little business. Vengeance against bad men. A whisper network of women will keep our secrets."

"We shouldn't joke like that," Risa says.

"You think I'm kidding?"

"Let's forget this right now and focus on the wedding, okay? This is a special night. Your big day's tomorrow. You're happy?"

"I'm happy. You're really gonna drink with me?"

"Why not?"

They clink glasses and put back their shots. The whiskey burns going down, and Risa feels like she might vomit. She follows Giulia's lead and chases the shot with a gulp of beer. Crazy to think it, but it's the first time she's ever had liquor or beer. Everything else has been wine or wine coolers. She doesn't feel like she's been missing much. The whiskey's warmed her up, sure, but it's also sent a wave of nausea through her and made her skin under her clothes all goose pimply.

"I can't believe I'm drinking with you," Giulia says, pulling her hair out of her face, drawing it back in a ponytail, and using a scrunchie from her wrist to keep it in place. She takes out her cigarettes and lights one, blowing a steam of smoke away from Risa. "Did I tell you how nice you look? Thanks for getting all dolled up for my dinner. I'm sorry I canceled. Was everyone upset?"

"Not upset. I think a little worried about you."

"I was a little worried about me, too. But whatever." She takes a pull from her beer. "Can I make a recommendation?"

"Sure?" Risa says, her voice rimmed with uncertainty.

Giulia ashes in a glass ashtray on the table between them. "I think you need to get some action. It's been too long. Hook up with someone for kicks. The options in here are, uh, limited, to put it kindly, but there's plenty of souls out on the sidewalk."

"I'm okay."

"Just an idea. You're drinking now. Might as well take it to the next step. Fully let loose."

"I don't think so," Risa says, sipping from her own beer, starting to feel the effects of the whiskey. Imagine her, going out and picking a stranger up for anonymous sex. She's thinking of *Looking for Mr. Goodbar*. She read the book and saw the movie. Look how that turned out. Anyhow, she doesn't want or need anything like that. She looks around the bar. It's not bad being here with her sister. She thought she'd feel worse. She's only a one-minute walk away from Fab, but she does feel like she's out on the town.

Fab.

She's been hiding the truth from him in the name of protection. Worried about the pitfalls and disasters that could arise from her coming clean or even hinting in the general direction of the truth. Losing track of how to best make him feel like he hadn't been abandoned or cheated. She's relied on silence, on keeping him in the dark. She wonders if a quiet lie is worse than a loud one in many ways. Eventually, Fab's questions will boil out of him. She can already see the angst creeping in. What happened with Father Tim is fuel. It's got Fab's wheels spinning. She can sense that.

Only recently has Risa been coming to terms with the fact that this kind of secret-keeping is in her blood. In her and Giulia's family tree, there were all sorts of lies that'd been covered up and never spoken of again. Apparently, one of their great-grandfathers, Alfredo Taverna, had another wife back in Italy before he came to America and met Nana Sabina. There was an uncle, Pasquale, also in Italy, who was a close confidant and conspirator of Mussolini's. When she and Giulia were little—Risa didn't discover this until she was in her early twenties, and Giulia still doesn't know—it turns out their father had a mistress for several years. A woman he'd take to clubs in the city while their mother raised them. The news was broken to her unemotionally by her mother, and Risa's never repeated it or asked her mother why she'd stayed with him after that. She would've known the answer anyhow. Divorce wasn't something her mother would've ever considered. The history of his transgression will die with them. Risa had learned, quietly, to forgive her father and to forget he'd ever had that affair.

But she needs to figure out a new way of dealing with this all when it comes to Fab. Those old ways lead to worse things. He's not going to be a little kid much longer. Maybe isn't now. Secrets and lies and silence won't hold. The foundation will start to rot if it hasn't already. She needs to make this up to him. She needs him to know that what happened was an accident but that there probably wasn't any other way, not if they wanted to be free of the violence and ugliness Sav brought into their lives. *Fab, I'm sorry*, she's thinking. *Everything's for you.* She'll give herself some time before she talks to him—really *talks* to him—but she promises herself she'll do it. How can she ever say some of what she'll need to say? How they washed away all that blood. Sav's grave in the moonlight. The dirt Fab ate.

She takes another pull of her beer and watches as Giulia makes an accordion of her cigarette in the ashtray. She thinks of Father Tim out on the sidewalk, hauling around his ideas about her, and pathetic Religious Pete, who wore an aggressive cross around his neck and brought her those nice books once, and what he could've possibly overheard. She looks for answers in the smoke ribboning up between them but only sees more question marks.

12.

Fab's still in bed. Restless. Seems like a couple of hours have passed. He finally gets up to pee. On his way out of the bathroom, he notices that Uncle Chooch is asleep on the couch in the living room, the TV playing some dumb movie. He goes into the kitchen and gets a drink of water straight from the tap. He can't remember the last time his mother went out for anything other than shopping or school or church. One strange thing after the next today. The apartment's quiet except for the noise from the TV and Uncle Chooch's snoring.

He has so many questions and nobody's got answers. They duck him. It's like watching one of those boxing matches where the fighters just dance around, evade each other. Why's everything gotta be so secretive? Why's he gotta get shut out? He just wants someone to tell him something real, even if it's bad.

Back in his bedroom, he sits on the floor up against the bed and flips through the latest *X-Men* he has. He tosses it aside.

Uncle Chooch gave him money to get the most recent issue, but he's going to get something else, something more dangerous, more grown-up. He picks up a copy of the newest issue of *The Punisher* and tries that. He's having trouble focusing. He's thinking about Justin jumping between roofs. He's thinking about how he didn't have the courage to do it. He wonders if he'll ever have the courage to do anything risky. Then his thoughts shift to Aunt Giulia getting married tomorrow. He wonders if she and Stan will have kids right away. That'd make him the baby's cousin. He hates the word *cousin.*

A knock on the nearby window stuns him. He can't see anything. He stands and moves there, his knees pressed against the radiator, cupping his hand to the glass, looking out at the dark backyard through the glass and the bars. His mom had the bars put in when he was maybe seven or eight after a few break-ins on the block. It was either that or an alarm. A ground-floor apartment without either of those things makes it tough to sleep. He sees a green hose coiled on the shadowy slab of concrete under the window. A couple of overturned buckets. A bunch of stakes in the ground where the concrete gives way to grass and dirt from when his mom tried growing tomatoes. The fences to the neighbors' yards on all sides. A looming telephone pole and its wires. The sycamore one house over that's erupted the concrete all around it and sheds leaves everywhere. He tells himself no one knocked. Something must've hit the window somehow. A fluke.

But then Justin jumps out into his field of vision. He's wearing his heavy coat and hat and has a scarf wrapped around his neck. He must've been pressed up against the back wall, hiding, waiting for an opportunity to spook Fab. He gives a little yell and laughs.

Fab jolts back. He puts his hand over his chest and then smiles. He unlatches the window and pushes it up. His mother forgot to reinstall the storm window behind it, so he talks to Justin through the screen and the bars. He can see, in the shadows, that Justin's face is messed up. A shiner. Some bruises on his cheeks. "You scared the shit out of me," Fab says. "What're you doing here?"

"Breaking you out," Justin says.

"What happened to your face?"

"Knucks got pissed at me. It's nothing."

"He hit you?"

"Come outside."

"I'll be right there." Fab closes the window and rushes out of the room. He tiptoes through the dining room, peeking in on Uncle Chooch, who's snoring harder now. He opens the hall closet, trying not to let it squeak on its hinges, and gets his coat and hat and bundles up quietly, pulling the zipper inch by inch. He heads out the front door, opening and closing both the main door and the storm door as gently as he possibly can. Once outside, the air seeming even colder now, he races around to the backyard and finds Justin sitting on one of the overturned buckets.

"What're you doing here?" Fab asks again.

"Where's your mom?"

"She went out."

"What happened to that dinner?"

"Got canceled. My uncle's here."

"Uncle Chooch?"

"Yeah. Why'd your grandpa hit you?"

"Fuck it. Doesn't matter. I got an idea."

"What?"

"We break into Perpetual Surrender. The school, not the church. We go up to the convent. Do some spy shit. See if Sister Val really sleeps under a Nazi flag. Get some photographic evidence." He taps his front pocket, unzips it, pulls out a throw-away camera—the yellow kind wrapped in a foil bag—and then drops it back in. "I want to see if they got my beeper up there, too. Sister Carm pinched it off me last week. Probably got it in a big box of shit they've stolen from us. Eddie Giangrande's Game Boy. Antonia DiPaola's Furby. Mikey Redden's *Anaconda* tape. We find that stuff, we'll be heroes."

"You crazy? We'll get in trouble. Suspended. Maybe thrown out. They might even call the cops."

"They ain't gonna arrest seventh graders. And you think I give a shit if I get thrown out? I'll go to Cavallaro like a normal person. I don't even know why Knucks makes me go to that fucking school."

"I'm more scared of the nuns than I am the cops. Sister Val catches us, she'll tear our ears off. I heard a story about this kid Antonio Belcastro from maybe ten years ago—he broke into the nuns' private bathroom on the first floor and hid out in one of the stalls and was listening to them pee and talk and stuff. They caught him and brought him up to the convent and nobody ever saw him again."

"The nuns made that story up to keep pervy boys from sneaking into their special bathroom. They probably sit around just making shit up to scare us."

"I don't know. I wouldn't put it past them to have weapons. Sister Val's probably got a gun." Fab bets she's been waiting her whole life to shoot an intruder. People like that exist. They buy guns, and they pray one day they get to use them on an intruder. He bets that's what all her prayers are. Nothing about feeding the hungry and giving toys to needy children. A mean-ass nun with a gun.

"I'm gonna go," Justin says.

Fab searches the dark sky. What's the worst thing that happens? They can't get in? Or they get in, the nuns chase them out, and they book it home? Adventure's what he needs. Trouble's what he needs. He wishes it wasn't cold, though. Wishes for summer weather, even if only briefly. He feels the sting in his hands and buries them deep in his pockets. He touches what he thinks is a stray Swedish Fish at the bottom of one. About three days a week, he goes to the bodega on Twenty-Third Avenue across from his school and buys brown bags of Swedish Fish from the jars with whatever money he has. The guy there, Len, weighs them on a scale. Fab thinks about their texture in his mouth. He thinks he's getting too old for such things. Spending his money on candy and comics. Little-kid shit. "Okay, let's do it," he says finally.

"Fresh," Justin says, slapping him five.

Fab follows Justin out of the yard and away from the apartment, hustling up the block toward Benson Avenue. He tries not to think of how his mother will panic when she gets home and finds him gone and Uncle Chooch asleep. Justin's bouncing around, hanging from gates, kicking fences and garbage cans, bending back antennas on parked cars, walking on the curb like it's a tightrope.

"How we gonna get in?" Fab asks.

"I'm thinking one of those basement windows," Justin says.

They cross Eighty-Sixth Street under the El and hug the buildings on the wide sidewalk. Bad Boyz Pizza is open, but the other nearby stores are closed. They turn right at the bank. Fab counts his steps the rest of the way. His stomach's doing flips. He feels like he might puke. A girl passes them talking loudly on a cell phone. No one he knows has a cell—it's still weird to see.

When they get to Our Lady of Perpetual Surrender, right there on the corner of Eighty-Fifth Street and Twenty-Third Avenue, they stand in front of the apartment building across the way and take in the facade of the school. It's not enormous in any real sense—compared to tall buildings in the city—but it's the biggest building he knows of in the neighborhood other than P.S. 101 and the complex where Justin lives, and it seems even bigger now. The bright red bricks. The darkened windows. He wishes he could close his eyes and make it disappear and then they'd marvel at the magic of that instead of busting a window and sneaking inside.

On the Eighty-Fourth Street side, there's a sunken area maybe seven or eight feet deep between the building and the sidewalk. A metal railing runs the length of it. When he was younger, Fab used to hide down there when they were playing Manhunt on the block after school. There are a few storm grates at the bottom and weeds growing up from the concrete and always some scattered trash. Fab used to think of it like a moat around a castle in a fairy tale except there's no water and it's easy enough to climb down. That's where Justin wants to go now.

Before they hoist themselves over the railing, though, they look around to make sure no one's watching. About fifty feet away, right past the church, Fab notices Father Tim stumbling out of the rectory. His face looks bruised. Hadn't been like that back at the apartment. He opens the gate and goes to the edge of the sidewalk by a parked car, leaning against a telephone pole. He unzips his pants and pisses on the wheel of the car. He's jolting his body around, so the piss is making squiggles in the air. Kind of the way a kid moves a sparkler on the Fourth of July to make shapes with the smoke. Fab can't believe he's seeing a priest in this state. He's still thinking about what Father Tim said about his dad.

Justin points and laughs. "Father Tim's fucked up, yo," he says.

"He was at my apartment a couple of hours ago," Fab says. "He was drinking wine."

"*Father Tim* was in your *apartment*? What the fuck?"

"I don't know why."

"Damn, that's gross."

Father Tim finishes pissing and then staggers into the parking lot between the church and the school, taking a shortcut to the Eighty-Fifth Street side. He loses his footing on a storm drain and face-plants on the blacktop. A howl of pain turns into laughter. He gets back to his feet and continues undeterred.

If the guy wasn't such a fucking disaster right now, Fab thinks he might catch up to him and ask what he was getting at before.

Justin shrugs. "He ain't gonna notice us," he says. He hops over the railing, balancing momentarily on the edge, and then jumps down into the pit.

Fab follows him. His nerves settle. No one can see them where they are.

Justin touches the dark windows that line the base of the wall. He's checking to see if the maintenance guy has accidentally left any open. No such luck. He loosens one of the storm grates, a long, two-inch-thick metal slab pimpled with small holes, and manages to pull it out, leaving a hellish little opening in the ground. He slams it nonchalantly against the glass of the closest window.

The glass looks strong, but it shatters.

Fab's uneasy again. He knows someone must've heard that. It's dark and otherwise quiet out. He's not even sure of the time. Later than eight, for sure. Might be after nine. He's halfway expecting an alarm to start blaring next. Doesn't happen.

Justin reaches in through the broken window and unlatches the lock. He pushes up the frame, more broken glass raining down on the ground, but the jagged edges are now out of the way and the window's properly open.

Justin climbs in first, avoiding the glass.

Fab follows him, getting a thin splinter of glass wedged in his palm as he seeks purchase on his way in. He scratches at it and feels it come out. He can't see. The basement's dark.

"We should've brought a flashlight," Justin says.

They search around for a light and finally find a switch on the wall, which turns on a series of overhead fluorescents that emit a too-bright glow, the bulbs sizzling. Fab looks around. It's an eerie room. The boiler. A few mops in buckets. An army of brooms. Sawhorses and stanchions and wooden folding chairs. Dusty gym equipment. A cage full of basketballs.

Justin kicks over one of the mop buckets. Dirty water puddles across the floor.

Fab's never been down here. Neither has Justin. Probably no student has. It's got an off-limits feel to it, even though it's nothing special.

They go to the scuffed wooden door at the far end of the room. Justin unlatches the lock, turns the knob, and opens it. He shuts the light in the boiler room behind them. They come out at the bottom of the main staircase. The steps are gray and severe. The walls are cinder blocks layered thickly with green paint. It's dark on the stairs except for a shaft of moonlight filtering in through a window one flight up.

"We should go," Fab says.

"Nah, we made it this far," Justin says. "Almost there."

They walk upstairs and go through another door onto the dark first floor of the building. This is where the kindergarten and pre-K classrooms are, as well as the main office, the nurse's office, the auditorium, and the private bathroom the nuns have in the school part of the building. Justin finds another switch and turns the lights on in the hallway. There are no windows in the hallway—only in the classrooms—so the light probably won't be visible from outside, but Fab still thinks it's a rotten idea. The hallway's so empty and abandoned-seeming at night like this. The walls are lined with Thanksgiving drawings from the little kids. Turkeys and pilgrims and all that shit. Those paper letters spelling out the grade over each door. Justin starts ripping down drawings and crumpling them.

"Don't do that," Fab says, imagining mean old Sister Bernadette emerging from her classroom, ruler in hand. Fab's still traumatized by how she threatened him and others with that ruler in kindergarten.

"You gonna be a cop the whole time?" Justin asks. He continues tearing down the drawings, leaving them scattered on the vinyl tile floors.

They're surprised to find the door to the main office unlocked. They go in, and Justin again turns on the lights. Thankfully, there are no windows in the main office either. It's spooky to be in there, a place Fab never wants to be during the school day. This is the waiting room part of the office. Winding up there means doom. Means a teacher sending a student to be disciplined by the principal, a tiny nun with a helmet of black hair named Sister Constance. Fab had never been sent to the office until this year and now he's been sent seven times by Sister Val, mostly for stuff he and Justin have done during class but occasionally for a schoolyard fracas. Justin's down here all the time.

The secretary is an old woman name Agnesia. Everyone calls her Milk of Agnesia. Must be seventy-five. Blue hair, wears perfume that smells like a funeral, always dresses to the nines. Justin sits at her desk. An electric typewriter. A black office phone with about fifty buttons. A crystal bowl full of starlight mints. A glass vase stuffed with fake purple flowers. Fab pockets a couple of the mints.

Justin goes over and tries the door to Sister Constance's actual office. It's locked. He attempts to pick it with a paperclip to no avail. Instead, he unzips his pants and pees in the wastebasket next to Agnesia's desk. Disgusting. The sound of the piss in the wastebasket makes Fab feel alone. It's an act he just doesn't understand, like ripping down the drawings in the hallway. He imagines poor Milk of Agnesia throttled by the ammonia smell first thing Monday morning. Fab doesn't protest. Justin finishes, zips up, and then goes through the desk drawers and finds a small flashlight. He tests it. Works.

"Dope," Fab says, trying to sound casual. "Maybe we shouldn't keep the lights on. Ain't no windows but someone might still see from outside."

"Okay," Justin says.

They leave, Fab flicking off the lights in the office on the way out. He finds another switch for the hallway lights and thumbs it off just to be safe.

Justin guides the way with the flashlight now, the beam fluttering across the darkness.

They walk up the hall to the nuns' private bathroom. The walls are pink tile. There are three stalls and three sinks. A large, clean mirror. It smells like bleach. A radiator rattles and hisses. Justin unravels a bunch of toilet paper from the dispenser in one of the stalls and begins tearing off long sections and filling the toilet. When the whole bowl is full of paper, he flushes, and the ensuing clog sends water rising over the rim and dribbling onto the floor.

Fab's not sure why Justin's set on all this destruction. That's not what they'd talked about, but it's as if Justin just can't help it.

Back out in the hallway, they stand in front of the elevator. Justin presses the button to go up. The second floor has the classrooms for first through fifth grade. The third floor has sixth, seventh, and eighth. Above that is the convent. They get in the elevator, and Justin thumbs the button for the typically off-limits fourth floor. Fab's shaking. Justin holds the flashlight under his chin so his face glows golden and red. He makes a ghost noise.

When the doors flutter open and they step out, they're in yet another dark hallway. Justin bounces the light around. At the end of the hallway are the two intimidating doors that lead into the convent. The elevator closes behind them, and Fab gulps. He wants to go back. All they've done so far—well, all Justin's done, Fab's only been along for the ride—they can walk away from, and no one will know it was them. There aren't any cameras in the building. But if they go into the convent and get made, that's it. He imagines being in Sister Constance's office with his mother on Monday. Sister Constance, as she has a few times on his visits to the office, saying he's turning into a bad seed like his father and uncle were. The police getting involved. Suspension. Maybe they'd even wind up expelled. Having to shovel his ass off this winter to make money to pay for the damages. "I'm gonna go home," he says in a whisper.

"Look how close we are," Justin says.

"To what?"

"Finding out about Sister Val. That box of stolen stuff."

"We don't even know if those things are real."

"That's the point."

Fab turns and presses the button to go down in the elevator. A ding. It's still there. The doors open, and he gets back in. He hits the button for the first floor, figuring on retracing his steps past the main office and the kindergarten and pre-K classrooms in the dark, back down the staircase to the basement and out the window. He'll leave Justin to his own devices. He wants to get caught, let him.

Justin gives him a disgusted look.

The doors close between them.

Back on the first floor, Fab takes a deep breath. When Justin gets pinched by Sister Val or Sister Constance or whoever, he'll be long gone. He bets Justin will rat on him and say he was there anyway. He'll deny it. He'll get back into his bed at home. Uncle Chooch will still be sleeping, and his mom won't be back yet. That way he'll have an alibi. Uncle Chooch will say, "No, the kid was here all night. Never left his room except to get water in the kitchen."

As Fab hustles down the hallway headed for the door to the staircase, he hears something behind him.

13.

Father Tim remembers Christmas mornings in the orphanage when he was a boy. The feeling of wanting a life he'd never have. Maybe his fate was sealed then. He'd always be yearning.

Things had not gone well with Risa—him, a blackmailer, ha—and then he'd returned to the rectory and been confronted by Monsignor Terrone while trying to bust open the safe in the office where they kept petty cash. Terrone had rolled up his sleeves and thrown some punches. Big bastard used to be a Golden Gloves prizefighter before becoming a priest. Father Tim took a couple to the jaw and a hard right to the eye. His vision's blotchy. His head pounds. He can feel the bruises on his face, like his skin is full of television static. Terrone had opened the safe and crumpled up two twenties and thrown them at his feet. He'd shamefully collected them.

Some priest. Wasted like this. More scrapes on his chin and

cheeks from where he'd flopped in the parking lot. What he's done. When's the bell ring? He wants a do-over. Go back to the orphanage. Take all different roads than the ones he took. Could've been an engineer or a sportswriter. The self-hate has kicked in. No stranger to him.

He's heading back to Blue Sticks now.

These woozy blocks. Stumbling. Strangers thrusting past. The blurred faces of a familiar parishioner or two. Shock. One saying, "Father?" Concern in her voice. Piss stains on his jeans. Reaching for fences. Crossing streets in a haze. Almost clipped by a bus. Stopping at a liquor store on Bay Parkway for a cheap pint of peppermint schnapps. Downing it on the sidewalk until he chokes. The night gauzy. His laces undone. Another fall in the cards soon. Falling forever.

When he gets to Blue Sticks, he pushes through the heavy door, the money he has left from Terrone clutched in his fist, and he goes to Joey Sends in a candlelit booth back by the kitchen and tells him he wants in on a card game.

Joey Sends laughs. "This fucking guy," he says. "You look like shit, Father, you know that? You try to rip off the wrong little old lady?"

Father Tim collapses into the booth across from Joey. "Please," he says. He puts the money on the table.

Joey Sends looks at it and laughs. "That's how much you came up with? Father, you've fucked with our goodwill one too many times."

Two goons—one tall, one short—approach the booth, grab him under the arms, drag him out. Never sweet for this world. He's being handled like a broken butterfly by a monstrous child. A dose of guilt over his predicament assails him.

"Take him out to the alley," Joey Sends says.

"He's a priest," the small goon says.

"I know what the fuck he is."

"I'm sorry," Father Tim says, and he starts bawling, his bruises aching with each tear. He's sorry for gambling and drinking, sorry for breaching the trust of faithful parishioners, sorry for Religious Pete, sorry for Risa and her sister and her son, sorry for striking out hard, sorry for living the way he's lived, sorry to God, sorry sorry sorry.

Too late. His feet scraping the wooden floor, thudding over the threshold as they slam through an emergency door under a red light.

Dark alley. Cold. A street side and a wall side. Garbage cans. Boarded windows. Graffiti on the bricks. Nothing ever as planned. The goons holding him up.

Joey Sends in front of him suddenly. "You got some balls coming right back here like this," he says. "Death wish territory."

Father Tim's face strung with snot, cheeks hot with tears. His mouth making words that don't feel like words. "One more chance. Please. Didn't work out." Thinking if he gets out of this with a warning or a broken thumb, he'll go home, pack a bag, get on a train to the city, go to the Port Authority, leave, head somewhere else. Go to New England. A town with a beach. Live in a rooming house. Spend his days in the library. Be a stranger. Get help. Go to meetings. Forget everything. Live a purgatorial existence devoted to atonement.

"You want out?" Joey Sends asks. "That's what you want, Father? You want to take a trip in the trunk to Staten Island? We'll have a nice little funeral for you in the dumps."

"No," Father Tim says. "One more chance."

But Joey Sends has a gun in his hand suddenly. From where? His waistband? A hidden pocket? A long slim barrel. Muzzle like an angry little mouth. He's pushing it into Father Tim's gut. "What I said before, about us giving you leeway because you're a man of the cloth, fuck that. You don't deserve that. You did this to yourself."

Father Tim vacates his bowels. The men around him groan. He waits for a muffled blast to signal his descent to hell. He's still waiting when he feels a big hand clomp down on his shoulder and squeeze tight.

14.

Risa gets it now. What being drunk does to a person. The appeal. Everything's in focus. Her body's fighting back against the pain and regret usually coursing through her blood. Every move she's made has been the right one. Sav deserved what happened to him. Roberto wrote his own fate too, and his poor parents just got caught in the crosshairs. Fab will be fine. She's a good mother, and he'll turn out to be a fine man. Fuck Father Tim. He can shove his blackmail up his ass. She's got *sway*. She'll go to Monsignor Terrone and get Father Tim banished to Utica or Rochester or some other godforsaken place in western New York. She has to, she'll put the gloves on. She's thinking tough and feeling indestructible. *Bring it.*

She's forgotten all about time. There's not a clock on the wall in the Crisscross and she's not wearing a watch, and she's totally unconcerned with how many minutes or hours have passed. She can't remember a day in her life when she wasn't painfully aware of the time.

Giulia's going on and on about Stan and Lola and Marco. She does that thing she often does a few drinks in, arching her back, her voice getting faster and more rambunctious.

Risa tunes her out.

One of the women from the bar comes over and joins them in the booth. The woman everyone calls Jane the Stain. She's probably around Giulia's age, a little younger than Risa. She's tall and pretty in a ravaged way, wearing a blue dress suit and a white blouse. From a distance, it looked like a nice skirt and blazer, but Risa can see now the fabric is ragged, worn thin. Jane has the withered eyes of an alcoholic. Dark hair with gray streaks. She introduces herself to Risa. Giulia says they've been coming in here together for years. She says Jane used to work at a garage too, not Sid and Eddie's, but now she's got a job in the city. "I don't want to talk about work," Jane says.

"What's your nickname all about?" Risa asks, a question she might not have asked if she wasn't drinking.

"It's a long story. Got in a fight in the schoolyard up the block when I was a girl. Made the other girl bleed pretty good, and there was blood all over my shirt. Everyone started calling me 'Jane the Bloodstain.' I liked it. Sounded like a pirate name. Eventually, because people are lazy, it got shortened to Jane the Stain."

Risa drinks some more of her beer.

"You know," Jane continues, "I've been coming in here for years and years, like your sister said. I've heard your name, and I used to see Sav in here a lot. It's like meeting a myth. You drink now?"

"Tonight I do," Risa says.

"Don't let what Marie said about Chooch getting Jimmy fired up bug you. I was in here that day. Jimmy was a ticking time bomb. Wasn't only Chooch coming to report that Roberto was hounding you. A dozen people got in touch with him about the guy in the span of an hour."

"Okay, I won't." Risa means it. Under normal circumstances, she'd get hung up thinking about how they were all judging that situation. Chooch coming into the Crisscross with the implicit aim of getting Roberto greased on her behalf.

"Anyhow," Jane says, smiling, "Jimmy and Roberto were both pieces of shit. The parents I feel bad for."

Giulia gets another round of drinks for the three of them. Risa is eager to be drunker. She wants to see how far she can take it. She's made bad choices, sure, and she married the wrong guy, but she's never gotten wasted the way people do, never done anything truly wild and reckless. She's lived all tightened up. Her stupid code. Quietly punishing herself for marrying Sav and for what she had to do to him. Saying her prayers, asking God to forgive or condone. Always putting Fab first at the expense of her own pleasure. It's necessary to put him first, to make a good life for him, but she doesn't have to forget about her own desires. She's not thinking about tomorrow, about what it'll take to recover for the wedding, about all the ibuprofen and Gatorade she'll have to down, about the cold showers she'll have to take, about standing next to her sister in that banquet hall with booze seeping from her pores. She's thinking about *now*.

When Giulia goes to bathroom, Risa falls into an intimate conversation with Jane. They're whispering across the table at each other. She feels so familiar, this stranger who spends her nights in this dive bar down the block from Risa's apartment. Jane's telling all her dashed dreams and darkest dramas. Her abusive old man. Wanting to be an actor and then realizing she wasn't good enough. Wanting to play tennis and then realizing she wasn't good enough. Sleeping around with loser men until she realized she didn't like men. Failed relationships with tough women. A girlfriend from the Village who worked on Wall Street and moonlighted as a bondage queen. Another girlfriend from Staten Island who coached basketball and used her whistle when they were having arguments. The constant refuge of booze. Risa guesses she's known a few secret lesbians before, or women who were rumored to be lesbians, but she's never known someone to speak as frankly about it as Jane is.

Risa sees Giulia come out of the bathroom, look over at them, and then drift toward the bar. She wonders if this is a setup. Giulia thinking that Jane would be a good match for her. Forget trying with men—they're all skeezy.

Jane *is* charming. Or she seems charming in the boozy haze. Her voice is melodious. Thick with the crust of the neighborhood and yet somehow sugary sweet.

"You're different than I thought you'd be," Jane says to Risa.

"Tonight, I'm different than I've ever been," Risa says.

Jane smiles.

Giulia finally comes back over. "You two look like you're hitting it off," she says.

A moment of panic creeps into Risa's consciousness. What's she doing? She's got to get home to Fab. Giulia's getting married tomorrow, and she's going to have a wicked hangover for the first time in her life.

But time swirls on, and she pushes the panic off to the side. Giulia and Jane are laughing. Giulia's doing an impression of Stan.

Risa gets up to use the bathroom. Giulia reaches out and puts a hand on her arm. "You're not going home, right?"

"Not yet," Risa says. She's wobbly. She was so disgusted by seeing Father Tim's drunken display and here she is a couple of hours later, unsteady on her feet, words syrupy in her mouth.

In the bathroom, she squats over the toilet, not wanting to touch the actual seat. She reads the graffiti on the tiled walls. She focuses in on one piece in red marker: FOR A GOOD TIME, CALL SANDRA. The number below it scratched out.

Bitch, she thinks.

She stands and washes her hands and goes back to the booth.

She thinks maybe she should use the pay phone to call Chooch. Or she could run home, duck in to check on them, and then come back. Giulia talks her out of it. "They're fine," she says.

"Please stay longer," Jane says, putting her hand over Risa's. She obviously chews her nails. Her cuticles are red and raw. She's written something on the back of her hand in blue ink, but the letters are smudged and faded.

"Aren't you worried about Stan and the wedding?" Risa asks Giulia, her practicality breaking through again for a moment.

"Doesn't matter if I'm hungover," Giulia says. "I'll be better off. You will, too. You know there's only one true cure, right? Start drinking again. There's an open bar at the reception. We'll be fine. A couple of midafternoon Bloody Marys will set us straight."

After a few minutes, Giulia drifts away to play pool. Risa and Jane are left alone at the table. "What kind of music do you like?" Jane asks.

Risa shrugs. "The Beatles. The Carpenters. Joni Mitchell. Girl groups. Paul Simon. You?"

"I'm boring with my classical."

"Classical is nice," Risa says, though she's never had that thought, never yearned for classical music, never remembers listening to it unless it happened to be playing in some waiting room or supermarket.

"I'm having a great time," Risa says.

"Yeah?" Jane says.

"Yeah."

Jane leans across the table and kisses Risa.

Risa's surprised by it. She can taste booze and the sweat on Jane's upper lip. To be kissed like that, so unexpectedly, and by a woman, it's nice. Gentle. Her lips against Risa's lips. Nothing forceful. Doesn't feel like Jane's doing it as any sort of power thing.

Jane falls back into her seat and says, "I'm sorry."

Risa touches her mouth. "It's okay," she says.

15.

Chooch awakens to the closing credits of the channel 11 movie. He sits up on the couch. He stands, shaking out his numb limbs, and goes to the kitchen for water.

He's surprised Risa's not back yet. He doesn't know exactly how long it's been. He looks at the clock on the wall. It's close to ten. He can't remember what time she left. He really didn't figure her long for the Crisscross.

He supposes he should check in on Fab.

Standing there in the kitchen, he considers a few things he might say to Fab about the world if the kid's still up and reading. He hasn't done much with himself, sure, and he's naïve about many things, but he's learned enough to give advice to a twelve-year-old. He wants to tell him to be good to his mom. He's got to treat her right. A lot of kids his age, they start experimenting with treating their moms like shit, seeing how far they can take it, how far a woman can be bent before she breaks, if the love's as deep as she makes it out. Chooch remembers going through that to a certain extent. He got over it, and he'll tell Fab he needs to avoid it as much as he can. Be a helper. Make her life easier. Act grateful for what she's given him.

The other thing—and it's cheesy, but it's true—he wants to tell the kid to chase his dreams and not have any regrets. If he doesn't have any dreams, get them. He's young enough, those dreams can become a reality. Look at Marco LaRocca. Well, before he croaked. Time passes fast. In six short years, Fab's eighteen, maybe going to college, trying to figure out how to be an adult. He likes comics, he should learn to draw. He likes music, pick up an instrument. Whatever. Get a dream. Follow it. Those collages Chooch used to make, he's not sure what he could've done with something like that, but it was close to a dream, and he just let it drift away.

Another voice in his head, a sinister one, imagines saying what really needs to be said, *You don't want to wind up like your old man, you really fucking don't.* But to say that is to explain where exactly it is he'd wind up. Dead under all the leaves and dirt. Flesh eaten by worms. Strangled by gnarly tree roots.

Chooch tries not to think about upstate these days. Upstate is ruined for him. Everything beyond the George Washington Bridge, sprawling all the way through the Hudson Valley and into the Catskills, is one big grave. His mother hasn't pressed any more on selling the house, seemingly content to let it rot.

You go too far down a troubled path, Fab, upstate's where you're headed.

He goes into the bedroom. He looks around at Risa's side. The shadowy crucifix on the wall. An ornament that seems to judge him. He wants to take it down, put it away in her dresser drawer, see if she notices.

He passes through the curtain, expecting to see Fab on his bed, reading or just lying there, but the kid's gone. An empty feeling settles in Chooch's gut. He checks the rest of the apartment before going into full panic mode. Not in the bathroom. Not hiding in the closet. Not in any of the obvious places, the kitchen or living room or dining room. Gone.

He sits down at the table and tries to get his bearings. He had one job, to keep an eye on Fab, and he fucked it up. Slept through Fab sneaking out. The possibility hadn't occurred to him. He's not sure why. He plays through his options. He can go to the Crisscross and tell Risa, or he can head out and try to find Fab. But where would he even start? And what if she comes home while he's out and finds them both missing? He can also wait here and hope Fab returns before Risa. The panic kicks into high gear.

16.

Fab's first thought is it's a ghost behind him. The ghost of some ancient nun who died in the convent and haunts these halls. He's heard stories. He thinks he believes in ghosts. Has read that their appearance is often accompanied by the smell of gardenias or cigarettes, and he's sure his nostrils are filling with both those scents.

Down the stairs to the basement and back into the room with the mops, buckets, chairs, and the cage of basketballs. In a dull bloom of light seeping in from a streetlamp outside, Fab can see that the puddle Justin made has spread farther. He props a chair in the scatter of broken glass in front of the window they came through and climbs out, sidestepping the exposed hole in the ground where the grate had been. He exhales, but he's not in the clear yet. He still needs to escape this weird little pit. Scale the wall, get a grip on the edge, latch on to the railing and pull himself up and over. He's done it before, playing around, no pressure. Now's different.

He looks up. Lights turn on in the dark windows of the school. He figures Justin's been caught. He expects to see nuns popping their heads from open windows, pointing at him, accusing him. *It wasn't me who flooded the toilet and pissed in Milk of Agnesia's wastebasket, I swear!*

He jumps and grabs the edge of the wall and pulls himself up. He then uses one hand to grip the railing and now he knows he's okay, he won't fall, he's almost all the way there. He pushes himself through the wide gap between the side rails and rolls onto the sidewalk.

He stands. As he's about to make a break for home, he hears Justin's voice: "Help me up!"

Justin's emerged from the window not far behind Fab.

"What happened?" Fab asks.

"Sister Val's after me," Justin says.

Fab gets back on the ground and reaches down to help Justin get out of the pit. Justin struggles, pressing his sneakers against the wall, almost falling, but eventually Fab yanks him free.

They run toward the corner, turning onto Twenty-Third Avenue, and then booking it to Eighty-Sixth Street. They duck into a little alleyway next to the bank to catch their breath. Justin's panting. He takes the pack of Winstons out of his pocket, feels around for and eventually finds a little yellow Bic, and lights one. He holds the pack out, but Fab can't imagine smoking another cigarette right now.

"What happened?" Fab asks.

"Sister Val came out of the convent with a baseball bat. She had cream all over her face, but I could tell it was her. She was wearing flannel pajamas and slippers that looked like rabbits. No Nazi shit I could see."

"She knew it was you?"

"I don't know. It was dark. I dropped the flashlight." Justin pauses. "We should go. They're probably gonna have the Six-Two over there any minute."

"Go where?"

Justin points up at the El. "Get on a train. Head into the city."

"What are we gonna do in the city?"

"Hide out."

"It's cold."

"I ain't going back to Knucks."

"We can't sleep outside, and I don't have no money."

"We'll sneak into an all-night movie or something."

Fab tries to imagine sneaking past a ticket-taker and hiding out in a dark theater. *Do they even show movies all night anymore?*

Justin starts walking on Eighty-Sixth Street toward the Bay Parkway station. Fab trails behind him. All the stores they're passing are closed, riot gates down, lights off, except for a couple of Chinese restaurants whose red lights glow somberly in their foggy windows.

When they get to the El, Justin flicks his cigarette into the street. At the top of the stairs, he turns to Fab and says, "You ever hop a turnstile before?"

Fab shakes his head.

"Well, we wait here, outside the doors, until we hear the train. When we hear it coming into the station, we run in, jump over the turnstiles, zoom upstairs onto the platform, and get in a car as soon as the doors open. That way, the clerk in the booth doesn't have time to do anything."

Fab pictures an army of nuns charging up the stairs and capturing them before any train shows up. Then he tries to see himself doing what Justin described. Bolting past the booth. The clerk probably yelling from his glass enclosure for them to stop. Launching himself somehow over the turnstile. He'd seen it done in movies and shows but is worried he won't be able to pull it off with any sort of grace. What if he trips? What if his legs don't clear the top of the turnstile and he goes lurching forward? He's worried he'll wind up in the grip of some cop before the night's out.

After a few minutes, they hear the rumble of an approaching train.

"How do we know if it's going to the city or Coney Island?" Fab asks. They can't see the tracks from where they're standing, so he knows it's a good question. They go up the wrong steps, they're fucked. And if it's headed to Coney Island, they certainly don't want to wind up there at this hour, though he supposes they could transfer for a city-bound B at that last Stillwell stop.

"I can hear it's coming from Twenty-Fifth Avenue," Justin says, pointing in the direction they came from. "If it was going to Coney, the sound would be coming from over by Lenny's."

"Right."

"Ready to go?" Justin asks.

Fab nods.

They run past the clerk, whose profanity-laden protestations echo through the station. Fab doesn't look at him. Focuses on the task at hand. He watches Justin leap over the turnstile smoothly like a pro. He goes second. It's not perfect—he bangs his leg on the way over—but he gets the job done.

In two seconds flat, they're up the stairs to the open-air platform and the train is rolling in. There are other people waiting there, a woman in her twenties or thirties and a much older man, and they're flustered by the presence of these out-of-breath boys. Nobody wants to see out-of-breath boys getting on a train. The others avoid them, make sure they're not stuck getting in the same car.

The doors burst open, and Fab and Justin hop into the first car they see. It's empty except for a man with a small foldable shopping cart full of newspapers and plastic bottles who keeps his head down and doesn't look at them.

The conductor is a few cars up. They're both praying he pulls out fast. If he doesn't, that'll give the clerk time to come aboard and drag them off.

"Fuck, fuck, fuck," Justin says, talking under his breath. "Come on, dude. Go."

The doors ding and close. The train moves. Fab's relieved.

Justin laughs. "You see that clerk? Too lazy to chase us."

"I didn't really see him," Fab says.

Justin takes a marker out of his pocket and tags the back of the orange seat across from him. His tag is DREX, and he writes it in thick gothic lettering. When he's done with that, he tags the window and the glass over the MTA map. Then he gets to work on another seat, drawing a quick gun with their area code, 718, written on the handle. The drawing of the gun is surprisingly good. Fab's only seen Justin just do tags before. Justin digs around in his pocket for the little throwaway camera, rips the foil off it, and snaps pictures of everything he's done.

A thought occurs to Fab. "You draw people?" he asks.

"I draw Knucks all the time," Justin says, putting the camera back in his pocket. "Got a whole book of drawings of Knucks. In one, he's getting attacked by a shark. Another one, he's got his regular face and the body of a toad."

"You think you could draw me my father if I gave you a picture?" Fab asks.

"Shit, sure," Justin says. "Five bucks. You even got any pictures of your old man?"

Fab thinks of the fiver Uncle Chooch gave him. He left it on his dresser. "Deal," he says. "I've got the five bucks at home. I'll find a picture."

"Cool." Justin pauses and stuffs the marker back in his pocket. "City's gonna be dope, I'm telling you."

The train stops at Twentieth Avenue. The doors whoosh open. No one gets on. They close.

Justin stands. "Let's go to another car," he says. He struts to the back of the car, past the man with the carriage, and opens the end door.

Fab follows him. They step out into the open space between cars. A gap beneath them. Fab can feel the connected cars shifting under his feet. He holds one of the rubber barriers to keep his balance. Eighty-Sixth Street rooftops rush by on both sides. The tracks turn right up New Utrecht Avenue.

"Let's stay out here," Justin says, putting his arms out, not holding on to anything, as if he's steadying himself on a surfboard. His shiner seems darker, more menacing. The car jolts to a stop at Eighteenth Avenue and then they're off again.

Fab tries to push past him and enter the next car, but Justin puts his hand out to stop him. Fab stays put.

Justin digs around in his pocket for his marker, finds it, and leans forward to tag the body of the car. He gets as close to the steel frame as he can to put a finishing touch on his tag. As he does, he loses his footing. Fab reaches out to help him, makes a clumsy grab for his coat, figuring he'll bunch it in his fist and pull Justin to him. Instead, because of the rattling of the train, he winds up thrusting his hand into Justin's right shoulder blade and pushing him to the side.

Words catch in Fab's mouth. In the next instant, Justin falls between the cars. It's like a magic trick. One minute he's there, the next he's disappeared.

All Fab can hear is the whooshing of the train against the night. No sound accompanied Justin falling. He didn't even scream.

Fab can't believe it. His heart's racing.

Justin must've found a way to cling to the side of the car. He's gonna come back, smiling, laughing.

Nope.

Fab thinks: *Did I do it? Was it me grabbing for him that made him fall?*

He fucking *fell.*

Fab thinks: *Jesus Christ. Please. No.*

Fab thinks: *It didn't happen. Couldn't have. I'm not even here. This isn't real.*

Fab thinks: *Rewind the tape. Bring us back to right before we got on the train. I'll go home. Fuck the city. I don't get on the train, this doesn't go down.*

Fab thinks: *They find the camera in Justin's pocket and salvage the film somehow, there's no pictures of me, only his lonesome tags.*

He moves into the connected car. No one's there. He sits down, rocking back and forth, hyperventilating.

When the train makes its next stop at Seventy-Ninth Street, he gets off and avoids the gaze of the glassed-in clerk as he exits the station and goes down to the street. Once on the ground, he leans against a telephone pole and vomits in the gutter.

He begins walking home. He refuses to think about Justin splattered on the tracks under the train. Maybe it was a gag. Like that scene in *Saturday Night Fever* where they pretend to jump off the Verrazano but there's a platform below for them to land on. Or maybe it's like what happens at the end of that movie—there's no platform, the dude simply loses his balance and flops into the water.

He puts his hands in his pockets. He clutches his jacket tight around his neck. He takes the starlight mint from Milk of Agnesia's desk out of his pocket and pops it in his mouth, trying to erase the taste of puke.

The whole way home, he keeps the same thought in his head: *I wasn't there. Nothing happened.* He won't tell Uncle Chooch or his mom or Aunt Giulia. If they catch him coming in, he'll say he needed some air. Went for a long walk. What'll they say? Maybe they'll put things together when the nuns report there was a break-in at the school or when Justin's body is discovered, but no one saw him at the school and hopefully no one will remember him from the train. He remembers the two people on the platform when they got on, the shopping cart guy in the car, the clerk who saw them hop the turnstiles, the clerk just now who saw him leave alone.

Justin's twelve, same as him. *Was* twelve. Fuck. No way he survived that. The closest thing Fab has to a best friend. Kid worked hard at his tags. Had it tough with Knucks and was always doing stupid shit, but he was gonna draw Fab's old man for him.

Living on the edge means taking risks, Justin knew that. Jumping rooftops. Riding between cars. The risk was the thrill for him.

No one will know. He keeps telling himself that. Aims to make it feel true. He was nervous about the wedding, that's all. He was sick of his room and needed time to think. Last time he saw Justin was when Uncle Chooch came and got him from the roof. Justin busted into the school on his own, was on the train by himself. The lie starts feeling true.

When he arrives back on his block, he looks at P.S. 101. Thinks about Uncle Chooch saying he used to go up on the roof of the school to listen to music and watch the stars and look down on the neighborhood. He can't picture it.

If he hadn't gone to Justin's after school and hadn't gone up on his roof, maybe Justin never would've come around with the convent idea.

The block feels different. He's noticed things changing over the last few years—people leaving, new people arriving—but not that kind of different. It's him that's different. Happens that fast. Get knowledge you don't want in the blink of a fucking eye. All death suddenly possible. Future mistakes dripping with doom.

He passes statues of the Virgin Mary and Jesus in front yard grottoes, and he wants to pray. Can't remember the last time he wanted to, though his mother makes him get down on his knees at his bedside every night and pray before going to sleep. Always a burden. Now a strange necessity. He knows all his prayers from school and church. Religion classes and CCD. A million Saturday masses at 5 P.M. at Our Lady of Perpetual Surrender with his mother. All the kneeling and incense. He recites the prayers fast in his mind. The Lord's Prayer. Hail Mary. He thinks the more times he can say them, the better off he'll be. Confession always ends with the priest saying something like, "Say ten Hail Marys and five Our Fathers." He'll say a thousand of each. Ten thousand. The priest in the confessional. He imagines having to confront Monsignor Terrone or Father Tim behind that screen, lie about everything, withhold. He thinks of Father Tim drunk in his apartment and drunker on the sidewalk outside the rectory. He thinks about his dad. He loses track of his prayers. They're not making him feel anything.

He stops in the middle of the block and takes a few deep breaths. He keeps replaying the scene from between the subway cars on a loop in his mind. Grabbing for Justin's jacket. Accidentally shoving him. Not only was he there, but it was probably his fault that Justin fell. He just wanted to get into the next car. He was just trying to help Justin after he stumbled.

Keep telling yourself that.

Part 4

SO MUCH COULD GO WRONG

Saturday, July 24 & Sunday, July 25

2004

1.

Fab walks up the front steps of the house in Rosendale and rings the doorbell. It makes a loud buzzing noise. As he waits for an answer, he takes in his surroundings. The house is almost fully obscured by trees at the end of a gravel parking lot. The railings on the porch are rotted. Gray paint is peeling off the siding alongside several broken shutters. Overall, the place is much bigger than he'd expected. He'd come down Main Street from the bus station to get here, passing a stonework library and an old-school movie theater. A railroad trestle looms over the small town. He takes a deep breath. He hasn't left the city much in his life. The air's so much cleaner upstate. It's quiet, too. Aside from a few passing cars, all he can hear are the trees moving in the wind and the flowing creek nearby.

A crust punk answers the door, standing on the other side of the screen. Shirtless, wearing black jean shorts. Crude tattoos all over his chest and arms and neck. Names and dates.

An arrow. What looks like a section of a map. Pierced nose and eyebrows. Green paw print tattooed on his chin. Head shaved and scarred.

"What?" Chin Tat asks.

"I'm looking for Stevie Scivetti," Fab says.

"Christ." Chin Tat turns around, calls out Stevie's name and says that someone's here for him, and then turns and disappears back into the darkness of the house.

Fab waits. He almost can't believe Stevie's here, that it really might be him. He takes a few steps to the left and looks at his reflection in the dirty glass of a window on the porch. He's wearing an army surplus jacket, an Anthrax T-shirt he bought off some guy who said he'd gotten it at a L'Amour show in 1984, jeans with frayed holes in the knees, and faded black Chucks. The knapsack slung over his shoulder contains clothes—a few shirts, jeans, boxers, socks—and some other necessities: his Walkman, CDs he'd stolen from Sam Goody, a toothbrush, deodorant, a hairbrush, a switchblade for protection. He's got long hair his mom's always begging him to cut. It gets knotty. He likes it in his face. He likes to hide behind it. He's got acne scars on his cheeks.

He feels old, searching on his own like this. A high school dropout, trying to make sense of who he is and where he comes from. He thinks about his mother, how mad she'll be when she discovers he's trying to track down his old man. He left a vague note for her about where he was going, told her he'd call when he got the chance. He knows she'll be sick with worry. *Let her worry.* He might not call at all.

Things hadn't been the same between them since he'd left Narrows Academy in Bay Ridge. A tense quiet formed in the space between Fab and his mother's expectations. A profound disappointment took root. "All that tuition money down the drain," she'd said. But he couldn't take it anymore. Teachers who acted like cops. All that God talk. Fab knew she'd put a lot of dough into Narrows Academy, just as she'd put a lot into grade school at Our Lady of Perpetual Surrender. He fended off this guilt with defensiveness.

"I didn't ask to go there," he'd said. "I could've gone to Lafayette for free. You and Dad went to Lafayette."

A big blowout. She bugged him every day thereafter, practically every hour, about getting his GED and thinking about college. She insisted he wasn't going to loaf around.

The door opens. Fab drifts back over. A man in gray sweats and with a messy white beard stands there. Double Stevie. Fab knows this guy's older than his father—early fifties, he's guessing—but he looks more ancient than that. Emaciated. Smoking a cigarette. His cheeks drawn in. Jaundiced skin.

Double Stevie gives Fab a menacing once-over through the dark screen. "You don't look like a Jehovah's Witness and you're not from the court, so fill me in on who the fuck you are and what the fuck you want," he says.

"I'm Sav Franzone's son," Fab says. He waits a beat, then information spills out of him. "I found Skeevy Ed on MySpace. He told me where you lived. Said I should I talk to you. I took a Trailways bus up here. I—"

"You kidding me?" Double Stevie pushes open the screen door and hobbles outside on what appears to be his one good leg. He puts his hand on Fab's shoulder as if they're old pals. "Holy shit, you're the spitting image of your dad under all that hair."

"Yeah?" Fab says, hopeful.

"Yeah. I think he had that same shirt, too." Double Stevie thumbs the black fabric of the Anthrax shirt. "You're how old?"

"Eighteen."

"Time's a bitch. I'm in my fucking fifties. Never thought I'd see the other side of thirty-five. Probably would've been better off." Double Stevie pauses, seems to contemplate the fact that Fab has come to him for some reason or another, trying to figure an angle. His face suddenly radiates worry. He flicks his cigarette off the porch into the front yard. Anger pours down from his forehead to his eyes to his clenched mouth. It's as if he's considered being kind and has decided against it. "What do you want, kid?"

Fab tries to maintain his confidence. "I'm looking for my dad. Skeevy Ed, he said if anybody knows where he is, it might be you."

"I ain't seen your father." Double Stevie's face softens.

The scent of lingering cigarette smoke overwhelms Fab almost more than the disappointment of the news.

"Look, kid, I'm sorry," Double Stevie continues.

Fab doesn't move, doesn't speak, just stands there. He refuses to believe Double Stevie almost out of spite. Or desperation. He'd come all this way, used the computers at the Ulmer Park Library for months to search for any news about his dad—finding Skeevy Ed online had been dumb luck. Not to mention going behind his mother's back to get money from Uncle Chooch for the trip. Five hundred bucks, he'd asked for. Told him it was to enroll in a GED class. Uncle Chooch was happy to help. Truth is, Fab owes Charlie Cee and Carmine Perasso in the neighborhood of eight grand after a string of bad bets, and he should be using the money to pay off the vig before their main goon, Joey Sends, comes knocking. And never mind that he's done other stuff to massively piss them off—stealing a few Italian suits off one of their trucks and selling them to Billy Marsh in Coney Island and then saying the wrong thing to the wrong girl, Joey's niece, Concetta, at a club over on Highlawn last night. It wasn't even that bad what he said. Called her a cunt because she wouldn't hook up with him. This off-the-boat Irish guy he knows from Bay Ridge tosses that word around like it's second nature. Fab's botched things pretty goddamn good. Part of his thinking is, if he finds his father, maybe the old man can help him get out of this jam he's in. Or maybe he can teach him how to escape. A father like that—that's what he'd be good at.

"I've gotta go to work in an hour," Double Stevie says. "I wash dishes at a restaurant in High Falls. Very extravagant life I got. I work, I come home, I get on my PlayStation. Got a Camry with three hundred thousand miles on it and a bunch of shit-ass crusty punks for housemates. Plumbing barely works. Joint's a hovel. Your father isn't here, and you should be happy about that."

"You never even heard from my dad?" Fab asks.

"Not so much as a peep. Left town that night in eighty-six and that was that."

"What happened? I've heard different stuff."

"I'm sure you have. We broke into this guy Gilly's house. Got wind there was a stash of money in his attic. Me, your old man, and Chooch Gardini."

"Uncle Chooch was there?"

"You bet. Feeding Gilly's cats. Whining for us to quit and

get out of the place. We found some money—not a ton, six large maybe—and we went to L'Amour and partied. I don't know how much you know and don't know, so I'm sorry if I'm spoiling any illusions you have about your old man, but he was banging this broad on the side. Sandra was her name. They were talking about running away together. I drop him at home. He's good and loaded. I tell him goodbye. He says him and Sandra are gonna screw their way to Florida. Says no more dirty diapers for him. Not that he ever changed a single fucking diaper. That upset you?"

Fab shakes his head. "I know about her."

"Thing that happened earlier that night might. He had this piece he scored somewhere. Wasn't loaded at the time, but he pointed it at you and your mom. I says to myself, 'Stevie, you're crazy, but Sav's even more of a fucking nutjob.'"

"He pointed the gun at us?"

"Really upset your mom. This was before Gilly's."

"And what happened the next day?"

"Next day, I went over, and Risa said he stormed out in the middle of the night and never came back. She was broken up. I felt for her, I did. You, too. A baby. Sav was my friend, but he wasn't cut out to be anybody's old man."

"You see Sandra after that?"

"Oh boy, was she pissed. Figured she got played. Everybody always making promises to her and then forgetting those promises. Curse of being who she was. I dated her for maybe a week afterwards." He pauses. "I got the hell out of Brooklyn right around then. People knew we'd knocked off Gilly. Broke a bunch of valuable records. Heat was coming down. I went to live with my cousin in Poughkeepsie and then I got a job washing dishes at this restaurant in New Paltz and, after a while, even New Paltz started to feel too big, so I came up the road to Rosendale."

"Can you tell me anything else about him?"

"I don't know. He was a ballsy guy. Someone said don't do something, he did it. Hated to be bored. Nothing more boring than being married. Him and your mother were a bad match. I don't even know how they ever got together. She still around, your old lady?"

"Yeah," Fab says. "She and I are very different."

"Never took up with anyone else, I bet. Another guy, I mean."

"Nope. You think he's alive, my father?"

"Don't you think you'd feel it in your bones if he was dead?"

"I don't know. I used to think I felt it, but how could I?"

"You took the bus up?"

"Yeah."

"Where you staying?"

Fab shrugs.

"Not a planner. You thought maybe your old man would be hiding out up here with me."

"I don't know what I thought."

"Fathers who leave don't want to be found."

"I guess."

Double Stevie takes a pack of Old Gold cigarettes out of his pocket. He holds the pack out to Fab, who makes a hand motion refusing. Double Stevie shakes one loose for himself, lighting it with a book of matches from a bar called the Cement Factory. He takes a deep drag and exhales a cloud of smoke. "You should check out some of the caves up here," Double

Stevie says. "Ain't got that shit down in Brooklyn. I'll tell you where you can sneak onto Turco Brothers Water and Iron Mountain property to explore. Nothing like being in one of those caves. Makes it feel like you're in another century. Get to thinking about all the ways people lived and survived. Next time someone attacks America, I'm ducking into one of those caves, and I ain't coming out."

Fab tries to picture himself in a cave. Shadows on a wall. Stalactites. Stalagmites. Whatever the fuck. Cold breath in the air.

"And here's my other advice," Double Stevie continues. "Change of scenery's good. Go hang in New Paltz. Lots of college-age kids. Bars and the like. At least a couple will serve you. They got a hostel there now. You can walk over on the rail trail. Nice hike. This local band I like, Sorcery Blowjob, is playing a house show somewhere on Church Street tomorrow night."

"I might try to find Sandra. Skeevy Ed told me she's in Ridgewood. I have her address."

"Let sleeping dogs lie is what I suggest."

Fab feels like he's run out of things to say. He should have more lines of inquiry. More he wants to know about his old man.

Double Stevie breaks the silence: "That was terrible about your Uncle Roberto and your grandparents. I heard all about it."

Fab still remembers it all vividly. He was five, and it seemed like his whole life was funerals and wakes for about a week. Sitting on folding chairs, staring at closed coffins. Sitting in church pews. Strong smell of flowers. Sitting in the backs of limos, headed out to the cemetery on Long Island, staring at zooming guardrails on the Belt Parkway. Surrounded by his mom and Aunt Giulia and Uncle Chooch. His inability to speak yet. Expecting his dad to show up. Uncle Chooch giving him a "Macho Man" Randy Savage wrestling figure to play with. All those wailing neighbors at the wakes for his grandparents. No one was too terribly upset or surprised by his Uncle Roberto's death. But his grandparents were another story.

"Tell me about Chooch," Double Stevie says. "I always figured he'd turn into one of those guys who marries somebody's daughter nobody else wants to marry."

"Not much to tell. His mom died. He's alone. He helps us out."

"Probably got a lot of dough, the bastard. Inherited that house. Rolling around like a pig in shit, I bet. You like him?"

Fab shrugs again.

Double Stevie stands up. He draws on his cigarette. Long sizzling noise. "Well, kid, it's been swell, but I don't know what else I could possibly tell you. You find your old man, tell him I say hey. I wish you well on your journey." He goes back inside, leaving a vapory smoke trail in the air, the door slamming shut behind him.

Fab's left sitting there on the saggy, rotting wood. Strange porch and strange town and strange everything. The whole bus ride up, he gave a lot of thought to how this would all play out. Didn't really plan on it being over so fast.

2.

Risa's returned home from a long and frustrating shift at Saints Joachim and Anne. There'd been a delay on the train ride from Coney Island, which had only deepened her aggravation. She's tired and her feet are sore. Her blue scrubs are sweaty and smell strongly of the sad, bland food they serve in the cafeteria at the nursing home. She wants nothing more than to take a hot shower. The whole time she was working—feeding old-timers in worn sweaters, cleaning them, making beds, whatever, all of it—she was dreaming about her shower. Lighting a vanilla candle and leaving it burning on the edge of the sink. Stripping down and stepping into the tub. The water blasting down on her back. Steam. Shampoo and conditioner in her hair. Soap on her hands and on her body. Decompressing. Washing the smell off. She's become an enigma to herself. Work hard. Provide for Fab. Play everything close to the vest. Keep all the regret buried.

Maintain the lie, even though she'd promised herself countless times she'd tell Fab the truth.

Before she can make it to the bathroom, she notices that there's a folded note on the table. She picks it up and reads. It's from Fab. She slowly deciphers his sloppy handwriting. He's gone to look for Sav. He wants to find his father, who he believes is still alive. No particulars. Just that's what he's doing. No *I love you*. No *goodbye*. Says he'll call when he can. He doesn't have a cell phone. She doesn't either. Another thing she regrets. She should've gotten him one at least so he can call from anywhere if he gets in trouble. She should get one for herself too, like Chooch did, so anyone can reach her at work without a problem.

She feels sick to her stomach. She sits at the table and stares at dust gleaming on the glasses in the china closet. She hadn't expected Fab to be home—he's always out somewhere—but now that he's *gone*-gone, the silence of the apartment is a knife in her heart.

She's tried hard with Fab. Tried to create opportunities for him. Devoted herself to being a mother who doesn't miss things, who talks to his teachers, who gets him extra help when he needs it, who tries not to fly off the handle. She's always put him first.

She had that one night with Jane the Stain on the eve of Giulia's wedding where she edged up against what she can only perceive as selfishness. The drunkest she's ever been, by far. It'd been reckless fun in a woozy moment. She'd never experienced anything else like it and probably never will again. She went home with Jane. They slept together. Clothes strewn on the floor. Bodies tangled. Finding some relief from years of frustration and repression. The next day, the guilt kicked in. Why? Because Jane was a woman, and Risa still considered herself a devout Catholic? Because she'd prioritized her own desires for once? She'd felt like it was an out-of-body experience. Someone else making decisions for her. Then it got worse when she heard about Fab's friend Justin getting killed on the tracks. He was a bad influence on her boy, sure, but he was a kid. She had to keep drinking through Giulia's wedding to avoid dealing with any of it. She decided to bury the encounter with Jane. For Fab's sake. To hide what had been revealed. She avoided Jane after that. Jane called and left her notes and tried to get in touch through Giulia for a few weeks, but Risa walled herself away. Jane gave up without a fuss. Months later, Risa saw her smoking a cigarette outside the Crisscross, and they waved at each other, and that was that. Giulia was the only person who knew what had gone on between them, and it was Giulia who broke the news that Jane died of cirrhosis in late 2000. She was thirty-seven. There was no ceremony. She got cremated. No grave to visit. Risa thinks of her often and wonders what might've been if she'd followed the yearning she felt. Too late for that now. She's given her life to Fab, and this is what's come of it.

Fab's got his father's blood in him, no doubt about it. He's developed a taste for danger. Justin was just the beginning. Fab was in constant trouble at Narrows Academy. Talking back to teachers, stealing, playing hooky, fights. He's gone through the whole rebellious-kid playbook, growing more and more distant from her. Nothing can erase what she did that night eighteen years ago. A deep, festering splinter. The skin's grown over it, but it's as present as ever. Long and jagged and aching beneath the surface. She knows the wedge between her and Fab originated then. She'll never escape it. And now she'll suffer through Fab's departure, considering how things might've been different.

She wonders where he might've gone. Back when Sav first disappeared, there was a lot of conjecture about where he disappeared to, but Fab wouldn't have been privy to that information. Her goal has been to keep Sav's memory somewhat alive, to make Fab feel like he had a father and that she was angry he'd abandoned them, but that he was nonetheless Fab's father. She'd decided on that strategy and stuck to it. Erasing Sav totally—with Frank and Arlene and Roberto gone—could've been possible over time. She suspects her true plan was to breed anger at Sav in Fab, but the plan's backfired. Fab wants to find his father and *know* him, though there's no him left to find or know.

She's never really come close to sitting Fab down and telling him the truth, though she lies to herself often about her intentions in that regard. Her main issue has been thinking about how he might react. She doesn't believe he'll say he understands, or he knows she was acting to save him and Aunt Giulia and herself. She doesn't believe he'll think burying the body made any sense. She's considered that he'll probably ask very tough questions: *If it was self-defense, why not call the cops? Why get rid of him upstate in the fucking woods?* And if he found out he was there, crawling on his father's grave, what then? She can't see past any of that. She's always imagined he'd pack a bag and leave in such a situation. Call her a murderer on the way out.

But what's the difference? He's gone now anyhow. Chasing what he believes is true but blind to the actual truth.

She stands and goes to the phone and dials Chooch. He answers after one ring. She asks him to come over.

He's there in five minutes. Always ready to help her when she needs it. Since Vi passed away, he seems to have gotten much older. Gray in his hair. A slouched posture. His hearing starting to go. He's smiling when she lets him in. "How was work?" he asks.

"Don't ask," she says.

Chooch quit his job after his mom's death. He had everything his parents had left him—the house across the street and the house upstate, some money and bonds, the car, a few stocks—and he settled into a life of leisure, rarely leaving his house unless it was to go to the market on Eighty-Sixth Street or to do something for her or Fab. He's still so devoted to them. A lot of days, she forgets to feel thankful enough for him. That he's there whenever she needs him. Comes when she calls. Like now.

For Risa, going back to night school and then getting the job at the nursing home had been a way of getting her head straight. A way of bringing in more money for Fab's education, though he bailed on high school and seems to have no interest in college. She's still got that CD at the bank for him. The idea was he could use it for college. She had some hope he'd get back on track but that seems to have gone out the window. Most of the rest of the money she inherited from Frank and Arlene is gone. Bills and repairs and tuition and donations to the church and paying for care for her parents. She's always tired these days. Work has ceased being an escape and is more of a burden now. She's thought a lot about tapping into Fab's savings and quitting. Chooch has offered her money again and again, but she won't take anything from him.

Now Chooch sits at the dining room table. So much of their relationship has centered around this table. From Sav to Father Tim and everything in between. Still there despite what Roberto had told her about screwing Ginny Saggese on it. Too much of a hassle to dump. She thinks of Father Tim's behavior that same night she met Jane. Coming around with accusations. Getting wasted. What Grazia told them at the wedding about Monsignor Terrone throwing him a beatdown in the rectory. His hush-hush disappearance. The threat he'd presented thankfully went away with him. It all started right here at this table. If she hadn't been drinking in response to his drinking, she might not have had that wonderful night with Jane and might never have had the sense of longing for that connection that filled her for years after. This damn table. Maybe it's cursed or maybe it's protected them somehow—they've dodged so many bullets.

She doesn't have to ask Chooch what he wants. She goes into the kitchen and puts on a pot of coffee and grabs a bag of savoiardi from Villabate Alba off the counter. Fresh. She brings the bag to the table and sets a plate in front of him, a plastic Yankees plate that Fab used a lot as a kid. She goes back to the stove and waits for the coffee to boil.

"What's wrong?" Chooch says from the table. "I can tell something's up."

She nods in the direction of the note on the table, within Chooch's reach. "Read the note. Fab left. Went to look for Sav." She pauses, puts her hands on the corners of the stove, feels momentarily as if she'll lose her balance.

Chooch comes over and stands next to her and braces his body against hers. "That's what he said, he went to look for his dad?"

"That's my son. Doesn't let me know his plans. Just leaves. Gone to look for a dead man."

Chooch doesn't say anything.

Risa pulls away from him. She knows Fab has asked Chooch for help every now and again. She's accepted a lot from him but never money. Fab, on the other hand, has discovered that Uncle Chooch is happy to give him handouts. Probably it's all the guilt. Chooch trying to make up for things going the way they've gone.

"You knew, didn't you?" Risa asks.

"I didn't."

"You're lying."

Chooch heads back to the table and reads the note. "He'll be back."

"Where did he go? Where could he possibly have gone?"

"I don't know. Really. Let him look. Gets it out of his system. Let him have that hope."

"'Hope'? It's a dead end, Christopher. What I did. What *we* did. I need to tell him the truth."

"We've been through this."

"Where is he?"

"I told you. I don't know."

"You gave him money though?"

"Not much. He said it was for a GED class he needed to take."

"He's taking advantage of you. You're too nice to him."

"He's not a bad kid. He's having a hard time. It's understandable."

Risa watches the coffee swirl around in the glass bulb on top of the pot. She shuts the gas and allows it to settle and then pours a cup in Sav's old Belmont Park mug for Chooch, handing it to him along with a speckled paper napkin. She goes to the dining room table and yanks a chair out, dragging its feet over the floor. She huffs and sits down. The smell of nursing home food on her uniform hits her in the face again and makes her want to gag.

Chooch sits across from her. "Don't be mad at me. Please."

"I'm not mad at you. Can you go look for him?"

"Look where?"

"Where would he start?"

"He'll be back. Watch. Give him a day or two. He's eighteen. He spends the money I gave him on a bus or train ticket, on food, on motels, it'll be gone in a flash. He doesn't know how that stuff works."

"What if I get a call that he's in trouble? What if he winds up dead out there? So much could go wrong."

"Give it until tomorrow before we hit the panic button—how about that? He's an adult. He's not a missing person."

"When Fab gets back, I'm gonna tell him the truth. Finally."

"You're being irrational. This was Sav's fault. Forget him. Keep acting like he left. Who knows how Fab will react? You and me, we could wind up in jail. Or worse. Fab goes off the deep end and pulls a Jimmy Tomasullo."

"He's not capable of that. He'll understand. Then the truth will be on the table, and we won't have this wall between us. No more hiding."

"You think so? I'm telling you, this kid feels connected to his old man. Despite everything." Chooch drinks coffee. Sits back in his chair. Crosses his arms.

Risa picks up Fab's note and rereads it. She pictures him

wandering around the Port Authority or Grand Central. She wonders if he's thinking about her. All the ways she'd thought he might turn out, she never figured on him simply disliking her. Again, she blames herself. She folds the note and unfolds it again. She traces her finger over his handwriting. "I think I need to be alone," she says to Chooch.

He takes another sip of coffee. "You're kicking me out?"

"Take the savoiardi with you," she says. "I don't need them."

"Ris. Come on. I'm just trying to help."

"Go."

He picks up the bag of cookies and leaves the apartment, looking back once on his way out the door, waiting to see if she'll say his name, ask him not to leave. She doesn't say anything else. She sits there and watches him go. She sits there with Fab's note and pounds her fist against the table. She's alone. So terribly alone.

3.

Giulia sits at her dining room table with a glass of wine, listening to Marco's lone solo album, *Forty Shots to the Heart*, on a little red off-brand boombox she bought on Eighty-Sixth Street for thirty bucks. She's hung up on one song in particular, "Bowery," reading the lyrics in the CD booklet, made to look like they're handwritten on a legal pad, and trying to see herself between the lines. "*The girl had hair as pretty as flowers, and we danced in the rain down on the Bowery*," Marco sings, and Giulia traces her finger over the words. They'd been to the Bowery together at least once, and she's half-certain it might've rained that day.

When the phone in the kitchen rings, she lets it go. Probably Stan. She can only listen to Marco's music when he's out. He gets so jealous these days. He didn't like Marco's picture being up in the Crisscross either. It went missing a few years ago, and Widow Marie pinned it on some fans who'd made a pilgrimage to the block, but Giulia secretly suspects Stan.

The phone keeps ringing. Seven, eight times. Could be Risa. Giulia hasn't heard from her in a couple of days. She's being silly anyway with these lyrics. Obsessing over lost time. She presses stop on the boombox, pushes back from the table, lifts the wineglass by its stem and downs a quick sip, and then goes to the phone on the wall, picking up the receiver after the ninth ring. "Hello?" she says.

"It's me." Risa's voice. "Can you come over? Fab's gone. He went to look for his father."

"Went to look for him where?"

"I don't know."

"Poor kid." She pictures Fab out in the world, hoping to encounter Sav. She wonders where he might even start looking. Working in the garage, she knows there's been neighborhood conjecture over the years. People suggest Sav's in Florida like Roberto had been or that he's gone to the Dominican Republic or Puerto Rico or the Bahamas. Others say Italy. This one guy, Vito Amendolara, is always in the garage and he knows Risa is Giulia's sister, and he talks about his cousin Gennaro back in Naples who insists he spotted Sav at some nightclub over there. Giulia has given up her hope of ever making it back to Naples, so she's jealous even though she knows it isn't true. *Naples.* The name sits in her mind like cement. If she'd managed to get back while still in her twenties, maybe she would've stayed there, learned the language, lived a life where she rode cobbled streets on a bicycle to late-night gatherings with friends at pizzerias and wine bars in secret alleyways.

"I'm going to tell Fab the truth," Risa says. "When he comes back, I'm going to tell him what happened that night."

"Ris."

"Christopher already gave me all the reasons why I shouldn't again."

"I'll be over in a bit, okay?"

"Okay."

Giulia hangs up and returns to the table, finishing the last swallow of wine. She grabs the boombox and the *Forty Shots to the Heart* CD case—which features a picture of Marco in an abandoned warehouse on the cover—and buries them in the hall closet under a pile of winter hats and gloves.

She leaves a note for Stan. Brings her wineglass to the sink and rinses it. Stops at the mirror in the foyer and sees herself. So much older in the eyes. Gray streaked all the way through her hair now and her too lazy to dye it. She decides she needs to change out of the yoga pants and tank top she's wearing.

She goes up to the bedroom and takes off the pants and tank top, leaving them on the closet floor, which drives Stan nuts. She puts on jeans and a bra and then digs around until she finds her favorite denim shirt.

If she's going to go, she wants to get out before Stan comes home. Stan will have something to say. He likes Risa but he hates Fab, and he'll go off on some rant about how that kid needs to get a job and quit taking advantage of his mother and giving her heartache. This from a guy who never left home, who lived with his parents until they croaked.

She leaves the house and heads for Risa's. It's a walk she makes pretty much every day one way or another since she's either heading to the garage around the corner, going to the

Crisscross, or checking in with Risa. She has it timed. She walks fast, she can do it in six minutes. She walks leisurely, it's more like eight. She decides she'll stop in for a quick one at the Crisscross. Her usual routine after work, but she feels like she needs one now. Widow Marie is still kicking. Eighty if she's a day.

The front door is propped open. Widow Marie's behind the bar. The place is never crowded. There's a disgusting melancholy in there that Giulia still adores. Smell of peanuts and bleach and cigarettes. Smoking inside had been banned in the city the year before, but that doesn't stop the few denizens of the Crisscross. A couple of others sit hunched at the bar. Cursed Roy and All Bad Allie.

Widow Marie's lost a couple of inches over the years. She drinks diet cola from an empty ricotta container. She wears sweaters in the summer. She seems bent. Arms all bony. Voice gruffer. She greets Giulia with her usual.

Giulia takes out her cigarettes—Widow Marie isn't frightened by the prospect of a fine—and lights one. She thinks back to that dramatic night Risa came in here with her. She still can't believe Risa got loaded and went home with Jane the Stain, who's gone now. Risa had been a different woman. Makes Giulia sad to think of the life Risa might've had if she put her own joy first like she did that time. Same's true of her when it comes right down to it.

The picture of Marco that used to be behind the bar but got snagged has been replaced by an eight-by-ten of the Twin Towers, the words NEVER FORGET emblazoned in gold across the bottom of the frame. They watched on TV in the bar that day. Everyone left work and stayed glued to the screen, only occasionally venturing outside to look up at the smoke in the sky. Even the worst alkies gasped and cried when the towers crumbled to dust. Almost three years later now, but it still feels like that smoke and ash is hanging in the air all over the city. Put things into perspective for Giulia for a stretch, though that perspective's starting to fade. Sometimes she feels as dumb as she did at thirteen: *What's it all fucking for?*

Cursed Roy sidles up next to Giulia now, sitting one stool over.

"I'd like to ask you something," Cursed Roy says.

"Back up," Giulia says.

"The smell?"

"The smell."

"It's my lower back. I've gotta really lay that cream on thick."

"It's not only that."

"Sauerkraut's my main source of nutrition. Good for the gut."

"What do you want to ask me, Roy?"

"Stan ever fart when he's fucking you?"

"Excuse me?"

"Mid-hump, he lets one rip? That kind of thing. I'm talking about a real thunderous blast. None of that silent but deadly shit. I'm taking a poll. I'm thinking about going to grad school, and I'm gonna do my thesis on farting while fucking."

Giulia laughs. "Sometimes I think about the choices I made in my life and how they've led me to moments like this and I really question my own judgment."

"Give me an honest answer."

"Why when he's fucking me and not when I'm fucking him?"

"Touché. Even better, how about Marco LaRocca? The world wants to know."

"I'll give you ten thousand dollars," Widow Marie says to Giulia, "if you bring Roy out back and chop his head off with my new axe."

"You have an axe?" Giulia asks.

"Got it on Mother's Day this year." Widow Marie reaches under the bar and pulls out a small, shiny axe with a hardware store label still on the handle.

"You don't have any kids."

"I didn't say I got it *for* Mother's Day. Went to the store that day and decided I needed an axe for protection."

"I wish I was dead," All Bad Allie says.

"Don't we all," Widow Marie says.

Giulia puts back her shot and takes a couple of long swigs of beer and then puts out her cigarette in an ashtray and leaves a ten on the bar. She scooches sideways off her stool and says, "That's enough for me."

"You going to your sister's?" Cursed Roy asks.

"Why do you care?"

"That nephew of yours is in some deep shit."

"He's just a kid."

"Betting over his head with Charlie and Carmine. Some other stuff he's done to get their balls twisted. Joey Sends is steaming mad."

She knows those names mean trouble. Blue Sticks is a bar farther up Bath Avenue she's never been to. Charlie Cee and Carmine Perasso run their gambling operation out of a back room there. Joey Sends has a reputation as an old-school leg-breaker. He's no spring chicken, but he's still adept at taking a tire iron to degenerates who owe. That doesn't work, word on the street is he takes people to a salvage yard on Stillwell Avenue that butts up against Coney Island Creek or to the dumps in Staten Island and makes them disappear. She suspects Joey was responsible for Father Tim's abrupt departure. Fab must be betting heavy on sports. It's summer, so he's not even betting on football or basketball. Probably baseball. She nods. "I'll check in with the kid," she says. "Make sure he keeps his nose clean. What's 'other stuff' mean?"

"Just some rumblings I'm hearing. He stole something didn't belong to him is what I ascertain. Maybe said a few nasty words to Joey's niece."

"Christ."

"Yeah, Christ is right, bud."

"I've gotta go."

Widow Marie advises Giulia to be careful out in the world. All Bad Allie gives a half-nod. Cursed Roy goes back to the seat he moved from.

Giulia leaves the bar.

She walks up the block to Risa's, thinking about the ways it's changed since she moved in. At least twenty years she's here. Maybe nineteen. Minchia. Time. Twenty more years, she'll be fucking sixty-one and then what? What will her life be? The old ladies she knows, they have church and bingo and feeding their families to keep them going. She doesn't want any of those things. Her and Risa's parents are in the home where Risa works, living on borrowed time. She doesn't want that. Back to the block. Lots of new faces. The Chang family. The Abdallahs. Ricky Genyuk and his girlfriend, Biana. The Lius. Many of the old-timers dead or gone to Jersey, Staten Island, or Long Island with their families. The long arms of gentrification haven't reached the neighborhood. Ethnicities have started to change but the working-class vibe has remained the same. Some new condos erected in place of the old frame houses that got torn down. Lola died in '99, her house was immediately demolished, and the ugliest condo on the block got put up in its place. No plaque. No more makeshift memorials for Marco. Chooch's house is still the same. Looking more run-down than ever. Overgrown garden. Faded, dangling shingles on the roof. Dirty siding. And Risa owns the building with her apartment since the Franzones died. Upkeep's been a bitch. Risa the landlord. Crazy. Giulia always thinks that when Stan dies or when she divorces him, whichever comes first, she'll move into one of the apartments above Risa and they can get old together.

When Giulia gets to Risa's, she knocks and Risa's there almost instantly, thrusting open the door, wrapping her sister in a hug.

"Oh, sweetie," Giulia says. "It's fine. Don't worry. He'll be back."

"I don't know."

Giulia goes in and sits at the dining room table. Risa sits across from her and asks if she can get her anything to drink.

"You don't have to play host," Giulia says. "I'm your sister. I lived here ten years. If I want something, I can get it, okay? Can I get *you* anything?"

Risa shakes her head. She pushes a folded piece of paper across to Giulia. "That's his note."

Giulia reads it and doesn't say anything. She can say, "Don't worry, he'll be back" until she's blue in the face, but she knows where Risa's mind is. She's sick because of the lie that everything's built on. She believes she's lost her son for good because of it. He might not be gone forever this time, but he'll disappear one day, and he won't call or leave a note or anything. Giulia can read every worry in her sister's eyes. Risa's only four years older than her, but she looks even older. Crow's feet. Bags under her eyes. A certain leaden quality that their mother also took on in middle age. A gelatinous panic molded into her features. Pushing herself to the limit at work. Pushing herself to the limit over the path Fab's on.

"You said you're going to tell Fab the truth," Giulia says.

"Soon as I can."

"You think this through?"

"What's broken between us can only get better one way."

Giulia flattens the note with her palm. Looks away from Risa. She's not sure what else to say. They've been over this before. Eventually, Risa's going to crack. She tells Fab, Giulia has no idea what will happen next. Maybe the floodgates open. Maybe Risa goes to Monsignor Terrone or that new Congolese priest she's so fond of, Father Augustus. Maybe she goes to the Sixty-Second Precinct with her goddamn wrists out, ready to have cuffs slapped on.

"I wasn't expecting him to turn out so much like his father," Risa says. "I thought I was molding him to be the *opposite* of Sav."

"You can't mold people, I guess," Giulia says. "Where you think he went? What'd Chooch say?"

"He gave Fab money, but he didn't know he was using it to go somewhere."

"He could be anywhere. People still talk in the garage occasionally. I hear theories. Sav went to the Caribbean. He went to Italy. Maybe Fab heard something like that."

"Fab's barely been out of Brooklyn. Anything could happen."

"Don't think the worst." Giulia grips Risa's hand on the table over Fab's note.

"I'm going to tell him the truth when he comes home," Risa says.

"You do what you need to do," Giulia says.

4.

Double Stevie was a bust. Fab should've guessed it would happen like that. It's true, part of him was imagining it playing out like he'd dreamed. He goes to see Double Stevie, asking for dope on his old man, and his old man's there, hiding out with his pal the whole time. Things don't happen like that. What Double Stevie said hit him hard in the heart. *Fathers who leave don't want to be found.* Dude didn't look like he should be able to say profound things.

What's he gonna do? Go to Jersey and find Sandra Carbonari and no doubt strike out with her and then have zero options left? His old man could be anywhere. Probably has a new wife, new kids.

Fab stops in front of the Rosendale Café. A woman he'd met getting off the bus—she had on a Black Crowes shirt, a hippie skirt, and Western boots embroidered with yellow flowers—mentioned she works at this place when he asked her for directions to Double Stevie's. Light reflects off the front windows. An old-fashioned sign hangs overhead. The building sits on the ground like it belongs there; not all buildings belong where they are. Peeling blue paint. The gravel parking lot next to it. Seating in the back garden. Smells like they serve health food. Not reminiscent of any restaurant in his neighborhood. He stands on the sidewalk and thinks twice about going in. He wishes he were better at doing things in the world. He wishes he had some swagger. Could go in there and order and flirt with the waitresses and wait for the woman from the bus to show up. Something he likes about her. Just a quick glance made him realize she's so different from girls he's known.

Instead, he sits on the curb out front. A few cars pass. Drivers and passengers take notice of him. He guesses he looks like a runaway. Folks never say he looks older than he is. Doesn't have a beard or wise eyes. Just the long, scraggly hair and acne scars. He's eighteen, sure, but he could easily pass for sixteen. He wishes he looked like a man.

His mind turns to Charlie Cee, Carmine Perasso, and Joey Sends. He's in way over his head. His pal Vinny—who he sometimes gets high with over at Jenny Pirello's place by Most Precious Blood—has warned him about Joey's extreme methods in dealing with problems like him. The dude once burned out Paul Profaci's right eye with a cigarette lighter over seven hundred bucks. Fab's in the hole for eight grand, and Vinny doesn't even know about the suits he snagged or the misfortunate encounter with Joey's stuck-up niece. Fab's pretty sure that alkie from the Crisscross, Cursed Roy, is scouting for Joey. He had to duck him on the way to the subway earlier. Maybe Fab should just stay away. Then again, there are guys like Danny Matasso and Dante Lo Buglio who owe big, and they still have all their arms and legs as far as Fab knows, but it might only be because they're related to the Gambino crime family.

The betting started small. His friend Gene got him going. It was easy. During football season, he put a few bucks down on the Giants. Then he got into betting on the Knicks and that turned into college basketball. He had a run of good luck. When he owed, he owed small, and what he hit Uncle Chooch up for would often cover his debt. Lately, he's been betting the over/under on the Yanks, and he's been on a bad cold streak. The suits seemed like a solution, but he gambled away the money he got from Billy Marsh, too. Debt blooms, sometimes the easiest thing is to just ignore it and take off. He'll keep it as tomorrow or the next day's problem.

An hour passes. Maybe more. Fab drifts in and out of sleep. He dreams of that moment when his friend Justin fell on the tracks between subway cars almost six years before. He can't shake it. The way Fab grabbed for Justin before he fell and accidentally shoved him. He's always back there in his dreams. Justin's body was discovered quickly, and Sister Val had seen him in the hallway outside the convent, so a narrative was built about him breaking into the school and then hopping on the train to escape and falling as he ran between cars. No one fingered Fab as his accomplice. No one remembered them together, not any of the strangers they saw on the El platform, or they simply didn't speak up. His mom didn't come home that night—she got wasted the one time in her life and stayed gone. Uncle Chooch claimed he bought Fab's story about going for a little walk to clear his mind, and they made a pact not to mention to his mom or anyone that he'd left the apartment. If Uncle Chooch put two and two together after word started to spread about Justin's death the next morning, he didn't say anything, though he gave Fab a couple of suspicious looks at Aunt Giulia's wedding. He was obviously more concerned that he'd failed to keep an eye on Fab the one night his mom wanted to let loose.

He gives himself a little smack to stay awake. He doesn't have any idea what time it is, and he's pretty sure there's not a bus back to the city today. Maybe he'll sneak into one of those caves Double Stevie mentioned and spend the night there. Probably shit his pants, he does that. Double Stevie also said he could walk on the rail trail to that other town the bus stopped at on the way here. New Paltz. Couldn't have been more than seven or eight miles. A long walk. It'd probably start getting dark a couple of miles in—it must be late afternoon or early evening—and then what would he do? His only options are to find somewhere to crash in Rosendale for the night and then wait for a bus tomorrow or to set out early and walk to New Paltz, figuring buses are more frequent there, maybe killing a bit of time at one of those college bars if they don't card him. Must be a motel around. He'll look for a phone booth. Search the yellow pages. In a motel, there'll be a TV and a vending machine.

A car pulls into the lot. Black Civic with mud on the tires and scratches on the hood. Sunlight gleams in the scratches. He can see that the woman from the bus station is driving. She parks in the gravel lot and gets out. She's changed her clothes. She's wearing black pants and a yellow blouse. Some makeup.

Clutching a bag under her arm. She notices him and comes over. "Hey, it's the bus station kid," she says.

That's what she thinks of him. *Kid.*

She continues: "You lost? Why you sitting out here?"

"I'm not lost," he says.

"What, then?"

He hesitates to say anything. He doesn't have any sense of how to formulate the words. How to boil it down. He wants her to feel bad for him. He wants her to take over and help him. "Came up here to see some guy," Fab says. "I saw him. Asked the questions I wanted to ask. That's it. Now I'm done, and I'm not sure where to go."

"You don't have somewhere to stay?"

"Not really."

"How old are you?"

He thinks better of saying his real age. "Twenty-one."

"More like seventeen or eighteen, I'd say. What's your name?"

"Fab."

"Like *fabulous*?"

"Like Fabrizio. What's yours?"

"Aries."

"Aries is your real name?"

"Sure is. You hungry? Come in. We'll get you something to eat."

He thanks her and follows her up a ramp on the side of the building to a door. What he was smelling outside is even stronger inside. It's cramped and homey. Wood floors. Scattered tables. A front counter. A bar. Chalkboard and whiteboard menus. Paintings and photos on the wall. Aries sets him up at a single table and introduces him to another woman named Michelle who's working there. Michelle is tall with loads of dark, curly hair and smiling eyes. Probably mid-twenties too. Wearing a white shirt and jeans. She brings him a glass of water. Aries asks what he wants. He shrugs. He can't decide. He doesn't know a lot of stuff on the menu. She says it's all vegetarian. She says she'll bring him the Café Nachos and a grilled cheese. He didn't notice those on the menu, but he nods. She goes back into the kitchen. He examines the menu again and realizes the grilled cheese is on the kid part down at the bottom.

A few other patrons come and go in the café.

When Aries next checks in with him, Fab takes out his wallet. "I have money," he says. "I can pay for my food."

She puts her hand over his. "No, the meal's on me," she says. "Save your money. I'm sure you'll need it."

He looks down at the table, thumbs the dulled edge of a butter knife.

"I can drive you over to New Paltz after I get off," she continues. "I know a guy who works at the 87 Motel right off the Thruway who can cut you a good rate on a room. That sound okay?"

"Yeah, thanks." He pauses. "Why are you being so nice to me?"

"When I got here from Syracuse, I was running away from a bad situation. I was a lost little lamb and some nice people stepped in to help me out. I try to pay that kindness back in life."

He guesses he believes her. He guesses he's feeling relaxed. It won't last.

5.

Giulia picks up the phone in the kitchen and calls Stan. "I won't be home tonight," she says. "Fab's gone. I'm staying with Risa."

"You're lying," Stan says.

"You think I'd lie about that? You want me to put Risa on?"

"You're going out with some guy you met at the garage or at the bar."

"I'm not."

"I don't trust you no more."

"What'd I ever do to lose your trust? I never ran around on you once."

"I see the way guys look."

"Stan, fuck off." She puts her hand over the mouthpiece and talks to Risa: "You mind coming over here and telling my husband what's going on? He thinks I'm off having a torrid affair."

Risa gets up from her chair and walks over to her. She takes the phone. "Stan, yeah, it's Ris," she says. "Giulia's with me. I'm having a bit of a crisis. Fab's gone, I don't know where."

Giulia can hear Stan on the other end of the line, apologizing profusely, saying if he can do anything let him know, saying he knows a guy whose cousin is a private eye.

"Thanks for letting me hang onto her tonight, Stan," Risa says, handing the phone back to Giulia.

Giulia returns the receiver to her ear, and she can hear Stan's breathing. She doesn't say anything for a few seconds, but then she puts her lips close to the mouthpiece and says, "There you go, you paranoid fuck. I'll take my apology in writing."

"Okay, okay," Stan says.

"You've got some nerve."

"I'm a jealous guy. I get worried you're gonna run off on me."

"I think doing all that electrical work in all those subway tunnels is messing up your mind."

"Maybe. I love you, babe."

"I love you, too. Okay?"

"Okay."

She hangs up the phone. "You believe this guy?" she asks Risa.

They go back to the table. Giulia almost makes a joke about wishing Risa would take a cast-iron pan to Stan's fucking head, but she thinks better of it. Poor taste. Anyhow, Stan's not Sav. He's fine. Maybe he feels like he's losing her. Maybe he *is* losing her. Maybe she should try to be happier with him. Maybe they both deserve that.

Giulia can see that Risa's folding in on herself. Whatever's going through her mind about Fab is all over her face.

She launches into a monologue about Stan in the hopes of distracting Risa: "Stan clips his fingernails and toenails over the garbage in the kitchen, you know that? 'Clip them in hiding like a normal person,' I says. He's got all this hair in his ears. You know what his favorite TV show is? *The Apprentice*. Jesus Christ. Guy used to read books about New York history. He goes on and on about all this boring electrician shit. What it's like down in the subway tunnels. This or that he was doing at the Javits Center. He's more of a snooze than teachers I had in high school. I took him to Joe's of Avenue U last week and told him he had to get the pasta con sarde and vastedda. You know what he ordered? A meatball sandwich. Nothing against their meatball sandwiches—it's just, I don't know, disappointing. And he still talks about us having kids. I don't think so."

Risa laughs a little during Giulia's diatribe.

"I'm sorry," Giulia says. "I'm venting."

"You're trying to get my mind off Fab," Risa says.

"A little, sure. What good's it gonna do to wonder where he is?"

"I don't know."

A loud knocking on the door. Risa jumps up. Giulia can tell she thinks it's Fab, but it's weird he wouldn't just barge in as usual. She follows her sister to the door.

When Risa opens up, she's confused by the stranger who's standing there on the other side of the screen, but Giulia knows exactly who he is. Joey Sends. He's a little shorter than them. Dark tan, leathery skin. Almost seventy but strong-looking and fit, muscles tense in his neck. He's got on a black porkpie hat, a blue soccer shirt with the Italian flag on it, and red trackpants. He has a memo pad in his hand and a pair of thick-framed reading glasses on a chain around his neck—he puts them on to consult his pad. "Fabrizio Franzone here?" he asks.

"Who're you?" Risa says.

He looks up at her and smiles. "He's not around? Tell me when you expect him."

"I'm his mother. Why're you looking for him?"

Giulia nudges Risa, as if to say, *Don't push this guy.*

"Let's just say I'm a guy who checks in on things," Joey Sends says. "And sometimes I gotta do more than check. Did Fabrizio skip town?"

"My son caused you some kind of problem?" Risa asks, forgoing Giulia's warning.

"For starters, he's got a nasty mouth on him is what I hear from my niece. And—I know a mother hates to hear it—he's very reckless. Got the wrong people preturbed." He says the word incorrectly like that—*preturbed* instead of *perturbed*—and then takes off his glasses and lets them drop back around his neck. "Your son's a big boy. I'm gonna talk to *him*."

"What'd he do exactly? He owes how much?"

"I don't do sleep, so I'll be back at some point soon," Joey Sends says, ignoring her questions. He turns and walks away.

"Just tell me what's going on," Risa calls out to him, as he opens and closes the gate like a real goddamn gentleman. He crosses the sidewalk and gets into a brown Cadillac Eldorado—looks like an '85 to Giulia—with a gleaming grille and rims. A beautiful boat of a car.

Giulia shuts the door and takes Risa by the arm.

"You didn't say anything," Risa says. "You know who he is?"

"That's Giuseppe Senzamica, otherwise known as Joey Sends," Giulia says. "He works for Charlie Cee and Carmine

Perasso. Fab must be gambling for real. Cursed Roy warned me he was in trouble."

"He doesn't pay up what he owes, this guy'll break his fingers or something?"

"Or something. Roy said he'd pissed these guys off in other ways, too." Giulia thinks it's best not to go into specifics. The money, the stolen suits, and disrespecting a made guy's niece sounds exactly like the kind of toxic cocktail of transgressions that could get a nobody clipped.

"What should I do?"

Giulia thinks about it. Whatever Fab owes, maybe they can scrape it together. Get Chooch involved. That'd be a start. "Chooch will help us out, I'm sure," she says.

"I don't want to ask Chooch for money," Risa says.

"Maybe we'll be able to cover it. I've got some cash hidden away from Stan."

"I don't want to take your money for this."

"We'll figure it out." Giulia doesn't like the idea of Joey Sends hanging around, keeping an eye on Risa, waiting for Fab. Her mind travels around the corner to the safe in the garage. They need to be ready. She continues: "Sid and Eddie keep a gun in their safe. I'm gonna go get it. You need protection over here."

"You know I don't like guns."

"It's not a matter of liking." She pauses. "Come with me. I don't want to leave you here."

"You think this guy's coming back right now? You think he's gonna try something?"

"I don't know what to think. Joey Sends has a reputation."

"He kills people?"

"What I hear, that's how he got his name. He sends people to early graves."

"He's an old man."

"Let's just go get the gun. Better to be overcautious."

Before they leave, Risa checks the windows to make sure they're locked even though she's got the bars. Then she locks the door behind them on the way out, confirming that the dead bolt is engaged, letting the screen bang shut.

They walk around the corner, past the Crisscross, to Sid and Eddie's garage. Giulia takes out her keys, opens the graffiti-covered riot gate on the office and yanks it halfway up. They crouch under it. She unlocks the front door and pushes it open. Once inside, she punches in the alarm code. Searches around for the light switch in the dark and finally finds it.

It's stuffy in the office. All the years she's worked here, she's not sure if Risa's ever come inside. They met on the sidewalk outside plenty of times, for sure, but she can't picture her sister in the actual office. Giulia's done a lot of complaining about the job, but this cramped room has been something of a sanctuary for her. She feels comfortable when she's on the clock. Safe. Knows where everything is. Has some Marco memorabilia she hides in her desk and likes to go through it when no one's around.

"They're gonna be okay with this, Sid and Eddie?" Risa asks.

"Fine," Giulia says. She kneels in front of the safe and spins the dial, working slowly through the combination. When it clicks, she opens the door and feels around for the gun. It's there. She takes it out and puts it on the desk and locks the safe.

She shows the gun to Risa. "You'll feel peace of mind just knowing this is an option," Giulia says.

"It's loaded?"

"Yeah. We've gotta be careful."

"I don't even know how to handle it," Risa says.

"I'm with you tonight. I'll walk you through everything. Joey Sends comes around when I'm gone tomorrow or the next day, you just point it at him and tell him to get lost."

"This is a mess."

Giulia tucks the gun into her waistband under her shirt, asking Risa to wait outside. She puts the alarm on, flips off the lights, locks the door, and then closes and bolts the riot gate.

They go back to the apartment. Giulia checks around for Joey Sends. Doesn't see him watching.

Inside, they settle at the table. Risa puts out an Entenmann's crumb cake.

Giulia removes the gun from her waistline so she can sit comfortably and places it on the lace doily in the center of the table next to a small wicker basket full of potpourri.

Risa stares at the gun. "When Fab comes home," she says, "I want it out of here."

"Of course," Giulia says, knowing it's just a precaution.

6.

The motel's a dump. Across from the entrance to the Thruway in New Paltz. Fab had passed it on the bus earlier but hadn't taken notice. The sign overhead a glowing yellow circle with 87 MOTEL in black letters. Nestled back behind a gas station and next to a dive buffet restaurant. Aries has driven him there after her shift in her beater Civic, the air conditioner broken, a Ben Harper CD playing. She talked over the music the whole way, smoking a cigarette out the window, her pack of yellow American Spirits propped crookedly in an ashtray overflowing with butts and blackened coins. Fab's not sure of the time, but he watched the sky go pink and purple and then dark through the window of the café. Must be nine thirtyish. Maybe ten. The dark up here is different than Brooklyn dark.

Aries's friend is the night auditor at the motel. He's behind the desk when they push in through the dirty glass door, and he bounds out immediately to greet Aries, who protects her cigarette pack in her breast pocket as he hugs her. He's massively tall, maybe six-five or six-six, over three hundred pounds, wearing a flannel shirt with the sleeves cut off to the shoulders and above-the-knee jean shorts with frayed edges and Birkenstocks. Long, yellowed toenails. Legs shaved smooth. He's got a wild mop of brown hair and a stubbly face and blotchy birthmark on his cheek.

"Who's this?" he says to Aries.

"Herbie, meet Fab. Fab, Herbie," Aries says.

Herbie puts out his big mitt of a hand. Fab notices a tattoo on his inner wrist. Looks like a bluebird. He reaches out and shakes. Herbie's a gentle hand-shaker. Not what Fab expects from someone his size. "Hi," he says.

"Any pal of Aries," Herbie says.

"Fab needs a place to stay for the night," Aries says. "Thought if the place isn't full, you could let him have one of the unoccupied rooms cheap."

"You know that's no problem," Herbie says.

"You sure?" Fab asks.

"This place is a shithole, that's the rub. It's rarely full. My boss is a drunk. He doesn't check in much. I often let people I know stay in one of the empties if they throw me ten bucks or buy me a six-pack. No skin off my back. Don't expect the world-class service I'm sure you're used to. Where you from?"

"Brooklyn."

"You got Brooklyn written all over you. My old man was from Midwood. Moved up here the year before I was born. What neighborhood?"

"Gravesend."

Herbie gives him a strange look. Makes Fab's skin crawl. "Let me show you back to your room."

Fab nods. He's having second thoughts. Aries is nice enough, but something's off about this Herbie guy. Then again, it's this or curl up outside somewhere and hope the cops don't notice. He'll keep the door dead-bolted. He'll keep his folded switchblade palmed and at the ready. First thing in the morning, he'll see about catching a bus. The park-and-ride is across the street, but he wonders if he needs to get a ticket at the station in town or if he can board there and pay on the bus.

"Don't be nervous," Herbie says. Flashing a big smile. Mangled, brown-tinted teeth.

Aries puts a hand on Fab's shoulder.

They go outside. The motel has two separate buildings, spreading from the office in a V-configuration. Herbie leads them to the block of rooms on the left. Maybe three cars in the lot. Gauzy lights behind drawn shades in two rooms. They go all the way to the last room at the back. Desolate. Dark. A dysfunctional overhead light in the parking lot strobing them. Herbie's talking the whole time. Saying a lot of names. Talking about that same band Double Stevie mentioned, Sorcery Blowjob. He keys open the heavy door. Room nineteen. The black sticker numbers faded where they're affixed on the wood.

Herbie turns on a light in the room. It's not one of those harsh, bright bulbs. Softer. Gives the room a hue the color of piss. Sad paintings of rivers and trees over two double beds with burgundy duvets. Flattened carpet. Age-stained herringbone wallpaper peeling back at the edges. A Gideon's

Bible on the nightstand. A TV chained to the wall behind the bureau on which it's propped. A green rotary phone on the desk closest to the door.

"Girl last week, Scary Mary McIntyre, she OD'd on me in the can," Herbie says. "You're not gonna do that, right? I don't like dealing with junkies."

Fab shakes his head.

"You got the ten bucks?"

Fab riffles through his pockets and comes out with two wrinkled fives. He hands them to Herbie, who folds and flattens them and puts them in the chest pocket of his vest-shirt.

"How old are you?" Herbie asks.

Fab's reluctant to answer. He already tried lying to Aries and she saw right through him. His thinking is if he tells people his actual age, they'll believe he doesn't know shit about surviving out in the world.

"Old enough he's got things he's running away from," Aries says.

"Fair enough," Herbie says. "Two more things of note: don't use the phone, and you don't get a key. You're here, you're in for the night. You go out in the lot to smoke or something, leave the door propped or unlocked. No complaints either. A roach in the tub? Blood on the sheets? Don't give a fuck. Part of the bargain." Another greasy smile from Herbie.

Fab nods again.

"Well, I'll leave you with Aries. You're in good hands. Duty calls. Never know who'll stumble in from the Thruway." Herbie leaves the room, shutting the door behind him.

Fab throws his knapsack on the bed closest to them. "Thanks for this," he says to Aries.

"Of course. You mind if I stay a bit?" Aries goes over to the other bed and sits down and kicks off her shoes.

"I don't mind," Fab says, though he's honestly confounded by the interest she's taken in him. Why she's being so nice. Why she wants to sit here and talk to him. The thought passes through his mind that she's hustling him somehow. Maybe she and Herbie are in cahoots. This room's her web, and he walked right into it. Doesn't make sense. There's nothing he has she could possibly want. She doesn't know about the few hundred bucks he has squirreled away for this impromptu journey. Could be she figures it, though. Kid like him. Brooklyn. Doesn't travel broke. Another thought occurs to him. A wild one. She's a vampire. Vampires are real, and she's a fucking vampire. He'll be dead in ten minutes. Her teeth sunk into his neck. This is the way it happens. Vampires feed on runaways. Lost and searching kids. He pictures her fangs in his neck. Sees his blood running over his Anthrax shirt. This room's his fate. A heap of drained victims in a ditch out back probably.

"You're not used to strangers being nice," Aries says. A statement of fact, not a question.

"What do you want? Why are you helping me?"

"See."

"See what?"

"There doesn't have to be a reason. Like I said before. I'm paying it back."

"Is Herbie bad?"

"No way. He's a sweetheart." She pauses, considers her words. "Okay. Can I admit something to you?"

"Sure."

"Maybe I have an ulterior motive." She pulls a small notebook out of her pocket. A blue pen with a chewed cap jammed into the tunnel of its spirals.

"What?"

"I collect stories. I know a lot of homeless kids. Living in tents off the rail trail. Crust punks. Kids leaving bad homes. Even some wrapped up with this culty group called Golden Mountains. Seems like around here is a haven or a magnet for kids like that. I ask questions and then write out the stories in first person. I'm a writer. I want to be a writer. I took classes at SUNY. I had this teacher Pauline who gave me the idea for this big collection of all these stories. Some of them are a few pages. Some longer. I have sixteen so far. I'm calling it *Catching Rats and Other Tragedies*. One of the stories is about this kid, Redline, who catches rats for food in Kingston. That was the first one I wrote. I'm rambling. You want to tell me your story?"

"I'm not a runaway. I told you before. I came up to see this guy used to know my father. I thought maybe he had an idea where he was. He's been missing a long time. I'm trying to find my father, that's all."

"Trying to find your father's an interesting story. He left when you were young?"

Fab gets up and paces. He goes to the window and pushes back the musty shade a bit, staring out at the parking lot, a ring of quivering moonlight reflected in a garbage-strewn puddle on the blacktop. A buzzing from somewhere in the distance. That flickering light. Dark trees at the edge of the lot. Aries isn't the kind of vampire he thought initially, but she's still a fucking vampire. "I shouldn't be here," he says.

"I freaked you out," Aries says. "I'm sorry. We don't have to do this. Look. I'm putting away my notebook. Sometimes I'm selfish. Sometimes all I can think about is collecting stories for my project."

"Other people's stories. That doesn't make you feel gross? Stealing them like that."

"I'm not stealing them."

Fab's angry. He feels betrayed. Letting himself be taken like this. Doesn't matter how trivial her angle is. All that kindness. Only to find out it's for some bullshit reason. Kindness is a lie. Always some—what'd she say—*ulterior motive.*

"You don't want to talk to me," Aries says. "That's fine. I'm not forcing you."

He has an idea then. One that really opens things up for him. Once he thinks it, his adrenaline starts pumping and he knows he'll never sleep anyway, so he might as well go for it. She steals so recklessly from others, well, he's going to steal from her in return. He goes back to the bed and opens his knapsack and takes out the switchblade. He flips it open and holds it out in front of him. He got the knife his freshman year. Georgie Renner was starting shit with him every afternoon, and he wanted to be ready for a fight. Georgie was all muscles. Took steroids and pumped weights. Fab figured a knife was his chance to spook him. He bought it at a shop next to the Kent Theater. Scared off Georgie with it.

Aries puts her hands up. "What the fuck, dude? I've been nothing but nice to you."

"Give me your car keys," Fab says.

"You're gonna steal my car?"

"I'm getting you back for all those stories you took."

"I thought you were a nice kid. I fed you. I hooked you up with this room."

Fab waves the blade in the air.

Aries takes her keys out of her pocket and throws them on the bed. "Can I at least take my other keys off the ring? That's work and my apartment. Come on, Fab. Don't do this."

"Leave everything. Get in the bathroom."

Aries shakes her head. "I don't believe this. I've got shit I need in my car." She walks into the bathroom's dull butterscotch glow. Mildewed shower curtains. Narrow window that looks like it's covered in burnt sugar. The door locks from the inside, of course, but it opens out into the room, so he figures he'll have to shove something in front of it to block her in. The window's too small for escape.

Aries sits on the toilet and takes out her cigarettes and lights one. She gives him a frustrated glance.

He closes the door and then puts the knife in his pocket. He goes over to the bureau and begins pushing it along the worn carpet. The television slowly edges off as he moves the bureau, thumping against the wall, where it remains hanging from the chain. He pushes the bureau's butt end up against the bathroom door, ripping a gash in the carpet.

Aries is talking to him, but he's trying not to listen. He's sweaty and nerved up. He takes her keys off the bed. He considers removing the other keys she needs from the ring, but he decides against it. He grabs his knapsack.

Outside, he thinks about how best to approach Aries's car. It's parked in front of the motel office, and he worries Herbie might see him through the window and figure out something's amiss.

Fab's plan is to drive straight to Sandra Carbonari in Jersey. Doesn't matter what time he arrives. He has her address in Ridgewood from Skeevy Ed. Hopefully she still lives there. He's not sure what Sandra will say that Double Stevie didn't, but he needs to see this through.

Fab approaches the Civic and squats down as he opens the door, careful to stay out of Herbie's line of sight. He can see him in the office, his back to the window, doing some weird stretches. Fab gets under the wheel. Throws his knapsack on the passenger seat. The car smells like Aries. Vanilla. Cigarettes. He wishes he hadn't told her his real name. He doesn't have his own car back home and his mom doesn't have a car he can borrow, but he took driver's ed and Uncle Chooch has let him take out his old piece-of-shit Citation that feels like driving a fucking *Flintstones* car. As far as driving goes, he's okay. Never hit anybody or anything. Has good vision. Keeps his hands on the wheel.

Key in the ignition. Lights off until he rolls out of the lot. He lowers the radio and presses the gas. The tires on the craggy blacktop sound loud to him, but he's sure it's his nerves amplifying the sound. Doubts Herbie can hear it.

Once out of the lot, he flips the lights on and makes a left and then cuts a quick right to get to the Thruway entrance. Soon enough, he's cruising south in the dark. He ejects Aries's Ben Harper disc and throws it out the window. He feels around in his knapsack for his CD Walkman. Gets it open and takes out Black Sabbath's *Paranoid* and crams it in the slot. "War Pigs" comes on. He turns it up. He pounds his hands against the wheel. Looks at the dash. The speedometer needle is pushing seventy, though it feels like he's doing a hundred. The whole car's rattling.

About ten miles down the road, there's a rest area. He goes in and buys a map that includes Jersey. He uses the bathroom. He comes back out and drives the car over to the gas station and fills the tank. Before getting back on the highway, he examines the map under the dome light. It's not far to Ridgewood. Maybe an hour. The Thruway is also 87. He'll stay on that to 17. Then take the exit toward Ho-Ho-Kus. From there, it's a couple of miles on Sheridan Avenue and North Maple Avenue. He scours around in his bag for the Win-4 lotto ticket on the back of which he wrote the address Skeevy Ed sent him. Godwin Avenue.

He gets back on the road, *Paranoid* blaring.

The drive's fast this time of night. Not much traffic. He only almost gets in one accident. Not his fault. Some asshole cutting him off. He thinks of Aries stuck in that bathroom. He doesn't feel bad for taking her car. His *story*. She wanted his fucking *story*. That's what he's hunting for.

He pulls into a spot across the street from a bar called Tain's. Sandra Carbonari apparently lives upstairs with Iron Andy and Sally Boy Lafragola. It's a dive. A green neon sign over the door. Christmas lights strung in the window. The apartment over the bar—accessed by a stairwell on the side of the building—looks dark.

Fab puts his knapsack in the backseat and covers it with some of Aries's assorted junk. Stray shirts. Cardboard. Copies of a magazine called *Chronogram.* CD liner notes and empty jewel cases. Crumpled American Spirit packages. He gets out and locks the door and looks at the car sitting there under a streetlamp that seems to be funneling down muted light.

He goes up the staircase and tries the bell. No answer. He knocks on the paint-chipped white door. Nothing. He raps the palm of his hand against the door harder. Still nothing. Tries the handle. Locked.

He goes down to the bar and expects to be bodychecked by a bouncer before crossing the threshold, but there's no one to stop him. The joint's not much from the outside and it's even less on the inside. A half-moon bar framed by glistening bottles and a dirty mirror. About eight swivel stools with chrome legs. A few tables and booths. A pinball machine. A jukebox playing Bon Jovi. Maybe twenty people filling the place. Not a ton but they're packed in like sardines. All of them older. In their forties and fifties at least. One or two even older than that. A handful of them look up at him as he enters. Not a regular. Disturbing their peace. It's hot and stinky in there. Booze. Bleach. Cigarettes. Dirty mop water. Something that smells vaguely electrical, like a hair dryer left on too long.

The bartender is a woman wearing a white crop top striped with flames, a black patch affixed over her left eye. She has frazzled brown hair. She sits behind the bar on a high stool with the authority of a prison guard. She's got a cigarette in her mouth. Smoke drifting up and framing her face.

Fab goes up to the bar. "Is Sandra here?" he asks the bartender.

She leans closer. "Say again."

"I'm looking for a woman named Sandra. I'm the son of an old friend of hers."

"Son of who?"

"Saverio Franzone."

"I don't give a fuck." The bartender cackles. Aims her thumb in the direction of the jukebox. "Back booth. Follow the scent."

Another cackle that turns into a dramatic cough. She hacks up some mucus and spits it into an empty bottle on the counter next to her.

Fab heads back to the booth the bartender indicated. The woman there can't be the Sandra Carbonari that his dad made time with. She's maybe two hundred pounds. Stringy dark hair. A square bald patch over her right ear like a sad alley dog. Wearing a hot pink tank top accentuating folds of skin. KILL 'EM ALL tattooed on her left arm in heavy metal font. Bloodred lipstick clashing against mangled yellow teeth. Smudges of darkness under her eyes. A nose full of burst blood vessels. Maybe the hint of some long-gone beauty underneath it all, but she's been ravaged by booze and time and whatever else. He's been picturing someone far prettier than his mom, and he's wound up in the presence of this beast. She's sitting across from a scrawny man with a gray stubbled face. His mouth hanging open. More rotten teeth. Gigantic, drooping earlobes. His chin melting into his neck. Scars on his cheeks like shards of glass had peppered his skin there and been tweezed out. He's wearing a satin softball jacket and a dust-flecked Devils cap. Empty glasses and bottles fill the table between them. An ashtray mountained with lipstick-edged butts.

"Sandra Carbonari?" Fab says.

"Who the fuck's asking?" she says, her voice simultaneously high and guttural.

"My name's Fabrizio. I'm Saverio's son."

"Saverio?"

"Sav."

"Sav Franzone? No shit. You look like him. Except for the long hair."

"You *are* Sandra Carbonari?"

"What do you want with me?"

"I'm sorry to bother you. I'm looking for answers. Looking for my old man."

Sandra explores the table for a bottle or glass that's not empty. No luck. "Buy me a drink, and I'll tell you everything you ever wanted to know. And buy one for Sally Boy here, too."

The man in the satin softball jacket lifts his hand from his lap and gives a salute.

"What kind of drinks?" Fab asks.

"Two double whiskeys on the rocks and two beers. And whatever Sally Boy wants." She laughs a thick, throaty smoker's laugh. The bar is full of that same kind of awful laughter. First the bartender and now Sandra, and Fab can hear it all around him like a deranged chorus. The joint's a real den for degenerate drunks. All he can think is they were once little kids. Stood in schoolyards and mouthed the Pledge of Allegiance. Ate their sack lunches. Said their prayers.

Fab retreats to the bar and orders the drinks. He has enough money in his pocket to pay for them. It takes him two trips. First, he brings the whiskeys and then he brings the beers. Sandra's half done with her whiskey by the time he's back with the beer. Sally Boy's struggling with his. Hands shaking.

"Nothing for you?" Sandra says.

"Not now," Fab says, sitting down next to Sally Boy. He can drink but not in a place like this. Makes him want to vomit seeing these old boozers. A real graveyard.

"I don't trust a teetotaler."

"I'm not that."

"What are you?"

"I told you. I'm Sav's son."

"I bet you don't think much of me. You're probably thinking your old man had rotten taste. I used to be a hot fucking tamale. Believe me. Right, Sally Boy?"

Sally Boy nods. Still trying to make the whiskey go down without slopping it everywhere.

"'Used to be,'" Sandra continues. "Say that a lot these days. Me and Sav had some good times. He was like me. Enjoyed the edge. You gave him two options, he chose the wrong one every time. His big mistake was marrying your mother. Prude. Last thing he needed in his life. He loved you. He did. Those first months, sure, he was out a lot and a big part of him didn't want a kid, but he was proud he had a boy. Said you were gonna grow up like Popeye. Strong. Eating your spinach. He was afraid, I guess. We're all afraid." She gets a bit lost looking longingly into her whiskey and then downs the rest of it. She reaches across and helps Sally Boy bring his glass up to his lips, letting him sip from the glass as she holds it, tilts carefully. Some of the booze runs out of the corners of his mouth. It's like a scene from the nursing home where his mother works but with booze replacing watered-down juice.

"I'm trying to piece things together," Fab says. "Figure out where he could've gone."

"That's rich. Good luck."

"What do you mean?"

"What I mean is your old man did want to leave, but he was leaving with me. That last night before he disappeared, it was all we was talking about. Over at L'Amour. After. We was gonna go to Florida. Me and him. A lot of days, I think about what my life would've been if that'd happened. Different. Shit. I'd be tan. I wouldn't be in Jersey. Nobody ever wants to wind up in Jersey, and yet so many of us do. Look at me. I'm fucking articulate tonight. Wistful. Sav. He was a romantic, you ask me. At heart. Me and him had some good times. We was gonna split. Sure, he was on the fence about leaving you. Tiny baby. But we was angling for good times. No more winter. No more this one or that one breathing down our necks."

"You don't think he would've left without you?"

"Nope." She smacks her lips together and moves on to her beer.

"What do you think happened?"

"You don't want to know what I think."

"I do. I want to find him. Anything could help."

"You ask me, you won't find him."

"Because he doesn't want to be found?"

She shakes her head. "I don't want to say it, kid. Hurts me to look at you. Dead ringer for him." She juts her hand across the table and strokes his cheek. Her hand drifts down to his shirt. Taking a bit of the black fabric between her fingers. "This his shirt?"

"No, I bought it from some guy."

"Sav had one just like it. One time, he was wearing it, and we was out in the East Village. Some little club. Seeing this band a friend of a friend was in. Wound up at this roof party. Drank a ton of beers. Laid on our backs looking up at the moon. Talked about our dreams. I told him I wanted to be a dental hygienist. Or run my own salon. Never told anyone that shit. He urged me to do it. He said he'd help me. That was when we started talking about Florida. That was the place where our dreams was gonna come true. He didn't really have that kind of dream yet, but he was hunting for one. Said I was his dream. Sweet talker when he wanted to be."

Fab wants to push Sandra for more. She's getting somewhere, hinting at something.

Before he can ask her to elaborate, Sandra puts up her hand and says, "How about one more double?" She holds up her glass and rattles around the ice at the bottom. "And then I'll tell you my theory."

Fab figures there's no harm. A few drinks are a small price to pay for information that might bring him closer to finding out what happened with his old man.

He goes back to the bar and orders another double from Eyepatch. Didn't even occur to him last time that she didn't ask to see his license. Place like this, they'd probably serve middle schoolers if they came in. Thing is, they don't. He bets he's the first person under thirty to walk through those doors in a while.

Back at the table, Sandra grabs for the glass and says, "You're a good kid. I can tell that. Lot of your old man in you. Nobody thought he was any good. I did. That's why he liked me. That's why we was gonna run off together. I got around. Never been shy about that. Sav didn't hold it against me. Lotta others did. Fucking sewing circles. People I called friends. Get branded a hooer, and your goose is cooked. Lotta people don't spread their legs think they ain't hooers. The way they're hooers is just different. They sell their fucking souls."

Sally Boy nods along like he's listening to a particularly good homily in church.

Sandra lifts her drink and says, "To Sav. I never said it out loud before, but he was the love of my life. Only one who loved me for me. Not even my mother did that. She wanted me different. She wanted grandkids getting their Communion. Parties in the fucking driveway. Sunday dinners. A son-in-law with a Rolex. None of that shit's for me. Not then. Not now. Hangs up when I call these days. Tells me what a disappointment I am."

Fab tries to rein her in. "You said *theory*. You think you know what happened with my dad."

Sandra leans forward on her elbows. "Oh, I think I know. Said it a couple of times here and there, and people looked at me like I had three heads, so I clammed up. Told your uncle and look what happened to him. People don't want the truth. They want the thing they find acceptable. Sav splitting like that on you and your mother was the acceptable version of events. Acceptable because he would've done it given the opportunity. Would've done it with me. But he didn't leave."

"You told my uncle? What do you mean?"

"I saw Roberto a little while before he died. He came into the Wrong Number looking for me. Just like you right now. Thought something was off."

"Jesus."

"Yeah, you put two and two together."

"And what do you mean about my dad not leaving?" Fab thinks of a story he had to read in high school. He can't remember the name and can only vaguely remember the plot. Guy ditches his family and lives near them and watches them for many years. A weird one. He remembers his English teacher junior year, Mrs. H, going on and on about it. For a second, he's thinking that's what his father did. He lives a couple of blocks away. Has kept tabs on Fab his whole life.

Sandra continues: "I think Risa and Chooch Gardini have a thing, and I think they killed your father. Oldest story in the book. Chooch has always been in love with your mother. He'd do anything for her. *Anything*. Mark my words. Sounds crazy. They don't look like killers, but you tell me how they act. Doing something like that changes people. I'm sorry to be the bearer of bad news, but your old man's kaput. Buried. Burned. I don't know how they did any of it. Don't have any proof. Just my instincts. You can think I'm a drunk. You can think I'm a nobody. I *am* a nobody. No skin off my back."

Fab's about to say, "Come on, seriously?" But he holds his tongue. Thinks of all the ways his mother and Uncle Chooch got weird when his father's name came up over the years. He always chalked it up to discomfort over the situation he was in—a kid abandoned by his old man, nobody wants to be that—but now he's seeing it through new eyes. Still, he would've known if they had some kind of relationship going. All these years, there was nothing like that between them that he could sense or see.

"I think Risa had enough," Sandra goes on. "Your old man cheating. Stealing. Coming home all hours. Messing with me. Saying we were running away. And he'd gotten a gun."

"Double Stevie said my dad pointed it at us. Me and my mom. Said he was there when it happened."

"You saw Double Stevie?"

"Right before this. Went upstate to find him."

"I don't know about Sav doing that."

"You know about him robbing Gilly the Gambler? Double Stevie said Uncle Chooch was there. I'd never heard that."

"*Uncle Chooch*. That's cute. He was there when they did that.

We were all at L'Amour right after. Chooch left early. Double Stevie took your old man back home. He was gonna pack a bag and come to my place. Next morning, we were gonna hop on a plane or a train or a bus or steal a car. Who knows? Whole fucking world was our oyster. I think your father told your mother he was leaving for good with me and then things got ugly."

Fab's trying to buy it, he is. A big part of him wants to buy it. A lot of questions would be answered. But he can't picture either his mom or Uncle Chooch being violent enough to go through with that. Whatever else he thinks of them, they're both soft. Unless they poisoned his dad's food or something. Can't imagine them burying him or feeding him into an incinerator or dropping him off the bridge into the Narrows.

"You don't believe me," Sandra says, then downs the rest of her whiskey. "It's okay. Nobody ever believes me."

Sure, she doesn't have any proof—only a feeling she's going on—but it's nothing he's ever even considered before. Start seeing plots and schemes everywhere, and anything can seem plausible. Two softies brought to the edge by his old man's antics. Not textbook but not out of the question.

"I didn't say I don't believe you," Fab says.

"You do believe me? Wahoo. Buy the kid a fucking balloon." She straightens in her seat, knocking her knees against the underside of the table, toppling a couple of bottles in the process. "Your mother must've really done a number on you. Let me guess. A lot of guilt and force-feeding and church."

"Me and my mom are really different."

"You're all Sav."

"I mean, I think so. Last time I saw him I was eight months old. I got no memories."

"You are."

"I wanted to find him, that's it. Could use his advice on some trouble I'm in. I thought he was out in the world living without me. Never really considered the kind of thing you're talking about. I mean, I wondered if maybe he was dead now and again, but not dead like this."

"Your old man was an expert regarding trouble. He'd help." Her eyes go glimmery. She didn't expect him to believe her and now she's maybe got a bit of remorse running through her veins and is trying to walk it back. "Kid, it's a theory. Don't base your life on it. Keep digging. Maybe Sav turns up somewhere. That's the case, you let me know. I want to know why the fucker left without me."

"The way they act, my mom and Uncle Chooch, it's always like they're hiding something. Aunt Giulia, too. My dad's name comes up, and everything's wrong."

"Could be a lot of reasons."

"You were saying it just to say it?"

"I told you. A hunch. I don't want you flying off the handle. Don't want to wake up to news reports that some scrawny fuck shot his mother and his sad-sack neighbor to death on a fucking hunch. Hunches come from the sky. The gut."

"Now you're saying it's not true?" Fab asks. "You don't *really* think my mom and Uncle Chooch killed my dad?"

"I didn't say that. But I'm not signing my name to it, okay? I don't want you going apeshit based on me making a guess."

"You didn't think I'd take you seriously?"

"No, I didn't think you'd take me seriously. Doesn't mean I don't believe what I said. Listen. How old are you?"

"Eighteen."

"Eighteen. Okay. Do what your dad couldn't do. Leave. Don't make the mistake of going back like your fucking uncle. You want to get even with your mom? Whether she offed Sav or not, you leaving will crush her."

He thinks about the money he has. How far could it possibly take him? A week? A couple of weeks? And then what? He's on the street somewhere? He wants to be gone, but he wants the truth worse. Fuck's that word? *Closure.* He doesn't want maybes or might've-beens. He wants the blood and guts of it. He's going to either find his old man or find out what happened to him and then he'll think about leaving for good. He thinks he could easily knock Uncle Chooch off for more of his bankroll. It's all tied together anyhow. He's got to go home. He's got to confront his mom and Uncle Chooch and take it from there. The wrong things get turned up, revenge is a possibility. Justice. He foresees that scenario.

"I see your brain working," Sandra says.

"I got a lot to process," Fab says, standing. "Thanks for talking to me." He leaves Tain's. Moves fast. He's back at the Civic in no time. Thinking about what time it is and what time he'll arrive home and what will happen when he goes to his mom and demands, for once in her fucking life, she tell the truth about his old man.

7.

Risa goes into the living room and puts a light blanket over Giulia on the couch. Typical Giulia to be able to sleep while a crisis comes crashing down. Not just Fab gone now, but this Joey Sends guy on his trail over a gambling debt and more. *Jesus, Mary, and Saint Joseph.*

It always brought Risa some sense of peace having her sister under the same roof as them. It lasted a whole decade, the time moving so quickly. Fab grew up. He loved his aunt. Even as he got older and meaner and more dismissive of Risa, he'd always soften up around Giulia. Maybe having Giulia around will help if he calls or comes back.

Her brain starts spinning again. *What if Fab doesn't call? Doesn't come back? What if he's gone forever?* A mother could go the rest of her life without hearing from her son. Happens all the time. She pictures herself in ten years—2014, a date that seems so futuristic and foreign—all severeness and sharp edges, in her mid-fifties, still yearning for word from Fab. He'd be in his late twenties at that point, and she'd be wondering if he had a wife, a family, and if he was terrible to them, or if he'd wound up in jail or a vagrant. Would he come back like Roberto, with trouble hanging from his neck like heavy chains? What if life simply continues, and she gets older and older, and there's no contact, only silence, only the sidewalks between here and church and the lonely train ride to her job in Coney Island, and she never knows anything, never has an opportunity to tell Fab the truth, to clear her conscience, only to let it all eat away at her like acid? What then? She'd still have Giulia and Chooch, but for how long? What if her punishment is that she just keeps living? She sees herself at ninety-five, a resident in the nursing home where she works now, whiskers on her face, milky eyes, alone and wretched. Everyone else gone. No visits from her son. No knowledge of him. No grandkids. No conversations with God. Nothing. Occasional sunlight on her face when she's wheeled into the courtyard to stare out at the boardwalk and the beach.

Then again, she thinks, *what if he does come back and Joey Sends does what he does? That early grave like Giulia mentioned.*

She paces in front of the dining room table. She hasn't changed out of her scrubs yet. She really should. She's not comfortable. She knows that much. She won't sleep. She's off tomorrow and the day after that, thankfully. She'll stare at the phone on the wall, willing it to ring. She walks over and picks it up now to make sure there's a dial tone. There is. She listens to it long enough that an automated operator comes on and says, "If you'd like to make a call, please hang up and try again." She jumps when she hears a noise outside, thinking it's Joey Sends stalking them, waiting for Fab to reappear.

She looks at the gun on the table. Back to where it all started in a sense. She reaches out and touches it. Remembers Sav aiming his gun at her and Fab right here eighteen years ago, how she cowered under his gaze. How he smiled at her. She imagines herself having to pick it up to use it. Giulia showed her a few things—how easy it is to grip, to put her finger over the trigger. Hardest part is not shaking too much. She imagines Joey Sends coming down the hallway and her screaming for him to stop, the gun in her right hand, her left hand clenched around her right forearm to keep it steady and straight.

Tomorrow, she guesses, she'll kill time going up to Eighty-Sixth Street and then making food. Maybe she can bring lasagna to Monsignor Terrone and Father Augustus. She remembers the lasagna she was cornered into serving Father Tim and wonders if Fab will encounter him out there in the land of the lost, crossing paths in some forlorn bus station or end-of-the-world rooming house where runaway priests and runaway sons hide forever.

Or maybe she'll make spedini for Chooch. He loves her spedini. She's not mad at him. He's trying to help her. His heart's in the right place. Still, he shouldn't have given Fab money. It occurs to her that Chooch giving Fab money is why he was able to place these bets that started the trouble with Charlie Cee and Carmine Perasso. They get out of this, she's going to have to put her foot down and demand Chooch stop giving Fab handouts.

She fixes herself a cup of tea in the kitchen and then sits at the dining room table with it, clanking her spoon against the sides of the cup. She's not so much interested in drinking the tea as she is in the ritual of preparing it and sitting there with it and using it as a tool for pondering. She looks down into the cup. A fleck of leaf that escaped the bag is floating in the water. People read tea leaves. *How? What does that mean?* So much she doesn't know. Maybe she can drink the tea and slice open the bag and the leaves will give her answers about Fab, give her guidance on how to help him.

The clock on the wall tells her it's after three in the morning now.

As she stares up at the ticking minute hand, car lights quickly streak across the apartment through the kitchen window, shaking her to her core. Someone has pulled onto the sidewalk in front of the driveway, even though the iron gate is closed. The lights snap off and the same darkness returns. A rustling outside. The whine of a car door.

Gotta be Joey Sends. "I don't do sleep," he'd said.

She stands, taking the gun with her, and rushes to the window and peers out. A car in the dark. It's not the Eldorado Joey Sends was driving. Someone emerges from the driver's side. A shadowy shape reaching into the car and grabbing a knapsack.

Takes her a second to realize it's Fab. She should've known from his body language. She lets out a breath and lowers the gun.

The car, she doesn't recognize. She wonders where he got it. Thinks maybe he stole it. Great. A hot car parked haphazardly on the sidewalk in front of their place.

Risa doesn't want Fab to see the gun. She gathers herself and brings it into the living room, stuffs it under the cushion of the couch where Giulia's sleeping. Giulia turns on her side but doesn't wake up.

Risa goes to the door and unlocks it. Takes another deep breath. She's glad he's okay. Glad he's back. Mothering instincts kick in. Give him hell for splitting like that. Let him know it's not acceptable. That she's been beyond worried. Ask him about the car. Where he went. Ask him about how much he owes Charlie and Carmine, how he got in so deep, what else he did to earn an extra portion of their wrath. And then she can sit him down—maybe he's hungry, wants some reheated macaroni—and start telling the truth.

She pushes open the screen and whisper-yells his name.

He walks toward the door. Looks like he hasn't slept. He stops in front of her.

"Whose car is that?" she asks.

"A friend of mine's," he says.

"What friend?"

"You don't know her. I should've figured you wouldn't be sleeping."

"I was worried sick." She drapes her arm around his neck and pulls him into an embrace. His body stiffens. He accepts the hug with reluctance. She continues: "Where on earth did you go?"

"Around," he says. He moves past her into the apartment. She follows fast on his heels. He drops his knapsack on the floor by the dining room table and gazes into the living room at Giulia, sprawled on the couch. "What's Aunt Gee doing here?"

"She came over to sit with me," Risa says. "I was so worried. And then, Fab, someone came around looking for you. Joey Sends? You're in trouble over this gambling you do—why didn't you tell me?"

He keeps his eyes fixed on her for a minute. Doesn't say anything.

"Are you hungry?" Risa asks. "You must be hungry. You didn't eat anything, did you?"

"I ate," Fab says.

"What'd you eat? A candy bar from a vending machine? Let me heat up some macaroni."

"I had a big meal. I'm not hungry."

"Where?"

"This restaurant upstate."

"What were you doing upstate?"

"I went to see Double Stevie Scivetti in the Hudson Valley."

"You *what*? Who told you he was up there?"

"Skeevy Ed."

"Where do you know him from?"

"MySpace." Fab sits at the table. He picks up the note he left and folds it in half, running the tip of his pointer finger around the edge, seeming to be begging for a paper cut.

"You'll cut yourself." Risa reaches out and grabs the note from him. She sits across the table in front of her half-finished tea. "Did you find Stevie?"

"I did."

"What'd he say?"

"Not much. No idea where Dad is. Told me to quit looking for a guy who doesn't want to be found. Said Chooch was with them when they robbed that Gilly guy."

"You leaving made me realize I have some stuff I want to tell you," Risa says. "You're a man now."

He laughs. "Yeah, sure. But let me tell you the rest of where I went."

"There's nowhere else to go."

"I saw Sandra Carbonari. Found her in Jersey." He stares at Risa and waits for her to react.

Risa's whole body tightens. Even saying that name aloud is a challenge. He knows how she feels about Sandra. How Sandra made her look like a fool for months and months, and then lingered in the neighborhood for years, her presence always an insult. "That woman was a cheap tramp eighteen years ago, and I'm sure she's still a cheap tramp."

"You don't think if Jesus came back, that he'd be hanging out with someone like her? Washing her feet? I think he would."

"Why'd you go see her?"

"Same reason I went to find Double Stevie. Looking for answers."

Fab seeing Sandra does make Risa angry. Sick to her stomach. Sav running around with her like he did. "Let me get you something to eat," Risa says. "Tomorrow, we'll do what we gotta do to deal with what you owe those men. Then I'll get you help. There are meetings. Programs."

"Meetings and programs for what?"

"Gambling addiction."

"I'm not a fucking gambling addict."

"People who aren't addicts don't have hoods showing up at their door looking for blood."

"It's just an intimidation tactic."

"You're not scared?"

"Not really," he says, twitchy, and she can tell it's a lie.

"You should be." She pauses. Thinks about bringing up her parents. Fab hasn't seemed to care much about them in the last few years, even less since they moved to the home. Their house still sits vacant, and she's asked him several times to go over there with her and help organize stuff and he's refused. She hopes mentioning them will ground him a little, make him remember what it was like to be a kid and to visit them on Sundays and to have them dote on him. She risks it: "And I want you to go see your grandparents. They ask about you every day. You never visit them anymore. You've gotta show people you love them while they're still around."

"Like you show me?" Fab says.

"What's that supposed to mean?"

"You don't want to hear about Sandra?" he asks. "How she looks? What she said?"

"I've got zero interest in that woman."

"She looks like shit, if it's any consolation."

"Watch your mouth."

Giulia stirs in the living room. She yawns. Tosses and turns. Stands finally. Maybe she's been faking sleep the whole time since Fab got home. She comes out to the dining room and passes behind Fab, stooping to kiss him on top of his head. "Look who's back," she says. "I told your mom not to worry. Said you'd come home in no time flat. How was your adventure?"

"Fine," Fab says.

Giulia takes the seat between them closest to the wall. She makes eye contact with Risa, seeming to ask with a nod of her head where they stand. Then she faces Fab: "Joey Sends is a big deal."

"I'll take care of it," Fab snaps back.

"My son's not scared at all," Risa says.

"Don't take this lightly," Giulia says. "These guys don't mess around."

"Also, Fab was telling me he went upstate to see Double Stevie," Risa says. She's struck by how much this night feels like the night Sav died, except it's Fab bursting in late, and she and Giulia are so much older. Fab's also not drunk or high, as far as she can tell. "You believe that?"

"I'm surprised he's still alive," Giulia says.

"I also went to see Sandra Carbonari," Fab says.

"Oh yeah? Any sign of your pop?"

Fab bites his lower lip. "Nope. She's a disaster. Hangs out at this dive bar in Ridgewood, New Jersey. Had some interesting theories about what happened to my dad."

"Sandra's an airhead," Giulia says. "Anything she says, I'd take with a grain of salt. She used to talk shit in the Crisscross all the time."

Fab's uncomfortable. Shifting around in his seat.

"Go shower," Risa says. "Get cleaned up. Your hair's so greasy. Then we can talk."

"I'm good," Fab says.

The way he's sitting there, he's so much like Sav. Too much. Wearing a shirt she's sure Sav had—where'd he even get it? The way it hangs on his bony frame. Fab has sinewy arms like his father. The same color hair and skin. There's a tension in everything he's doing now. Every movement in his chair. The way he's gazing down at the table.

Risa starts: "What happened with your dad . . ." She lets the sentence drift away, feeling Giulia's eyes on her. Her sister's supportive aura radiates outward, but it's crusted thickly with a layer of doubt. No turning back once the words escape her lips. She finally manages to say what she wants to say: "I'm gonna tell you the truth."

"Hold off for a sec," Fab says. "I want to tell you what Sandra told me. Her theory."

"It's taken me a long time to get here. Let me finish."

Fab ignores her. "Sandra said she thinks you and Chooch killed my father," he says. "Said you were having an affair and you killed him to get him out of the way. Made it look like he disappeared."

Risa's startled. Can feel the red rising in her cheeks. "You've been here your whole life. Have me and Chooch ever been together?"

"He's in love with you."

"It didn't happen like that."

"But."

"Maybe we should all get some rest and talk about this tomorrow," Giulia says.

"There's no tomorrow anymore," Fab says. "There's only right now."

"It was an accident," Risa says. "The way he was being, I had to put a stop to it. I didn't think I'd hurt him that bad."

"What are you saying?" Fab asks.

Risa draws in a deep breath. "It's not how Sandra said. Nothing like that. I did what I did to protect us. I didn't mean to kill him."

Fab stands, the chair screaming across the floor and bumping the wall. "What the fuck are you saying?"

Risa's shaking. She tries to lay it all out as calmly as she can: "He was very, very drunk. He had a gun. Earlier in the night, he'd pointed it at me and you as a joke. Can you imagine that? A man pointing a gun at his wife and baby?"

"Double Stevie told me."

"He was here for that part, yeah. Uncle Chooch was, too. Then, later, your father attacked Aunt Giulia. Put his hand around her neck. I didn't know what he was capable of."

Fab looks to Giulia.

"It's the truth," Giulia says.

"Attacked you how?" Fab asks.

"He was gonna hurt me."

"And what happened?"

"I had this cast-iron pan on the stove I used when I was frying cutlets," Risa says. "I grabbed it and swung it at him. I was thinking I'd slow him down. He'd run off, holding his head. Go bleed on Sandra's pillows. Maybe I'd knock him out. I didn't think I'd kill him. I didn't know he'd hit his head on the table as he fell."

"He died instantly?" Fab asks.

"He had two big gashes in his head, and he was bleeding a lot. We didn't know what to do. I ran across the street and got Christopher." She won't mention that they waited even longer than that—Giulia going to the Crisscross for cigarettes.

"Instead of calling an ambulance, you got Uncle Chooch?"

"He came over. We were gonna call for an ambulance but—next thing you know—Christopher is feeling your dad's neck, and there's no pulse."

"I don't fucking believe this. You murdered him."

"I was protecting us. I swear. I didn't mean to." The emotion coming through in her voice. Fighting back a breakdown. "In a lot of ways, I don't care I did it. He deserved it. But it built up this wall between me and you. Nothing could ever really feel right. For that reason alone, I wish I could rewind to that night. I do. Find some other way to chase him off. Let him leave town with Sandra."

"It all happened so fast," Giulia says.

"What'd you do with him?" Fab asks. So many questions.

"We took his body upstate to Christopher's country house and buried him in the woods," Risa says matter-of-factly.

"You brought me with you?"

She nods. "You were just a baby."

"Christ. I thought you were a boring-ass mom who goes to church and wipes old people's asses for a living, but you're a fucking monster." He turns to Giulia. "You were there the whole time?"

"I was," Giulia says.

"I'm not a monster," Risa says. "I was protecting you."

"You keep saying that," Fab says.

"I was."

"You robbed me of my old man, and you hid it from me my whole life. No wonder I'm so fucked in the head."

"Don't say that. I've tried to tell you over the years. Living with the lie was too much." Risa's crying now. She uses her sleeve to catch tears on her cheek, dark spots spreading on the blue fabric. "You have a right to know the truth. When I came home from work and got your note, I knew I'd finally tell you first chance I got. I knew we couldn't go on like this."

Fab doesn't say anything for a minute.

"I'm sorry, baby," Risa continues. "I'm so, so sorry. What are you thinking? You believe what I'm telling you, right? That's the way it happened. Can you ever forgive me? Can you understand?" Desperation in Risa's voice. Maybe if Fab could see into the moment—like looking into a crystal ball and watching the memory—he could understand how it all went down and grasp what state his father was in and have some sympathy for why they had to do things that way.

"You kill Uncle Roberto, too?" Fab asks. "And Nana and Papa Franzone?"

"That was Jimmy Tomasullo going nuts," Giulia says, then she shoots Risa a look that indicates she's not going to come fully clean about the role she and Chooch played in getting Jimmy agitated about Roberto's return.

"I want to go over to Uncle Chooch's right now," Fab says.

"Why?" Risa asks.

"I want you all together, and I want you to take me up to my father's grave."

"It's the middle of the night," Risa says. "In a few hours, we'll go over, okay?"

His face goes red with anger. "I said *right fucking now.*"

8.

Chooch can't sleep, tossing around in his bed, readjusting his body to try to make himself more comfortable. He's second-guessing everything he said and didn't say to Risa. He's never seen her get mad at him the way she did before. Fab leaving is a big deal. He understands how hard it's hit her. He's sorry he gave the kid all that dough without her say-so. He believes what he said to be true, though. Fab will be home soon. Maybe he'll come back nicer, seeing that it's a tough world out there, that not everyone wants to help him the way his mother does. Whatever Risa wants to do regarding telling Fab the truth, he'll go along with. No matter the consequences.

He also couldn't bring himself to tell her something. Late last week, he got a letter about a natural gas pipeline project in Sullivan County and the desire on the part of the company to cut through his property, so he's worried that eventually Sav will be found in those woods. He's been thinking he'll have to move Sav's bones or burn them. But maybe the gas pipeline won't happen, and he can just continue to ignore it.

The unsettled feeling gets stronger, so he turns on the television. After his mom passed away, he got cable. She'd been steadfastly against it, insisting it was a waste, questioning the need for all those stupid channels. Now, he wonders how he ever lived without it. All those stupid channels keep him company. A night like this, the wheels spinning endlessly in his mind, it's good to zone out on something.

He keeps a news channel on for a minute because he likes the anchor. She's wearing red and has a pleasant voice. The 9/11 Commission released its report a couple of days ago. A bench-clearing brawl in the Yankees–Red Sox game. Some press conference with Bush.

Chooch stares at his walls, which are now bare—the pictures and posters taken down and trashed because they made him feel like an old man trying to stay a kid—except for the faded black Saint of the Narrows Street sign he repurposed all those years ago. He gets up. He needs to use the bathroom. As he stands, he feels something in his left leg pop. Right above his knee. A pain booms up his thigh. He falls back into a sitting position on the bed, wincing, grabbing his thigh in pain. *Jesus Christ*, he thinks, *I pulled a fucking muscle getting out of bed.* Saddest shit he could've imagined. He thinks how alone he is. He could take a tumble in the house and croak. He's only forty-fucking-four, not in his eighties or nineties. He kneads his thigh, pressing the heel of his palm over the muscle, and feels exactly where the pull is.

All he's got to show for his age is a body full of wear and

tear from doing nothing. When his father was forty-four, he was an old man who had accomplished things. White hair with glorious Ernest Borgnine muttonchops. Bushy eyebrows. Had been doing his job for over twenty years and was speaking of retirement. Had received recognition for contributing to the workings of the city. Had an identity as a New Yorker and as an Italian American. Chooch doesn't have anything except what his parents left him. He's skipped straight ahead to the old man part without having had a family or a good job or a sense of purpose beyond helping Risa.

He moves the wrong way, his leg hurts an awful lot. Other positions, it's fine, there's only an echo of pain. He pushes on the bed with both hands and stands, attempting to keep his left leg stiff and straight, putting all his weight on his right side. It mostly works. He's standing. He lurches forward, dragging his left leg. Seems like the pain is at its worst when he's in the act of sitting or standing or otherwise flexing the muscle. He keeps it straight, there's the promise of pain, the very real threat that he'll move a way he shouldn't move, and it'll hit him like a shock wave, but it mostly quiets down.

By the time he gets to the bathroom and flicks the light on, he's laughing. A madman alone in his house, making a fucking odyssey out of a simple journey to the can. He's relieved all he needs to do is piss because he fears the pain in his leg that would no doubt accompany a shitting session. He makes a vow right then and there. Whatever else he does, he's going to start taking long walks down by the water. He can go all the way to the Sixty-Ninth Street pier and back on the promenade. Listen to music. After his leg heals. Stretch beforehand. People who stretch, they don't pull muscles getting out of bed to squirt in the middle of the night. After a while, maybe he builds up from walking to jogging. He doesn't do something like that, it could be a lot more than a muscle pull that blindsides him. Say he has a fucking heart attack. He's at that age. Guys like him—gaining weight progressively over the years, doesn't exercise a lick, mostly still eats whatever the fuck he wants—have heart attacks and drop dead all the time. He thinks of his arteries like old pipes. He can't remember the last time he even got his heart rate up in a way that would suggest physical exertion. Carrying clean clothes up from the cellar maybe.

He hates the bathroom, especially at this time of night. The tiled walls. Mold in the grout. His scummy sink. The toilet with its rust-colored rings. The black brush sitting in a puddle of bleach in its black stand. Folded towels on the counter. His scrunched toothpaste tube. His toothbrush with its battered blue bristles. A bar of Ivory soap in a tray next to the sink, flecked with coils of hair. The medicine chest full of his mother's old prescriptions. All of it illuminated by the jarring white light.

When he's done, he flushes, watching the water swirl, listening to the tank hum.

He struggles down the dark hallway back to his bedroom, being careful with his bad leg. How quickly he thinks of it as his bad leg. He assumes it'll heal within a few days or a week, but what if it doesn't? What if this is the way it stays? What if he's a hobbled old-timer from here on out? What if he needs to use one of those motorized scooters when he goes to Pathmark or Waldbaum's? What if he needs one of those lifts to carry him up and down the stairs? He's sure Risa will tell him to go see a doctor. He hates doctors. He hasn't been to one in years.

The television still being on in his room brings Chooch comfort. Reluctant to sit, he goes over to the window and holds back the curtain and looks outside. It's quiet. Streetlights throwing an orangish hue over the blacktop and sidewalks and parked cars. A black wire on the apartment building next to Risa's hanging loose from the roof and swaying in a light breeze. Rugs and dish towels put out to dry on fire escapes. The soft murmuring of the block's few trees. Clotheslines stretched in the backyards of the adjoining block. Darkened windows in all the buildings and houses. Except one.

The lights are on in Risa's apartment. He imagines she's up worrying, nursing a cup of tea, pretending to work on a crossword puzzle, hoping for the phone to ring. It takes him a second to notice something out of the ordinary. The car pulled up on the sidewalk outside her front gate. Not a huge deal during normal hours. People will pull in anywhere while they're waiting for someone or dropping something off or running into the bodega. He's even seen people park there like that and pop into the Crisscross Cocktail Lounge for a quick drink. But something's off about this. He doesn't recognize the car. He waits and watches.

He'll call her, that's what he'll do. She's up, no doubt. He'll check in. He's sure she's okay other than being worried about Fab. He's sure this strange car's a fluke. Nothing to do with her.

His mind goes wild. But what if some men broke in and are holding her hostage? What men? Why her? He heard a story once. This family on Long Island. Father, mother, two daughters, a son. They're sitting around one Sunday night. Boom. Three men in ski masks storm in. Guns blazing. Demand to know where the drugs are. "What drugs?" the father asks. This makes the guys mad. They beat him to a bloody pulp. The daughters and son are crying. The mother's saying they've got the wrong place. The guys go apeshit. Tear the place up. Kill the family. Turns out—the cops discover later—they had the wrong address. A goof on their part. True story. He can't remember where he heard it, but it's true. He wants to say it was in Valley Stream. Really stayed with him. What if it's something like that? A home invasion. Wrong address. Whatever the fuck. Risa all alone.

Chooch digs around on his desk, looking for his cell phone. He's not even sure why he has one, he doesn't get many calls, but it seemed like the thing to do. Everyone walking around with them. Got a computer too finally, a desktop, so he could play games and write emails and get on MySpace. He has five friends on MySpace—some women from the office where he used to work, plus Fab. He knocks over a stack of shrink-wrapped DVDs he bought from the sale rack at Best Buy in Ceasar's Bay Bazaar. Just a few weeks before, he'd upgraded to a Sony DVD player and was buying discs whenever he saw them. Wolfman's had closed the year before, and VHS tapes had become mostly irrelevant—another way he was catching up with the times. He finds his phone behind the nameplate that Fab gave him as a gift for his thirty-first birthday and flips it open. It lights up. The power's almost drained.

He forgets about his leg for a second and moves awkwardly. A pain shoots through him, making him double over the desk. His mouth is dry. The nausea passes. He dials Risa's number. It rings and rings. Goes to her answering machine.

He decides he'll make his way downstairs and then across the street. He moves forward. Slowly. Counts his steps seven at a time to try to calm himself. The pain burns through his leg. Seems to rise like steam through his torso and his arms.

Just as he gets downstairs, out of nowhere, there's a reckless pounding on the front door that rattles the house, trailed by a scratchy voice. It's Fab, and he's pissed.

9.

Giulia guesses she's always known it would come to something like this. Part of her feels bad for Fab. The other part only sees his old man in his eyes.

Fab's pushing for them to go across to Chooch's, and Giulia's wondering what the hell Risa did with the gun. Joey Sends could be outside somewhere, watching, waiting. If he's not, maybe he has some underling keeping an eye on the joint and he'll be back soon. She goes over to Risa and says, "In case Joey's outside, what'd you do with the gun?"

Risa leans close to her: "Under the couch cushion."

"What're you two whispering about?" Fab says.

"Nothing," Giulia says.

She watches as Fab squats over his knapsack on the floor, fiddling around with the zipper, finally getting it open and jamming his hand inside. While he's distracted searching for something, she ducks into the living room and feels around under the cushion and finds Sid and Eddie's gun. She shoves it back in her waistline like she knows what she's doing and looks over at Fab to check if he'd seen what she'd done. Doesn't seem like it. Joey Sends surprises them, she's gonna be ready. Just then, she notices as Fab's hand emerges from the backpack with his switchblade. She's seen it before—he got it because there was a bully busting his chops at school. He pockets it. He's sweating, nervous. All that he's learned in this little bit of time. Must be terrible. Must feel like the whole world's a lie.

They move across the street. The night's all silhouettes. The sky and the tops of the buildings around them look like rough, sandy lines drawn on an Etch A Sketch. Little slivers of glinting light in the blacktop under their feet. Stardust caught in the ground. Giulia heard somewhere they use ground-up glass in asphalt. She looks around for a sign of Joey Sends's Eldorado. Doesn't see it. But there's a guy leaning against the telephone pole over by Mr. Vistocci's place, maybe watching them, maybe not. Thinks maybe—though there's a bit of distance between them—that it's Cursed Roy. Could he be doing reconnaissance for Joey? *Fuck.*

"Let's leave Christopher out of it for now," Risa says to Fab. "It can wait until tomorrow. We'll give him a heart attack at this hour."

"I'm done being patient," Fab says.

Giulia puts in her two cents: "Joey Sends comes back around, you'll be done with a lot of things." She's thinking maybe if she scares Fab enough about Joey Sends, she can keep this from going way off the rails.

"I don't give a fuck," Fab says.

As they step onto the sidewalk in front of Chooch's house, Giulia looks at Fab. Under the waning moon, there in the wee small hours, inching closer and closer to dawn, he seems to have totally transformed into his old man. His lanky body. His movements. Even his voice.

At Chooch's door, Fab holds open the screen and knocks loudly, using his fist and forearm. She's sure lights will snap on in windows. People will look outside and scream for him to shut the fuck up. Won't care at all about what danger anyone's in, only that their sleep's been disturbed. The guy she thought might be Cursed Roy hustles away up the block.

Chooch opens the door. He's wearing basketball shorts and a Megadeth muscle shirt. He's standing in a strange leaning position. Maybe he's hurt. Putting all his weight on one leg.

"Christopher, I'm so sorry," Risa says.

"We're coming in," Fab says.

"Sure," Chooch says. He waves them in. "What's going on?"

Fab, Risa, and Giulia flow into the dark house like something being swallowed. Chooch flips on a light. He's limping. He leads them into the kitchen, where the fluorescent overheads rumble on. The refrigerator makes its postmidnight noises.

"Can I put on coffee?" Chooch says. His calm presence seems to be defusing Fab a bit.

"Put on what you want," Fab says.

"What happened to your leg?" Risa asks.

"I don't know," Chooch says. "Pulled a muscle getting out of bed to pee. You believe that? I'm an old man."

"You should sit. I'll make the coffee."

Chooch seems relieved. "Thanks, Ris. I know you won't

be lazy like me and do the instant." He sits at the table. He's really struggling.

Giulia sits next to Chooch. Fab across from him. Risa goes to the cabinet and gets the coffeepot and fills the reservoir with tap water. She finds the can of coffee and spoons grounds into the basket and then sets the pot on the burner, the blue flame rising under it. She joins them at the table.

Giulia's thinking about the time they've spent at tables. Sunday dinners. Talking sessions. Drama. Always around tables. Now this. She's also thinking of Jimmy Tomasullo. The way he gunned down Roberto, Frank, and Arlene at a table not unlike this, in a situation not unlike this. Fab full of rage the way Jimmy was full of rage. She's glad she's the one with the gun and not the kid.

"I don't have much in the way of food to offer," Chooch says. "Might be some Ding Dongs in the cabinet."

"Listen to this fucking guy," Fab says. "He wants me to eat Ding Dongs."

"Oh, take it easy. I'm just trying to be polite."

"Yeah, *polite*. That's funny. You three are so fucking polite."

Risa cuts in: "I told Fab everything, Christopher. Everything that happened that night."

"Okay," Chooch says, searching for something to occupy his hands, settling on bending and reshaping a stray paper clip.

"The version you decided was the truth, anyhow," Fab says.

"I told you the truth," Risa says to Fab. "I wouldn't lie to you."

"You wouldn't lie? Your whole life's been a lie. *My* whole life's been a lie."

"Don't say that."

"Dad might've had problems, but he didn't deserve what you guys did to him."

"Fab saw Sandra," Risa says to Chooch. "She had some big ideas. Told him it was a plot. That we conspired to get Sav out of the way."

"Sandra has no idea what happened," Giulia says. "It's like your mother said before. She was protecting us from your father. He was a mad dog. Wasted. He had that gun."

"Everybody was protecting everybody, I know," Fab says.

"I didn't mean to kill him," Risa says. "If he hadn't—"

"Yeah. Right."

The coffee begins to percolate on the stove. Sputtering up into the glass bulb.

"I want to tell you something," Chooch says to Fab. "You're like a son to me. Whatever I did, it was because I didn't want you to grow up without your mom. Your dad forced her into a bad spot. She didn't mean to hurt him as bad as she did, but if she didn't act, there's no knowing what he would've done. He'd been wrong in the head for a while before that night. No one loves you as much as your mom. No one ever will."

"If I feel like a son to you, that's pathetic," Fab says. "I'm not your son. I'm Saverio Franzone's son."

Risa gets up and tends to the coffee. She brings the pot back and sets it on an oven mitt in the center of the table. She finds four mugs in the cabinet and teaspoons in the drawer over by the stove and then retrieves a quart of milk and the sugar bowl from the fridge, setting them next to the coffee.

Giulia's the first one to pour herself a cup. She needs it bad.

"All these fucking stupid rituals," Fab continues. "Coffee. Sitting around, having big meals. Going to church. Visiting

Nana and Papa on Sunday. Going to the bakery. School. Everything I ever did in my fucking life, every way you ever talked to me. None of it was real. None of it was anything. You were just hiding what you did. You were just keeping me from knowing who I really am."

"Fab, please," Risa says.

"I wish I could go back to that night and save him."

"I told you I didn't mean for it to happen. You've gotta believe me."

"I don't *gotta believe* shit." Fab yawns. Pours himself a cup of coffee. Spoons in four sugars. He's nerved up. Hands shaking worse. Body wired and tense. "I wanna go upstate. Now. I got this car, we'll all drive up. I wanna see where you buried him."

Chooch also pours himself some coffee. "What's the point?" he asks. "There's nothing there. Just bones in the ground. It's been such a long time."

Fab takes a long slurp of coffee. He seems to be formulating a plan. Switching gears. Giulia feels like she can see his thought process: there's no use in going to the grave after all. "You're right," Fab says to Chooch. "What's the fucking point?" He pauses. "You have money. Your mother left you loads. You mentioned to me your old man was paranoid and he'd hidden a bunch in the house. I want—"

"Don't," Risa says.

Fab searches for a number. "I want fifty thousand dollars. You don't have it in the house, we'll go to the bank first thing. Soon as I have the money, I'm leaving. I'm getting the fuck out of here. I'm going away like my father never had the chance to."

"I have a CD for you at the bank," Risa says. "Money we inherited from your dad's folks. I always figured it'd be for your college. I don't know if the CD has matured yet, but we can get it soon probably."

"Fuck that. I want what Uncle Chooch has now. I'm leaving as soon as I get it." Fab reaches into his pocket and takes out the switchblade, flicking it open. "Leave all this shit behind."

"Fab, you put that knife down," Risa says.

"Whoa, kid," Chooch says, putting up his hands in surrender. "I'll give you the money. I got maybe that much around. Maybe more, maybe less. I'll give you whatever I have. You take it and go wherever you're gonna go. You need my car, you can take that, too."

"Christopher, no," Risa says.

"I already told you I got a car," Fab says.

Chooch tilts himself toward Risa. "We thought we were doing the right thing that night," he says. "Fab can't see it. Maybe if he has time in the world on his own, he'll come to some different conclusions. Money's just money."

Giulia's wondering if she's going to need to pull this gun she has on her nephew. Walk him back a bit. She does that, Risa might not forgive her. She puts her elbows on the table, drops her forearms, and accidentally knocks into her coffee mug as she's swiping her hands down. The mug rattles onto its side, a big strip of coffee puddling toward Chooch. He stands and backs away from the table before the coffee drips off the edge onto his lap. It's a big dramatic move to save his shitty shorts from a coffee spill. His hurt leg gives out. He grabs his thigh. Winces. He says, "Ouch, fuck me." And then he loses his footing and falls backward onto the linoleum floor. Hits like a ton of bricks. He's lying there, writhing around, cursing.

Risa scrambles to find some paper towels in the cabinet under the sink and begins mopping up the coffee on the table, which is now cascading onto the floor next to Chooch's feet. She falls to her knees and scrunches up a few paper towel squares over the coffee collected there. She puts her hand on Chooch's shin. "Are you okay?" she asks, without looking at him, focusing on the coffee. That's Risa. Always focused on mopping up the spill.

"I don't know if I can walk," Chooch says. "I can feel the pull's worse than before."

Fab gets up and approaches Chooch, avoiding the coffee, the blade still open in his hand. "You were never my father's friend," he says, stepping forward and putting his foot down on Chooch's bad leg.

Chooch howls.

Fab continues: "Now get up and get me my fucking money."

Risa's still on the floor. She's backed away from the coffee-darkened paper towels, sitting now against the legs of the chair she'd been in. Something beyond worry and fear has stormed across her face.

Giulia's heart is in her throat. Fab's got this look like he's been yearning for this moment his whole goddamn life. He's lost it. Has been waiting to lose it. It was one thing to think his father had left him, to wonder if he was dead or alive, but all this news has catapulted him into some new stratosphere of hatred and resentment. Even as he'd edged into bad behavior over the last several years, he'd maintained a bit of the kid she always knew. That kid's totally gone now.

"Fabrizio, I'm asking you nice as I can, *please* don't do this," Risa says. "I know you're angry. You've got every right to be angry. But something like this isn't *you*. Not deep down. You think you're like your father, but you're not. You're like me."

"I'm nothing like you," Fab says. He turns his head to Giulia and flashes the blade. "Help get Uncle Chooch up. He's gonna show me where this money is. It's mine. He owes me. You all owe me."

Giulia thinks again of the gun cool against her hip. She nods.

10.

Risa's mind flashes to Fab as a boy on a long-ago Christmas morning, wearing his *Star Wars* onesie pajamas. So excited to open his presents. Racing into the living room from their bedroom. The tree set up next to the television. That red felt pad on the floor under the tree. The nativity scene. A scuffed Baby Jesus figurine in a manger, surrounded by Mary, Joseph, and the Three Wise Men in a dilapidated stable. Toy trains circling them. Stacks of presents. Giulia drinking coffee on the couch while Risa took pictures of Fab tearing off the wrapping paper and ribbons and tossing them up in the air. So sweet, her little boy.

Not so sweet now. Stomping on Chooch's injured leg. Talking about retribution for the wrongs done him. Demanding money.

Her eyes drift over to the refrigerator. The magnets look like little pieces of fruit. A bright red apple. A banana. A bunch of grapes. A pear. A pineapple. They hold pictures in place. Vi near the end in her hospital bed, hair combed, playing cards laid out on a tray in front of her next to a Dixie Cup and a bowl of orange Jell-O. Chooch's father at their house upstate. Fab's third-grade picture. His short hair gelled neatly, so different from the greasy, knotty long hair he has these days. He's wearing his blue Our Lady of Perpetual Surrender sweater, smiling in front of a blue-sky backdrop crisscrossed with red laser beams. A shot of her and Fab at his ninth birthday party, which Chooch and his mom let them have in their backyard. The trees dangled with streamers. A card table covered with a plastic tablecloth and paper plates and a rainbow cake that Risa worked hard on. A small crowd of folks gathered there. That bastard Father Tim—*What the hell was he doing there?*—forking a piece of cake into his mouth. She's got her arm thrown around Fab, and they're both smiling wide. She's wearing a black blouse she bought for the occasion. She looks at this picture, she sees a different woman. A happy mother. And Fab looks like the most content kid in the world. Risa hasn't been inside Chooch's house in a long time. She's surprised to see this picture on the fridge.

Over the past six years, as Fab really started to change, she often thought about how he could've continued as a happy-go-lucky kid. She wondered about what college he'd go to. She figured somewhere upstate. Maybe a SUNY school. She daydreamed about him falling in love. She'd imagined a whole alternate future for him and for herself, and it'd felt true. He met a sweet-natured girl from Albany named Helen at orientation. They took classes together and got married after graduation. Risa gave them the apartment upstairs. They had a baby boy they named Sandro. Risa was so excited to be a grandmother. She retired from the nursing home and spent her days walking Sandro around in a stroller, showing him the sights of the neighborhood. The rattling El. Eighty-Sixth Street with its hosed-down sidewalks and fruit stalls. The time capsule buried in front of Our Lady of Perpetual Surrender. Outside Lenny's pizza shop, where they filmed John Travolta doing his double-slice strut for *Saturday Night Fever*. The guy's house on Eighty-Fifth Street with all the statues: Elvis, Marilyn, Betty Boop, Humphrey Bogart, Batman, Superman, Dracula, and Frankenstein. Thudding along over the concrete. Sandro cooing, sucking on a pacifier. Fab got a good job somewhere. Maybe with the city. And Helen was ambitious. Attended Brooklyn Law. Wanted to be a trial lawyer. They talked about whether Sandro would grow up to be a ballplayer or a movie director or a politician. It'd all felt true, but none of it was. There won't be a Sandro.

Where can they go after this? If there is an *after this*.

"Fabrizio," she says again, his full first name sawing through the room. "Please stop. Don't do this."

Fab laughs. The laugh telling her he blames her for everything.

Chooch turns on his side and leans on his elbow. "Put the knife away," Chooch says to Fab.

Risa puts her hand on Chooch's shoulder.

"Can you walk?" Fab asks. "I want the money."

"I think maybe I can walk," Chooch says.

"Fabrizio, I want you to just stop and think about what you're doing," Risa says. "Who we are. I'm your mother. This is your Aunt Giulia and Uncle Chooch. We've been your whole life."

"Fuck you," Fab says.

She takes the words like a bullet to the chest. She thinks of her mother and reverts immediately to the old ways, the classic tactic: "You know what?" she says. "I wish you *would* stab me." Guilt. Martyrdom. Like building a dam to protect against a flood. And Risa means it. She *has to* mean it. Part of the formula. He stabs her, she can face down her sins and go to hell or purgatory or wherever God sees fit to throw her. Some broom closet.

"Don't say that," Chooch says.

"Get up," Fab says to Chooch.

Chooch rises, first to his hands and knees, and then Risa stands and helps him to his feet. He puts an arm around her shoulder. Fab makes Giulia get closer to them. He asks Chooch again where the money is. Chooch says the cellar. Fab motions with the switchblade for them to go downstairs.

Chooch retrieves a skeleton key from a hook on the wall over by the hallway. It's tied on to a big piece of fuzzy red yarn. He's moving slow, helped along by both Risa and Giulia now, but eventually he gets to the cellar entrance and inserts the key and backs away as Giulia pulls open the creaky door. Fab's behind them, demanding that they go down first. Risa knows he doesn't like cellars, has maybe watched one too many horror movies.

The stairs down aren't easy for Chooch. He's limping harder. Almost collapses once. Risa and Giulia save him from falling. The steps are three-inch slabs of wood that seem to be bowing. Risa doesn't know much about these things, but she's smart enough to ascertain that one day they'll start snapping. They need to be braced.

The cellar is cooler than the kitchen. Boxes and crates piled high against the walls. Oil burner. Dust-webbed bikes. Washing machine. Workbench. Risa's never been down here. It smells like dust and grease and ancient things. Chooch probably does have a bunch of money hidden somewhere. He's probably going to give it to Fab, no questions asked. It must be money his parents left for him. He'd do that. For her.

Suddenly, Risa feels like she's floating above it all. Chooch's arm is no longer around her shoulders. She can't feel the sweat-slickness of his skin through her shirt. Her hand's not meeting Giulia's hand in the middle of Chooch's back. She's floating in the cellar like people do in spaceships. Her back up against the plasterboard ceiling. Zero gravity. She's looking down at Fab. Knife in hand. Face dotted with perspiration. His posture a quick scribble of recklessness.

Whatever it was that made her feel that way, it's over. She's back. Helping Chooch forward on the cement floor. Struggling. Every bit of silence loud as hell.

"Where's the money?" Fab asks, obviously unnerved by the haunted stillness of the cellar.

"Scattered," Chooch says.

"Don't do this," Risa says.

She can feel Chooch shrug against her. "What's it matter?"

Fab begins frantically searching around. With his free hand, he picks up a weathered red suitcase stacked on top of a green plastic storage bin and unzips it, finding only coiled Christmas lights and an artificial wreath and blank gift tags.

"Not in there," Chooch says. "Take it easy. I'll tell you."

Fab throws the suitcase on the floor. Still open. The cord of Christmas lights spilling out like guts.

Chooch nods over to the shelves next to his dad's workbench. "There's a cardboard box for an Olivetti adding machine. A bunch is in there."

Fab rushes over. He puts the switchblade down on the workbench next to a radio and snaps on a nearby drop light. He yanks the box from the shelf, knocking over a stack of record needles in jewel cases and cardboard boxes of television tubes. Of all the awful things he's doing right now, it makes Risa sick to see that he hasn't picked up what he's knocked over and that he tossed that suitcase down the way he did. Not how she taught him to be. None of it. She raised him to be gentle and respectful. Thought she did, anyhow. Meant to, despite everything.

He peels back the flaps on the box, removes the adding machine, and then feels around on the bottom and comes out with a metal safe. He opens the lid, and it's full of cash. He smiles. "How much is here?"

"I don't know," Chooch says. "Maybe nine or ten grand."

Fab goes back and grabs the suitcase, emptying its contents on the floor. Dusty pile of Christmas stuff from the sixties and seventies. He fills the suitcase with the cash from the safe and then zips it shut. "Where else?"

Chooch nods his head to the opposite side of the room. A metal locker with a broken hasp.

Fab goes to it, thrusting open the door, revealing an orange extension cord hung from a thick metal hook. Some old car belts still in their original packaging propped atop a stack of manuals and magazines. A box that says it contains an eight-track player.

"Should be one of those little cases for forty-five records," Chooch says. "Blue handle. Might be buried."

Fab sets the suitcase down and kneels in front of the locker.

The switchblade's still on the workbench, illuminated under the light. He's forgotten about it.

Giulia snakes out from under Chooch's arm, leaving Risa holding him up on her own, and takes the gun she got from Sid and Eddie's safe out from under her shirt. Risa knew she brought it with her, afraid that Joey Sends might pounce in the night, but it didn't occur to her that she might pull it on Fab. Even after he showed the knife. Even after it started to make sense that someone might need to shock him into cooling down. "This stops now," Giulia says.

Fab turns and sits on the floor with his back against the locker, his legs outstretched, the suitcase cradled close by. "You're pointing a gun at me, Aunt Gee?" he asks. "Where'd you even get a gun?"

"I had to get it from Sid and Eddie's safe because Joey fucking Sends came around looking for you," Giulia says. "Jesus Christ, Fab. You're gonna put that blade away, leave Chooch's money alone, and you're gonna walk up those stairs and exit this house. Get in that car you showed up in and drive anywhere but here. Go get your head straight. Figure out a way to pay off Charlie and Carmine, to atone for whatever other ways you fucked up with them and Joey. What you learned tonight, you can do whatever you need to with that information, but don't do it like this, okay?"

"Giulia, put the gun down," Risa says.

"What do *you* want to do, Ris?"

"With me is his home. He's always welcome under my roof. Nothing changes that. Put the gun down, please. Fab, go back to the apartment."

"You were begging him to stab you five minutes ago, and now you're saying you'll tuck him in tonight?"

"He's my son. He's my responsibility. What he's going through, it's a lot."

"He's gone. I can see it in his eyes."

Risa feels the confusion thundering through her. She wants to die. She wants to live. She wants Fab to live. She wants Fab to love her. She wants all this sickness to fade. She wants a block party. A big folding table out in the street that everyone's assembled around. Sausage and peppers in steaming tin trays. A time of celebration. Her parents in good health. Giulia smilingly unmarried. Chooch and Vi. Fab a kid again. Sidewalk games. Hopscotch. Pitching pennies. Stoopball. She wants the Eighteenth Avenue Feast. She wants to be in church at Christmastime, the smell of frankincense and poinsettias hanging in the air. She wants a trip to her favorite market on Eighty-Sixth Street first thing in the morning, before they get too crowded. She wants broccoli rabe for a good price. She wants spumoni in a paper cup. She wants the week after Fab was born. Learning to nurse him. Barely leaving bed. Sipping water through straws. Eating ice chips. Her skin against his skin. Swaddling blankets. A small, perfect world. She wants only good memories to sing through her mind. "We'll get him back," she finally says.

"You won't get me back," Fab says.

Risa remains frozen. She can feel Chooch's heavy breathing. His heartbeat. She can almost feel the pain in his leg in her own leg.

"I'm not leaving until I get the rest of the money," Fab continues. "I leave here without the money, I'll tell everybody what you fuckers did. They'll find my father. It won't look like any accident. It'll look like what it was. Murder."

Fab leans into the locker, feeling around, yanking the case out by its cracked blue handle. He pulls it into his lap and thumbs open the silver latches and finds more money stashed there. Rubber-banded stacks. He empties the money, so it's piled all over his thighs and crotch. He unzips the suitcase enough so he can stuff the stacks in there one by one.

Risa's thinking again of Sandro, the grandson she'll never have. Her name for him. Her stupid name. The cross she'll never hang on his wall. The songs she'll never sing him to sleep to. Whatever happens now, however this goes, even if Fab miraculously begs their forgiveness and says he understands why they did what they did, understands what kind of man his father had become, there will never be a Sandro. The possibility has eroded totally. There's too much pain and not enough of the right kind of future. And, of course, Fab seems incapable of any such epiphany.

He pulls the zipper shut over the money and stands. Takes a step toward Giulia.

"Stay where you are," Giulia says.

"Put the gun down," Risa says again. "He needs help. A lot of help." She imagines Fab in bed like he's gone through a ten-round bout with a brutal fever. A wet washcloth on his head. Finished with the nightmare and coming out on the other side.

Giulia's biting her bottom lip. Her hand's shaking. She showed up tonight only to comfort Risa. She sure wasn't in the market for any of this. First Joey Sends and now a blade, a heist, a fucking showdown. She lowers her gun hand. The gun's in line with Fab's legs, not his chest.

Fab reaches back for the switchblade and grabs it. "I have to, I can get that gun away from you," he says.

"Giulia, please," Risa says. It's like she's seeing Sav corner her sister all over again. The same scene playing out a different way. Everything's a mess, but she's not watching her son get shot by her sister. No matter what else happens. No matter what he does to deserve it.

Giulia lowers the gun even farther but doesn't put it down all the way. Instead, she pulls the trigger. Guessing, Risa figures, it'll serve as a warning shot. Keep Fab from pressing forward. The noise is deafening. The bullet chunks against the cement floor by Fab's right foot. He jolts back and drops the knife.

11.

Fab leans over and picks up the switchblade. He can't believe how close that bullet was. Can't believe Aunt Giulia fired at him. Can't believe she's got a gun. Playing tough. Thinking she's gonna scare him off. There's no scaring him off, not knowing what he knows now. How his mother killed his father. How they all buried him and made him watch. Fuck them. And fuck Charlie Cee and Carmine Perasso and Joey Sends. He needs a new life to escape the lie. This money Uncle Chooch keeps down here in his fucking crypt is the key. By dawn, he'll be in Jersey, watching the light come up. He'll go to Atlantic City. He's always wanted to go there. Ditch the car. Get a motel. Stash the money in some locker at the bus station the way they do in movies. Bring a fold of cash in his pocket and play at the tables in the casinos. Put down a few bets at the sports book. Maybe fall in love with some waitress. He can imagine himself there, succeeding, thriving. Making a career out of gambling. He does well enough, maybe he can get out to Vegas. Who's he kidding? He's only bet on sports, has barely played poker or blackjack, and never even been near a slot machine—he thinks he's just gonna strut into that town and *succeed*? Still, the money's the key. If it's not Atlantic City he's going to, it's somewhere, and he's gonna be someone else, he's gonna be his dead father's son.

"Don't do that," Giulia says, her hand unsteady, the gun quavering in his general direction.

"You're gonna shoot at me again?" he asks. He knows she won't. One warning shot in close quarters is enough to prove her point, but her point's moot to him. He's getting out of this cellar with Uncle Chooch's dough.

There's more of it.

Fab turns to Uncle Chooch. "Where's the rest?"

"Wooden liquor box over behind those bicycles," Uncle Chooch says. "And then there's a cookie tin under a basket of clothespins next to the washing machine. I think that's it."

"You think?"

"Been a while since I've gone to all the spots."

"You don't have to do this," Fab's mother says to him. "It's a mistake."

"You know all about mistakes, huh?" Fab says. "I got news for you. Nobody's ever got to do anything. And I still have this knife. I'm still running the show."

"Take the money," Uncle Chooch says. "Go."

Fab turns back to Aunt Giulia and looks at her like he knows it's over, his gaze telling her she doesn't have to act like she's stopping him anymore. She lowers the gun and curses under her breath. He holds the knife at his side and picks up the suitcase with the other. He goes over by the bikes and finds one of those wooden boxes for fancy scotches. More like a minicrate really. Propped against the wall. Wouldn't think nothing to look at it. Script on the front. Words he can barely make out. Details about how long the scotch was aged and in what type of barrels. A drawstring to slide open the front part. Wood the color of a church pew. He puts the knife on the floor and yanks the string, pulling back the lid or top or whatever the fuck it's called. Plenty more dough hiding there. He unzips the suitcase again and starts grabbing fistfuls of money from the scotch box and shoving it in the open suitcase.

His mother and Uncle Chooch watch him. Still frozen. Aunt Giulia's sitting on the floor next to the workbench with her head in her hands, the gun in her lap.

Again, he zips the suitcase back up, grasps the knife and holds it out in front of him, and then heads over by the washing machine, where he quickly finds the cookie tin and the final stash of money. He repeats the process of opening the suitcase and, this time, he inserts the whole tin in there.

He carries the suitcase with him, the zipper undone maybe six inches. He's not sure how much money he has in total, but it's got to be close to fifty grand. That was just a number he picked out of the sky anyway. He comes back to Uncle Chooch. Presses the knife against his belly. Avoids looking at his mother, so close. Her sorrowful eyes sorrowing him with each glance. "I know you're holding out," he says to Uncle Chooch. "Where's the rest? I want every last dollar."

"There's no more I can remember," Uncle Chooch says.

"You're lying."

"Fabrizio," his mother says.

"Shut up," Fab says. "Stop calling me that."

"Don't talk to her like that," Uncle Chooch says, and he thrusts his forearm out at Fab. Catches him right in the center of the chest. Knocks him off balance.

Fab drops the suitcase but doesn't let go of the knife. He stabs Uncle Chooch in the stomach. A frantic urge. Not understanding, just doing. The blade going in doesn't feel like much to him. His hand around the grip. The gumminess of the silk-screened faded skull graphic on Uncle Chooch's shirt rubbing against his skin. Blood rising hot beneath the dark fabric. Uncle Chooch groaning forward. His mother gasping. Aunt Giulia gasping, not even instinctively reaching for the piece. The whole cellar a gasp. Fab's long hair in his face.

He withdraws the knife. Painted red with Uncle Chooch's blood. He looks at it and looks at his mother and then picks up the suitcase and books it upstairs. If they hadn't done what they'd done, this wouldn't be happening. He's telling himself that. He's gotta move fast. They call an ambulance, the cops wind up coming around, he needs to be as gone as he can be. He didn't mean to stab Uncle Chooch, not really, but it feels like some kind of proper revenge at least. He's got the money that he's got, and he's got the car. All he needs. He'll be over the Verrazano in fifteen minutes or less and then hauling ass on the Staten Island Expressway and following signs to the Jersey Turnpike. He makes it that far, maybe he's in the clear.

Outside, the gloom presses down on him. He scrambles across the blacktop and goes to the Civic and gets in. He tosses the suitcase in the backseat with all of Aries's shit. Wipes the blade off on his jeans—Uncle Chooch's blood streaked there—and then flicks it shut. Finds the keys in his pocket. Starts the car and turns on the headlights. Doesn't put on his seat belt. The engine hacks. Exhaust fumes under the shivering body, steaming up from the sidewalk like a crying cloud. He pounds the wheel and howls. He did *something*. He's got guts. He stood up against all the ways they'd fucked him over. This is it. This is *him*.

In the rearview mirror, he notices a car maybe fifteen feet behind him parked at the johnny pump. A big car. Its lights flash on. He sees the shape of a man in the driver's seat. As the car eases out of the spot and passes under a streetlamp, he gets a glimpse of Joey Sends behind the wheel of his neighborhood-famous Eldorado. *Fuck*. Lying in wait for him. Fab shouldn't have treated the situation so flippantly. Guy's relentless in the first place is what he's heard, but the thing with Concetta must've really sent him over the edge. Why else would he come hunting for Fab in the middle of the fucking night? It figures the pettiest bullshit comes back to bite him in the ass the hardest. Concetta thought she was above him—that art school she goes to in the city, her expensive dress and bleached-blond hair and press-on nails—and Fab called her what she deserved to be called. *Double fuck*. Now he's got this to contend with. As if running away and hoping the cops aren't on his trail for stabbing Uncle Chooch isn't enough. He pictures a high-speed chase on the Belt Parkway, Joey Sends's Eldorado bumping him, trying to make mincemeat of the plasticky Civic.

He slides the gear into reverse. Backs up fast. Hits the front fender of a Mercury Grand Marquis parked opposite. Puts the car in drive and peels out. Races up Saint of the Narrows. He's sweating. Swiping his hair from his face. In the rearview, all he can see are Joey Sends's lights, eating up his whole world. Illuminating the interior of his car. It's nowhere time. The block's dead. He blows the stop sign on the corner and takes the turn onto Benson Avenue with a heavy foot. Feels like he's up on two wheels. The sound of rubber squealing on blacktop. He tries to gain traction. Tries to straighten over the double-yellows. The steering wheel zipping through his hands as Joey Sends follows after him, easing that big boat of his around the corner.

Fab totally loses control. Speeds up onto the sidewalk and slams into a telephone pole midblock. The front end of the car crushes like a soda can. In slow motion, he feels the steering wheel press hard against his chest, taking the air from him. His head slams the windshield. His legs are trapped—he can't feel them. Smoke pours from under the hood and through crevices in the broken glass. He thinks about the suitcase in the backseat. He knows it's mostly closed, but he fears the money's spilled everywhere in the car. Blood maps his vision. All he can see is smoke, his head tilted slightly toward the passenger side. All he can hear is the low growling of the dying horn. He's in pain that feels more like pressure, as if he's shattered on the inside.

A car pulls up next to him. Idling. Must be Joey Sends. The whine of a car door. Feet on the blacktop, crunching glass and shattered plastic from the Civic.

Fab sees Joey Sends open the mangled passenger side door on the Civic; it falls off as he pulls it, the whole fucking door. In the smoky haze, Joey Sends resembles someone sent to save him. Fab knows better.

"Hell of an escape," Joey Sends says, his eyes traversing the wreckage engulfing Fab. "You fucked yourself up pretty good."

Fab's thinking, *He's gonna find the money, he's gonna find the money, he's gonna find the money.* The fucking guy can't know about it, there's no way. He won't think shit of the suitcase in the back. Probably just believes Fab was making a break for it because he couldn't pay up. Still, all it takes is one little look-see.

Fab's thinking, *I can still get free. I can climb out of this car and hobble to the Bay Parkway El station and catch a train into the city and go to the Port Authority and be gone somewhere soon.*

"Looks like you did my work for me, you cidrule," Joey Sends says. "The level of disregardlessness you've exhibited is fucking breathtaking. The money you was in the hole for, the suits you glommed, the nastiness you showed towards my niece—you're a worthless stain, that's it, and you think you got balls. Nothing I like more than seeing punks like you get their just deserts. Make an example for others. You encounter the chance again wherever the fuck it is you wind up, you should talk respectful to classy girls like Concetta."

The pressure builds. Fab's vision is going goopy. The last thing he sees is Joey Sends searching around in the car. Leaning finally into the backseat. Discovering the suitcase. Opening it. No doubt pleased with what he finds.

And then there's a wash of darkness.

12.

Chooch thinks of all he could have done differently. Starting with the haircut he got right before the first day of first grade. He's never liked getting haircuts. Too intimate. The Russian woman at John's Barber Shop on Bath Avenue who last cut his hair in '02 had sour breath and gnarly teeth, and she was wild with the electric razor. Does it all himself now with cheapo scissors. But that haircut he got for opening day of first grade. Bowl-shaped. Kind of like a medieval monk. Got dragged for that. Sav leading the charge.

Doesn't matter. He's thinking how he never went to a fucking high school dance. He could've asked someone. Who? Elaine from Cropsey. She was sweet. Quiet. Went to Kearney and got good grades and was at church every Saturday night. Might've said yes. He could've known what it felt like to have someone say yes. Walking into a dance in the gymnasium with a girl. He saw Elaine's mother on

Eighty-Sixth Street not too long ago. She's dead. Elaine, not her mother. Ovarian cancer. Nice person, not that they ever talked much.

So much he doesn't know about the world. Doesn't know anything about the past, not really. Those great-grandparents that came on boats from Italy. What they were running from and what they were running to. How they lived. Doesn't know history. Doesn't know how time works. Or memory. What he sees in his inner eye and how he sees it. Never know now. Never got smart enough. Too late.

Down on the cold concrete floor. Pain in his leg. Worse pain in his gut. Such pressure. Risa's holding him in her lap. Angelic in her blue scrubs. Has a towel she snagged over by the washing machine pressed against his midsection, trying to stanch the flow of blood. Looking up at her. Chin. Jawline. Brimming tears. Exhausted. Shocked about Fab. Skin drained of color but still stained-glass smooth.

The money. Chooch's father had stashed it for emergencies. House repairs. Unforeseen hospital bills. Trouble. Never had to use it for anything like that. Most of it gone in a flash. Fab carrying it out in that suitcase. He could've shown him only one of the hiding spots, but he knew the kid would need money to survive out there in the mean world. Needed it more than he needs it. He's got plenty. There are a couple of other spots Chooch withheld, though. Not even on purpose. Went blank. What his father and mother would say. How disappointed they'd be. How easily he'd let so much of their money go. Fab's great heel turn. Charlie and Carmine keep Joey Sends on his trail, Chooch will pay that debt off too. Doesn't want it hanging over Risa. Got enough on her plate.

Risa. The nursing home smell, but also her Prell shampoo and the cream rinse she uses. The Jergens lotion she rubs on her hands and arms every night and morning.

Chooch imagines a booming cartoon voice asking, "Is this the end of Christopher 'Chooch' Gardini?" Almost laughs. Resounding answer: "Who gives a fuck?" Fading like the McFlys fade from those pictures in *Back to the Future*. Won't *be* anymore. Never even *was*.

"You stay with me," Risa says. "I'm gonna pay you back every cent of your money."

He coughs up some words: "Forget the money."

"Giulia went up to call nine-one-one. An ambulance will be here soon. I'm so sorry about all this."

His mouth's dry. An ambulance. Carried out on a gurney. He worries over that. If he's in the ambulance and then the hospital, his house will be wide open.

Risa reads his mind. "Don't stress," she continues. "I'll lock up."

A nod in return.

Risa's trying hard not to cry more. Those tears in her eyes barely dotting her lashes. He can tell she's got a lot to say but doesn't know how to say it. He can tell she's torn between staying with him and running out after Fab. "I'm so, so sorry, Christopher," she says.

"Nothing to apologize for," Chooch says, the words seeming to drop from his mouth one at a time.

"Save your energy. Please. They'll be here soon." Risa pauses. "Where you think Fab's gonna go? My God. What kind of mother am I?"

He feels around for her hand. It's holding the towel in place against him. Blood blossoming rose-red there. He can see the outer ring of that redness. Puts his hand over her hand where it's tight against the towel. Can feel the raised tunnel of a vein under her knuckles.

From his low vantage point, he sees a piece of paper crumpled under his father's workbench. A note his father discarded? A receipt for a part? A tattered page from one of his many manuals? Yellowed with age. Chooch's eyes travel up to the surface of the workbench. The radio there. Crooners his father used to listen to while he toyed with a television or a radio or a typewriter. How content Chooch had been to sit and watch and listen. His father singing along. The radio still plugged in.

"Can you put it on?" Chooch asks Risa.

"Put what on?" Risa says.

Motioning as much as he can with his head. "The radio."

"I can do that," she says. She lets him down gently and makes sure the towel is in place. She gets up and goes over to the workbench and turns on the radio. Illuminated under the drop light, she looks like a woman doing something holy. An echo of watching her nurse Fab the night Sav died, except it's her back to him now. Holy like that. Such tenderness. As if she's retrieving the Eucharist from the tabernacle. Another image to hang in his imagination, for however long he's got one left. She turns the knob. His father's favorite station comes in full of static at first but then it clears up as Risa fiddles with the antenna.

A voice splinters through the static. Frank Sinatra in the middle of singing "I Guess I'll Have to Change My Plan." A song seeping from the edges of the past. He squints hard enough, he swears he can see his father stooped at the workbench.

While Risa's up, she retrieves the gun Giulia had, hiding it away at the bottom of a box of rusted plumbing parts. He knows she's doing it because the cops will want to come down here. He tries to picture cops in his cellar.

Risa returns to Chooch. He can see she's covered in his blood. She sits beside him. Takes him again in her arms. Strokes his hair.

Chooch visualizes the future. He's dead in his grave, and Risa visits him weekly. He's buried at St. John Cemetery in Queens with his parents. Lived his whole life in southern Brooklyn only to be buried in Queens. Where the family is. Where they've been. Always his mother's answer. A puzzle of headstones. Risa getting lost and bringing flowers every time. It's a regular grave. Dirt. A coffin piled over other coffins. Nothing special written under his name. The dates he was born and died. Not even BELOVED SON. But, as he pictures it, he can see out from the ground. See Risa kneeling there. Talking to him. Propping the flowers against a jutting rock. Clearing out the weeds and setting them aside.

But he's not dead yet. Not quite.

Giulia pokes her head down from upstairs. "Ambulance is on the way. Should be here in a minute or two."

"You hear that?" Risa says.

Chooch gives another little nod.

"You hold on."

His eyes drift shut and then he snaps them open. Sees her half-smiling in the flickering. For some reason, it feels like he's looking through a telescope at her. Not that he's looked through many. Went to the planetarium on a field trip in high school. Still recalls the peace of seeing stars freckling the darkness.

He counts to seven in his head.

His eyes fall back to the crumpled paper under the workbench. He's starting to fade. Numbness spreads through him.

The song on the radio's over. Buzzing static now, as if it had never been working.

He hears feet on the steps. The ambulance people. Giulia's voice talking to Risa about an accident up the block. Risa's hand on his hand as he's lifted into the air. "I'm with you," she says.

He manages to get out one fragile word: "Okay."

13.

When they're outside, the EMTs load Chooch into the back of the waiting ambulance. Risa looks down at herself. Chooch's blood is everywhere. Giulia's standing on the sidewalk, smoking a cigarette. Red lights strobe against the darkness. Risa can see more lights down at the end of the block. Another ambulance, a fire truck, and a couple of police cars. A blue sawhorse closing off entry to Benson Avenue from Saint of the Narrows. What Giulia mentioned. At first, Risa's not thinking at all, figuring she'll just climb into the ambulance with Chooch and accompany him to Maimonides. Then it hits her. The timing. Fab taking off the way he did. Whatever happened at the other end of the block no doubt involved him. *No. Please.*

She reaches up into the ambulance and gives Chooch's hand a little squeeze. "Is he gonna make it?" she asks one of the EMTs, a man with a gentle countenance. He reminds her of the actor Mathew St. Patrick, who'd done a stint on *All My Children* a handful of years ago and is now—she'd read somewhere—on that show *Six Feet Under*, which she hasn't seen.

"He'll be okay," St. Patrick says.

Chooch is out of it now. An oxygen mask affixed over his mouth and nose.

The other EMT is a woman Risa's seen at Our Lady of Perpetual Surrender. Her name's Melissa, and she's always acting ecstatic in church. Melissa cuts Chooch's shirt open down the center—Chooch won't like that his Megadeth shirt got sacrificed—and works on the wound. "You coming?" Melissa asks her.

Risa shakes her head. "I can't."

St. Patrick pulls the doors shut. The driver backs the ambulance off the block onto Bath Avenue, avoiding the mess by P.S. 101, and takes off, lights and sirens screaming.

"We have to go over there," Risa says to Giulia. She was expecting cops at Chooch's house too, but there's no one so far. Maybe they're tied up with whatever else is happening or they haven't been notified yet that Chooch was stabbed.

Giulia nods, dropping her cigarette on the ground. "You think it's Fab?"

"I hope not."

They move fast up the block together, arms linked. Risa's shaking like it's freezing out even though it's over seventy at 4 A.M., or whatever time it is. She's thinking the worst. She's thinking about that thug Joey Sends lying in wait for Fab and pouncing on him. Her son, stealing that money, believing suddenly he's a lion, and finding out real fast he's a lamb.

"I'm sorry about before," Giulia says. "Pointing the gun at

Fab like that. I didn't know what to do. I felt like I couldn't just let him steal from Chooch."

Risa's got tears in her eyes. "Maybe if I hadn't told him—"

"Don't second-guess yourself."

When they get to the corner, a cop steps in front of them, a tall and severe woman. Her nameplate says ACEVEDO. She blocks their way, putting up her hands and warning them they need to stay back. She seems surprised by the sight of Risa with the blood on her.

Risa asks what's going on. She's looking for her son, she says. She's worried about him. He took off in this direction.

The cop ignores her, reiterates again they need to step back.

All Risa can really see from this vantage point are the emergency vehicles with their red and blue lights, a huddle of men and women in uniforms. Some smoke drifting up by the telephone wires and streetlamps. They push closer to the northeastern corner, the cop easing off a little.

Risa leans over the hip-high wrought-iron fence surrounding the apartment building on the corner to get a better angle. She sees the car Fab arrived in, smashed against a telephone pole farther up the avenue, seeming to be almost cratered around it.

She loses it. She hops the fence and cuts through the yard, coming out the front gate, closer to the accident. She feels like she's in a tunnel full of blaring lights. All of time is closing in around her. She wants to break through the concrete and burrow into the earth. Find a secret lever that can stop the future from happening, that can reverse course, bring her back to some version of before. She doesn't want to go to that car and find Fab the way she knows he'll be. She wants a beginning again, not an ending. She knows now that no matter how hard she's tried to make life better for herself and for Fab, there's just no controlling it. If she had it all to do over, she'd release the reins. There's no key, no plan. Only the joy that's there to be held before it dissipates or decays.

Officer Acevedo halfheartedly chases after her, but lets her go, realizing a mother's concern for her son isn't going to be hindered.

Acevedo must've lost Giulia in the chaos of the moment because Risa turns quickly and sees Giulia threading herself between a fire truck and ambulance and rushing over to join her by the totaled Civic, its doors wedged off, broken glass oceaned around it on the blacktop.

Other cops descend on them. There's nobody behind the wheel, they can see that.

One of the cops, GUARINO his nameplate says, asks what the fuck they think they're doing.

"My son was driving that car," Risa says.

"I'm sorry," Officer Guarino says, taking off his hat and clutching it against his chest, and Risa *knows*, the cop doesn't have to say anything else. She knows Fab's dead, and she collapses against Giulia.

"No, please," Risa says.

"He's in the back of the ambulance," Guarino says. "It was fast. He wasn't wearing a belt. Took some elbow grease to get him out."

Elbow grease. The way he says it so casually, almost cruelly, makes her sick to her stomach. She pictures EMTs and firefighters struggling to free Fab from the wreckage.

"Oh, Risa," Giulia says.

Risa scans the sidewalk for Joey Sends, checks the street for his car. She doesn't see any sign of him but feels certain that he'd chased Fab up the block and forced him to crash, probably snagged Chooch's money. She wants to say Joey's name to Guarino, describe him, though she's sure every cop's already intimately familiar with the bastard. *He did this*. She imagines a scenario where Joey is wheeled into Saints Joachim and Anne a few years down the line as her patient, another bad man from the neighborhood crumbling to dust. She'll put a pillow over his face and press down.

She shakes back to now. Guarino guides them over to the ambulance. Giulia's holding her up. All these other people around, just doing their jobs.

Risa isn't prepared to see her son lying there under a white sheet. She isn't prepared when the sheet is peeled back. Fab stiff and empty in death. Blood crowning his forehead. Bruising on his nose and cheeks. His lips cut. Mouth frozen open, front teeth missing.

She thinks of the promises she'd made to him when he was small. Cities and countries they'd visit, landmarks they'd see, ways they'd be, the beauty of forever radiating from the place where their breaths touched. She's broken all those promises. She wants to say so much but can't make words. Her long list of regrets. She wishes she could've been the kind of person to pack the car, take him somewhere majestic, like a lake or a mountain upstate, start a bonfire, and sit around and be carefree. She regrets that she could never find a way for them to leave Saint of the Narrows Street and Gravesend. This neighborhood was all they ever knew. He said he'd gone to the Hudson Valley yesterday—she hopes he saw something beautiful there. She regrets not being happier. Not trying to be. Even after everything, she could've tried. She regrets carrying things the way she carried them. Regrets not reading to him every night. Regrets all the lies. Regrets not taking a million more pictures. Fab out on the sidewalk, bouncing around a Spaldeen or playing with his action figures. Her arm around him in their front yard, smiling for the camera. Shopping at the markets on Eighty-Sixth Street. Going for pizza and ices at Lenny's or Spumoni Gardens. She has pictures from birthday parties, his Communion and confirmation, his graduation from Perpetual Surrender, and that week he tried to be an altar boy, but the little things, the everyday things, are already fading, mere images in her mind being swallowed up by the dark mystery of existence. One wrong move, and it's all gone for keeps.

Risa touches Fab's arm, says, "I love you, I'm sorry," and then she goes ice-cold, feeling that his troubled soul has gone from him, whispering far away from his body. Emergency lights fog across them. Something old leaves her, and something new enters. A profound devastation. An awful, razor-edged wisdom. She takes her hand away from Fab and collapses against Giulia, pinned forever to the void of this moment, the terror of regret.

Acknowledgments

First off, unending thanks to Nick Whitney, my editor, who has been an absolute dream to work with. This book simply wouldn't exist in its current form without Nick's guiding hand. It felt great to have someone editing the book who understood—even more than me sometimes—what I was after. Thanks also to Bronwen Hruska, Juliet Grames, Rachel Kowal, Lily DeTaeye, Janine Agro, and everyone else at Soho. Thanks to Luke Bird for the killer cover.

Thanks to Nat Sobel and Judith Weber, as well as Keith Stillman and Jenny Lewis. I went through a long process with this book, and Nat and Judith always drove me to be better.

Thanks to Megan Abbott, Ace Atkins, Jack Pendarvis, and Jimmy Cajoleas—true pals.

Thanks to Stephen Monroe and everyone in my department at the University of Mississippi for support and encouragement.

Thanks to Bobby Rea, Greg Brownderville, and the whole *Southwest Review* crew.

Thanks to Oliver Gallmeister, François Guérif, and everyone else at Éditions Gallmeister. Thanks to my French translator,

Simon Baril. It's impossible to put into words how much François, Oliver, and Simon have meant in my life—I wouldn't have a career as a writer without them.

Thanks to my German publisher, Polar Verlag, and to my UK publisher, No Exit Press.

Thanks to booksellers, libraries (and librarians), and readers everywhere.

I could try to list all the writers, filmmakers, musicians, painters, and photographers who had some influence or impact on this book, but that'd take quite a while, and I'm sure I'll be writing essays and talking about that stuff at length down the road soon. I will say the music of Loren Connors was indispensable to me, particularly the album *Hell's Kitchen Park*. "Mother & Son" and "Child" are songs that feel like they provided a beating heart to the story.

Thanks to my mother, Geraldine Giannini, for everything and so much more. My grandparents are gone but they exist in all these stories, as ghosts, as memories, as voices, as do so many folks from the old block.

Thanks to my wife, Katie, for reading drafts before I have business showing them to anyone, for her critical eye, for her kindness and generosity and unwavering support. I think the moment I fell in love with her twenty-three years ago, after we'd just started dating, was when I went to pick her up from her waitressing shift and saw her reading Nikos Kazantzakis's *The Last Temptation of Christ* at the bar—it's been a hell of a great run. Love you to the max, Farrell. Thanks to our children, Eamon and Connolly, who make me see and think about the world in new ways every day. Love you guys.